OF WILD AND MERRY MEN

A Novel of Colonial New England's Forgotten Queer Utopian Experiment

GARRETT HUTSON

WARFLEIGH PUBLISHING

This book is a work of fiction. Aside from historical figures (as noted), all names, characters, events, and places are the works of the author's imagination. Any resemblance to actual events, places, or persons living or dead (except as otherwise noted) is entirely coincidental.

Warfleigh Publishing, first edition.

Cover design by Steven Novak

For more information, or to book an event, please contact the author at www.garretthutson.com.

ISBN 978-1-953846-16-7 (ebook)

ISBN 978-1-953846-17-4 (paperback)

ISBN 978-1-953846-18-1 (hard cover)

CONTENTS

For all the LGBTQ people who have searched for our own history in the popular accounts, and came away disappointed. This book is for you.

CHARACTERS AND HISTORICAL FIGURES

Fictional Characters:

1. Noah Bancroft – a young man from Lancashire who arrives in New England hoping to leave behind the record of his sins.

2. Jimmy Hawkey – the lone survivor of his native village, he is raised by Floyd Hawkey in Cornwall and Maine.

3. Floyd Hawkey – a widowed fisherman from Cornwall, he finds a native boy alone in the salt marshes of Massachusetts Bay, and adopts him. He fishes the waters off New England for years before opting to settle there.

4. Jack Cooper – a sailor on Captain Levett's ship.

5. Will Hailey – a carpenter from Yorkshire, recruited by Captain Levett for his new colony on the coast of Maine.

6. Roger Hodges – one of the indentured servants at David Thomson's estate.

7. John Small – a fisherman at Cape Ann, the future site of Gloucester, MA.

8. Benjamin Burton – an indentured servant at Mount Wollaston/Merrymount, recruited from the Bristol docks.

9. Robbie Ellis, Philip Davies, Leo Taylor, Sam Weaver, Ralph Mason – indentured servants at Mount Wollaston/Merrymount, recruited from the Bristol docks.

10. Andrew Blanford – a fisherman from Weymouth in Dorset, he befriends Jimmy Hawkey on Cape Cod.

11. Harry Colburn – a fisherman from Christchurch in Hampshire, he befriends Jimmy Hawkey on Cape Cod.

12. Jonathan Cheswick – a Puritan minister from Suffolk, who comes to minister at Weymouth Plantation.

Historical Figures:

1. Captain Christopher Levett – Adventurer from Yorkshire, associate of the Duke of Buckingham; sent by Sir Ferdinando Gorges to found a colony in Maine.

2. Captain Robert Gorges – son of Sir Ferdinando Gorges, he is appointed first governor of New England. Founder of Weymouth Plantation.

3. David Thomson – a Scotsman in Devonshire, recruited by the Council for New England to plant a colony; starts the first sawmill in New England.

4. Amias Thomson – wife of David Thomson.

5. Samuel Maverick – an eccentric young man from Devonshire, he comes to New England with Robert Gorges, and stays to become a "Lone Planter" on the future site of Boston.

6. William Blaxton – an Anglican minister from Lincolnshire, he comes to New England to preach to the Native Americans, and becomes a "Lone Planter" on the Charles River.

7. Thomas Walford – an adventurer from Devonshire, he comes to New England with his wife and daughter under Robert Gorges, and stays to become a "Lone Planter."

8. William Jefferies, John Bursley, and James Ludden – three servants left behind to "look after" Weymouth Plantation when Robert Gorges returns to England.

9. Thomas Morton – a lawyer from Devonshire, and a committed libertine, he founds a utopian colony on Massachusetts Bay that he names Merrymount.

10. Captain Richard Wollaston – an associate of Thomas Morton, he brings indentured servants to Morton's colony, but comes into conflict with Morton over these boys.

11. Mr. Rasdall and Lt. Fitcher – employees of Captain Wollaston, who help him run the venture.

12. Wonohaquaham – sachem of the Neponset band of Massachussett Indians.

13. Edward Gibbons – one of the indentured servants at Mount Wollaston/Merrymount, who later becomes a Puritan and betrays Thomas Morton.

14. Thomas Gardner and John Tylly – leaders of the Essex colony at Cape Ann.

15. Roger Conant – the leader of a group of Adventurers who

fled Plymouth Plantation to settle first at Cape Ann, and then founding Salem.

16. Christopher Conant – one of the Adventurers who fled Plymouth Plantation to settle first at Cape Ann, and then at Salem; brother of Roger.

17. John Oldham – a hot-tempered Puritan who fights with Miles Standish and is banished from Plymouth Plantation; settles first at Cape Ann, and then at Salem.

18. John Lyford – an Anglican minister from Ireland, he comes to New England to preach to the Plymouth Plantation separatists; he is banished from on the colony, and temporarily resides at Cape Ann before leaving for Virginia.

PART ONE

"WE DO NOT SEEK A UNIFORM LIFE."

"We do not seek a uniform life."

CHAPTER I

SEPTEMBER 1623 - MONHEGAN ISLAND

The coastline rising from the horizon was a welcome change from two months of unbroken sea, dark green against the deep blue of the Atlantic Ocean, and Noah Bancroft's heart quickened.

An unbroken vista of towering trees loomed closer as the ninety-foot pinnace bobbed on the swell. Those trees beckoned to a new life, where Noah could start afresh, unencumbered by his transgressions. He could hide here, far from home, where no one had ever heard of him.

"That coast be the Maine, lads," the First Mate said to the dozens of men who crowded the rail on the starboard side of the three-masted vessel. He pointed. "Monhegan Island dead ahead. There be a fishermen's plantation there, and a fine harbor."

Noah squinted against the sun. It took several minutes before he could discern a patch of trees distinct from the endless stretch of forested coastline beyond, growing taller with each rise and dip of the waves.

"Mind that line, boy," a black-bearded sailor growled to Noah. "There'll be time enough for gawking when we drop anchor. Bring the jib about."

"Aye, Jack." Noah hurried toward the line off the foremast, grabbed on with both hands--the blisters having some time ago hardened into callouses--and tugged hard, leaning backward to put all his weight into it.

He was only ten-stone-plus-four, but he'd learned to utilize that weight to supplement the meager strength in his arms.

The sailors liked to tease him about his slim frame. "No bigger'n a hedgehog," the black-bearded Jack Cooper often said, shaking his head. It wasn't Noah's fault he was so thin; he'd only just passed the seventeenth anniversary of his birth two weeks ago. His body was still stretching.

He only occasionally had to tug on the lines. He was indentured to Captain Christopher Levett shortly before they sailed, but most of his duties had been of the Ship's Boy variety--carrying messages, fetching items, and serving the captain's meals. It was humiliating at first to act as a servant, but Captain Levett was kind and cheerful, and Noah came to appreciate servant tasks over the grueling work of the sailors that shredded his palms and made his muscles ache.

And no one on the ship knew what he had done. That alone made all the work worthwhile.

The ship rounded the south end of the island, where waves crashed in white foam against jagged rocks. Noah gaped at the thick stand of pine trees, taller than the ship's masts. They had to be at least a hundred feet tall. And the trunks were packed so tightly together he couldn't see far inland. He'd never seen a forest in England to match it.

A harbor appeared between the western shore of Monhegan Island and two smaller isles. Captain Levett was on deck now, and he issued the order to reduce sail. Several sailors crowded around Noah, tugging down the jib, and then a slender red-haired sailor scampered up the foremast to tie it down. They did the same with the mainsail, and the ship's progress slowed to a crawl. The ocean breezes were more muted here, but still carried a chill hinting at the turn of the season.

A clearing spread across a low rise to their right, with a collection of ramshackle buildings scattered around it. Dozens of white men milled around, doing a variety of things, and several raised their arms and called "Halloo!" Beyond the docks, several brown canoes sat on the sand; Noah's eyes stopped on the handful of bare-chested men with long hair as black as raven feathers, and skin so brown it resembled old copper. He'd never seen men who looked like that.

"We go ashore, Bancroft."

Noah turned at the deep voice, startled. Captain Levett's piercing blue eyes bore into Noah above his wide brown mustache, curled at the ends and waxed to a point. The patch of brown beard at Levett's chin was likewise waxed to a point, but his cheeks were clean-shaven, in contrast to the sailors. His knee-length blue coat with brass buttons and gold embroidery also set him apart. A white waistcoat covered most of his linen shirt, and sported a gold pocket watch on a chain. The droop of his unstarched white ruff collar, however, showed his common origins. His gray breeches and knee-high brown boots completed the look of a man of authority.

Levett held out his hand. Noah took it and helped the captain step over the rail into the longboat lashed to the side of the ship. Then he scampered over the rail himself and sat on the bench behind the captain.

A tall lanky man with stringy brown hair and a mouthful of rotting teeth sat next to Noah. "I heard tell these are the best cod fishing waters in the world," he said in a high Yorkshire twang, nudging Noah with his elbow. Noah nodded without a word. Will Hailey was friendly enough, though his breath made Noah want to gag. He was one of the passengers, a colonist recruited for the new plantations Captain Levett intended to build on this coast. A master carpenter, he claimed.

The longboat lowered with a squeak of ropes through rusty pulleys, its side bouncing and scraping against the hull of the ship until it splashed in the water. Two oarsmen propelled it the fifty yards to the sandy patch at the edge of the clearing. The pungent smell of fish assaulted Noah's nostrils, growing stronger.

The boat slid onto the sand. He hurried over the side, his boots landing in foot-deep water, and took a step forward before holding his hand out to help Captain Levett ashore. A collection of perhaps thirty men had gathered on the grassy knoll above the little beach, woolsey shirts and dark trousers stained with fish oil, dirty faces partly obscured by scruffs of beard. Farther to their left, perhaps a half-dozen of the brown-skinned raven-haired men watched the goings-on with unreadable expressions.

"Those be the savage Indians," Will Hailey whispered next to Noah's ear, his gaze following Noah's. His rotten breath was even worse than the pervasive stench of drying fish. "They come to trade furs for things every house in England boasts aplenty—iron pots, steel knives, woolen blankets. They make none of it themselves."

Will's disparaging tone barely registered. Noah's attention was held by the strange clothing the Indian men wore; or rather, the near lack of it. From the distance of the ship, he hadn't realized they didn't wear proper pants; the tan leggings they wore left their hips bare, and half of their buttocks as well. Long strips of what looked like leather hung in front and back from a narrow band at their waist, concealing their groins but not the v-shaped lines that descended to that region, and hiding the cracks of their buttocks but barely half of the round muscles themselves.

"Practically naked, ain't they?" Will said.

Noah's face heated, and he looked away quickly. He had been careless. "It's unseemly." He couldn't imagine walking about in such a state. But the thought made his stomach flutter.

"Savages," Will repeated, shaking his head.

Noah turned to Captain Levett, who had stepped into the center of the collection of fishermen, raising his right arm.

"I am Captain Christopher Levett, His Majesty's Woodward of Somerset, charged by the Council of New England to establish upon these shores a permanent English colony in the name of our dread sovereign King James," Levett announced in the tone of self-importance appropriate to the leader of a fleet of six pinnaces, even though only one was present. "We bear you greetings from the Council, and seek your assistance to furnish our colony with stores of fish to last the coming winter."

The fishermen hardly looked impressed, staring at Levett with only mild curiosity. A few scratched at their cheeks, an impudent display of boredom. "What have ye to give?" one called out.

Levett glanced at one of his sailors, and the man launched into a litany of items they'd brought for trade. Copper pots, iron utensils of every variety, pewter mugs, musket balls and gunpowder—all got mild attention from the growing crowd of fishermen. The item that got the most excitement, strangely enough, was the barrel of butter.

Noah found it amusing that Captain Levett wasn't trading their barrels of ale. It hadn't even been mentioned.

Then a tall, lithe figure emerging from where the forest met the rocky shore to their right caught his attention. He was bare-chested, brown-skinned and raven-haired, like the Indians on the other side of them, but he wore dark blue trousers and scuffed leather boots. He was younger than the others, closer to Noah's age, and Noah couldn't peel his eyes away from the curves of the young man's chest, shoulders, and biceps. His skin was smooth, and glowed in the sunlight.

Noah no longer heard what Captain Levett and the fishermen were saying.

In his hands, the young Indian carried two cages of lashed sticks, containing the strangest-looking creatures Noah had ever laid eyes on. He set them on the ground near a stone hearth, and the red-haired man sitting there filleting cod looked up and grinned. A wooden bucket sat on the ground next to him, nearly full of slimy fish guts.

Noah edged closer.

"Four today," the young man said, in English, but with the lilting drawl of the Cornish or Welsh.

"A couple to eat, a couple to sell," the older red-head replied.

Noah wandered over, trying to keep his eyes on the strange living rocks inside the cages, and not on the buff torso of the young man standing between them. He wished he didn't feel this attraction, for boys instead of for girls. "What are those?" he asked, keeping his eyes down.

The older man stood, picked up a cage, and held it toward Noah. Beady black eyes near the front of the things inside made them look like strange green-black insects with antennae, but with wicked looking claws. "These ugly things? They're called lobsters. Thousands of 'em live in the water around here, crawling around the rocks under the waves. The natives catch them for food. They ain't much to look at, but their tails and their claws make for mighty good eating."

Noah curled up his nose. "What do they taste like?" He glanced back and forth between the older white man and the young Indian. Trying desperately not to stare at the young man's muscles.

A strange sort of smile crept along the older man's mouth, and he looked at the young Indian for a minute before returning his gaze to Noah. "You should try one. We have enough to share. Join us for dinner, would you?"

"Thank you." A tingling sensation rippled through Noah's midsection. "Do you eat anything else with them?"

"Cod, of course," the red-haired man said with a rough laugh. "I'm Floyd Hawkey, and this strapping lad here is my son, James."

Noah couldn't hide his surprise as he looked at the brown-skinned young man. "Your son?" he asked before he could stop himself. His mother would scold him for that, were she here. Asking impertinent questions, such manners!

Floyd cackled. "What, he don't look much like me? Aye, Jimmy here's adopted. He's a native of New England, a son of one of the American tribes. My pals and me found him wandering alone on the south shore of the Massachusetts' Bay seven years ago. He lost his whole family in a great plague, his whole clan even. They'd sent him off into the woods before it got too bad, and that's why he lived. He went back home to find his village deserted; by the living, that is. The dead were left lying about to fend for themselves."

"Papa and his friends took care of me that summer," Jimmy Hawkey said, and Noah allowed himself to look into the handsome young man's eyes. They weren't pitch black as he'd initially thought, but a very dark brown that nearly blended into his pupils.

"Aye, and when the autumn frosts came callin', we took him back home with us."

"Where's home?" Noah asked.

"Sennen Cove, in Cornwall." Floyd Hawkey scratched the gray stubble on his chin. "Most of the fishermen here are from Cornwall or Devon, and those what ain't are from either Jersey or Guernsey, in the Channel. You'll find us a friendly bunch."

"How many are here?"

"During the summer, we're about a hundred, most days," Floyd said. "Boats come and go, you see, travel to some of the other stations around. Most go back home in the fall, but I'd reckon about twenty of us hardy souls stick it out all winter. Jimmy and me, we've been doin' that a couple of years now."

"Mr. Bancroft!" Captain Levett's voice carried across the clearing, sharp and cross.

Noah made hasty apologies to Floyd and Jimmy and hurried toward Levett. "We go to trade, Mr. Bancroft. I'll require your assistance." Noah followed him up the rise to the stone trading post.

After an hour spent securing food stuffs sufficient to support the colonists for the coming months, Captain Levett released Noah for the remainder of the afternoon. Noah looked for Jimmy Hawkey, but didn't see the young man anywhere. Floyd Hawkey had returned to filleting cod, working alone.

Movement through the nearby trees caught his eye, where the lithe brown form of Jimmy Hawkey glided through the forest. Noah found the entrance to a trail, and after a quick look around to see if anyone was watching, he struck off in the direction Jimmy had gone. Jimmy was a ways ahead of him. Noah picked up his pace to shorten the distance. He'd call to Jimmy when he was closer.

The trail followed a creek into the hills, and some fifty yards from the clearing, a group of five men stood naked in a pool of thigh-deep water, splashing their torsos, armpits, and privy parts. Noah allowed a few seconds for his eyes to roam over the group, noting involuntarily that the water must be cold, for their privy parts had all shrunk into nubs. He looked away before they could catch him watching.

Another thirty yards up the trail, Jimmy Hawkey stepped onto the rocky bank, tugged off his boots, and pulled down his trousers. Noah stared at his back and backside, transfixed. His body was smooth like a little boy's, not even any hair on his legs. Jimmy took a step into the shallow water, only calf-deep here, and crouched down to put his hands in the water and splash his face. His privy parts dangled between his spread legs, and Noah's mouth went dry.

"Looking to take a bath?"

Noah about jumped out of his skin at the voice so close behind him. His heart pounded, and he struggled to catch his breath. He spun around to see Will Hailey standing a few feet from him. "You startled me, Will."

A smirk twisted up one corner of Will's mouth. "Get a good look, did you, boy?"

Noah's whole body went cold, and he stood rooted in place. Sweat ran down the back of his neck, and dampened his upper lip. Finally, he was able to work his mouth to speak. "I--I was looking at the trees. They're so different here."

"Aye ..." Will said drawing the word out.

"They're so tall!" Noah gushed, hurriedly. "I bet most of them are over a hundred feet tall. Two hundred feet, some of them."

Will nodded, appraising Noah for a few seconds. Then he gripped his shoulder with strong fingers, almost making Noah wince, and pulled him down the trail. "Let's have a look, shall we?"

Noah wanted to glance back at Jimmy Hawkey, but he didn't dare. He trudged along next to Will, deeper into the forest.

"How old are you, boy?"

"Seventeen years."

"That's old enough." They walked in silence for a moment before Will spoke again. "You're younger than everyone else, and it's plain as day you weren't used to hard work. I bet your father's a jurist or a clergyman, ain't he?"

"He's a physician." A rush of nerves tingled through Noah's midsection. He didn't want to talk about his past. Dangerous things lived there.

"I knew he weren't no artisan or laborer," Will said with a cackle. "So why did you sign on? Got sent away, didn't ya?"

Noah's insides went cold again. He wanted to deny it, but his mouth was dry and he couldn't form the lie.

"I know what you were lookin' at back there. And I've seen how you look away whenever any of the men on the ship get too close to you while they're workin'. You try to hide it, but I see."

Noah glanced around, desperate, hoping no one was around to hear Will's words. But they were alone. The thick canopy blocked most of the sunlight, and the forest floor was dark. It reminded him of warm summer nights of his childhood, when Percival Aubrey, their vicar's oldest son, told the village children fairy tales of the awful things that happened to bad children who wondered into the forests.

"You ain't the first one I've known. Sometimes boys do with boys. And sometimes they get caught." Will stopped and turned Noah to face him. "They get sent to the hangman, you know. You was lucky you just got sent away. Was it your daddy, the one what caught you?"

Panic tore through Noah, and every instinct said to run. But he couldn't move, not a single muscle. His breath came short and fast. His mouth opened, but he couldn't make his voice work.

Will stepped closer, keeping his tight grip on Noah's shoulder. "I can keep a secret," he said, almost a whisper.

His rank breath made Noah's stomach turn, but a wave of relief washed over him. He still couldn't speak, but he managed a weak smile to show his thanks.

"I ain't been with a woman since June," Will said, and his other hand stoked Noah's backside through his trousers. "Three months is a long time to go without, ain't it, boy?"

Noah shook his head. "I—I don't know."

A full smirk twisted Will's mouth as he took his right hand from Noah's shoulder and undid Noah's belt buckle. "Turn around."

Terror swept through Noah. He'd never ... "No," he said, pleading with his eyes.

Will tugged down Noah's trousers. His rough hand rubbed Noah's bare buttocks like sandpaper, and slipped in between. With his right hand, Will unfastened the front of his own trousers. "I said turn around. You do what I ask, and I won't tell the captain what a filthy pillicock you are."

He took Noah by the hips and spun him around. Noah's pulse roared in his ears, drowning out the sounds of birds in the trees. Seconds later, the hardness of Will's erection poked around the crack of his ass. It found the entrance it sought, and Will spit on it several times.

Noah squeezed his eyes shut. Lance Aubrey had never asked this of him. Their vicar's younger son had routinely slid his hardness in between Noah's thighs, but neither of them would have dreamed of doing *this*. This was sodomy, and one went to hell for it. It was also buggery, and one could hang for that. Noah had always enjoyed bending forward enough that Lance's pecker rubbed him on the taint, which sent shivers through his body, but that never crossed the forbidden line.

When the uncomfortable pressure turned into searing pain of a sort he'd never imagined, something rustled in the bush behind them. A shout of surprise rose from Will, followed by a thud. Will collapsed into the bush, his trousers still bunched around his knee, his erection jutting pathetically into the moss on the ground.

Noah twisted to see Jimmy Hawkey behind him, arm raised with a large rock in his hand. The ragged edge of the rock was red with blood.

A thousand thoughts swirled in Noah's head, and he had the presence of mind only to pull up his pants and cover his shame. His face burned and he looked down while buckling his belt. He felt the warmth of Jimmy's hand on his shoulder, and shrugged it away.

"Are you alright, Mr. Bancroft?" Jimmy asked, softly, letting his hand drop.

Noah was silent for a few seconds before nodding. He turned toward Jimmy, but could barely get himself to look at his rescuer. Every time Jimmy's dark eyes found his, he looked away, glancing back a few seconds later to see the other youth watching him. "Thank you. You can call me Noah."

"You're welcome." Jimmy took him by the arm and pulled him toward the trail. "We need to get you back to the camp before he wakes up and looks for us."

Noah trudged along beside Jimmy for several minutes, numb, barely aware of what was happening. Then, like a sudden wave, the pain rushed through his chest. He stopped, leaned against the giant trunk of a pine tree, and collapsed onto his butt on one of the roots. He buried his face in his hand.

Jimmy sat next to him, put his arm around his shoulder, and hugged him tight. Noah turned his face into Jimmy's bare chest and sobbed.

CHAPTER 2

OCTOBER 1623 - PISCATAQUA POINT

The fear was constant.

Noah avoided Will Hailey as best he could, but they were a small cohort, and it was impossible to stay away from him. He'd glared at Noah that day at Monhegan, when he stormed into the clearing an hour after being knocked in the head by a rock; the sight of Noah enjoying a dinner of cod and lobster beside Floyd and Jimmy Hawkey no doubt added fire to Will's anger, but he didn't approach them.

After lifting anchor the next morning and crossing the twelves miles to Pemaquid Point on the coast—site of a fishing station that Captain Levett thought would make a superior trading post to Monhegan—Levett let the sails luff to explore every bay and inlet down the coast.

Every evening when he brought the captain supper, Noah found Levett poring over maps and charts spread across his table. "Come, Noah, have a look," Levett would say, pointing to a spot on the map to explain their current location, and tracing his finger along where they'd travelled that day. He explained the differences between the charts, and the reason.

"This was drawn by Champlain in 1604, coming southward from Acadia. Do you read French?"

"No, sir."

Levett waved a hand in the air, dismissive. "No matter, his notes aren't important. Champlain didn't find a suitable location for a French colony along the Maine, and he turned back toward Acadia. Up here.

His charting is more detailed than Cabot's, but of limited use to us. This chart of Captain Weymouth's expedition in 1605 has proven worthless; it was drawn from the recollections of Mr. Rosier after they returned to England, and is wholly inaccurate. But this one by Popham in 1607 shows us more possibilities. Right here, at this bay, is where he laid his ill-fated plantation. All of the colonists returned to England the next year, abandoning the colony; but we shall visit it to determine if the fault lay in the terrain, or in the constitution of the colonists."

Levett's eyes glowed when he pulled the largest map closer. "Ah, but this one is Captain John Smith's chart from his 1614 voyage. It is the most detailed by far, and as you see here, and here, and here, and here, and so on, he made extensive notes of his observations."

"Have you found a place for your colony, sir?"

"Aye, I think perhaps I have. There were many suitable sites along Casco Bay, here." He ran his finger in a C around that bay southwest of Monhegan Island. "Further exploration is in order to confirm my suspicion. But first, we rendezvous with Captain Robert Gorges here"--his finger slapped onto a spot on the map--"at Piscataqua Point. Several colonies are being planted in New England this season, and we must inaugurate a government for His Majesty's new dominions."

It was the beginning of October when they finally reached the Isles of Shoals, seventy-two nautical miles south-southwest of Monhegan Island. They stopped at a seasonal fishing station—smaller and less impressive than the one on Monhegan, to Levett's disappointment—and met the other five pinnaces in their fleet, which had sailed separately and rendezvoused at the deep harbor formed by the cluster of the three largest Isles. Levett took a day to scout a suitable location for a permanent fishing station, deposited a few dozen of his recruits to build it and jaunted across the five miles of water to the mouth of the Piscataqua River.

Noah managed to steer clear of Will Hailey, keeping to the opposite railing until their arrival at Piscataqua Point, a spit of land jutting into the ocean on the south shore of the wide estuary.

The point was cleared of trees, and several fishermen's shacks clustered to the rocky shore near a collection of docks. Behind them, on the banks of the river, stood a large sawmill, and several sawyers carried lumber from inside and stacked it near a pile of logs. On higher ground near the back of the clearing stood a two-story stone house. Hardly a grand manor house, but substantial enough to impress. A pair of pinnaces sat at anchor in the mouth of the river, each flying the white and red banner of St. George, marking them as English ships. Surrounding the settlement on the landward sides were thick stands of deciduous trees, hints of yellow and orange joining the green of their leaves.

After aiding Captain Levett onto the boat that would row them to shore, Noah spotted Will Hailey in the crowd on deck. His eyes shot daggers at Noah. A chill ran through him, but he breathed easier when Will didn't join them.

The crowd gathered to greet them contained several men in fine attire of velvet, leather, and lace, in contrast to the fishermen in their stained clothing. Noah kept a step behind Levett, following closely at his elbow as he led his entourage ashore. The gentlemen there removed their wide-brimmed hats in a sweeping motion and bowed from the waist. Captain Levett did the same, and after a second's hesitation, Noah bowed as well; he wondered if the men behind them were bowing, but he dared not look back to find out.

"Captain Gorges," Levett said, face still to the ground, before slowly rising. "My ship and its men are at your service, sir."

"Welcome, Captain Levett." One of the gentlemen had separated himself from the others, standing a step in front. He was a few years younger than Levett, perhaps thirty years old, with flowing brown hair that hung in waves to his shoulders, a curled brown mustache and pointed chin beard. "You remember Captain West, of course. And I present Mr. David Thomson, founder of Pannaway Plantation, and our host for this gathering."

"I welcome you, Captain Levett," the man indicated as Thomson said in a Scottish burr. He was younger than the others, probably late twenties, with thick black hair hanging to his shoulders. His narrow blue eyes and thin lips gave him the appearance of a perpetual scowl.

None of the other men warranted an introduction, and Gorges suggested they retire to the house and proceed to the business of the colony.

"Mr. Bancroft, you shall act as my secretary," Levett said over his shoulder as they followed the others toward the stone house.

"Yes, sir." Noah's heart raced, and his palms grew clammy. He had only a vague sense of the manners of the gentry, having interacted with gentlefolk little back home in their village of Rosemeade, Lancashire. His family were of the upper middling sort, educated but unrefined. The elaborate display he'd witnessed increased his anxiety.

And he desperately wanted to do a good job so that Captain Levett would be pleased with him.

"I call to order the inaugural meeting of the Government of New England." Robert Gorges' voice reverberated around the room. He sat at the head of an unpolished wooden table, while Levett and Captain West sat on opposite sides from one another. A tall cup of beer stood before each of them. The chair at the other end of the table sat empty, though a piece of parchment and a quill in an inkwell occupied the space.

Secretaries sat in smaller chairs behind the three captains, a writing board on their knees. Noah was several years younger than the other two. A high window on the far wall let in daylight, its stone sill reflecting some of that autumn light. The interior walls were bare wood, unpainted and unadorned; only the quartet of silver candlesticks on the wooden credenza in the corner hinted at affluence.

"Let the record note that present are myself, Captain Robert Gorges, Governor of New England, Councilor; Captain Christopher Levett, Councilor; and Captain Frances West, Councilor. Absent from the meeting is Mr. William Bradford, Governor of New Plymouth, Councilor."

Noah struggled to keep up with his quill and prayed that no one noticed his struggle.

"Let the record also show that a copy of these proceedings will be sent to Mr. Bradford at New Plymouth Plantation." The haughty sneer on Gorges's face spoke volumes on his opinion about Bradford's absence. Gorges launched into a lengthy speech about how the Council for New England, meeting at Plymouth in the County of Devon, under charter from His Majesty King James, had named Sir Ferdinando Gorges—Robert's father, Captain Levett had said—to the post of Governor-General of all of New England from the fortieth parallel to the forty-eighth parallel, and had empowered him to appoint councilors. These councilors were to have power of law over land and sea, and any person or persons planting or trading in the province. Sir Ferdinando Gorges had thus appointed the three men present, plus the absent member, to that duty.

Noah hoped Captain Levett wouldn't mind if he only recorded the gist of Robert Gorges's speech. It was impossible to write down every word. He breathed easier when Gorges asked Levett to report on his exploration of the Maine, and his plans for colonization there; Noah was familiar with this, and wouldn't have to work so hard to record it.

Levett spoke at length about the condition of the fishing stations on Monhegan Island, Pemaquid Point, and Damariscove Island, and the conditions of the coast and inlets between there and here. He gave a detailed accounting of the men he'd recruited from Yorkshire for his proposed port city, which he would christen York after his sponsor city. Noah stiffened at the mention of two master carpenters.

"I have identified several viable locations for the new city, but further exploration is required to determine the best one. I shall make my determination at the earliest possible date, and will secure the claim with the leader of the local natives, to ensure the plantation's safety and prosperity. I will write to your excellencies forthwith."

Gorges asked Captain West to give a report of their new plantation at Weymouth.

West spoke about the town he and Gorges had planted that summer on the south shore of the Massachusetts' Bay, with a detailed listing of the planters by occupation and sex. It surprised Noah that several women had joined the expedition, though the majority were men. Captain Levett had said the Nonconformists at New Plymouth included whole families with women and children; but one could hardly expect them to behave rationally, given their outlaw status in England.

Listening to Captain West drone on, Noah wondered why Gorges didn't report all this himself, since he was clearly the leader of that expedition. West spared no opportunity to praise Gorges's leadership and judgment.

Once West had finished, Gorges straightened and announced with a sneer, "Let the record reflect that no report could be made on the conditions at the New Plymouth Plantation due to the absence of Mr. William Bradford, Governor of New Plymouth, at the meeting of the colony's councilors." A sniff punctuated his disapproval. "However, I shall report that our host, Mr. David Thomson, informed me that men from New Plymouth called upon him in July, begging fish to feed the colony. Mr. Thomson filled their shallop with codfish, accepting payment in furs. Let the record note that those furs were owed to the Council in payment of New Plymouth's debts."

Gorges paused for dramatic effect. "Captain West and I detained Mr. Thomas Weston upon his return from the Maine, on charges of neglecting his previous colony at Wessagusset—on which site we have planted our colony—and for selling firearms to the American tribes in violation of Royal decree." Gorges frowned. "Weston has pled innocent to the former, and guilty to the latter. I have accepted his plea and agreed that he may depart for Virginia within the fortnight."

Noah almost sighed with relief when Gorges concluded the meeting. His hand had cramped long ago, but he'd struggled on in silence.

They emerged from the room, Noah keeping a step behind Levett. David Thomson stood in the hall with a young gentlewoman at his side and slightly behind him, dressed in a silk frock with wine-colored skirt, cream bodice, and black leather jacket with lace at the cuffs and collar. She was younger than Thomson by several years, perhaps five years older than Noah. She had a kind face, with round cheeks punctuated with a hint of pink, and large blue eyes over a small nose. Her uncovered blond hair was curly, but pulled back from her face into a bun at the crown of her head.

"Gentlemen, I present to you my wife, Amias," David Thomson said. The young woman bowed her head, keeping silent.

"Mistress Thomson," Captain Levett said with a nod and a flourish of his hand.

"Mistress Thomson has the honor of being the sole woman at Pann-away Plantation." Robert Gorges looked at David Thomson and added, "Though doubtless others shall follow in short order."

Thomson swallowed visibly at the implied rebuke, his Adam's Apple working up and down. He nodded without a word.

"I plan to bring my family to my colony of York next year," Levett said. "They remain in England until we have secured the location."

"Indeed," Gorges said, regarding Levett with an unreadable expression.

Noah decided to stay as invisible as possible around Captain Robert Gorges.

He followed Captain Levett to the docks, but did a double-take when he spotted two familiar but unexpected faces. He grinned, and a wave of warmth spread through him when Jimmy Hawkey and his father Floyd smiled back.

"Pardon me, Captain, but do you require my services? Might I have a little time to explore the plantation before I return to the ship?"

"You may take your leisure, Mr. Bancroft. But mind the time and make certain to be back at your post prior to dinner."

"Yes, sir, I will," Noah said, fighting the smile that tugged at the ends of his mouth.

He waited until Levett's boat pushed off from the dock before he approached Jimmy and Floyd. "I didn't expect to see you again."

"We heard your ship was coming here," Jimmy said, and his eyes held Noah's. He was wearing a shirt today, though the laces hung untied, leaving the collar loose and exposing a third of his chest. Noah mostly avoided looking at that triangle of smooth brown skin.

"We often fish these waters 'round here," Floyd said, scratching his stubbly cheek. "It's on the way to or from the Massachusetts' Bay. We usually rest over at the Isles of Shoals, but my Jimmy was worried about you." The sideways look he gave his adopted son, with a hint of amusement in his pale eyes, said that he wasn't criticizing the change of plans.

Jimmy's dark eyes continued to stare into Noah's, and though the youth's face remained passive, Noah was sure he saw concern in those eyes.

"I'm glad to see you." Then he hastily added, "Both of you."

An amused chuckled escaped Floyd Hawkey's lips. "You lads share your news, while I go secure space on the racks for our day's catch."

"Was this an unplanned visit?" Noah dared not hope that the Hawkeys had travelled all this way only to see him, no matter what Floyd's words had implied.

Jimmy looked confused by the question, his black eyebrows knitting together. "Planned? We came here on purpose, if that's what you mean. We heard from others on Monhegan that your ship was bound here. When I saw that the man who tried to ... to hurt you ... when I saw he was on your ship, I was worried for you. I told my father I wanted to take one more trip south."

The warmth spreading through Noah's belly reached his cheeks. "Thank you for thinking of me. I'm glad it coincided with your fishing trip."

Jimmy shook his head. "I came to see if you're safe. We already passed through here this summer, on our way to and from the Massachusetts' Bay. We planned to remain on Monhegan until spring." He looked to where Floyd spoke with a group of fishermen at the drying racks, negotiating space for the next few days. "I made an excuse that the waters around Monhegan had grown too crowded, but I did not fool him. He says nothing, but I know."

Noah's cheeks flushed hotter. "I am well, thank you." He became aware of suspicious eyes watching them, and he shifted his feet. Seeing Jimmy staring at him, he looked down. A second later, he glanced back up to see if Jimmy were still looking at him, and a tingle ran up his spine when he was.

Jimmy's eyes held his several seconds longer, then he nodded his head toward the docks. "Let us take my father's boat and explore up the river."

Noah grinned, but then cast a glance toward Floyd Hawkey at the fish racks. "He won't mind?"

"Not if I unload our catch first. Come."

Noah followed him to a high-sided boat that wasn't much longer than twenty feet. One mast stood in the center of the flat bottom, a single sail tied to it. Another stretch of canvas over a metal frame covered the back three feet of the boat, giving a small amount of shelter. There were at least ten large woven baskets filled with codfish inside the boat, and Jimmy jumped down and hefted one up, then nimbly hopped onto the dock and strode toward shore.

Noah tried to lift a basket, and was stunned at how heavy it was. He hadn't expected that, with as easily as Jimmy had lifted one. He bent his knees more and put his legs into it. Once he had it lifted, he leaned back a little and let the basket rest on his chest. He climbed onto the dock—harder than it looked—and followed Jimmy.

By the time he was half-way to the drying racks, he was huffing from the effort. Fishermen watched him and laughed. "Put your back into it, lad! You'll get there."

"Work like that will make a man of you, that's certain!" another said, to raucous laughter.

He was almost to the racks, sweat running down the sides of his face, and Jimmy turned to return to the boat. His eyes widened. "That's my work. You don't have to help with it."

"I wanted to help," Noah said, managing not to sound too winded. He left unsaid that he was having second thoughts.

Jimmy patted his shoulder. "I'll do the rest. Stay here with my father. I'll be finished soon."

Noah dropped the basket next to the one Jimmy had left near Floyd, who sat on a stool with a metal pail and was already gutting the first cod.

"Take a rest." Floyd nodded toward an empty stool. "You ain't used to work like that, lad. Do a little more next time. Eventually, you'll be as big and strong as my Jimmy."

Noah took the stool, but his heart jumped at how a few of the fishermen were looking at him. Pity, that's what he saw on their faces. A chill ran up his spine. "I'll just rest here a minute, and then I'll bring another one."

Floyd shook his head. "Let Jimmy do it. It's his chore, not yours. It's kind of you to offer, but you've got your own work to do later, ain't that right?" At Noah's nod, he chuckled and said, "Then take your rest time when you can get it. It's a precious thing indeed."

Noah's breathing and pulse had returned to normal when Jimmy brought the last basket from the boat, and announced that was all. His face and that triangle of chest glistened, but no sweat ran down either after ten times the work that had caused Noah to drip.

"Are you ready to go?" Jimmy asked, staring at Noah with those deep, dark eyes.

"Aye," Noah said, mimicking the fishermen's favored term for yes, and leapt from his stool. He nearly forgot to bid Floyd goodbye in his hurry to walk beside Jimmy.

"Goodbye, lads." Floyd chuckled, a twinkle of amusement in his eyes.

Jimmy shifted the sail with one hand while his other worked the rudder, slight movements sending the boat exactly where he wanted it. Noah was impressed. Jimmy made it look effortless.

Tall grasses lined the shore between the river and the forest, green on the top, brown and stalky near the waterline. Their stately grace was shattered on occasion by the movements of small unseen creatures. Birds, judging by the chirping sounds.

"These salt marshes line most of the coast," Jimmy said, his voice surprisingly quiet. But the awesome stillness of the river, the marsh, and the forest beyond demanded respectful quiet from the human interlopers. "The water here is brackish, so you can't drink it. The river brings fresh water, but the tides bring in salt. River fish and ocean fish mix here and attract multitudes of birds, and the grasses shelter them."

"It's very peaceful," Noah said with a sigh. "And all the grass means you don't have to worry about what's hiding in the forest."

Jimmy was silent, but Noah swore his eyes narrowed a little. Was Jimmy offended because he thought Noah meant Indians? He'd really meant wild animals, not the Indians. Hadn't he? "Thank you for bringing me here," he hurried to say. Maybe his gratitude would cover up any unintentional gaffe.

"The marshes are special places." Jimmy looked off in the distance. "When I was a boy, our village was on a hill that looked over the Massachusetts' Bay. At the bottom of the hill were salt marshes like this one. The other boys and I would play hunter there, catching frogs and salamanders."

"Is that where Floyd found you?" Noah asked, and hoped he hadn't gotten too personal.

A strange look crossed Jimmy's face, but a second later, his expression returned to normal. "I went there after I found everyone dead."

He might as well have smacked Noah across the face. "What happened?"

"The sickness," Jimmy said, as if that explained everything. "After my father died—my first father—and then my little sister started coughing, my mother sent me away. She told me to hide in the woods and not talk to anyone. To not come back until the leaves turned colors. Like they are now. I knew how to sleep in the forest, knew how to snare rabbits and cook them. I wandered the hills for a few months, and when I came home, everyone was gone. There were dead bodies all around the village, and the others had disappeared, like a spirit took them away. I never found my mother or my sister. So I went down to the marsh. It felt safe there. The tide was out, and I walked all the way to the bay. That's where I saw Papa and his friends with their boat. They called to me and offered me food."

Noah couldn't imagine what that was like. "Does it make you sad to think about?"

Jimmy shrugged. "Sometimes. But my life is good. When we came back the next summer, we learned that the sickness was spreading from village to village. If Papa hadn't taken me back to England with him, I would have died, too."

They sat in silence. Jimmy watched the birds swooping in and out of the marsh grasses. Noah watched Jimmy. Then, on an impulse he couldn't control, he leaned forward and placed his lips on Jimmy's. He held them there for a couple of seconds before pulling back. Panic swept through him. If he'd misread Jimmy's interest, Jimmy would punch him in the face, toss him overboard, and sail away without him.

Jimmy stared at him for several seconds. The silence sank dread into the pit of Noah's stomach. "I'm ... I'm sorry," he stammered. But Jimmy leaned forward, put both hands on Noah's shoulders, and kissed him back.

CHAPTER 3

October 1623 – Pannaway Plantaton

Jimmy's lips were soft, but he pressed them too hard against Noah's. He had probably never done this before. Still, the touch of his lips, the closeness and heat of his body, sent a jolt of electricity down Noah's spine, through his belly, and straight to his groin. His cheeks flushed hot as his member stiffened in his pants, and he squeezed his thighs together to hide it.

They broke the kiss after several seconds, and Noah looked down in embarrassment. And inadvertently his eyes went straight to the front of Jimmy's pants, which poked outward as if a pole had been planted there. His cheeks and neck grew even hotter, if that were possible.

He looked away in a hurry, hoping Jimmy hadn't noticed where he'd been looking. "Did you like that?"

Jimmy nodded.

"You've never done that before, have you?"

"No one here does that. I never saw kissing before I went to England."

Noah ventured a glance. Jimmy was staring at him. "You want to do it again?"

"Yes." Jimmy leaned forward, eyelids half-closed, lips puckering.

Noah leaned back, thinking of what Will Hailey had said on Monhegan, and what Captain Gorges had said about Amias Thomson. Was he just practice? "Wait. I wonder ... would you rather do this with a girl? If there were girls here, would you choose one of them to kiss?"

A hint of smile curled the corners of Jimmy's mouth. He shook his head. "There are girls here. Just not English girls." He leaned into Noah, their lips touching again, but their torsos touching as well. Jimmy put his hands on Noah's arms and moved them around his back.

Noah let his hands hold Jimmy, and then dared to slip one under the tail of his shirt, touching the soft skin over firm ridges around the valley of Jimmy's spine. Jimmy's hands slipped under Noah's shirt, warm against his back.

Noah lay back into the bow of the boat, pulling Jimmy down with him, their kiss lasting until they were both out of breath.

"We should get back, before anyone wonders what we're doing," Noah said, bolting upright and looking around. The river was silent save for the calls of birds in the marsh grasses and the occasional splash of a fish leaping to catch an insect.

Jimmy raised onto his elbow, and his hand settled on Noah's forearm. "We're exploring the river. Everyone will believe that."

Noah looked at Jimmy, almost getting lost in the confidence in those dark eyes. "Aren't you afraid someone will think that we ..." His voice trailed off, and his cheeks heated.

Jimmy shrugged. "No one would think that unless they've done it themselves."

Noah took a moment to ponder that. "On Monhegan Island, does anyone ..." he couldn't get himself to finish the sentence, his throat going dry.

A wry smile curled the corners of Jimmy's mouth. "I don't know. But I think probably yes." He rose and sat facing Noah. "Most of the men at Monhegan come in May to fish for cod, and return to England in

September or October because they have wives and children waiting for them. But a few years ago, some of us stayed over the winter, all men without wives. Most years we are about fifteen souls, and I suspect a few are companions."

A strange mix of realization and excitement swept through Noah. "I never thought of it that way." Then another thought occurred to him. "Your father ...?"

Jimmy's expression grew serious, and he looked off in thought. "I don't think so. He had a wife, and a daughter, too. They died the winter before his first voyage to America with his friends. Almost eight years ago. When they found me by the shore of the Bay, I think taking care of me was what he needed to fill his heart again. I don't think he wants another woman, but not because he is like us."

"But you think there are others ... like us ... here?"

Jimmy stared into Noah's eyes, and his hand caressed Noah's arm. "I am certain of it." He leaned in, and they dropped back to the floor, kissing.

Dusk was slipping into twilight when Jimmy pulled the boat alongside the pinnace, and hallooed the crew, who sent down a rope ladder. Noah thanked him, careful not to touch him, and scrambled up the ladder, which swayed against the side of the ship. He scampered over the rail, waved, and rushed toward the captain's quarters.

But came face-to-face with Will Hailey.

"Did you have yourself a merry time with the Indian?" Will asked with a smirk, and the accusatory look in his eyes made Noah feel like Will could read his mind, could see what they had done on the river.

He didn't meet Will's eyes. "It was very enjoyable. We explored up the river. There's much good country there. I mean to tell the captain about it." He took a step to bypass Will, but the man stepped in front of him again.

"It would serve you well to be wary of the savages. Even one raised by an Englishman. His nature is still of the savage, no matter what English habits he's learned. The men will question your judgment."

Noah swallowed, took a second to think of a response. "He was an excellent guide. Now let me return to my duties, so I can tell the captain what I've learned about the country."

Will grabbed Noah's arm on his way past. "If you've been cavorting with the savage instead of doing my bidding, I'll see your neck in a noose before the week's out," he said, loud enough for Noah's ears only. He nodded his chin up at the yardarm. "I'll hoist you up there meself. You know, boy, in England they'd cut your balls off before they hanged you. Not sure if Captain Levett would let me do it, but I'd sure like to."

Noah went cold, and stared back at Will, open-mouthed.

"This passenger bothering you, Bancroft?" Jack Cooper's gruff voice said. The big, black-bearded sailor stood close to Hailey, glaring down at his hand gripping Noah's arm.

Noah swallowed hard, fought to control his breathing so he could speak. "I was telling him about exploring the river with that son of Floyd Hawkey," Noah managed to say while sounding only a little breathless.

Jack chuckled. "That sounds like a merry old time, that does. A fine adventure. I'm glad you made a friend your age. Hurry on, now; the captain be wantin' his supper 'fore the clock strikes."

"Wait a moment Bancroft, before you remove those dishes," Captain Levett said, barely glancing up from his writing. His quill moved furiously across the parchment as he signed something, then he folded it in thirds, dripped candle wax onto the edge, and sealed it with his signet ring. He handed it to Noah. "This needs to be taken to the captain of the *Anne* tonight. They depart with the morning tide. I'm sending them to Cape Ann to plant a station on the Massachusetts' Bay." He beckoned with his hand. "Come here, I'll show you."

Noah left the dirty dishes and walked around the table. Levett had Captain John Smith's map spread on the end of the table, and he stood and met Noah there. "We're here, at the Piscataqua River. Down here is the point Captain Smith named after the queen, Cape Ann. It guards the entrance to the Massachusetts' Bay, this body of water here. It's ideal for a permanent station, and eventually a fort as well, to keep the French out."

"That leaves five ships for your new colony."

Levett's finger ran back up the coast toward their present location. "My mission from the Council was to plant many permanent stations in New England this season. The Council want fishermen who will stay year round, and that's what we brought aboard our other ships. Some we will leave here, at Pannaway Plantation. Others I'll send to Monhegan Island, Pemaquid, and Damariscove Island. And we planted some on the Isles of Shoals, over here. But the men aboard this ship are meant for my colony of York, which we'll plant somewhere along here." He ran his finger over the coast of the Maine. He straightened and nodded at the sealed message in Noah's hand. "Now, remove those dishes and take that message to Mr. Holloway. Tell him you need to take it forthwith to the *Anne*."

A wistful look came to Jimmy's eyes the next day when Noah told him about the *Anne*'s mission. They were tramping through the forest a mile west of Pannaway.

"Jack Cooper rowed me to the *Anne* last night, and I delivered Captain Levett's message directly to her captain," Noah said, breathless all over again with the same excitement he'd felt in the moment. "Her captain said he was glad to have their orders, so his crew could plant their passengers and return to England before winter takes hold."

"Winter takes hold here many weeks before it does in England," Jimmy said. "You'll see soon."

Noah contemplated that, but Jimmy's point of reference in Cornwall might not be the same as his in Lancashire. He shrugged it off. "Will the new station there—at Cape Ann, I mean—will it make it easier for you and your father when you travel to the Massachusetts' Bay next summer?"

Jimmy didn't answer immediately. "Perhaps. It might offer us a place we can stay, should we require it."

"You were from there, weren't you? When you were a boy?"

Jimmy nodded. "But my people lived on the south shore of the bay. Cape Ann is on the north shore, and farther to the east, where the bay meets the ocean. I have never set foot there, though I have seen it from our boat."

"Is it a good place for a new station?"

Jimmy brought his musket up to his chest, put his finger to his mouth. Noah fell silent. His heart leapt into his throat as he glanced around, trying to see what Jimmy had seen. But nothing stood out except trees, endless trees. Jimmy raised his musket and aimed off into the woods. Noah could barely breathe.

The gun fired with a loud crack, and Jimmy's shoulder came back from the force of it. A bird squawked, and long brown feathers scattered to the wind. The carcass fell to the ground some twenty yards away.

Jimmy grunted in satisfaction, nodding to himself, and trudged off toward the grouse. He knelt and picked it up by the feet, and held it aloft for Noah to see. "Dinner tonight."

"I wish I could join you," Noah said, and meant that.

"Tell Captain Levett you're staying here tonight."

Noah looked away. "I wish I could."

"Why can't you?"

Noah didn't look at him. "I have to do what he says. He owns my indenture."

Jimmy was silent for several long seconds. "I didn't know. I thought you were free. An adventurer." He paused another couple of seconds before adding, "You don't seem like the kind of boy who would sell himself for a passage to America."

Noah's lips pursed. "I wasn't given a choice."

Jimmy grunted, and Noah wondered what he was thinking. "Did someone see you kiss another boy?" he finally asked.

Not kissing. A wooded hundred outside their village, a mossy log near a stream, well distant from the cow path and hidden in a shallow ravine. No one should have seen. A little pool in the stream, ideal for skinny dipping in the warmth of May, the cold water bringing hardness to their privy parts. The way Lance slid his between Noah's legs, moving back and forth, pressing upward against his taint ... How could they have known the vicar knew the spot, came there for contemplation when he was at a loss of what to say in his homily? Noah's face burned at the memory, and he wondered if it were now as red as the vicar's—Lance's father's—that day.

Jimmy grunted again, looking sideways at him. Noah's face grew hotter, and he looked down at the trail.

Three figures stepped from behind a large tree some twenty yards in front of them, and the boys stopped in their tracks. Noah's heart skipped a beat at the sight of the trio of Indian men, a few years older than them. Blocking their path. They dressed like the Indians on Monhegan Island, with the partial pant leg that failed to cover their hips and half-exposed buttocks. Their hands rested on stone axe blades at their hips, and Noah's breath came short and shallow.

He looked at Jimmy, who had lifted his musket to his chest and gripped it in both hands, white-knuckled. The grouse had fallen to his feet. Then he raised his right hand, palm outward, and said a few strange words, deep and guttural.

The three men in front of them kept their hands at their axes, but one said something back. Jimmy replied, but his body tensed. A brief conversation of short, clipped phrases ensued, and then all fell silent.

"What's happening?" Noah whispered.

"They are Abenaki," Jimmy said, keeping his voice low and talking out the side of his mouth, his eyes never wavering from the trio. "I can't speak their language, but I know words of greeting. They didn't return the greeting, but asked about the Strangers—the English at the point. I tried to say in my first language that the Strangers want only to fish and trade, but I don't know if they understood."

Noah looked at their faces, but their expressions were unreadable. Their dark eyes were like stones staring back. "Will they let us pass?"

Jimmy didn't answer, but knelt slowly, keeping his eyes on the three men. He picked up the grouse in his left hand, keeping his musket in his right, and slowly stood. Then he held the bird out, toward the men, and said a few words in that strange language that didn't sound like anything Noah had ever heard.

One of the men grunted, and then the three of them laughed. Noah wasn't sure what was happening, but they stepped to the side of the trail, backs to the largest tree.

Jimmy said a word, his tone sullen, and then he said to Noah, "Come on, but keep behind me."

Noah stuck close to Jimmy's side a half-step behind him, until they passed the spot where the three men stood, watching them with vaguely amused looks. Jimmy veered as widely around them as was possible on the trail, and Noah stepped into the bramble at the edge to keep himself on the opposite side of his friend. Jimmy walked backwards for several yards, keeping the men in sight. When they slipped into the forest and disappeared, he finally turned back forward and picked up his pace.

"I believe we are safe, but let's not dawdle."

"What was that about?" Noah asked once they'd put some distance between them and the place where they'd passed the men.

"I think they wanted to intimidate us. When I wasn't intimidated, they mocked us instead. At least, I think that's why they laughed when I offered them our catch. Their language differs from mine, but some words are similar."

"Like English and Dutch?"

Jimmy shrugged. "I don't know any Dutch."

Noah had heard some Dutch a few times, on trips to market at Chester with his family, from sailors ashore from trading vessels. His mother—an educated woman who valued learning above almost anything—had told him that Dutch was like a funny form of English when written, familiar words spelled in strange new ways, but pronounced even more strangely so as to be incomprehensible to an English ear.

The trail widened as it approached the clearing, and the buildings of Pannaway Plantation came into view. Noah breathed easy for the first time in twenty minutes.

Until he spotted Will Hailey among a crowd of men near the sawmill. Will's eyes met his for a second, and he smirked. Noah looked away and hurried past.

Noah spotted the falls before the sound of the rushing water reached his ears. This was their farthest trip yet up the Piscataqua River, almost a dozen miles from the point, and the salt marshes had given way to unbroken forest. Jimmy lowered their sail, tied it up, and dropped anchor in the middle of the river. The boat's forward progress halted, and the bow turned in the current. Noah watched the water tumbling over the rocks in the low c-shaped falls and then looked back at Jimmy.

As they'd done every day for the last two weeks, they came together without a word, mouths meeting and arms embracing, hands roaming under shirts, and they lowered to the bottom of the boat.

It got easier each time, and by now they were familiar enough with the feel of each other's bodies pressed close that neither was embarrassed that the other felt the hardness that sprang between his legs within a minute of kissing. No longer did they keep their hips back to hide it, but allowed every part of themselves to touch while they kissed.

After some time, Jimmy pulled away and tugged his shirt over his head. Then he put his hands under Noah's shirt and lifted it up, raising Noah's arm's. Noah shivered, the chill of the October air raising goosebumps across his torso and down his arms. But then Jimmy pressed against him, soft and warm skin against skin, and his stomach went light.

Jimmy's right hand roamed down his belly, sending tingles up his spine. But then his palm ran past the waist of his pants, gliding down the stiff shape of Noah's prick under the fabric. Noah gasped. Jimmy's mouth moved down his chin to the tender flesh of his throat, kissing and nibbling with his lips, sending shivers down Noah's spine. And all the while, his hand moved slowly up and down over the stiff rod inside Noah's trousers.

A wave rushed through Noah, and he breathlessly said, "Stop!" Jimmy's hand paused, but it was too late. Noah pulled his hips away, clenched every muscle in his lower torso in a vain attempt to halt the natural reaction. Sweat sprang from every pore, his breath caught, and the spasms below sent a rush of wetness into the front of his pants.

"I'm sorry," he breathed, but Jimmy put his finger to Noah's lips. He pulled Noah's hand to the front of his pants, wrapped Noah's fingers around the hardness barely concealed within. They kissed again, and Noah lost himself in the feel of Jimmy's lips on his.

"Halloo!"

The call jolted them both. It wasn't far off. A chill shot through Noah's body, and Jimmy's eyes grew wide. They pulled away from each other without thinking, each reaching for his shirt bunched up beneath them.

"Halloo!" the voice called again, even closer. "Ahoy there. Anyone aboard?"

Noah tugged his shirt over his head, getting it twisted around him as he sat up and looked over the side.

Six men occupied the boat approaching theirs, but Noah's eyes fell upon the smirking face of Will Hailey in the bow, and his breath caught in his throat.

"What are ya doin' lyin' on the bottom of your boat, lad?" Will asked, the words clipped, his narrowed eyes accusing.

"We were napping," Noah said.

"Your face is awfully red for just awaking from slumber."

"You startled us," Jimmy said.

"Foolhardy, the both of ye," a fisherman said in a slow drawl, and nodded toward the trees on the nearest bank. "The savage Indians could've fallen upon ye before ye had any time to react. Ye'd both be dead now."

Noah glanced at Jimmy, worried how he'd feel about the fisherman's words. But Jimmy's face was calm, and he replied, "That's good advice. We thank you."

"Too much work to be done, hauling in the catch before winter," another fisherman drawled. "'Tis a waste of time to nap now. Ye can nap when the snows come. I wouldn't like to speak to your father about it, young Mr. Hawkey."

Jimmy straightened tall. "My father and I finished our catch for today, Mr. Penley. I am at ease for the afternoon, and I brought Mr. Bancroft on a quest to find the falls."

"At ease or no, you'd best store up extra for the coming winter," Penley replied.

"I thank you for your kind advice," Jimmy said, and hauled in the anchor. "Raise the sail," he said to Noah.

Will Hailey glared at Noah as Jimmy's boat sped past theirs. Noah's whole body burned with shame and anger. This was not over.

Captain Levett called him over the night after next, as he gathered the captain's dirty dishes. "A word please, young man."

"Yes, sir?" Noah barely kept the tremor from his voice as he stood in front of the captain, dishes in-hand. Levett's tone had been more serious than was usual in private.

"There have been reports made to me these last two days concerning you and certain aspects of your behavior on shore."

Noah stiffened. It was a wonder he didn't drop the dishes to the floor, his hands trembled so much. "What rumors be there, sir?" His voice most definitely wobbled that time.

"I won't repeat the worst one, since it is unsubstantiated," Levett said with a note of distaste. "I have no use for false witness. But I cannot ignore its spread among the passengers and crew of this ship. I have a mission to lead, a colony to plant. I cannot have ... distractions. We mustn't ignore that you have been incautious in your interactions, which have led to certain assumptions spreading among the men, leading to these reports."

Noah's mouth had gone dry, but he managed to swallow and croak out, "Do you believe them, sir?"

Levett stared at him for many long seconds. "Not the worst of it, no." He sat forward, folded his hands on the table and looked down for a few seconds. Then he took a deep breath. "It is natural for men to form close and intimate bonds, and such bonds form the more easily when women are not present. Every sea captain knows this, though it is not discussed publicly. But it must never become a distraction, or it must be dealt with."

"Am I to be punished?"

Levett shook his head and stood. "I have sold your indenture. To Mr. Thomson of Pannaway Plantation. His household is in need of an additional servant, and you will go to his house tomorrow morning. Our ship will depart soon, but you are to remain here."

Noah wasn't sure how to feel—relieved that he wasn't being flogged, or hanged; but also trepidatious about his future with the Thomsons.

Captain Levett stepped closer, and his eyes held a sad sort of kindness. "This is the last we shall see each other for some time, and I bid thee good bye, Noah. I wish thee well."

Captain Levett's final words to him—using not only his first name, as he often had in private, but also the familiar "thee" for the first time—ran through his mind on repeat while two sailors rowed him to shore in the misty gray light of dawn.

One nail near the bow of the rowboat wasn't flush with the plank, its rusty head sitting a half-inch off the wood. Noah had never noticed it before. It could snag his hose and rip a tear if he weren't cautious, and he didn't have another pair. How fortunate he'd never caught himself on it before, the countless times he'd clambered over the side of this very boat. How many near-misses had he suffered without ever knowing? If he snagged it hard enough, it might draw blood. Gangrene could take someone's foot. If the nail came any looser, the boat might spring a leak. Cold water would flood in, its icy fingers surrounding their feet and climbing their legs. The ocean would swallow them up, its depths holding them down like a frigid hand on their chests, wrapping them in death's embrace.

The boat bumped against the dock.

"Farewell, lad. You're Mr. Thomson's now." Jack stared off into the distance.

Noah climbed out, swinging his leg wide of the loose nail. He faced the stone house on the rise, his earthly belongings in a pack over his shoulder. He took a breath and trudged up the path.

CHAPTER 4
MARCH 1623/24 - MAINE

The storm came suddenly.

The wind whipped the waves into whitecaps, tossing the ketch like a toy boat. Sudden, hard rain blew in sheets, drenching them.

"Get the net aboard!" Floyd Hawkey shouted over the howl, but Jimmy was already tugging with all his might. A high wave rocked the boat hard, and his feet slipped, cracking his back against the seat.

It took a second to regain his breath, but then he braced his feet against the sides of the boat, wide-legged, knees bent to absorb the motion, and tugged again at the net. Floyd released the rudder and appeared at Jimmy's side, lending his strength.

The weight of the caught fish disappeared in an instant, and the tattered remains of the net flew out of the water and struck them in their faces.

"We have to make for Damariscove!" Floyd shouted, returning to the rudder. "It's our only hope."

They'd been almost five miles south of Pemaquid Point when the storm hit, putting them less than two miles from Damariscove Island. The wind and waves, coming out of the north-east, would drive them south of the island, and Floyd grunted with effort, pulling at the rudder. Jimmy tightened the lines on the flapping canvas cover at the stern and joined Floyd on the bench. He grabbed the rudder from the other side, helping Floyd hold it in place against the mighty force of the churning water.

The tall pine stands of Damariscove Island came into view, black against the slate gray sky. The rain morphed into the whiteness of blowing snow, blinding, but wet enough that it still swept over them in sheets like driven rain.

Miraculously, they found the entrance to the deep cove that cut through the center of the island, for which it was named. But their struggle didn't end. The side of the ketch bumped hard against the jagged rocks that bordered the opening, and the heart-breaking splintering of wood cracked over the roar of the northeastern winds. Jimmy pushed hard against the rock, and they slipped past it into the more sheltered water, but still tossed about.

A half-dozen fishing huts came into view, and then the docks in front of them, and Floyd adjusted the rudder. Men poured out of the huts, thick coats and hats bundled against the wind and snow, and flagged them toward a strip of pebble beach.

"Too early to be out in deep water," one of the fishermen said in a drawling Somerset accent, handing a steaming bowl to Jimmy. He took the bowl gratefully, hot in his icy hands. He huddled naked under a thick blanket, while their dripping clothes hung on a cord above the fire, threatening to douse it.

"Nay!" Floyd said, the indignation coming loud and clear. "'Tis safe past the Ides of March. Everyone knows that."

"In the English Channel, aye. But not in New England." He handed a bowl to Floyd, who accepted it in silence.

"But you're new to this country, aren't ye?" Jimmy said between swallows of thick fish stew. "Captain Levett planted this station last fall."

"Aye," another fisherman said, also with a Somerset drawl. "But the captain, he spoke with more'n a dozen fishermen what stay year-round, at Monhegan and Pemaquid. Wait 'til the new year, that's what they all said."

"I spoke with him meself, and I said no such thing," Floyd muttered, but didn't belabor the point.

"It's only ten days later, Papa," Jimmy said under his breath.

Floyd didn't acknowledge Jimmy's comment. Instead, he stared at his bowl and slurped his stew.

"You're an American, aren't you?" the first Somerset man said. His gaze on Jimmy's face was steady, as if studying him. But neither his expression nor the tone of his question seemed hostile.

"Yes," Jimmy said, without further explanation.

"He's me son," Floyd said, a touch of indignation still present in his voice. "Found him when he was a wee lad, all alone. He's been with me almost eight years now."

"We heard there was a pestilence in the country," the second Somerset man said. "Many dead, whole villages, even. Some say seven years, some say eight."

"It lasted two years," Floyd said, scraping the bottom of his bowl and gobbling the last of the stew. His raised the bowl toward their hosts before setting it down on the nearby table. "We thank ye. My boy Jimmy and me, we're grateful to ye for takin' us in and feedin' us."

"Your boat will need repairin'," the first one said. "Ye can stay as long as ye need."

"And we'll need a new net," Floyd said between bites of stew. "If ye can spare one, we can help ye lads around here for a couple of weeks in exchange."

"We can spare a net, no trouble."

"What news have you of Captain Levett and his colony?" Jimmy asked. He hadn't intended his voice to sound so eager, and his cheeks heated. But maybe that was just the warmth of the stew, and the nearness of the fire.

"The captain himself went back to England," the first man announced, plopping into a chair opposite them and rubbing his hands over the fire. "Gone to fetch his wife and children. I expect he'll return in a few months. By the autumn, at the latest."

Noah would be with the captain, wouldn't he? He'd said he was indentured to him. Jimmy hid his disappointment. But still ... "Did he plant his colony before he left?"

"Aye. Built a fine house on Casco Bay. Left ten Yorkshire men there to hold it for him 'til he comes back. Gave us a map to it. He stopped by here on his way back to England."

Jimmy wasn't bold enough to ask if Levett had had a young servant boy with him when he stopped here. He stared at the bottom of his bowl and spooned up the last of the stew.

"We'll call there in a couple of weeks ... once it's safe to go out in deep water." A twitch at the corner of the fisherman's mouth said that this jab at Floyd was meant as a jest.

"Hardy har," Floyd said.

But Jimmy's mind was already playing out the scene in two weeks' time, when they pulled up to the York colony at Casco Bay, and Noah came out from the house. Their eyes would meet, and his friend's smile would light up his face. Jimmy would talk his father into staying in Casco Bay for the spring—it was a big bay, full of fish.

And in the afternoons, after the fish were laid out on the racks to dry, he and Noah could take their boat exploring.

The sun came out the next morning, revealing a world covered in almost a foot of snow. Mist shrouded the forest and swirled in whisps over the water.

"The damndest weather in this part of the world," Floyd muttered, tugging his hat lower over his ears. "After the Ides of March, it should be springtime. Well, come along, lad. Our boat needs mendin'. Best get to it."

The Damariscove fishermen took some time to inspect their own boats, which remained tied to the wharfs, but showed a few signs of battering. The wind and waves had banged them against the side of the dock, leaving behind deep scratches; but none needed serious repairs.

Except the Hawkeys' ketch. At least three of the boards along the port side were nearly gashed through from the encounter with the rocks, being dangerously thin in places. Jimmy shivered as he ran his fingers along the thinnest part, right where he had been sitting. It had been a narrow escape.

"It'll take a few days to cut and plane new boards," Floyd said to the pair of fishermen who had hosted them overnight. There were thirteen of them who had stayed permanently on the island. More would come for the summer—this was a favorite spot for the seasonal visitors from England—but that was a month off, at least.

"We'll help with that," one of their hosts replied. "We can have it all finished by tomorrow."

The kindness of these strangers overwhelmed Jimmy. "Thank you." The words were hardly enough.

"We're much obliged to you," Floyd said. "For the safe shelter, for the dinner, and for your help with our boat. It ain't no wonder the good Lord chose fishermen when he started teaching. Once we're back on the water, my boy Jimmy and I will stay with ye a few weeks and contribute to your labors."

Their hosts chuckled. "We're here together, and we'll survive it to-gether."

The snow melted away after a couple of days, and overnight the decid-uous trees growing in the shade of the giant pines sprouted pale green buds. Jimmy and Floyd joined their hosts every frosty morning on the rocky shore, collecting clams and oysters in buckets. Jimmy set out their lobster traps after their third day on Damariscove, and caught some of the spiny creatures. At least one or two of the locals dropped a line into the water each day, and came home hours later with three or four halibut. And from this bounty arose a rich stew every night.

On March 26th, the second day of the new year, a group of them set sail for Casco Bay.

Jimmy's nerves tingled. But it wasn't until his father pointed it out that he realized his movements were jerky, and even a bit absent-minded.

"Don't worry lad, we ain't gettin' caught in a storm twice," Floyd said with a chuckle.

But that wasn't the reason Jimmy was nervous. He'd carefully avoided bringing up the subject of the York colony after their first night on Damariscove Island, lest he seem over-eager. But the possibility of seeing Noah there kept it on his mind—when he paused from digging clams to gaze across the ocean at the distant shore, when he lay down to sleep every night and imagined Noah's lips on his ... and when he turned onto his side and pulled his knees to his chest so his erection didn't show under the blankets. He didn't need strangers seeing *that* and commenting on it in the morning. Or his father.

The boats didn't pause until they'd reached the mouth of Casco Bay, some ten miles southwest of Damariscove Island, and then they threw their nets off the sides. Jimmy concentrated on the work and tried not to wonder how far away the York colony sat from their position. Could the colonists see their sails on the horizon? Was Noah looking out over the water right now, seeing fishing boats and wondering about Jimmy?

It was impossible to know. The jagged shoreline of the giant bay ran for hundreds of miles. There were twenty miles of open water across the mouth of the bay alone, and it extended into the forests some ten or twelve miles in most places, dotted with dozens of islands big and small, and broken by the mouths of countless streams and small rivers. Captain Levett could have chosen any number of spots for his new city.

It might take weeks to find it on their own. He couldn't expect to impose on the Damariscove Islanders, sharing their lodging and food, for that long. Sooner or later, Jimmy would have to open his mouth and risk asking.

He let most of the morning pass before he worked up the courage to raise the question on one of their near passes with another boat.

"Where is the York colony from here?" he shouted, cupping his hand around his mouth to make sure his voice carried over the water. They'd been drifting south-westward all morning, trawling into the bay itself, each boat making wide loops and hauling in the nets when they were full. The stiff breeze had them moving at about seven knots, and some of the islands now loomed close, only two or three miles away.

"That-a-way," one of the trio of fishermen in the nearest boat shouted back, pointing toward the south shore of the bay, where a cluster of islands guarded an inlet.

"We'll stop there later," one of his companions shouted. "See if they want to trade for some of our catch."

Jimmy's heart fluttered. He'd find out soon enough if his friend were still in this country.

"We won't have time for a long stay," Floyd said as their fish-laden boats navigated the broad inlet at the south end of Casco Bay. The sky was gray with thick cloud cover, but he held his thumb toward the sky and closed one eye until he was satisfied he knew where the sun sat. "'Twill be dark in five hours."

The lead boat pulled close to the mouth of a river, trimming its sail. Jimmy worked to trim their sail and slow them, but cast glances at the thick forests, watching for any sign of a clearing.

That clearing appeared some fifty yards upstream from the river mouth, and a giant stone house loomed out of the trees some twenty yards from the riverbank. "Strange no one's come out to meet us," Floyd muttered, putting voice to Jimmy's own thoughts.

A nerve twitched at the back of his neck.

The boats pulled onto the sandy bank alongside one another. Everything was quiet. Even the fishermen kept silent.

"This ain't right," the leader of the group finally said. Everyone else nodded, but none had the courage to halloo into the woods.

"No one's been here for a long time," Floyd said, and pointed at the house. "Those grasses ain't been trampled by anyone in weeks. Look at 'em."

Jimmy's heart had risen into his throat. It was true, the weeds along the side of the house had grown a foot-high already, including directly in front of the door. The wild grasses stretching from the riverbank toward the house were undisturbed by anything so large as a human. Scanning the meadow, he saw signs of the passing of small animals and deer only.

"There's no sign of attack," he said aloud, as much for his own reassurance as everyone else's. No arrows littered the ground near the house, no muskets dropped into the grasses and lost. A battle, even among as few as two dozen, would have trampled the meadow.

"Captain Levett believed the Penobscot Sachem when he called the captain 'friend,'" one of the fishermen said, with a note of bitterness that made Jimmy flinch. The side-eyed glances his direction from the other fishermen were impossible to miss.

He wanted to say anything, but his mouth was dry and his mind devoid of any response.

"We should check the house," the leader said, mouth set in a grim line. He waved them forward, and they marched across the narrow meadow toward the door.

The interior of the house was musty, and dust motes swirled in the afternoon sunlight streaming through the windows. Small cobwebs occupied the corners where walls met ceiling. Dishes and silverware were set on the dining table, ten place-settings, their sheen dulled by a thin coating of dust.

Upstairs, the beds were made. Clothes lay folded in half-full trunks. But there were no shoes anywhere, no footprints on the dusty wooden floors. It was as if the York colonists had left for an afternoon outing, intending to return.

Only they hadn't returned.

None of them spoke a word. But Jimmy could feel the Damariscove fishermen's gaze on the back of his head. He didn't need to turn around and look.

Or maybe he didn't dare confront their suspicions face-to-face.

"No one's been here for a month at least, maybe six weeks," the leader of the Damariscove fishermen said when they'd gathered back outside. "Wherever they went, their footprints were left in the snow, and that's long since melted away."

"That's ten good Englishmen, gone missing in the wilderness," another said, his Somerset drawl somehow managing to be accusing and melancholy at the same time.

But the only Englishman Jimmy could think of was Noah Bancroft. He silently prayed to the Creator that Noah had gone back to England with Captain Levett, and wasn't left behind at this house. *Please, let him not have been left behind.* If Noah were in England, he'd be safe. Here, Jimmy could only fear what might have befallen him.

And his stomach was an icy stone in his gut at the thought.

CHAPTER 5

APRIL 1624 – NEW ENGLAND

"We won't have to remind you of your moral duty in our new home, will we, Mr. Bancroft?" David Thomson asked, stern eyes narrowed and brows knit tightly together in disapproval. "I trust I won't find you touching yourself in an unseemly manner again?"

Noah rubbed his red and swollen hands, not making eye contact with his master. Instead, staring at the yardstick in Mr. Thomson's hand. "No, sir."

"No, sir, what?"

"No, sir, I won't touch myself in an unseemly manner again, Mr. Thomson."

"Good. See that you don't."

Noah nodded, still looking down, and hurried away. It wasn't his fault. He couldn't help that thoughts of Jimmy Hawkey still came to mind unbidden, months after they'd last seen each other. And he couldn't help the physical reaction that those thoughts often brought. It wasn't his fault there was only one effective way to deal with that reaction before anyone saw it. The broom closet had become his refuge for such moments, and the pile of old rags his friends.

But Mr. Thomson was a wily Scotsman, and somehow he always knew when Noah snuck off there. It was as if the walls whispered to him. Except that Mr. Thomson was far too pious to engage in such witchcraft.

"Now get back to work," Mr. Thomson called after him. "There is much still to be done before we depart."

From the central hall, Noah picked up a crate and carried it to a cart in front of the house. His pulse quickened, and he glanced at the woods. When the spring thaws finally came in mid-March, they had brought with them swift raids from the Indians, who appeared from the edge of the trees as if conjured by a sorcerer and shot arrows at the servants tending Mr. Thomson's cattle and sheep, before disappearing into the darkness of the forest. They came three or four times a week, and though no one had been killed, one cowherd had taken an arrow to the shoulder a couple of weeks ago. He nearly lost the arm to infection.

Noah's most hated chore became collecting armloads of firewood in the evenings; the stacks of chopped wood sat along the side of the stone house, and the edge of the woods was only about twenty yards from there. Here at the front of the house, it was closer to thirty yards, but still too near to relax while he stacked another box onto the cart.

These raids had been the final straw for Mrs. Thomson. Noah had overheard her complain to her husband about the harsh winter when they thought no one was near. Now, the fear of Indian attack had pushed her to insist, in front of the servants, that they move to a safer location. "We can't raise our children in such a dangerous place."

Noah sympathized with Mrs. Thomson. It had been the coldest winter he'd ever known, and his most miserable chore was twice daily scraping the frost from the insides of the windows. The thin rag he used offered no protection, and his fingers hurt. While the snow that piled two or three feet high in the clearing was beautiful, and Noah had taken the occasional peaceful moment to stare down the slope toward the fishing village at the point, or toward the sawmill on the riverbank, with nothing but the winter stillness to interrupt his thoughts; once the fierce north winds howled down from the Maine coast, he came to dread even a moment outside of the house to fetch wood.

But the primary cause of his unhappiness was the stern and strict manner in which Mr. Thomson dealt with the indentured servants. And of the ten of them, he treated Noah the harshest. Noah worked long hours into the cold dark nights, and slept a mere six hours on a musty pallet on the floor of a room not much bigger than a cupboard, with a thin cotton blanket his only protection from the cold. Even the two enormous fireplaces—which Noah and the other servants kept continuously stoked—barely warmed the house. Or so it seemed, until he had to go fetch more firewood.

Noah hauled several other heavy crates from the hall to the cart, his heart in his throat and constantly glancing at the forest, wondering if any moment might be his last. At least it would end his tenure under Mr. Thomson. Once the cart was full, he helped Rodger Hodges drive the ox down the lane toward the docks.

Mr. Thomson's new shallop lay tethered to the largest dock. She was a thirty-foot double-masted beauty, built in November with lumber from Mr. Thomson's sawmill. In addition to her twin sails, she had four sets of oars should the wind fail her. It would be a snug voyage for the sixteen of them—the Thomsons plus ten servants—exposed to the elements on the open deck, but at least it wasn't far. A journey of sixty miles should only take a couple of days.

But Noah doubted a move of just sixty miles to the south would give Mrs. Thomson the escape from the harsh winters she sought. Childhood trips from his home in Lancashire to Chester in Cheshire had also been about sixty miles south, and the weather was no different there.

Noah and Roger transferred the crates and trunks from the cart to the boat, where three other servants arranged them at the front. "Now we go back for the furniture," Roger said when they'd finished. Noah's arms were already weak from the heavy work, and he wondered if he'd be able to lift heavy furniture. Would Mr. Thomson beat him if he dropped something? He had no doubt. He would surely lay down with many bruises tonight.

They rounded Cape Ann late-morning of the second day. Noah stood at the rail, staring across two miles of choppy water at the collection of cottages clustered on the rocky shore, tiny in the distance. It would be so easy to slip overboard, unnoticed. He could swim for it. He glanced around to see if anyone was watching him. Mr. Thomson would be red with rage, but what could he do? He'd hardly jump in after Noah.

But the fear wrapped its icy fingers around Noah's heart, and he knew deep down that he'd never make it. He'd drown in the rough and frigid water.

He stepped back from the rail.

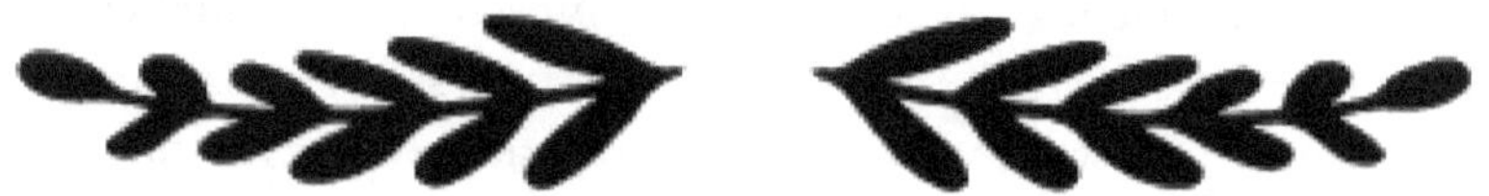

A half-mile away, a twenty-two foot ketch bobbed on the waves, its sail driving it toward the cape. In its stern, Floyd Hawkey and his new partner, John Small, scaled and gutted cod from the morning's catch.

In the center of the boat, Jimmy Hawkey adjusted the sail, and the boat turned. He gazed for a few seconds at the sleek shallop that had passed in front of them, an unexpected sight in these waters. Probably carrying some new planters arrived from England. Gentlemen, most likely, judging by the newness and fine build of the boat.

They would soon have their dreams of easy riches in the New World dashed by reality. Jimmy turned his attention back to the wind and guided the boat back to the Essex station.

They'd sailed down from Damariscove Island after the somber discovery of the abandoned York colony, and stopped over at Cape Ann. Thomas Gardner and John Tylly—the leaders of the Essex colony—had welcomed them so warmly they decided to relocate here. They took one of the abandoned cottages, some of the original party of thirty-two having returned to England on the first supply ship of the spring.

The colonists from Dorchester, Dorset were Presbyterian Puritans—but unlike what everyone in Cornwall said about Puritans, these sturdy burgesses weren't cold judgmental zealots who turned their noses up at merriment. Everyone was friendly, and it pleasantly surprised Jimmy to get only a few curious looks upon arrival, and not a single rude stare.

There was no one at the Essex colony like him—and Jimmy pushed aside the memories of Noah Bancroft at Piscataqua—but he felt welcome nonetheless.

As welcome as he would ever feel anywhere, that is.

It was dusk when the Shallop slowed in the channel that separated the wooded island from the thick forests of the mainland, which looked dark and foreboding in the fading light. Noah shivered at the thought of what might lurk in that forest, watching them. To their left, a large clearing spread up a low rise, filled with the stumps of felled trees. At the top of the rise sat a timbered house, tall and fortified with multiple gun slits.

The shallop put into a cove on the southwest corner of the island, and Mr. Thomson issued orders. "Trim those sails. Back-paddle the oars and slow the craft." Noah jumped onto a set of oars, paddling backward against their forward momentum, leaning back with all his might, and slowing the shallop until it bumped gently onto the sandy shore. His breath heaved with the effort, and his forehead beaded with sweat despite the coolness of the evening.

"You see, my dear, there's no way for the savages to approach us here unseen," David Thomson assured his wife, motioning across the channel toward the mainland. "I knew it was ideal when I first saw it five years ago, with Captain Dermer. A hostile force must cross a thousand feet of water to reach the island. This house will not be so vulnerable as our last one."

"That is a relief," Amias Thomson said, their year-old son on her hip, their other three children clinging to her skirt. She looked around for a moment, and nodded appreciatively. "I will feel much safer here."

"I might have claimed the island back then, had not Mr. Noddle left the expedition to claim it immediately for himself," Thomson said, lips tight and nose curled. But then he raised his chin as he surveyed their new home. "We'll expand the clearing, and once we're settled, I will send back to Pannaway for the cattle."

Thomson turned toward Noah and the other nine servants lined up along the port rail. "Men, take the furniture into the house first, and then the crates. Ye may have your supper only after ye have moved everything inside."

Noah glanced at the darkening sky, and almost groaned before he stopped himself. Any hint of complaint would bring a back-hand slap across the face. He joined the others in saying, "Yes, sir, Mr. Thomson."

Noah spent the next week and a half swinging an axe to fell trees and expand Mr. Thomson's cattle pasture. His muscles ached constantly, and by the end of every day, his arms felt like wet noodles that he could barely lift. But after it got dark every evening, he had to work inside the house, catching up on the cleaning and serving. He collapsed on his pallet every night, but the next thing he knew, the rooster crow awakened him, and it was time to get back to work.

Over and over. Day in and day out.

But on their eleventh day on the island, Mr. Thomson announced that he was going to pay a visit the next day to Captain Robert Gorges, Governor of New England. "Mr. Hodges, Mr. Bancroft, ye shall accompany me to Weymouth Plantation."

The sea breeze on Noah's face the next day was cool and salty, and he closed his eyes to relish its contrast with the warmth of the late April sun. It was exhilarating being away from the island, like those days last fall when he and Jimmy Hawkey explored the salt marshes of the Piscataqua ...

Blood flowed to his lower regions, and he turned sideways so Mr. Thomson wouldn't see the physical reaction. Thank God it receded quickly at the mere thought of anyone noticing.

With the wind behind them, their shallop made the ten-mile passage along the southern shore of the Massachusetts' Bay in just over an hour. The tall hills rising in a line to their south looked blue in the haze. They put into a long inlet, salt marshes on either side, and glided toward the collection of houses two miles in, sitting on a low rise between the marshes and the hills behind. A single wharf jutted through the marshes and into the inlet, Captain Gorges's pinnace tethered to it. Men onshore hallooed, and came down to meet them, catching the ropes Noah and Roger tossed to them.

Mr. Thomson wasted no time. "I am Mr. David Thomson, of Pann-away Plantation and Noddle's Island, come to call on Governor Gorges. Kindly direct me thither."

"I'll take ye there," a young man said, and strode back up the raised trail through the salt marsh, and up the rise.

The village was a cluster of some thirty houses, timbered in the old English style with high thatched roofs. In the center was a longer tim-bered building; the trading post and meeting house, presumably. As they approached the largest of the houses, only then did Noah notice several jagged blackened stubs of wood in rectangles of charred earth on the farthest side of the village, across the creek. At least four houses had burned to the ground.

Robert Gorges sat behind a table wearing a coat of burgundy velvet, with lace cuffs and starched ruffled collar. Two stacks of papers sat before him, and he inserted his quill back into the inkwell when they entered. He didn't rise. "Mr. Thomson, to what purpose do I owe this visit?"

Mr. Thomson bowed his head in deference. "Governor, I thank you for receiving me. I come to report that I made the purchase of Mr. Noddle's Island, opposite the mouths of the Charles and Mystic rivers. My family and I have lately relocated there, finding it safer from the Indians than our previous house."

Robert Gorges looked as if he'd swallowed something sour. "Indeed. We ourselves have had trouble with the Americans in this vicinity. They have proven themselves hostile to our position here, and the damnable

non-conformists at New Plymouth Plantation have been no help to us."
He sniffed his displeasure. "The hostility of the natives is entirely their
fault, I may add, owing to the rash actions of their militia at this very
location a year ago. Their past actions have spoiled our hopes of trade
with the local tribes."

"That is indeed regrettable, sir."

Noah thought he detected a note of unease in Mr. Thomson's voice,
an uncommon wariness in his eyes. He was frightened.

"Have ye abandoned your Pannaway Plantation, then?" Gorges asked,
sounding accusatory.

Mr. Thomson shook his head, his confidence returning. "Nay. The
plantation is secure; only the position of the manor house beside the
forest was an unfortunate vulnerability. In due time, the needs of the
sawmill will see to it that the wilderness recedes from it."

Gorges pursed his lips, and Noah wondered why.

"We have been working steadily to clear the wilderness from our corner of the island," Mr. Thomson continued. "It enhances our security,
surely, and also expands our cattle pasture."

"'Tis a pity you have had to clear the land yourself," Gorges said,
his tone of condescension unmissable. "We were fortunate to find a
grand clearing here, as if waiting for our arrival. I don't often agree with
Governor Bradford of New Plymouth Plantation, but it doth seem that
God smote the savages to clear the way for us."

Noah pictured Jimmy Hawkey, crying in a salt marsh because his
family had all died, and the heat of anger rushed through him. "Why
would God want to kill so many people?" he asked before he could stop
himself. "The plague killed children, even, by the thousands. Why would
God do such a thing?"

The room was silent for several seconds. Robert Gorges, still seated,
stared at Noah with narrowed eyes. "God smote the heathen Canaanites,
and the Midianites, and the Philistines, all for the benefit of the People
of Israel. Is it so remarkable, young man, that in our own day he should
smite the heathen Indians for the benefit of Christian Englishmen?"

Noah couldn't make himself believe that. How often had their vicar
preached that God loved humanity so much that he'd sent his Son to

live among us? That kind of love wouldn't kill thousands; nay, tens of thousands. He just couldn't believe that.

Then he looked at Mr. Thomson's face, and icy fear gripped his chest.

"Mr. Thomson, it is your Christian duty to see to the proper instruction of your household," Robert Gorges said. "See that your servant is corrected."

"I will, sir. Allow me a moment to accomplish the task." Thomson grabbed Noah's ear and yanked him out the door. Noah winced and hurried to keep up.

Once outside, Thomson turned on him and boxed him on both ears. The sudden impact rattled Noah's brain, sending an instant jolt of pain through his head and crashing against the inside of his forehead. His ears burned, and the ringing in his right ear was the only thing he could hear for several seconds.

"You shall not speak to your betters until spoken to, Mr. Bancroft," Thomson said through gritted teeth, the sound muffled as if through a long hollow tube. "We will revisit your impudence once we have returned to the island. For now, you will remain here until I have concluded my business with Captain Gorges. Do not move from this spot."

Mr. Thomson marched back into the house, and Noah's eyes followed him with unmasked hatred. For a moment, he didn't care if his master looked back and noticed.

But then the foolishness of that unguarded moment swept over him, and he looked around to see if anyone had seen the hatred on his face. But the colonists went about their work and paid him little mind.

The sounds of the village were slowly returning through the ringing in his ear, and he noticed the man beside him—the one who had brought them here from the wharf—trying to get his attention.

"We be leaving within the fortnight," he said in a sort of whisper, but loud enough for Noah to hear it. "This place will be abandoned again. Plenty of empty abodes there will be for anyone what wants to hide out."

It took a moment for the implication to settle in Noah's mind. *A place to hide out.* "Everyone is leaving?"

The man nodded. "Aye. Most of the wheat crop failed because of the dreadful winter, and we don't have enough flour to last the summer. The Indians won't trade with us, so Captain Gorges announced we sail back to England so we don't starve. Mr. Walford, Mr. Maverick and Reverend Blaxton are staying, along with the Mrs. Walford—but not here; Captain Gorges has granted them land on the Charles River."

Noah's mind raced. The Charles River, named after the Prince of Wales, emptied into the bay near Noddle's Island, to the southwest of it. This village was about ten miles east of the island. That would leave no one near Weymouth Plantation. He could hide here, but he would be utterly alone. "You are certain no one is staying here, in this place?"

The man shrugged. "I can't speak for everyone, but I know not a single soul that wishes to stay in this accursed place." He paused as if in thought, and then added, "There is Nantasket, a little spit of land a few miles northeast of here, where four fishermen live. They're under the authority of the nonconformists at New Plymouth, so it would be a brave man who might want to join them. 'Tis possible, though."

After seven months in New England, Noah had yet to hear a kind word from anyone regarding New Plymouth Plantation, so he ruled out that possibility. His hope of escape shriveled and blew away in the wind.

Mr. Thomson emerged from the house, Roger Hodges a step behind him. "Come, Mr. Bancroft. We go to the trading post to replenish our beer. You and Mr. Hodges will need to roll a barrel back to the ship."

"Yes, Mr. Thomson." Noah nodded thanks to the young man and hurried after his master.

David Thomson called Noah into his study after they returned to the island. "Stand against the wall, Mr. Bancroft," he said, taking his birch rod from a cupboard. "Lean forward, legs apart."

The first whack of the stick made Noah wince and suck in his breath.

"Your behavior embarrassed me in front of our betters," Mr. Thomson said. The second whack forced the air out of Noah's lungs in a hard burst. "You have the devil in you." The third whack made him squeeze his eyes shut. "And we must drive him out." The fourth whack caused tears to escape, no matter how tightly he clenched his eyes closed.

The fifth and final whack made his stomach hurt, and it was with desperate relief that he rushed from the room when Mr. Thomson announced they had finished.

CHAPTER 6

MAY 1624 - MASSACHUSETTS BAY

"Hallooo!"

Noah looked up from the tree he was halfway through felling with his axe. A shallop approached from the southeast. A cow bellowed its anxiety behind him, and from the back of the clearing a cowherd shook his cowbell and called the animal's name.

"I'll tell Mr. Thomson we have visitors," Roger Hodges said, driving his axe into the trunk of the tree he'd been working on, and hurried to the house.

Noah suspected Roger had been quick to volunteer for that duty to gain a respite from the grueling work. Not that he blamed him. "They'll need help to tie up," he said to the other indentured servants working nearby, and hurried toward the wharf.

The shallop carried three men and a woman with an infant in her arms. One man wore the black shirt and white collar of a clergyman, and the other two wore the velvet coats and wide-rimmed black hats of gentlemen, though minus the starched ruff collars. As the boat glided to their wharf, the youngest of the men—this one only a few years older than Noah—threw him a rope. "Thank you, my good man," he said in a genteel drawl when Noah tied it off.

Mr. Thomson hurried down from the house, his wife and children scampering to catch up. "Greetings, my good fellows," he said, his voice betraying only a hint of breathlessness.

The other gentleman followed the youngest one off the boat, and turned to give the young woman a hand, while the clergyman stood behind her with a hand on the elbow that cradled the baby.

"You must be Mr. David Thomson of Noddles Island, I presume?" the youngest one said, and a hint of smile brightened his face.

He's a cheeky one. Noah immediately liked him.

"I am he."

"Allow me to introduce myself, sir. I am Samuel Maverick, of Plymouth in Devonshire, though late of Weymouth Plantation in this country." He had the diction of a southwestern gentleman, but the bold manners of someone unaccustomed to worry over what others thought.

"And I am Thomas Walford," the other young gentleman said. He was a few years older than Maverick, perhaps twenty-five. "My wife Jane, and our daughter Jane."

"You must be the Reverend Mr. Blaxton, Captain Gorges's chaplain," Thomson said to the clergyman. "I was told you were coming to this area. You seek to convert the savages to Christ."

The clergyman nodded. "I am called to bring the Gospel to the Americans of the Charles River. The Massachusett tribe." Clearly the oldest of the three, Blaxton was still no more than thirty, and probably in his late twenties like Mr. Thomson.

"That is a dangerous endeavor, Reverend," Thomson said, his tone suddenly grave. "The Americans are a hostile race. We shall pray for your safety."

An impish gleam came to young Samuel Maverick's eyes. "If one treats one's neighbors with kindness, they usually return the kindness."

Noah couldn't help but smile at that.

Mr. Thomson's lips pursed, but he nodded. "That is so."

"We are your new neighbors, my good man," Maverick said with a grin. He pointed toward the Charles River. "Reverend Blaxton to the south there; Mr. Walford to the north on the Mystic River, yonder; and I on the peninsula between them, across this pleasant channel from your own most fortified residence. Seeing as we are each of us lone planters here, we would be much obliged to you if you might offer assistance to your neighbors with the construction of our abodes. As indeed we are told, the Good Samaritan helped the injured stranger."

More cheekiness! This endeared Mr. Maverick to Noah all the more. At Mr. Thomson's stunned hesitation, he spoke up. "I would be happy to help the endeavor, Mr. Thomson."

A flash of anger crossed Thomson's eyes, but quickly disappeared. He bowed his head to the visitors. "I am happy to offer an exchange of neighborly assistance. My servants, Mr. Bancroft and Mr. Hodges, will aid your construction, so that you may not be obliged to sleep in the open any longer than necessary. And once your shelter has been secure, I will gladly accept the grace of your aid in expanding my clearing."

"Most gracious of you, kind sir!" Maverick said, grinning and bowing with a flourish of his hand.

Behind her husband, Amias Thomson giggled and covered her mouth. David Thomson's posture stiffened.

"You are most kind, Mr. Thomson," Walford said with a more demure nod, but a hint of amusement twinkled in his eyes.

"Your wife and child shall stay with us in our home until you have constructed yours, Mr. Walford."

Maverick took a step toward Noah. "As my need is less pressing than that of the others, this young man and I will devote ourselves first to the construction of Reverend Blaxton's mission, and only then to my own abode."

"A most noble proposal, Mr. Maverick," Thomson said, mouth held tight. He turned to Roger. "Mr. Hodges, you shall accompany Mr. Walford to his land."

"How old are you, Noah Bancroft?" Samuel Maverick asked, handing the oars to Noah for his turn rowing their boat up the Charles River, and then plopping down on the seat Noah vacated.

"I'm seventeen years. I'll be eighteen this summer." Noah started rowing, and then cocked his head at Maverick. "How old are you?"

Maverick threw his head back in laughter. "Very good! One should never ask a question one isn't prepared to answer oneself. I am twenty-two years old."

From the bow of the rowboat, Reverend Blaxton shook his head, but a tiny smile curled the corners of his mouth. "What impertinent conversation."

Maverick laughed again, then leaned toward Noah, put a hand next to his mouth in dramatic fashion, and said in a stage whisper, "Mr. Blaxton won't say it, but I happen to know he's the same age as Captain Gorges. They're both twenty-nine years."

"What impertinence!" Blaxton said, but then chuckled and looked off at the forests lining the riverbank.

A trio of birch canoes rounded a bend ahead of them, paddling swiftly in their direction. Noah stopped rowing at the sight of six Indian men wielding the paddles, and a chill ran through him. A seventh man, older than the others, with streaks of gray in his black hair and several feathers adorning his headband and armbands, stood in the middle of the largest canoe. When they drew near the boat, he raised his right hand, palm out.

Reverend Blaxton stood carefully in the boat and raised his hand in return greeting. "Peace!"

Water dripped from the oars Noah held suspended, and they glided to a stop. "You are Englishmen?" the standing Indian said, his voice deep and guttural.

"We are," Blaxton replied. "Our countrymen have gone home to England, but we few have stayed to work with your people."

Noah held his breath. His heart pounded.

The older man grunted, then said something to the younger men resting their paddles across the tops of the canoes. They steered toward a rocky outcropping on the riverbank. "We talk," the older man said, pointing at the rocks.

"Follow them," Maverick told Noah. Noah swung the right oar several times to bring them around and then rowed hard toward the shore. The current was slow, but it still took effort not to drift downstream. He managed to ground the bow of the boat below the rocks where the Indian men had pulled the three canoes out of the water.

"I'll speak to them alone," Blaxton said to Maverick and Noah. "It will be less threatening to them. You men wait here."

Noah watched Blaxton speak with the older Indian, with the six younger ones behind and around him in an arc. He couldn't hear what they were saying, but both gestured with their hands. "What do you suppose they're saying?"

"Mr. Blaxton seeks their permission to settle on their land," Maverick said, awfully nonchalant under the circumstances.

After a while, the seven Indians got back in their canoes and paddled away without a glance at the two white men in the rowboat.

"Pull the boat from the water. We stay here," Reverend Blaxton said. "Their sachem, Chickatawbut, has given this rocky point and all land between the mudflats for our mission."

"This is a pleasant spot." Maverick looked around and nodded. "Easy to reach. Not much more than a mile from the mouth of the river."

"Their village is not far," Blaxton said. "This is God's work. Let us begin it."

Sweat stung Noah's eye while he and Samuel Maverick worked the saw back and forth through the trunk of a young oak tree. It would break their rhythm if he stopped, so he squeezed that eye shut and squinted the other so the sweat would roll away. Finally, their saw broke through, and they stood back as the twenty-foot tree crashed to the ground near the shore of the river. He wiped at his eyes with his sleeve.

Maverick was bare-chested, his lean torso glistening with sweat in the sunshine. He was compact, his muscles small but tight, and Noah cast many quick glances while they rested. Maverick's white shirt lay draped across a nearby bush, along with his hat, and sawdust coated his black breeches, stockings, and leather shoes.

It wasn't just Maverick's torso that drew careful, hurried glances from Noah; without his shirt tails tucked around them, the outline and movement of Maverick's privy parts showed plainly at the front of his breeches. This sent butterflies tumbling through Noah's midsection. He was glad they were hot from labor, otherwise his cheeks would show his blush.

With the tree felled, they took their little hatchets and hacked off the branches, tossing them onto a pile of others they'd cut that morning.

"I'll say it again, my boy—you would be much more comfortable working without your shirt," Maverick said, huffing from the labor. "'Tis hot as midsummer, and there are none but me to see you, so you needn't feel shame."

It wasn't the kind of shame Maverick thought, but Noah kept silent.

The last of the branches removed, they rolled the log toward the collection of logs they'd accumulated to be chopped into firewood. A five-foot pile of rocks stood nearby, waiting to be formed into Reverend Blaxton's new mission once they'd cleared enough space for it. Maverick fetched the saw. "On to the next one."

Pulling the twin-handled saw back and forth was grueling work, but at least it added variety compared to the axe he used at Mr. Thomson's island. And the work allowed him to stare brazenly at the ripples of Samuel Maverick's flat stomach—including the narrow trail of hair that disappeared beneath the waist of his breeches—while appearing to merely focus on the work.

Sweat stung both eyes this time, but he gritted his teeth and worked through it. Once they'd finished and the tree fell, he hesitated before grabbing his hatchet. Then, before he could change his mind, he pulled his shirt from his trousers, the tails unwrapping from around his privies; then he tugged it over his head and tossed it aside.

"That's a good boy," Maverick said with a grin. "Now I don't have to feel alone in my half-nakedness."

Noah had to smile at Maverick's reference. They were hardly half-naked, not in comparison with the Indian men who'd called on Reverend Blaxton that morning. He took his hatchet and leaned down to chop at the nearest branch.

Maverick's smile faded at the sight of the bruises that covered his back. Noah looked away, avoiding Maverick's eye, and focused on hacking off the branch.

"You should know, Mr. Blaxton wasn't entirely honest when he told the Indians that *all* the others had returned to England," Maverick said, quiet. "Captain Gorges left three of his servants at Weymouth Plantation, to 'look after it' for him. But I doubt the captain plans to return."

Why had Maverick mentioned that now?

They worked the rest of the day in silence.

"My father's a vicar," Samuel Maverick said, lashing two large sticks together to form a three-foot cross that would top the roof.

"I didn't realize," Noah said. An image of Lance Aubrey sprang to mind. He stole a glance at Maverick's shirtless torso, pink with sunburn, but looked away quickly. No good could come from involvement with vicars' sons.

He looked toward the river instead, where Reverend Blaxton was climbing into the rowboat to call on the Indians upriver. He had said he'd be back for supper. Noah's imagination played through what he and Maverick might get up to alone in the woods. But he forced that image from his head the moment he felt stirring in his groin and wiped at his mouth with his sleeve. They had just finished their lunch of salt pork and stale bread, and there might be crumbs in the stubble on his lip.

"Is he High Church, or Low Church? Mr. Braxton, I mean." Noah asked, nodding toward the departing rowboat.

Maverick laughed. Noah's cheeks flushed. "That's not a question I expected from a youth," Maverick said, still chuckling.

"I think my father is Low Church," Noah said. "He used to complain that our vicar was a 'damned High Churchman.' I think my mother was indifferent to the vicar, though. She never talked about the church. She preferred to discuss books."

"A woman after my own heart," Maverick said with a grin. "As for our Mr. Blaxton, he's neither High Church nor Low Church. He falls in the middle." Maverick cocked his head and regarded Noah with an amused expression. "And which are you, young Noah Bancroft?"

Noah thought for a second, and then shrugged. "I don't know."

Maverick nodded knowingly. "Then you must be like your mother."

The thought pleased Noah, though he couldn't say why. A warmth passed through him. "Which are you, Mr. Maverick?"

"I rest in the middle, like our Mr. Blaxton." He looked off in thought for a moment. "My father is a Low Churchman, I think. He conforms, of course; but remembering the words he says and how he prays at home, I think he's Low Church. But hardly a Puritan, at least! He agitates not for reform." A wry grin lit up his face. "And like our Mr. Blaxton, he is tolerant of different views. *Unlike* the Puritans. We are a broad church, after all. Good Queen Bess wanted not to make windows into men's souls, only to bring uniformity in practice."

Maverick stood and stretched. Noah couldn't help that his eyes went to Maverick's flat stomach; and the way his hips pushed forward while he arched his back, the outline of his pillicock was quite obvious against the stretched fabric ... Noah looked away quickly.

"The Act of *Uniformity*," Maverick said, his nose curling slightly on that last word. "One understands why it was necessary to end the civil strife between Protestants and Catholics. It was indeed common sense."

He leaned down and picked up one end of the saw. Noah hurried to take the other end, avoiding looking at the way Maverick's pillicock flopped loosely beneath his breeches as he moved. And almost succeeding.

"But religious matters aside, I do not seek a uniform life." A half-smile tugged up one corner of Maverick's mouth as he looked at Noah. "And neither should you, Noah Bancroft."

CHAPTER 7

MAY 1624 - MASSACHUSETTS BAY

A grassy meadow spread across the low ground at the end of the peninsula the Indians called Shawmut. The meadow wrapped around a string of hills running the length of the peninsula, and facing Noddle's Island.

"My new home," Samuel Maverick said with a grin, and pointed toward a sandy spot a hundred yards above the mouth of the Charles River. Noah rowed them there, and they pulled the boat onto the shore. "We can put a dock here. And the house shall be … over there." He pointed at a flat stretch above the meadow, halfway between the river and the tree line.

But Noah was looking toward the bay, and the clearing of Mr. Thomson's home across the channel. The two-story house looked tiny in the distance, and little dots of color on the far side of the clearing were probably the cattle, though he couldn't make them out.

"It's a third of a mile away," Maverick's voice said, startlingly close by. His hand planted on Noah's shoulder. "Unless Mr. Thomson is staring out the window through his spyglass, he doesn't know we've arrived from Mr. Blaxton's. I shouldn't expect him to come calling anytime soon."

Noah nodded, but stayed silent. It had taken a week to build Reverend Blaxton's mission and home. With any luck, it would take another week to build Mr. Maverick's home; but it would probably be sooner than that, and the realization sent a cold stone of dread sinking through his belly.

Three days later, they mixed a batch of pine tar in a large iron kettle over an open fire, and then stepped back, grimy and dripping sweat from every pore. They had left the wood beams of Reverend Braxton's pier untarred, since the water flowing past the mission was fresh. But at Mr. Maverick's house closer to the edge the bay, the water was brackish, and his beams would need tarring for protection. It was an unpleasant, but necessary, chore.

"You haven't got a change of trousers, have you?" Maverick said, nodding at the filthy pants Noah wore.

Noah shook his head. "No, these are the only pair I own."

"I thought so," Maverick said, and unbuckled his belt. "Off with them! You don't want to ruin them. I'll take mine off, too, so you won't be alone." He kicked off his shoes, pulled off the filthy stockings, and then dropped his breeches to the ground and stepped out of them.

Noah's mouth dropped open in shock.

"Go on, now! Don't be prudish about it. Tarring a pier is filthy business; you'll end up covered in the stuff. It won't wash off your clothes, so unless you want to ruin them forever, you'll get out of them before you pick up the brush."

Noah glanced toward the channel, at Noddle's Island in the distance. "But they'll be able to see us from Mr. Thomson's house!"

Maverick laughed. "Mrs. Thomson won't be able to see a thing from over there, unless she steals her husband's spyglass." And with those words, Samuel Maverick took a bucket and dipped it in the pot, then strode naked toward the logs piled beside the reeds along the shore.

Noah swallowed hard, trying not to stare at Maverick's pale buttocks gleaming white in the sun. He filled the second bucket with tar and set it on the ground. His heart fluttered, and nervous tingles tickled the inside of his belly. Taking a deep breath, he unbuckled his belt and threw his pants down, kicking them off to the side. His cheeks burned, and he stared at the grass in front of him when he hurried toward the pile of logs with his pitch.

Maverick had rolled a log from the pile and crouched beside it, brushing dark pitch along the end and then working his way down the length. Noah tried to avoid looking at Maverick's privy parts dangling between his legs, and concentrated on rolling his own log off the pile. But his eyes couldn't resist the pull. He scolded himself, and looked at the ragged edges of the logs to remind himself that if Maverick caught him looking and punched him for it, he might tumble onto them and break his neck.

That would be faster than a hangman's noose, at least.

He focused on his work and brushed the pine tar onto the wood. By the time they finished the first beams, half of his arms were covered in sticky brown resin, along with his knees.

"Time to move to the next one," Maverick said, straightening and arching his back, putting a hand on the base of his spine. His eyes looked Noah up and down, and he laughed. "We'll most certainly require a bath when this work is finished! Come now, there are more to get done."

He strode back to the pile and grabbed another log in both hands, keeping his feet back and leaning forward to avoid crushing his toes. Noah's mouth had gone dry. Once Maverick had rolled his log away, blessedly out of Noah's eyesight, at least for the moment, Noah chose his next beam and resumed the messy work—this time, with his back toward his host.

The water sent shivers racing up Noah's legs and spine, raising gooseflesh all over his body, and shrinking his privy parts tight. But he plunged in after Samuel Maverick, his feet squishing into the mucky river bottom, until they were belly-deep.

"This will ruin my good bath brush," Maverick said, eyeing the fine horsehair brush with a sigh, but then scrubbing it across the tar residue on his chest.

Soap bubbles glistened across Maverick's torso, and Noah looked away. He barely glanced at the young man when he handed him the soap and the brush, and turned his back toward him to wash. He concentrated on his task, not listening to the splash of the water behind him, until his skin was pink from the scrubbing.

A force hit him from behind, knocking the soap right out of his hand, and wet arms wrapped around him and tugged him under. Maverick's deep laughter was the last thing he heard before his ears plunged into the cold water.

He rose, spitting water from his lips and wiping the hair from his eyes. But then strong legs wrapped around his thighs and clamped down, then twisted, knocking him off his feet and sending him sideways back into the water.

He came up face-to-face with Samuel Maverick, who laughed and splashed a handful of water at him. Noah had to laugh with him as he took a step back, and splashed two handfuls of water back. Then he lunged forward, throwing his arms around Maverick's shoulders and pushing him backward. Maverick managed to keep his head above water, just, and the two of them grappled under the surface and laughed until their sides hurt.

It was the most fun Noah had had in over a year. So much fun he almost forgot that niggling anxiety at the back of his brain that he might accidentally spring a plum branch.

Almost.

They were both panting with exhaustion when they finally stopped, stepping apart in the chest-deep water to catch their breath. "We'll call the day finished," Maverick said. "We can build the dock tomorrow." He clapped Noah on the back, and they waded out of the water arm-in-arm.

Dusk was falling, bathing the clouds above the bay in a pink glow. Noah stood at the end of Samuel Maverick's new dock, staring across the channel at Mr. Thomson's house in the distance. "I don't want to go back," he said, as much to the air as to the young gentleman standing next to him. Neither listener could do a damn thing about it, but he had to give it voice.

"I would happily let thee stay here with me," Maverick said, surprising Noah by slipping into the familiar. "But he owns thy indenture, and could claim thee from me. I haven't the funds to buy it from him."

"I won't go back there." Noah's voice was firmer this time. His hands fisted at his sides.

"New England is vast."

The implication was clear. He had his friend's blessing to disappear. He didn't need it—he'd already decided to run away—but it pleased him to have it.

"If thou don't return, Mr. Thomson will come here looking for thee. I can honestly tell him I do not know whither thou went."

Noah smiled. "He'll probably be as concerned about his boat as about my absence. He cares not for me."

Maverick turned from the view and faced Noah. "Mr. Noddle lived alone on that island for five years. The solitude nearly drove him to madness. Once we planted at Weymouth last summer, he came calling near every fortnight, talking without ceasing. When your Mr. Thomson's factor offered to buy his island, Noddle accepted without counter. He departed at once for Cape Ann. We heard he's built a house on the coast some miles from the Essex station, where he can live alone as he likes, but visit the village often."

Noah understood the warning about solitude. But Cape Ann was too far to go on his own, as inexperienced as he was on open water. And New Plymouth Plantation was out of the question, with their fanaticism.

But Maverick had intimated days ago that three men had stayed on at Weymouth Plantation...

Yes, that's where he'd go. Then sometime soon a supply ship would stop there, and he could take it to Monhegan Island. Jimmy Hawkey was there.

A thrill ran through him at the thought, but almost immediately vanished into nothing. He had no money to pay for passage to Monhegan. And he was sure as hell not going to sell himself into indenture again. And besides, being around Jimmy was dangerous. The temptation was too great. Someone had caught them once, they'd be caught again. And this time, they'd be hanged.

But if there were still three men at Weymouth Plantation, he wouldn't be alone.

"I'll find others, I promise." He shook Maverick's hand, and then climbed aboard the boat and took hold of the oars. Dusk was fading into twilight, and soon no one on Noddle's Island would see him in the dark.

"Remember, my friend—we do not seek a uniform life. Fare thee well, Noah Bancroft."

Noah waved and rowed as hard as he could toward the far side of the river. He needed to get as far as he could before he lost all light; it was too dangerous to cross open water in the dark. He got past the mouth of the river and a half-mile along the south shore of the bay before he had to stop and wait for moonrise.

It gave him an hour to rest at the edge of the salt marsh, and reflect on his position. With any luck, the three men remaining at Weymouth Plantation would have no recollection of him being Mr. Thomson's indentured servant. *Please, God*.

The moon rose over the waves an hour later, bathing the bay in silver, the dark shore a stark contrast. He resumed his journey, his easterly path leaving Noddle's Island in view behind him. He watched it recede in the distance until it faded from sight.

PART TWO

"Come, let us make merry!"

"Come, let us make merry!"

CHAPTER 8

JUNE-JULY 1624 - ESSEX COLONY, CAPE ANN

The heat of the afternoon told Floyd and Jimmy it was time to put back into shore. The codfish had sunk to cooler waters, and the last haul of their nets had yielded little. Still, their baskets were nearly filled, so it was a good day at sea.

In the bow, under the shade of the canvas tarp, Floyd and their partner, John Small, knocked the cod on the heads to stop their flopping and sorted the last catch by size, tossing them into various baskets. Jimmy raised the sail and adjusted it to catch the wind. Stepping to the stern, he swung the rudder toward Cape Ann. Toward home.

Jimmy and Floyd were not the only newcomers that spring. A fellow named William Noddle showed up and talked everyone's ears off for a day. He'd spent the last several years alone on an island. He slipped away as suddenly as he appeared, and built a house a few miles up the coast. A few weeks later, fishermen from the Isles of Shoals arrived, having abandoned that station because of the lack of wood and other resources. John Small had been among those. "A few went back to England," he'd said of his fellow fishermen at the Isles. "But most went down to Virginia. What's left of us came here. Ain't no better cod fishing in the world. Not in Virginia, that's certain."

The rocky shore of Cape Ann and the great forests beyond were a thin green line on the horizon from their favorite fishing spot, some ten to twelve miles out. Jimmy loved watching it slowly grow as they bobbed toward it. By the time they were a couple of miles away, he could make out the village as little brown dots.

A shallop appeared on their left, coming from the south in a trajectory that would intersect theirs near the cape. They were about the same distance from shore, moving at a comparable speed. Jimmy adjusted the sail to eke a bit more speed from the wind. If they got there first, they could claim the closest spot on the wharf and not have to carry their load as far.

The shallop came into port behind them. It was old and sun-faded, its hull bearing the nicks of years of use. Quite a contrast to that sleek new shallop that had sailed past a couple of months before, without stopping at the cape. That one had carried more than a dozen people, while Jimmy counted only four men on this one.

"This wharf is the property of Plymouth Plantation," one of those men shouted when Floyd and John wrapped their ropes around the wharf posts and tied off. His voice carried the nasal whine of the eastern shires. "Any fishing done from this wharf belongs to the Plymouth Plantation."

"Is that so?" Floyd said, scratching the stubble on his cheek. "We joined this colony weeks ago, and ain't nobody here what belongs to that plantation."

Jimmy turned away so no one would see him almost laugh at the way his father goaded them. Every newcomer in the village had heard the tale of the emissaries from New Plymouth who'd come at the first thaw, complaining that the new colony was trespassing, and they already had a wharf and salting racks here to prove it. Mr. Tylly never tired of recounting how he had rebuffed the four dour men, showing the copy of their patent from the Dorchester Company. Jimmy suspected the tale might be a tad exaggerated, but it was always entertaining. "Ye were the ones who trespassed beyond your own borders when you built it, so it's forfeit," Tylly claimed to have said.

And now Mr. Tylly and Mr. Gardner hurried down the wharf. "Are ye back to cause more trouble?" Tylly called.

"We brought our patent as proof this time."

"We showed you *our* patent last time," Mr. Gardner said, uncharacteristically sharp. "It's from the Council for New England, and it grants the Dorchester Company the right to plant a colony at Cape Ann."

"It's not valid if our patent was issued first," one man on the shallop retorted.

"Let us see it," Mr. Tylly said, holding out his hand.

Jimmy had work to do, but he kept his attention on the little drama playing out in front of them. He tied up the sail more slowly than usual. And he couldn't help noticing that his father and John Small worked much more slowly than usual, folding the nets and shifting the baskets of fish.

Mr. Tylly stared at the document in his hand, frowning. "This bears the same date as our own patent! The council have made a mistake. They granted two patents for the same land on the same day—one to the Dorchester Company to start a colony, and one to the New Plymouth colony to build a wharf and establish a fishing and salting station."

"Our charter is older than your charter. Ye know that," the man said, reaching for the patent. Tylly didn't hand it back yet. The man huffed, and continued. "Ye know well the story. After we landed in New England in the cold of winter, 1620, we wrote back to the company the following spring for guidance, since we landed outside of our charter. The Council for New England wrote back that we could stay where we'd planted. Since our charter was three years before your colony's charter, our patent prevails over yours."

Mr. Tylly opened his mouth to retort, but Gardner was faster. "I'm no lawyer," he said, his tone warm and conciliatory. "But it stands to reason that the Council has authority over both charters equally. They would adjudicate rival patents, don't ye agree?"

"Indeed."

Gardner smiled. "In the meantime, since we have possession of the wharf, and we maintain it at our own expense and labor, we will keep the right to it until the Council informs us otherwise. If ye have no other business with us, then ye best be on your way home. Good day, my good fellows."

Jimmy nearly busted out laughing at the red-faced reaction from the New Plymouth men. But Gardner and Tylly merely touched the rims of their hats and strode back to the village.

"Ye heard the man," Floyd said, heaving a basket of fish onto the wharf. "Off with ye."

The men scowled at Floyd, unfastened their knots without a word, leapt aboard their old shallop, and pushed off.

The ocean waves washing onto Cape Ann were still frightfully cold on June 19. Nonetheless, Jimmy stripped off his clothes on the far side of the rocky promontory that sheltered the colony's harbor, and took the plunge into the waist-deep water, dipping down to his shoulders and briskly scrubbing his arms and chest.

While the Dorchester men bathed in their homes on Saturday evenings, the Hawkeys, like other fishermen, did not own a wooden tub, and so had to wash up in the surf. While many did this in sight of the village, Jimmy preferred to go off on his own.

He remained in the water only a moment, and as soon as it cleansed his body of any fish stink, he climbed back onto the rocks. He leaned down to grab his shirt and trousers, and crouched to dip them into the crashing waves, scrubbing them together until the dried remains of fish parts were carried away, and only the permanent stain of fish oil remained. Then he did the same with his stockings.

"Jimmy Hawkey! Jimmy Hawkey!"

The urgency of the cry snapped Jimmy from his hypnotic work, and he looked toward the top of the promontory.

"Jimmy Hawkey! Where are you, Jimmy Hawkey?"

He scrambled into his still soaked trousers and stockings, and slung the dripping shirt over his shoulder. He shoved his feet into his boots but did not lace them, and scampered over the rocks, jumping down onto the sandy shore of their harbor, and sprinted toward the village.

The colonists stood in a cluster at the edge of the village, staring up at the low ridge that ran the length of the cape's south shore. Jimmy followed their gaze—at eight Indian men standing in a line at the crest, staring down at the colonists.

"Thank God you are here, Jimmy Hawkey," Mr. Gardner said, sounding quite relieved indeed. "We've hailed them, asking what they want, but I don't think they understand English. We haven't a trading post to draw such visitors. Can you speak to them? Your father says you can remember the Indian tongue."

One of them. Jimmy swallowed annoyance at the assumption all the native peoples of New England spoke the same tongue. "I will speak to them."

The request filled him with anxiety, given the communication miscues with the Abnaki trio last fall. That memory triggered others, of afternoons spent kissing Noah Bancroft in the bow of his father's ketch ...

Jimmy approached the staring men with trembling fingers. He raised his right hand and greeted them. The oldest man returned the greeting. He was about forty, his hair still black but his face lined. "Why have you come here?" Jimmy asked in the language of his childhood.

"We come here every summer, since time immemorial," the man said. "We travel four days from our village to return to our summer camp."

Jimmy's shoulders relaxed. They spoke the same language! He explained that the English had come here last fall from far away, to build a new home. The older man said that they were Pawtucket. As they conversed, Jimmy noticed minor differences from the language he'd spoken as a child.

"This clearing was once our summer home, but the great plague eight years ago killed all but twenty-five of our number." The man motioned toward the colony. "We do not need all of it any longer, and can share with the English. We ask only that we may camp here so that we can fish and clam as we always have. We will stay there." He pointed to a flat spot above the promontory.

Jimmy nodded. "Go to that place. I will tell the English you mean no harm to them. Welcome."

Jimmy spotted the three masts before Floyd and raised their spyglass for a closer look. The banner of St. George snapping in the ocean breeze identified it as an English ship. "A supply ship's coming in, Papa." The older man sat on their stoop, sharpening his filet knives on a whetstone.

"Always nice to have visitors," Floyd said without looking up, checking the edge of his knife with a calloused thumb. "I think this one's unexpected—I've heard nothing about it." He looked up then, toward where Jimmy pointed, shielding his eyes with one hand. "It'll be a while yet. Probably still six or seven miles out. Don't neglect your work now; be a good lad and prepare supper for us."

"Yes, Papa." Jimmy grabbed the pail of shellfish he'd collected from the rocks that afternoon—oysters, clams, and mussels—and shucked them into a bowl. He'd cut them up to mix into their oat porridge when it simmered later. But while he worked, he daydreamed about what the approaching ship might bring.

It had been three weeks since the encounter with the men from New Plymouth; too soon for word to have reached the Council regarding the dispute and the rival patents causing it. Any decision would be months away still. This approaching ship would bring supplies of one variety or another, and maybe some new colonists.

It was an hour before the pinnace drew up, and Floyd and Jimmy sat on their stoop eating warm bowls of thick seafood oat porridge. The white background of its English flag glowed yellow in the evening sun. It was a few days past Midsummer, and the evening sun dropped slowly, lingering warm and bright well beyond supper time.

The name *Unity* stretched across the bow in black. Jimmy counted over forty men crowded along the railing, too many for just crew. "That ship carries passengers."

"We should greet them, that's the neighborly thing," Floyd said between bites. "Eat faster. Not much worse than cold porridge."

Jimmy wolfed down the last of his bowl.

They joined the two-and-a-half dozen Essex station colonists at the shore end of the dock. Mr. Gardner and Mr. Tylly stood on the wharf near the ship with a tall, stern-looking gentleman in the blue coat of a ship's captain. Eight young men from the ship rolled four barrels down the wharf.

"What'dja bring us?" John Small called to the nearest duo.

"A barrel of salt, and three barrels of beer," one boy replied, only slightly breathless.

"Three hundred pounds of salt!" Floyd said with a grin. "That'll last us all year."

"But that half-ton of beer won't last so long, eh?" John Small chuckled and poked an elbow into Floyd's arm.

But Jimmy's attention focused on the young men rolling the barrels onto shore. They were about his age, maybe a year or two older. Nineteen to twenty-one, that was his guess. They didn't dress like sailors—passengers meant for this colony? It would be nice to have others his age around. Mr. Gardner's children were young, and the rest of the colonists were several years older than him.

Glancing back at the rail of the pinnace, it seemed most of those passengers were young men around his age. Three older men contrasted with the others, one of them quite a bit older indeed—at least forty-five or fifty. Easily the oldest white man Jimmy had seen this side of the Atlantic. This one wore the clothes of a gentleman—broad hat with a feather, fine velvet jacket, lace-fronted shirt, lace cuffs, starched collar, fine leather boots with gold buckles—and descended the plank to the wharf. He strode toward the ship's captain standing with Gardner and Tylly, grinned broadly, and thrust out his hand.

His voice carried. "Thomas Morton, late of Devon and London, at your service, my fine fellows. I see you've met our Captain Wollaston."

Wollaston looked annoyed.

"He's a dandy, that one," John Small muttered out the side of his mouth. "Just what we need."

Jimmy stiffened, and Floyd cast him a sideways glance.

Mr. Gardner and Mr. Tylly led Morton and Wollaston toward shore. Gardner spoke. "Welcome to Essex station, gentlemen. Are ye staying?"

"Only for the night," Wollaston said. "We sail at dawn with the tide."

"But we remain in this vicinity," Morton said. "I bear charter from the Council to plant a colony on the south shore of the Massachusetts' Bay. Captain Wollaston has partnered with me on the venture, and we bring forty indentured boys, along with Captain Wollaston's lieutenant, Mr. Fitcher, and his factor, Mr. Rasdall. We are indeed eager to establish ourselves, and so we cannot tarry here long. But first we explore the region, and introduce ourselves to the neighbors, planters and natives alike."

"Thank the lord they aren't staying with us," John Small muttered to Floyd and Jimmy. "Can ye imagine listening to that bag of wind every day?"

Floyd chuckled and shook his head. Jimmy just shrugged. He glanced back at the deck of the pinnace, but no one stood at the rail any longer. The two older men—Lieutenant Fitcher and Mr. Rasdall, presumably—had put the young men back to work.

Jimmy couldn't help the sinking disappointment that these young men were bound elsewhere. He stood at a distance and watched the four pairs rolling their barrels into the supply house.

"The eight boys I brought ashore are for sale," a voice said behind him. It took Jimmy a second to realize Captain Wollaston of the *Unity* was speaking. He didn't turn his head or move, but his eyes scanned the village until he saw Mr. Gardner leading that Mr. Morton around, almost a hundred yards away.

"Have they any skills?" Mr. Tylly asked behind Jimmy.

"Nay, but they're stout laborers. I'm sure ye could use four pairs of workers for general labor," Wollaston said.

Jimmy's pulse quickened. Perhaps he'd have companions here after all. He kept still, looking toward the storehouse; there were others milling about, but he tuned his ear to Wollaston and Tylly.

"At what cost?"

"Five pounds per boy, for a term of five years."

Tylly was quiet for several seconds. "I'll speak with Mr. Gardner about it. Silver coins are dear ... but perhaps we could collect enough to pay you four pounds per boy."

"It must be five pounds apiece. I require forty pounds for the eight to cover the expense of their passage. And you can see that they are fine sturdy boys, accustomed to hard work on the Bristol docks."

"Mr. Gardner and I will confer with the others."

"I must have your decision before nightfall," Wollaston said. "And I ask your discretion when you confer with your fellows—this is a private transaction between ye and me, and does not involve Thomas Morton. You may discuss it only with me, or with my factor, Mr. Rasdall. I expect him ashore presently."

Jimmy crouched below the open window at the corner of the Great House, a large two-story framed structure plus a garret which housed Mr. Gardner and his family, plus Mr. Tylly, and a community meeting room. Being younger than twenty-one years, they did not include him when the colonists met to discuss or vote on some question.

"If we agree to share the cost equally, we will share in their labor equally," Mr. Garnder said inside. "The method for sharing can be determined once the deal is made."

"Who shall house them?" someone asked. "There are more than eight of us abiding here, so which of us bears the extra burden of boarding?" Murmurs of agreement rose.

Gardner spoke again. "We can agree that the boys move from home to home, staying where they labor the day, according to the method we decide."

"We fishermen have no need of a servant's labor," Floyd said from the far side of the room. Jimmy held his breath below the window. "And we have no coin to contribute, even if we did."

"Aye!" John Small shouted.

Jimmy's fingers tingled. It surprised him how much he wanted the colony to take on the eight young men. He hoped his father's words wouldn't dissuade the majority.

"We will not ask the fishermen to contribute to the cost," Mr. Tylly said. "The Dorchester men can buy the indentures, and share the labor amongst ourselves. If ye fishermen should decide in the future that ye need the labor of these indentured boys for a day, we can arrange for you to pay the colony in trade."

"'Tis fair," one of the other fishermen said, and the others voiced agreement.

Jimmy exhaled in relief.

"Then it be three pounds apiece from each Dorchester man," Mr. Garnder said. "That makes thirty-nine. We'll take a pound from the general fund."

"What man can spare three pounds?" someone asked. "But if we put in a pound apiece, plus two pounds from the general fund, we can buy three of them." This met with hearty agreement.

A strange mix of excitement and disappointment mixed in Jimmy's gut. He would get companions his age—but only three. Eight would have been better.

Gardner said, "If any man objects, let him speak now."

Jimmy held his breath again. Only silence came through the window.

"Then Mr. Gardner and I shall collect the coin," Tylly said. "I will take the fifteen pounds to Captain Wollaston and his factor."

Jimmy crept away from the window, smiling.

Evenings at the Essex station were some of Jimmy's favorite times. These summer evenings especially, when the sun sank slowly in the western sky, bathing everything in a soft glow. He sucked in another baked clam, washed it down with a gulp of strong ale, and laughed at the men and women frolicking beside the fire.

They were more than forty souls here now, including now a handful of women. They gathered around a bonfire every evening, swapped tales from the day, shared the catch, and—after eating and drinking sufficient beer—made music and dance. Four of the colonists had sent home for their wives at the first thaws, and their arrival from England this week had caused a grand celebration.

Jimmy's eyes lingered on the trio of young men sitting together on a rocky outcropping some twenty yards on the other side of the bonfire. Even after three weeks here, the indentured servants—called "the Bristol boys" by everyone else—kept to themselves when they weren't working. Jimmy wished to get to know them, be part of their group, but there never seemed an opportunity to start a conversation.

He took another clam out of the iron pot half buried in the sand between him and his father. As he tipped his head back to suck it into his mouth, his eyes looked toward the rocky neck at the far edge of the colony's clearing, where a cluster of five wigwams had gone up. Jimmy was proud of his role in convincing the colony's leaders that the Pawtucket would make good neighbors for the summer.

"Is it tempting to join them?" Floyd asked, catching the direction of his gaze.

The question caught Jimmy off guard. "No, of course not." He wasn't one of them. In more ways than one.

Jimmy shifted his butt in the sand and looked back at the dancers around the bonfire. Floyd watched him for a moment. "Thou could, if it pleased thee to do it. Thou art a man now, Jimmy. Nineteen years old. I can't expect thee to stay with me forever."

Jimmy looked down at the sand between his crossed legs. "I have no reason to leave thee, Papa."

"Hmmm ..." Floyd tilted his head back and sucked in a clam. "Thou might go to Casco Bay. Captain Levett is returning soon with his family. And with more colonists, I suspect. He'll stay at his York plantation. And so will thy friend, our Mr. Bancroft." There was a knowing look in his eyes.

Jimmy ignored it. It was true, though. They'd heard this from many sources, and the thought of Noah's return to New England sent a flutter through Jimmy's chest. He'd known Noah for less than two months; and yet, nine months later, Noah came often to mind. Not to mention his occasional appearance in Jimmy's dreams, in which they did more than kiss, things they hadn't done in reality ...

He shrugged and reached for another clam in the pot. He didn't want his father to know how much he thought about seeing Noah again.

Even though Papa probably already knew that.

That night, Jimmy spread his pallet on the grass in front of their cottage, rolled his shirt to form a sort of pillow, and laid back to stare at the stars.

A few people still sat around the bonfire on the beach, talking and drinking beer; it was Saturday night, so none of them would cast off at dawn, not on the Lord's day. They could linger into the night. But they were thirty yards away, at least, and their chatter was but a dull murmur on his ear. A southerly breeze came off the bay tonight, somehow warm and cool at the same time, and the waves beating against the rocky neck to his left lulled him into a dreamlike state, halfway between waking and sleep.

He and Noah were in the boat somewhere up the Piscataqua River beside the salt marshes, shirts off, kissing. A breeze like this one tonight kissed their skin, cool in contrast to the warmth radiating between their bodies. In his mind's eye, their pants came off, too. And Noah was beautiful. So beautiful.

Jimmy slipped his hand down the front of his pants.

CHAPTER 9

AUGUST 1624 – WEYMOUTH PLANTATION

Noah awoke to the sound of rustling in the corner of the cottage. It took a second to crack open his eyes, and realize something was nosing around in his dirty dishes, left as usual atop the barrels in the corner.

It must be those damned raccoons again. When would he learn? The wily creatures were incorrigible, overcoming every obstacle he placed for them. Once the summer heat subsided, he could take to closing his door at night; but for now he needed the airflow to have any chance of sleeping.

He raised his head slowly from the pile of straw that had been his bed for three months, and then his shoulders. If he rose slowly enough, the blasted creatures might remain too consumed with his scraps to notice him coming upon them. But as he lifted halfway, he saw not a collection of raccoon tails, but the slender hind end of a dog. It had pushed aside the upturned rakes Noah had laid out around the barrels, and stretched its neck to lick at the plate.

"Hello, there," Noah said, smiling. The dog startled, looked at him for a second with plaintive brown eyes, and tentatively wagged its tail. Then it turned back to the plate and resumed licking.

Noah stood and took a careful step toward it. "Where did you come from?" The dog was slender, but he could only just make out the outlines of its ribs, so it wasn't starving. It looked young, not much more than a puppy, perhaps four to six months. It was light brown, with patches of darker brown here and there, legs a bit too long in proportion to the rest of it, and its tail was long and narrow.

Noah walked around the side of it. He'd seen no balls from behind, but at this angle, it was definitely a boy. And definitely not more than a puppy, his testicles having not descended yet. The plate Noah had left on the barrel looked as clean as if he'd already washed it in the creek, and the dog finally stopped licking to look at him in earnest. His tail wagged with more enthusiasm now, and he took a couple of steps toward Noah, a tiny whine escaping his throat.

Noah reached out slowly, and tentatively touched the pup's ears. The tail wagged even faster. Then he nudged his muzzle into Noah's palm and licked the underside of his wrist. This made Noah laugh, and he dropped his hands to the dog's shoulders, scratching him. "What am I going to do with you?"

The dog cocked his head, and then sat facing Noah, staring at him with big brown eyes.

"Let's see if I have any food for you." Noah checked the cabinet above the barrels and found a crusty remnant of a bread loaf which had begun to molder. He pinched off the moldy part and tossed the stale end to the floor. The dog wolfed it down with barely a chew, then sat again and stared at Noah. "The porridge is for me. But I'll let you lick the bowl when I'm finished."

Noah was true to his word, and after finishing his oatmeal porridge, he set the bowl at his feet. The dog licked it clean. Beyond clean. Once the dog finally finished and looked back up at Noah, he walked toward the open door, motioning for the dog to follow. "Come along. Let's see if the others know where you came from."

He glanced toward the bean and squash patches on the edge of the village, but they stood empty at this hour. He found the other three at work at the trading post—which, in practice, was just a storehouse without customers.

"I saw him nosing around the edge of the marsh yesterday," Will Jefferies said. "If I were you, I'd shoo him back into the woods."

Noah looked at the dog, who sat calmly next to him, looking up at him with his head cocked. He couldn't send him away. "Maybe I'll keep him. He's friendly, and maybe he could help us."

"If you keep him, you feed him out of your ration," John Bursley said. "We can't give you more than your share because you want to care for some found dog."

"So be it," Noah said.

Over the next week, Noah took the dog with him through the woods near their clearing, and to his surprise, the dog caught quail, grouse, and wood ducks. He chased many rabbits as well, though he wasn't successful at catching any. Yet. But he brought the bird carcasses to Noah when called, and that gave them meat every night for the first time since Noah had arrived at Weymouth Plantation. He caught so many ducks, in fact, that Noah decided on the fifth day to name him Drake.

For the first few nights, the dog slept in the open doorway of Noah's cottage; but by the fourth night, he had curled up next to Noah on the pile of straw.

They went down to the salt marsh beside the bay on the afternoon of the eighth day. As usual, Drake ran ahead, frolicking in the tall grass along the edge of the reeds, sending song birds scattering. But then he stopped, nose in the air, sniffing. After several seconds, he bounded across the high grass along the cove to the raised boardwalk that led to the wharf, barking at the water. He ran to the end of the wharf, barking an alarm off into the bay somewhere.

"What is it, boy?" Noah called, hurrying after him. He had taken a few steps down the wharf when the mast of a pinnace appeared beyond the mouth of the estuary. The ship glided past, about two miles away, headed west. Several dozen men milling around the deck meant it carried passengers as well as crew. The deep, howling barks of hounds echoed across the water, barking back at Drake.

The ship made no move to enter the inlet, but continued westward.

The sense of apprehension at the sight of strangers was automatic now, after three months of hiding from Mr. Thomson. They couldn't possibly know who he was, or that he had run away from his indenture. But the fear prickling the back of his neck wouldn't leave.

Drake stopped barking only after the ship's stern disappeared behind the distant trees on the point. Then he loped back to Noah and stood in front of him, tail wagging, his face looking like he was grinning. He thought he'd chased off the strangers. Noah laughed and scratched behind the dog's ears. "Good boy, Drake."

He hiked back up the path to the village, Drake bounding around in concentric circles beside him. New colonists had arrived, but they weren't coming here, where empty buildings sat awaiting reoccupation. How curious. He needed to tell the others.

"Perhaps they mean to plant at the Charles River," young James Ludden said. "There be a fine harbor there, and they could command the whole bay from it."

"As long as they aren't from the New Plymouth Plantation, I welcome new arrivals," John Bursley said.

Dread sank into the pit of Noah's stomach at the thought that one of them might suggest joining the larger colony. He couldn't risk returning that close to Mr. Thomson's house. Ten miles was plenty close enough. He would have preferred farther than this if a suitable option had existed.

"Halloooo!" The call from the forest caught them by surprise two days later. Even Drake, who dashed toward the trail leading into the hills, hackles up, barking for all his slender body was worth.

Noah and the three others reached for their muskets, but the middle-aged man who emerged from the forest in the elegant velvet, silk, leather, and lace attire of a gentleman beamed from ear to ear. His eyes crinkled, and his beard contained as much gray as brown; Noah guessed him at least forty-five—easily the oldest man he'd encountered in New England.

"Good morrow to ye, my good fellows!" the man shouted, then stopped to pet the dog, who only stopped growling long enough to sniff the stranger's breeches. He had the drawl of the southwestern shires—Devon, Dorset, or Gloucester—which Noah recognized because of its commonality among the fishermen and planters of New England.

"Please allow me to introduce myself," the gentleman said, stopping to bow while sweeping off his wide-brimmed hat, the end of its feather grazing the dusty ground. "I am Thomas Morton, late of Devonshire and London, newly established on the next hilltop some five miles yonder. A lovely knoll the native savages call *Passonagessit*." He swept his hand back toward the west. "Captain Wollaston and I have planted a new colony there, along with his agent, Mr. Rasdall, Lt. Fitcher, and our company of thirty sturdy boys. I understood this to be the spot of Captain Robert Gorges's plantation, though I hear that Captain Gorges has departed with most of his colonists."

"Aye, he left some four months ago," Will Jefferies said. "Six of us stayed—three here and three up bay." He didn't bother explaining that there were four of them standing in front of Morton. Noah tensed and watched Morton's face, but the older man's visage only glowed with friendliness.

They took turns introducing themselves, and Noah went last. "I am Noah Bancroft, from Lancashire. And this is my dog, Drake."

Morton's grin was dazzling when Noah introduced his dog. "The settlement's protector, I see." He patted Drake's head, then straightened. "It is my great pleasure to make the acquaintance of ye. We desire good neighborly relations with our co-inhabitants of this country, so please accept my invitation to join our company in a feast of celebration this coming Saturday at dusk. And Drake is welcome, of course." He bowed to the dog, who remained seated beside Noah, but wagging his tail. Then he bowed again to the four humans. "Good day to ye, my good fellows. Until Saturday next."

"Should we attend?" Noah asked the others.

"We must see their new colony for ourselves," Will Jefferies said.

"Aye," John Bursley agreed. "If they build a trading post there, it will take some of the beaver trade from us."

"*What* beaver trade?" young James was brave enough to say, eliciting a sheepish shrug from Will Jefferies.

Noah wondered if David Thomson would also receive an invitation from this Thomas Morton. An icy thread raced through his chest at the thought. Of course he would. Perhaps Noah had best not venture near.

But the desire to see faces other than Will Jefferies, John Bursley, and James Ludden was so strong it was like a siren calling to him.

Noah told his companions he wasn't going to the feast. He stood in his doorway on Saturday afternoon, watching them disappear down the forest path leading west. He waited about fifteen minutes for them to get well ahead of him, and then motioned for Drake to come with him toward the trail.

The trail was wide and well-worn, but it was rugged and rocky as it generally followed the outline of the inlet, up-and-downhill, traversing many creeks that tumbled out of the high Blue Hills to the south.

The evening light was growing dim when sounds of laughter and conversation drifted through the woods. It had been a ninety-minute hike, but he was only slightly winded. Drake was panting, though his gait hadn't slowed; he looked happy for the rest when Noah veered into the brush at the first glimpse of a giant bonfire ahead.

Noah crept forward, bent low to stay in the cover of bushes, and Drake stayed a step behind him. When he got to a place that he could see clearly enough, he hunched down and motioned for Drake to lie down. He'd been working on those commands in his cottage every day, and the dog had gotten the hang of it quickly. He laid down and rested his chin between his paws, glancing at Noah from the sides of his eyes.

Noah pulled back a branch of the honeysuckle bush to peer at the gathering, careful that the movement was slow and not noticeable.

It was a large clearing—perhaps twice the size of the clearing at Weymouth Plantation—but not flat, rising to a central peak at the top of a high knoll. Several sturdy timbered structures formed a U-shape around a central stone hearth, from which a giant bonfire reached for the sky. Long wooden tables stood on the near side of the fire, while closer to the houses, several deer carcasses rotated on spits over smaller cooking fires. There had to be close to a hundred people in the clearing—and to Noah's surprise, more than half of them were Indians, and of these, at least half were women. Perhaps a dozen dogs ran around the gathering, more concerned with their own play than with the surrounding humans. Drake whimpered, but Noah put a hand on his head and whispered, "Shhhh."

Will Jefferies, John Bursley, and James Ludden sat together at a table with other young white men, tankards of beer in front of them. Noah scanned the crowd for any sign of Mr. or Mrs. Thomson. Then his eyes stopped at the sight of Samuel Maverick engaged in animated conversation with Thomas Morton.

It was tempting to step into the open and go talk to the only person who had shown him friendship since Jimmy Hawkey last year, but he couldn't help thinking that if Maverick had come, Mr. and Mrs.

Thomson might come, as well. Thomas Morton had clearly invited all neighbors; the Thomsons might walk into the clearing at any moment, Mr. Thomson would see Noah and claim him, and drag him back to Noddle's Island ...

He pictured the beating he would receive upon arrival there, and he had to shake his head to clear the image. Drake cocked his head and looked up at Noah with concerned eyes. "They will not catch me," Noah said to the dog, not much louder than a whisper. He crept back from the honeysuckle and slowly stood, careful not to make any sudden motion. Then he motioned for Drake and headed back to the trail.

And came face to face with a tall, lanky youth buckling his belt, splotches of crimson rising into his cheeks as he looked at Noah with wide blue eyes. The trunk of the big oak tree next to him had a large wet stain.

"Sorry, I didn't know anyone else was using this spot," the youth said, the words tumbling out. He had waves of brown hair cascading down the side of his neck, and one unruly dark lock swooped over his forehead when he looked down and away, and he had to push it back from his eyes. His skin was pale, except for the splashes of red still coloring his cheeks.

"No, I was just ..." Noah let his voice trail off, unable to come up with an explanation for what he'd been doing in the brush that didn't sound like he'd been spying.

"I haven't seen you yet," the young man said in a charming drawl, and his big blue eyes flicked down and up so fast Noah almost didn't notice it. Then he stuck out his hand. "I'm Benjamin Burton."

"Noah Bancroft." He shook Benjamin's hand, and it was warm and soft, and sent a jolt of electricity up his spine. Benjamin's long, slender fingers brushed the inside of his wrist, sending tingles through him. His cheeks heated, and he looked away—toward the gathering of people in the clearing. "We—that is, my dog Drake and I—we're just arriving. But I wasn't sure ..." his voice trailed off again, unable to come up with any words for why he'd been hanging back.

Benjamin smiled and put an arm around Noah's shoulder. "Come along, then. I'll get you a mug of beer, and we can eat some food."

The warmth of Benjamin's hand on his shoulder made Noah's stomach light as air. He grinned and whistled for Drake. The dog bounded ahead of them a few steps, bouncing around and wagging his tail.

Then icy fingers of fear gripped Noah's heart as they stepped into the clearing, and several people looked their way. He assured himself that even if Mr. and Mrs. Thomson accepted Thomas Morton's invitation, Mr. Thomson would take one look at the Indians in attendance and turn right back around.

With a joyful bark, Drake dashed off toward the group of dogs at play, jumping and running around with them.

"Don't worry, they don't run off. He'll be fine. This way," Benjamin said, steering Noah toward a tapped barrel. He released Noah's shoulder, but his fingers trailed down Noah's back as they fell, sending a pleasant shiver up his spine. He glanced around to see if anyone had noticed. Benjamin took two mugs from the nearby table and filled them, the foam spilling over the sides.

Noah thanked him and took a sip. The beer was rich and thick on his throat. "Do you live here? Or are you visiting?"

Benjamin responded with a crooked grin. "I live here. There are thirty of us boys, recruited from the Bristol docks by Mr. Morton. This is his colony. Captain Wollaston owns our indentures, though. That's him over yonder." He nodded toward a man in a blue coat, probably about forty, standing with a group of young men. Unlike Thomas Morton's gregarious manners, Wollaston stood with stiff posture.

Noah almost said that he was indentured as well, but thought better of it at the last moment and closed his mouth.

"There were forty of us at first," Benjamin said, stepping closer and dropping his volume. "Captain Wollaston sold a few at Cape Ann, and then several more at Monhegan Island. Mr. Morton was mad angry, yelled at Captain Wollaston that they had a deal, and we were all meant for *his* colony."

"What did he say?" Noah asked, eyes widening.

"Captain Wollaston? He stayed calm as an owl, told Mr. Morton we were his prerogative, and he needed to recover his expenses. He said that he would uphold his end of the bargain, and Mr. Morton would have plenty of workers left for his colony." Benjamin shrugged. "I understand

Mr. Morton's anger. It was him that recruited us personally from the Bristol docks. But it's Captain Wollaston's ship, so he gets our indentures for our passage."

Benjamin put his hand on the small of Noah's back, turning him toward a long table filled with platters and bowls. The half-carved carcass of a wild turkey sat on one platter, surrounded by bowls of peas and biscuits, and plates of bacon, salt pork, and dry cheese. The giant slab of butter grabbed Noah's attention. Butter! He hadn't had butter since he'd left the Thomsons' house. Several giant sea bass lay in the center of the table, pride of place.

"Mr. Morton catches them himself," Benjamin said, following Noah's gaze. "He baits his hook with *lobster* meat." He laughed and shook his head.

Noah took a pewter plate from a stack, and a spoon and knife, then filled the plate. He'd grown used to small meals at Weymouth, where they had limited stores, but the sight of all this food made his stomach rumble.

They sat at another table, where Benjamin introduced him to several of Mount Wollaston's indentured youths.

"Where do you stay, Mr. Bancroft? At Nantasket? Or at Weymouth Plantation?" a young man named Robbie Ellis asked.

"At Weymouth," Noah said after a second's hesitation. His instincts told him to reveal as little as possible; but they would surmise soon enough that he was no fisherman. Then a wave of panic swept through him at the realization he had already given his real name, and anyone here might speak of him to someone who might speak of him to Mr. Thomson. They were a small society in New England.

"That's nearby, I hear," Benjamin said, looking at Noah with those large blue eyes.

"Five miles." Noah looked away from Benjamin's gaze before it made him blush. "I walked here in less than two hours," he told the others.

"How are things there?" a young man named Philip Davies asked.

Noah shrugged, took a couple of seconds to weigh his answer. "It is fair. Most of our food stores came from the charity of New Plymouth Plantation. The trading post is full of unsold items because the Indians are suspicious of the colony. I dare say, I was surprised to see so many of the natives here at your feast."

The young men laughed.

"Mr. Morton is determined to be friendly with everyone," Benjamin said. "Even though he has legal right to the land by patent from the Council for New England, he insisted on buying it from the local Indian sachem the day we landed. He invited them to a feast before we'd built our shelters."

More laughter and head shaking by the group.

Noah supposed they thought it a waste to buy land one already had title to. "'Tis hardly a waste, though, if it makes the Indians friendly to the colony. We would have more food at Weymouth if they consented to trade it."

A wry smile turned up one side of Robbie Ellis's mouth. He raised his mug. "To the wisdom of Mr. Morton, may it prosper us all."

A pleasant buzz had settled over Noah by the time they finished eating. His head felt light, his belly warm, and his fingertips tingled in a not unpleasant way.

He was midway through his third mug of beer, which was more than he'd ever had in one sitting. But these boys he was with—all a year or two older than him—only grew more merry as they reached the bottoms of their mugs. Their laughter was contagious, even if Noah didn't know what they were talking about half the time.

He got up from the table to follow them back to the beer barrels and almost ran smack into Samuel Maverick. Noah put up a hand to stop himself, and his cheeks heated when he realized he'd laid his palm against Maverick's chest. He pulled it back in a hurry.

"Hallo!" Maverick said with a grin. Noah stared a bit too long at his perfect teeth. "I spotted you earlier, but you were having such a merry time that I did not wish to interrupt it."

"I'm glad to see you," Noah said, and then his cheeks heated again at the involuntary image of Maverick naked by the water. "I was afraid I'd encounter Mr. Thomson here, and I almost did not come."

Maverick chuckled. "A wise caution, to be sure, but you needn't have worried overmuch. I have nurtured friendly relations with Mr. and Mrs. Thomson these last months, and it surprises me not that he would decline Mr. Morton's invitation. I cannot imagine the two of them getting on in any amicable fashion."

Noah laughed, unconcerned that it might be unseemly to do so.

Maverick's grin widened. "You are enjoying yourself. That pleases me." Then he leaned closer and said more quietly. "But do be cautious, Noah. Excess drink loosens a man's lips. I would not want thee to say anything to endanger thyself."

Noah was too focused at first on the way Maverick had reverted to the familiar form of address that it took him a few seconds to grasp the implications of the warning. Not only might he reveal too much about his situation, being a runaway from indentured service; but far worse if he slipped up and said or did something more incriminating.

"I won't." A voice called his name, and he looked over at the beer barrels. Benjamin, with the others, waved to him.

"Go on, then," Maverick said with a chuckle, and Noah hurried to rejoin his new friends.

CHAPTER 10
August 1624 - Mount Wollaston

"It's too late to return to Weymouth tonight," Benjamin said, putting his arm around Noah's shoulder. "You'll fall in the dark and twist your ankle. The wolves might eat you. You must stay 'til morning."

The evening had grown cool, and the remaining guests coalesced with their hosts around the bonfire. The Indians had departed en masse some time ago, and Samuel Maverick had recently left; he had come by boat, and he also seemed much more clear-headed than Noah right now.

"I'll stay."

Benjamin grinned. "I'll fetch you a blanket. You can share my pallet."

A thrill rushed up Noah's spine, and he couldn't help the grin that stretched across his face as he followed Benjamin into the house. Once his eyes adjusted to the dimness, he found Benjamin standing in front of a row of pallets, spreading blankets over one. He shuffled over to join him.

Then a hint of fear crept through him when he saw several Mount Wollaston boys sprawled out on their pallets. "There's not enough room for the both of us," he whispered.

"There is if we lay on our sides." Benjamin dropped to his knees and patted the spot in front of him. "Come on."

Noah's belly went light as air. A thrill at the thought of lying so close to Benjamin competed with the familiar fear of being seen thusly; but the thrill came out on top. He stretched out on his side, facing away from Benjamin so he wouldn't stare into those big blue eyes. That would be too much to bear.

But once Benjamin covered them with the blanket, he scooted closer, then closer again, and again, inch by inch, until his body pressed against Noah from behind.

"But—" Noah started to protest, but Benjamin laid a finger over his lips.

"Shhh," he whispered, so quietly that Noah could only hear it because Benjamin's lips were mere inches from his ear. The heat of Benjamin's breath against his neck sent tingles all over him, and goosebumps rose on his arms.

Benjamin's arm came around him beneath the blanket, and his palm rested against Noah's belly, warm through the fabric of his shirt. Noah could barely breathe. Benjamin's hand inched lower, stopped for a second, and then wiggled its way under Noah's shirt. His palm was hot against Noah's navel, and now Noah's breath stopped completely for a few seconds.

It came out in a rush when Benjamin pushed down firmly against his belly, nudging him backward. Their hips pressed together, and there was an unmistakable hardness in the front of Benjamin's pants that rose along the curve of Noah's right buttock. Benjamin shifted, and it settled into the space between. Noah's physical reaction was immediate, and the fear of discovery had fled into the darkness.

"Shhh," Benjamin whispered again, as quietly as before. Noah nodded in silence, and Benjamin's hand slipped inside the front of his pants.

Noah awoke to the chirp of birdsong. A dull ache spread through his head, and it took a second to realize where he was. One of Benjamin's knees rested between his own, and Benjamin's hand lay atop his right hip. His shirt twisted around his midsection, and he briefly tried tugging it back into place, but it was hopelessly twisted.

He edged away from Benjamin, rising in a panic to see if anyone else were awake inside the big room. But only slumbered breathing greeted him. The indentured servants of Mount Wollaston all sprawled on their pallets as if they'd collapsed there and not moved all night. He exhaled in relief.

He slipped out from under the blanket and stood, stuffing the front of his shirt back into his pants so he could wrap the tails around his privy parts. But then panic set in again when he saw the large, crusted stain at the front of his trousers. He let his shirt fall over it, momentarily relieved that the long tails covered the evidence of last night's misdeed. Then shame crept through him when he pictured the looks of judgment he would receive for walking around with his shirt untucked, like some barbarian. But their judgment would be far worse if they saw the stain of his spilled seed. He left it.

Tendrils of smoke rose from the black and gray ash mounded where the bonfire had been. From a pile of dogs lying on the ground outside the house, Drake raised his head and looked at Noah. Noah motioned for him, and the dog disentangled himself from the others and took a moment to stretch before trotting over.

"Ah, Mr. Bancroft! You are an early riser, like myself."

Noah turned toward Thomas Morton sitting at one of the long tables. Beside him, looking dour, sat three other men—Captain Wollaston, his factor, Mr. Rasdall, and Lt. Fitcher. Morton rose, leaving the others in irritation at his abrupt departure, and strode toward Noah.

"I am indeed pleased that you availed yourself of our hospitality," Morton said, beaming. "Come, let us breakfast together, shall we? Bread and a little jam? Yes, perhaps—but by the looks of you, I think some eggs and bacon are more in order. Come along, let's visit the coop."

A pair of cows in a pen mooed at them, while the bull snorted and kept his eye on them as they passed. Hens of various colors, too many to count, scratched and pecked at the dirt in front of a long coop with a low door.

Drake kept the rooster occupied while Morton and Noah collected a half-dozen eggs. Within ten minutes, they sat on a wooden bench beside one of the little cooking fires, and Morton was scrambling the half-fried eggs together in a sizzling skillet.

"You fit in well among the lads here." Morton gave the skillet a little toss and held it back over the fire. "You would be a most welcome addition, should you choose to stay here instead of returning to Weymouth Plantation."

The thought of being part of this community was quite appealing, and Noah couldn't deny the warmth he felt picturing evening meals with this group of young men, and their easy camaraderie. But what had happened last night with Benjamin ...

That must never happen again. The danger of discovery was too great, and then they would find themselves hanging by their necks from a tree branch until they strangled to death.

He shook his head. "Thank you for the kind offer, sir, but I have a home I must return to."

"Perhaps it's best if you discuss the option with the other three," Morton said. "All four of you are welcome to join our company. It could only benefit all of us to collaborate."

Noah couldn't argue with the logic, so he remained silent.

"You would enjoy the company of our fine lads, methinks." Morton pulled the skillet from the fire and slid half the eggs onto each of the two plates he'd dipped in a rain barrel and wiped clean. "They are all good boys, you'll find, though unjustly cast out and scorned by society. There are many such wretched souls in Devon, left behind and forgotten. Many run off to Bristol in search of a new life, and I was proud to offer that to these lads. They are a good lot, my little Ganymedes."

Noah's fork stopped midway to his mouth, and his head spun in Morton's direction. He slowly dropped his fork onto his plate. Had Morton actually said what he thought he'd heard?

A wry half-smile crept across Morton's lips. "Ah, I see you know the story of Jupiter and Ganymede? Well, let it be our little secret." He winked and shoved a piece of bacon into his mouth.

Noah did indeed know the story, having read Greek mythology with his mother. Zeus, the king of the gods—whom the Romans called Jupiter—had looked down from Mount Olympus and beheld Ganymede, the most beautiful youth in all of Greece, and fell instantly in love with him. So Zeus had turned himself into an eagle, snatched Ganymede up, and carried him to Mount Olympus, where Zeus took him as his lover.

A shy smile slowly spread across Noah's lips as the full implication settled in. It was incredible to think, and he looked at Morton and raised a questioning eyebrow. How could it be? The other three men—Captain Wollaston, Lt. Fitcher, and Mr. Rasdall—would never allow it.

Morton chuckled, gave Noah another wink, and shoveled a spoonful of eggs into his mouth.

"Where did you live before Bristol?" Noah asked Benjamin an hour later. After Sunday morning prayers, the tall young man had readily agreed to come with Noah into the woods, and the two of them were following the trail east toward Weymouth Plantation. Drake trotted along beside Noah.

"A little village in Gloucestershire, called Littledean," Benjamin said, and Noah smiled that he'd been correct that Benjamin came from somewhere else. "I left when I was sixteen. I thought I might find more like myself in Bristol, so that's where I went."

Noah's belly tingled. "Did you find them? More like us, I mean."

Benjamin nodded. "There's a house by the Bristol docks that takes in boys like us. Not a public inn, just a plain house behind the docks. The hostelier was one of us once. Came there from Bath, I think, when he was our age. He keeps on the lookout for new arrivals of our kind, and takes 'em in. He gives you a bed for a farthing a night, and dinner for a penny."

They walked in silence for a moment, though Noah sensed there was more.

Finally, Benjamin spoke again. "There's plenty of work to be found at the docks—hauling crates, loading ships, scraping barnacles from the hulls. But you can earn the most from the sailors. The ones that want you take a back room at the inns, with a window over the alley, and at midnight they put their lamp in the window. That's the signal. You must climb through the window so no one will see—if the innkeeper catches you, there's hell to pay—but if you're careful, you can have a night's love and walk home with sixpence."

Noah shook his head in wonder. He'd felt so alone all these years, and all he could feel was awe that such a place existed. "I had no idea."

A mischievous grin twerked the corner of Benjamin's mouth. "Sailors are the best lovers. They spend months at sea, with no company but their shipmates. And one must be careful onboard ship, even if there are others like you. A strict captain might hang them from the yardarm. When they come ashore, most of them head straight for the inns, where they can find a bawdy wench to serve their needs. But some don't mind the months without women, and they know where to find boys like us when they get to port."

"The boys at Mount Wollaston—they're all like us, then?" The thought was incredible, but the possibility made Noah's skin tingle.

"Not all, but most." Benjamin shrugged. "There's lots of reasons young men leave their villages and come to Bristol. Not all of them are like us. Mr. Morton picked strapping lads who aren't afraid of work; but I think he also knew what kind a lot of us are. You can tell by the way he looks at us sometimes. Did you know he abandoned a wife in Devon? Some of the others told me. It was a scandal, and everyone in the shire was talking about it."

Noah thought of Captain Levett. He'd left his wife and children behind to plant his colony, but only temporarily; he was going back to fetch them. In fact, they would all be back in New England by now, somewhere up the coast of the Maine. "He won't send for her, then? For Mrs. Morton?"

Benjamin scoffed. "Not for a king's ransom! He's finally free, and he's not going back. None of us are."

I'm not, either. "The other men—Captain Wollaston, Lt. Fitcher, and Mr. Rasdall—do they know? What kind of boys we are, I mean."

Benjamin considered this for a moment. "I don't think so. No, I'm certain they don't. Mr. Morton is more worldly than they. Captain

Wollaston knows commerce. I think it best to remain circumspect in his presence."

That would have been Noah's default, anyway. Always best to hide it. They'd already been too indiscrete.

The cottages of Weymouth Plantation came into view down the trail, and Noah stopped to turn toward Benjamin. "Thank you for accompanying me home." He extended his hand.

Benjamin shook it. "The three others are home already, I presume?" When Noah nodded, he added. "Then I shall leave you here, so it won't raise uncomfortable questions. You should come visit us often." Then he leaned in quickly and kissed Noah's cheek before turning and striding back the way they'd come.

Noah watched him for a moment, the easy way his body moved, as if gliding over the uneven ground. It would be so easy ...

No! He shook his head to clear the thought. Danger lay that way. Danger and temptation. He turned back toward Weymouth Plantation and trudged home, Drake trotting along beside him. It might be a lonely little hamlet, but it was safe.

CHAPTER II

OCTOBER 1624 - NEW ENGLAND

Noah and Drake took their daily morning hike down to the salt marsh below Weymouth Plantation, the grass on the hill crunching underfoot with the previous night's frost. Their breaths crystallized in the crisp air, and a thin misty fog rolled in from the bay, stirred by the wind off the ocean. Ducks rising from the marsh as Drake ran around its edges looked gauzy in the thick moisture.

Noah trudged around the inlet toward the point to look out toward the bay. The fog was thin enough he could see past the end a short way, though the many wooded islands not far offshore hid from view, lost somewhere in the mist.

A splash rose to his left as Drake leapt off a rock and plunged into the water. Noah laughed and threw a stick, which the dog immediately swam toward and snatched from the water. Drake carried it back a way, but then let it go when something caught his attention and he dunked his head and shoulders into the dark water to snatch at something, but came back up with a strand of seaweed hanging from one side of his mouth.

"Silly dog! Those fish are too fast for you, boy."

The hull of a ship glided past, at the edge of his vision. Heading east, toward the ocean, it was the size of a pinnace, and he squinted to peer through the mistiness at it. It looked like the *Unity*, Captain Wollaston's ship.

A jolt of panic swept through him at the thought that the Mount Wollaston colonists would have abandoned their plantation without warning. Captain Gorges had abandoned Weymouth Plantation, after all; though he'd at least given notice to his colonists, and shared his plans with Mr. Thomson prior to departing. Noah couldn't imagine Mr. Morton not sharing such news with their indentured boys, and Benjamin would have sent Noah a message.

The four men of Weymouth Plantation had passed many a Saturday night at Mount Wollaston, though Noah had been fastidious about not drinking so much that he couldn't walk home. Not since that first time. And there had been no repeat of the dangerous clandestine stroking of that first night. Thank God.

But the way Benjamin touched his back when no one was looking brought temptation to bear, and there had been a few visits to the shadows behind the house, with a moment of furtive groping, brief and out-of-sight.

Too brief to satisfy the urge.

Noah shook his head. No, Benjamin would have found a way to get a message to him if they were leaving. Still, a tickle of fear lodged itself at the base of his torso, and wouldn't let go as he called Drake and hiked back to the village.

A big exhale of relief escaped his lungs when he rounded the last bend in the trail. Several young men moved around the clearing atop Mount Wollaston. He hadn't realized how shallow his breathing had become until his lungs refilled with air after that big involuntary exhale. The morning mist had thinned to a mere haziness, and the frost had melted away, leaving a slick of mud on the trail, or he might have broken into a run.

Drake barked to announce their arrival, and then dashed off to play with Mr. Morton's dogs. Several of the indentured boys waved and greeted Noah by name, and he smiled when he returned their greetings, happy to see each and every one of them.

He spotted Benjamin on the far side of the clearing, carrying an arm load of kindling wood toward a pile beside one of the houses.

"You alright?" Benjamin asked, dumping his load onto the pile.

"I'm glad to see you," Noah said. His cheeks heated at the admission, but he didn't care. It was true. "I saw the *Unity* heading out to sea, and I thought perhaps you'd all abandoned the plantation."

"Captain Wollaston left this morning, with his Mr. Rasdall. He sails for Virginia." Benjamin grinned. "Thought you'd missed me?"

Noah shrugged and looked down, embarrassed for real now. "Other colonies have been abandoned."

Benjamin laughed. "None of them were led by Mr. Thomas Morton! He would never."

Noah laughed with him, his relief rushing out with the laughter. He had to admit he couldn't picture Mr. Morton giving up on anything.

"Mr. Morton's in charge of us while Captain Wollaston's away, so our chores are light today," Benjamin said, nodding toward the pile of wood. "But I've still got to build this pile up to eye height before leisure. If you help me, I'll finish sooner."

"Of course I'll help."

Benjamin motioned his head toward the woods. "Come along, then."

They tramped into the woods, which were awash in autumn yellows, oranges, and reds. Benjamin stooped to pick up a large stick near the base of a small maple tree. "In a month's time, the snow will cover all the sticks. We have to collect a season's worth before then."

"I haven't done this since I was small." Noah grabbed at a collection of fallen branches and twigs under the soaring boughs of a giant oak tree, left by one of the summer's storms. Back in Lancashire, collecting sticks was a child's work, while grown men split logs into bigger pieces of firewood.

"Me, neither," Benjamin said with a grin. "But someone's got to do it, and this week the task fell to me."

"Why did Captain Wollaston sail for Virginia?"

"To replenish our stores. We've been doing fine trade with the Indians, and we might run out of trade goods before long. There are merchants at Jamestown who can sell him everything the colony needs, and Captain Wollaston took our furs to exchange. He said New England furs are in high demand in Virginia at the start of winter."

"Are you glad he's gone?"

Benjamin chuckled. "You guessed he's not as popular with the lads as Mr. Morton is?"

"I don't believe anyone could be as popular as Mr. Morton is."

Benjamin laughed. "That is true. Mr. Morton is truly unique."

They returned to the village clearing with their armloads of sticks, and Thomas Morton was passing by at that moment. "Ah, Mr. Bancroft! We rarely see you this early in the day. Have you joined our little company permanently?"

"He thought perhaps we'd abandoned the plantation when he saw the *Unity* departing," Benjamin answered for him.

"Never!" Morton said, but his broad grin indicated the idea amused him. "I am glad to see you, however, as I'd like to have a word with you about business. May I borrow him for a few moments, Mr. Burton?" There was a twinkle in Morton's eye when he said this last part, and a mischievous smile graced his lips.

"Of course, sir," Benjamin said. Then to Noah, "I'll see you after my next load of wood."

Noah dropped his armload of sticks onto the pile and hurried back to where Thomas Morton waited for him.

"I'm curious how trade goes with the Indians at your post there at Weymouth Plantation. If you don't mind divulging your business to this curious old man."

"Not very well, I'm afraid," Noah said. Visits from native fur trappers to Weymouth were rare indeed, and his three companions no longer even complained about it. Most of their miniscule trade came from the four fishermen at Nantasket, bringing cod fillets to trade for needed tools and utensils. "We worry that it will be a lean and desperate winter."

"I wondered about that." Morton stroked his chin and looked off in thought. "I confess, I am disappointed in the level of trade we have received here, though I have endeavored without ceasing to put the natives at ease with our presence. I know they are suspicious of Englishmen in their midst—due in no small part to the rash and reckless behavior of the militia from New Plymouth Plantation, the devils—and I have had to work diligently to assure them of our friendly intentions. It has born some fruit, to be sure, but we have not seen the profits that are expected by the Council for New England. Or by me."

Noah's eyes widened. "But Benjamin was only just telling me that Captain Wollaston sails for Virginia to replenish the trade goods you have sold, and takes the furs you have received in payment."

"Aye, 'tis true. But we should have needed to do that a month ago, were we to bring in the profit that is required. I do not wish to discourage you by saying this, but it is some small relief to me that your post at Weymouth Plantation is not taking trade away from us. It only bolsters my opinion that our two plantations should join forces, for the good of the venture, and of all involved."

This made good sense, and Noah knew in his mind that it was the only way forward; but in his heart he still feared encountering Mr. Thomson here at some point. At least at Weymouth he was well hidden, if lonely. "I'm quite comfortable where I am, sir."

The look on Morton's face said that he didn't believe it for a moment. "How old are you, Mr. Bancroft?"

"I'm eighteen years."

"Mmmm," Morton said, nodding. "Most of our lads are eighteen to twenty; a few of them a year or two older than that. The other fellows at Weymouth Plantation—I suspect Mr. Ludden is younger than you, but the other two are quite a bit older, are they not?"

Noah nodded. James claimed to be fifteen, though Noah suspected he was a year or two younger than that; and though they had never told him specifically, Noah suspected Will Jefferies to be mid-twenties, at least, and John Bursley was certainly older than thirty.

"Ye would all be welcome additions, of course—but you especially."

"Why me especially?"

"If one were to judge by the frequency of your visits to our little company, it would seem you prefer the camaraderie here to what you have at home."

Noah shrugged and avoided Mr. Morton's eyes.

Morton watched him for a few seconds before putting his hand on Noah's shoulder and guiding him away from the houses, down the slope overlooking the shore. "Answer me truly—are you indentured to someone, Mr. Bancroft? Have you run away?"

A cold jolt jabbed through Noah's chest, and he stiffened. Morton's hand, which had lain lightly on his shoulder, now gave it a squeeze.

"I deduce from your reaction that my presumption was correct. I have suspected this for some time. Do not be alarmed—I am a lawyer, you'll remember. And I shall act as your attorney should the need present itself. I made a career defending those who have been victimized by cruel circumstances in Devon. Now tell me—who has claim to your indenture? From whose cruel hand have you fled?"

Noah continued to hesitate. Mr. Morton seemed trustworthy ... but it wasn't safe to trust anyone.

"Go on," Morton prompted, giving Noah's shoulder another little squeeze. "It's best we be prepared."

But first Noah wanted to confirm something. Since Mr. Morton was a lawyer, he would know the truth. "Is it true that an indenture is voided if the master abuses the servant?"

"Of what form was the abuse, Noah?" Morton's voice was soft and kind, but his use of Noah's given name still startled him.

Noah took a deep breath, gathered his strength. But he couldn't meet Mr. Morton's eyes. "He would beat me. Often."

Morton nodded, took a breath. "Then indeed his claim on thee is null and void. I would argue for thy freedom if this devil ever came looking for thee. Now tell me who he is."

Morton's switch to the familiar form disarmed Noah. "Mr. David Thomson, on Noddle's Island."

"Mmmm," Morton said, nodding and stroking his chin. "I must say, that surprises me not. I have met this Mr. Thomson on a few occasions, and I found him quite cold indeed. Stern, if one is being kind. I sense a deep well of anger within him."

"I agree, sir." Noah said. Then an unexpected smile crept up on him. He felt light, as if Morton had lifted a weight from his shoulders.

Morton's jovial smile returned. "We mustn't be too judgmental of him. He is a Scotsman, and he probably had a hard time of it in England.

I deduce he was there many years, given that his wife is a daughter of Devonshire, and they had several children there before their transport to New England. And we know how we English feel about the Scotsmen who have descended upon us these last twenty years that our kingdoms have had the same king." He chuckled as if it were amusing.

"But Mr. Morton, sir—how would you defend me if Mr. Thomson came to claim me? There is no magistrate here."

Morton chuckled again and turned Noah back toward the hilltop. "Then our lads would defend thee with our guns."

Noah imagined Mr. Thomson's face, scarlet with outrage, and he laughed.

"Thou art indeed one of us, Noah. We will not let him take thee."

"Thank you, sir." Noah's voice was barely more than a whisper, but he feared it would croak with emotion otherwise.

"If I may ask, how did thee get to be in Mr. Thomson's service?"

"I came to New England with Captain Levett last year. He was a kind master. I liked him. But a black-heart named Will Hailey poisoned Captain Levett's mind against me. He told Captain Levett lies about me … and about my relationship with a native boy. He implied I'd … done … things … with this boy. But I didn't, I swear!"

Morton had nodded along. "I believe thee, Noah. Tell me, what did Captain Levett do?"

Noah swallowed, tried to tamp down the emotion threatening to take control. "Captain Levett said he couldn't keep me on the ship, and he sold me to Mr. Thomson." He sniffed, and wiped away a tear with the back of his hand, looking at the ground. "I should be grateful he didn't have me hanged."

Morton chuckled. "It surprises me not that Christopher Levett would find the most lenient and humane solution to an intractable situation such as that. I have met him back in Devonshire, and found him a most affable fellow. And it should be remembered that his dear friend, George Villiers, Duke of Buckingham, is a beloved favorite of the king."

He took Noah by the shoulder and stopped them before reaching the hilltop. He leaned close and said quietly, "I should not be the sort to repeat gossip, but in this situation I believe it might put thy heart at ease. Our sovereign, King James, is said to have a deep and intimate love of

Buckingham. And a wont to fondle the duke's privy parts, according to palace servants who would know."

Noah's eyes widened, and his mouth fell open. He had no words.

"It is a weakness among lords and gentlemen to never believe the word of a servant; but I find servants to be more truthful than the average gentleman, and they often know everything that's going on that lords and gentlemen don't see." Morton straightened and pointed a stern finger. "Mind, there has never been any accusation of sodomy against the king, and I shall not tolerate slander in this plantation. Is that understood, young man?"

Noah nodded. "Understood, sir."

"And I trust thou understand the difference between fondling and sodomizing? Need I explain further?"

Noah's cheeks heated. "No, sir. I understand."

Morton gave one firm nod. "Good. Remember, the king's own father engaged in sodomy with many a man in his household. That is the *real* reason his wife, the Queen of Scots, had him murdered. But alas, that was forty years ago, and I suspect young folk remember that not."

Noah smiled and shook his head. He'd never known that—the king's father, a sodomite! There truly *were* men like them everywhere, as Benjamin said. But Morton's warning was clear—while what he and Benjamin had done would be tolerated, anything further would put the colony in danger.

"I understand, sir." Fondling would not give way to sodomizing.

"That's a good lad." Morton patted him on the back with a jovial smile and strode back into the settlement.

CHAPTER 12

WINTER 1624-'25 - WEYMOUTH PLANTATION

Noah rubbed his hands together and blew warm air between them as he stepped out of his cottage. He shoved his hands inside his coat and pulled it snug in the front, several of the buttons having fallen off, and trudged toward the trading post. The dry snow crunched under foot, and Drake bounded from drift to drift, burying his nose and then tossing white fluff into the air, snapping his jaws as it fell back to Earth.

"Come along, silly dog!" Noah called with a laugh, motioning with one arm, his hand pulled into the sleeve for that modicum of protection from the frigid air.

Drake loped toward him, but then stopped, ears cocked, and looked off at the forest trail.

"Hallooo!"

Noah recognized the voice before Thomas Morton appeared around a bend, hiking down the trail with a strange pair of contraptions strapped to his feet, a long and crooked piece of wood smoothed of its bark as a walking stick in his right hand. Behind him he pulled a sled, loaded with stuffed canvas bags. A half-dozen of his dogs bounded past him, leaping over the frozen creek. Drake barked happily and play-bowed, then dashed off after them as they plowed through snow drifts in big circles.

"Good morrow, Noah Bancroft!" Morton called when he was still on the other side of the creek.

John Bursley came out the door of the trading post. "Wonder what he wants?" They'd just seen Morton a few days prior, when they'd visited Mount Wollaston for Christmas at his invitation. Will Jeffries and James Ludden came out of their cottages a moment later.

"Good morrow, my fine fellows!" Morton called, having leapt across the frozen creek and now climbing the bank toward them, lugging the sled behind him.

"What are those?" young James asked, pointing at the odd tear-drop shaped woven wooden contraptions strapped to Morton's boots.

"The local tribes make these, for venturing forth during the snowy months," Morton said, lifting one foot to show them. "It keeps them atop the snow, and makes movement much easier. A most ingenious people, the Americans. They're called 'savages' by most, but I find them more civilized than a great many Englishmen. They were good enough to give some to me." He then stomped his foot down to demonstrate that it didn't sink.

Noah was the first to notice another pair of the things, hanging from a shoulder strap down Morton's back. "You have a spare pair."

"Indeed, I do." A twinkle lit Morton's eyes. "I have come to keep company with you for the duration of the winter, and to make Weymouth Plantation my home base for the season's industry."

"Ha! What industry?" John Burlsey said. He swept his arm toward the empty woods, white and silent.

"Why, the beaver trade, of course! We shall tally forth into the snowy woods, my lads, up hill and down vale, and catch the furry little creatures where they damn up the streams. I appoint ye good men as my deputies in this enterprise."

"Why us, Mr. Morton?" Noah asked. "Why not the boys at Mount Wollaston?"

Morton's lips pursed for the barest of seconds. "Captain Wollaston doth not permit the use of 'his boys' for my 'private enterprise.' He is a man of commerce, but his vision for the colony is agrarian and mercantile, not industrial. I have a broader vision than he. And so I come to ye, inviting ye to join my venture."

"We can't just up and leave the plantation," Will Jeffries said.

John Bursley scoffed. "Why not? It ain't as if we'd miss any customers at the trading post."

"What if the fishermen from Nantasket come to trade fish for our wares?" young James asked. He had a point. The four fishermen residing at the end of the Nantasket peninsula were the only regular customers Noah had seen in his seven months at Weymouth.

John Burlsey scoffed some more. "In the winter? Not bloody likely."

Noah tried to remember the last time the Nantasket fishermen had come calling. It was about four weeks ago, a couple of weeks after the first snows.

"Captain Gorges entrusted us to watch over it for him," Will said.

"And what's going to happen to it while we're away? You think the bloody Indians are gonna burn it down, in the dead of winter?"

Will frowned. "No, they're not fool enough to go abroad in this weather." He cast a sideways glance at Thomas Morton.

"I offer generous terms, my good men!" Morton said, beaming. "As the originator of the scheme, and the supplier of the necessary traps, I shall keep fifty percent of the take. Ye four will split the remaining fifty percent. And when the trade ships come in the spring, we shall make ourselves a fortune. What say ye?"

Will and James gathered around John at the door of the trading post. Noah took a few steps closer, but remained a distance apart. "Those are good terms," John said, voice low for them alone. "And what else are we gonna do until spring?"

"What do we know about trapping furs?" Will whispered.

"Mr. Morton will teach us," Noah said, taking one step closer, but still several feet apart from their cluster.

"We'll freeze to death camping in the woods," young James said.

"Or catch our death of pneumonia," Will grumbled.

"Not if we bundle up properly," John said. "And we'll take along spare clothes in case we get wet. We can warm ourselves by the fire every night." He nodded over his shoulder into the trading post. "What are we to do in the springtime when the trade ships come, and we ain't got but a few furs to trade? Captain Gorges is countin' on us to run this plantation for him."

"You go, then, John Bursley," Will said, crossing his arms.

John scowled. "Morton's terms are based on the four of us goin' with him. If ye two back out, that drops the take, don't it? Mr. Morton knows that, and he'll change his terms if it ain't all four of us. He'll keep more than half, then, I guarantee."

"Captain Gorges won't be pleased if we don't send him many furs ..." Will said, his voice trailing off, sounding unsure.

"We can give it a try," Noah said, taking another step toward the threesome. "If ye don't get on well with it, we'll take our cut and end it. We're free, after all—we can come home whenever we like."

"Sounds fair to me," John said, looking at the other two.

"I'm up for it," James said.

Everyone watched Will Jeffries. He looked at the snowy ground, face screwed up in thought. Then he shrugged. "Why not?"

The four of them walked toward Thomas Morton. "We'll do it," John Bursley said, extending his hand.

"Excellent!" Morton beamed and shook hands all around. "Let us break fast together, and I will show ye how to set the traps."

Noah's feet were like blocks of stone by the time they stopped for the night, high in the Blue Hills south of the bay. He wiggled his toes, and could barely feel the movement. His fingers had hurt for hours, no matter how much he clapped his hands together, or shook them. Thomas Morton had given him a pair of woolen mittens before they set out, which felt luxuriously warm for about ten minutes. Now he wasn't sure his hands held the strength to pull them off and on.

The dogs seemed oblivious to the cold, still trotting along beside the men as if this were a jolly adventure. But they were too tired to run around and play when Morton selected their campsite in a hollow sheltered from the wind by a bluff overlooking a creek. Drake stayed close to Noah, panting big clouds of steam, but looking happy, as if he were grinning.

"Messers Bursley, Jeffries, and Ludden—strip the bark off those birch trees by the water," Morton said. "Mr. Bancroft, you will assist me with building our shelter."

Noah helped him bend pine boughs into a sort of half-dome facing toward the creek. His fingers barely moved anymore, and every time he had to hold a bough in place for Morton to lash it with the rope, he only hoped his grip stayed strong enough to last until Morton had tied off the knots. By the time he helped Morton spread a canvas tarp over the entire structure, including hanging over the opening, he was desperate to huddle inside the thing.

Morton kicked away the snow to clear a patch of ground in front of the shelter, and then directed the others to pile their armloads of birch bark there, strike their flints, and ignite the pile.

"A trick I learned from the Indians. Birch bark will burn no matter how wet it is. If any of you lads find yourselves alone in the wilderness, in the rain or snow, find a birch tree and build yourself a jolly campfire. Once it's hot enough, ye can throw on any wet wood and blow the flame to keep it going." He chuckled. "A wise lot, the Indians. We English can learn much from their ways."

The campfire did indeed grow quickly, and they collected around it to bask in its heat. Noah's fingers and toes began to tingle, and he wiggled them. They moved more easily now.

They warmed a pot of beans over the fire and fried some ham. They tapped into Morton's half-barrel of beer, leaving their own for later. It was a thick and strong winter ale, brewed to last the season without freezing.

And so it was with a full belly and a warm head that Noah crawled into the close space of the shelter with the others. The glow from the fire made their shadows dance in the dark space. The dogs poked their heads under the canvas flap after the men and watched.

"Take off your coats, and spread them across us like blankets," Morton instructed while he spread a thick woolen blanket over the ground, and unfolded two others. They lay down and huddled under their coats while Morton spread the remaining blankets over them. Then he crawled under as well. "Turn onto your sides, my boys, and pull close together, lest we not last the night."

The dogs filed inside the shelter and lay in a semi-circle around them. Drake lay his nose against the top of Noah's head, and the sigh he released blew Noah's hair and tickled his scalp. Morton pressed up behind Noah, who scooted closer to James. Morton stretched his arm across the both of them, pulling them still tighter together, leaving no air between them.

It was both snug and intimate. The shared warmth of the huddled men and dogs penetrated deep into Noah's bones. A sort of calm settled over him, a feeling of safety. This was that kernel of hope he'd clung to when his father sent him off to the New World as a servant—to find moments like this one among men, in a world with few women. Although it would never be possible to find love the way normal boys found love with girls, this was more than nothing.

They returned to Weymouth Plantation six days later, sleds piled with beaver furs.

Noah had never imagined he'd be so glad to see the cluster of shabby little cottages. But after six full days in the forest wading thigh-deep into icy beaver ponds to drive a stake and set a trap, shivering the whole time, and then repeating the process hours later to retrieve a trapped and drowned beaver from the bottom, he was finished with the whole business. Cold, exhausted, and nauseated by the whole process, he wanted nothing more than to return to the tedium of life in an isolated little colony.

"'Tis a fine haul, my lads," Morton said, sweeping his arm in a grand gesture over the sleds of furs. "'Twill bring a fine trade when the supply ships return. And ye will bring your master, Captain Gorges, a tidy profit in 'soft gold.'" He removed a mitten and stroked one of the shiny brown pelts.

"There were more to be had," John Bursley said, not the first time that day he'd grumbled about Morton's unilateral decision to leave after only half of the beavers in the area had been trapped.

"Aye, but one must think to the future," Morton said. "Leave enough of the furry creatures to breed more for next winter's haul. Just as a sheep farmer knows to spare a selection of lambs every year to maintain his flock. The American tribes treat the bounty of the forest in like manner, and we are wise to follow their example. We return from whence we came grateful for the bounty, and now we will merry ourselves at home these next many days, before our next sortie into the wilderness to venture to new territories."

Noah couldn't muster the courage to tell Mr. Morton that he didn't want to go on another trapping trip. He stared at the ground as they walked into the center of the village.

"Someone's pried open the storehouse door!" Will Jeffries pointed at the storehouse, mouth tight in outrage.

The dogs ran ahead of them, sniffing at the door frame. Their hackles rose, and several let out low growls. The men hurried to the door, which had been pulled closed but would no longer latch, the wood around the lock splintered.

"Look!" James Ludden pointed toward their bags of beans, barley, and wheat. "They took some of our food!"

"I told you we should have stayed and minded the store," Will said, looking at John with a scowl.

Morton held up his hands. "Put your minds at ease, lads. Before I set forth to pass the season at your plantation, I sent a message to my Indian friends at the Neponset village, using a messenger who spent some years in England, who can thus converse in both tongues. I thought it wise to inform them of my whereabouts these next months, lest they call for me at Passonagessit—their name for our Mount Wollaston—and find me absent. I suspect they came hither to trade for corn, and finding me not present, they helped themselves."

"That's thievery!" John said, crossing his arms and glaring at Morton. "Send for your 'friends' and make them answer for trespassing and stealing."

Morton bowed his head and held out one hand palm-up in a genteel show of acquiescence. "I will indeed. I assure ye, they intended no harm—otherwise, they would have taken all and left naught behind. They took only what they need, and left us the bulk. But I will insist on payment of ten beaver skins for the produce."

The skins would be valuable when the supply ships returned in the spring. More valuable than the food that was taken. Noah, Will, and James looked at John, who frowned while he considered it. "That's fair."

Morton clapped his hands once and smiled. "Excellent! I will sally forth and send word to their sachem on the morrow."

A party of Indians appeared five days later, brightly colored blankets pulled tight around them, draping from shoulders to feet. They tread across the packed snow in the same snowshoes Morton wore.

Noah hurried to the trading post ahead of them—not an effortless task when the snow was two feet deep. He threw the door open and scanned the large room until he spotted John and Will tallying the inventory in the back. He called their names.

"Shut the damned door," John grumbled, rubbing his arms.

"We have customers," Noah said, breathless. John and Will stared in surprise over his shoulder, and Noah turned to see the half-dozen visitors standing behind him. He stepped aside to allow them in, and closed the door behind them.

One man stepped forward and held up a hand, palm forward. "Peace, brothers. We come from the Neponset village, to make payment to our brother Morton for the food our young men took from this place on the last full moon." His voice was deep and resonant, and his words carried an odd sort of accent, like he always spoke from the back of his throat.

"Morton's not here," Will said.

"He told us to meet him at this place on this day." The man's expression registered neither surprise nor disappointment.

"He's gone hunting," Noah said. He was about to say that Morton would return in a few hours, but John spoke up first, a little too eager.

"We'll take the skins for him."

The man turned toward his companions and motioned with his arm. Two of them left, returning a moment later with a stack of five beaver skins apiece.

"Put 'em here, in the back," John said. After they'd deposited the ten furs on the ground in the back corner, John situated them behind a crate of salt biscuits.

"Give greetings to our brother Morton," the first man said. "We are sorry he was not here for us to greet him personally." The group of Indians left in silence, and Noah closed the door.

"Gents, I have an idea," John said, a devilish look in his ideas.

Noah glanced at where the furs lay hidden behind a crate, not visible from the front of the store. "What are you planning?" he asked, suspicious.

"When Morton gets back, none of us tell him the savages were here to deliver his furs. We keep quiet, understand? That way, we get to keep all ten."

Noah didn't like it, and not only because it was dishonest, and cheated Thomas Morton of five pelts. "But if Mr. Morton thinks they didn't bring his furs, he'll go himself to their village to demand them. He's bold like that. Then he'll find out we cheated him."

The other three laughed. "If he goes marching into an Indian village alone, demanding they pay him furs, they'll kill him!" Will said.

"Especially if he calls them cheats!" James added, eyes aglow with mirth.

Noah hardly found it funny. He scowled and crossed his arms. "We don't want him to get killed."

John Bursley came up close, and pointed a finger at his face, inches from his nose. "You listen good, mister. Don't go running your mouth and ruin this. We have needs here, and those ten furs are gonna get us what we need. We're not gonna let you ruin it, understand?" He made a fist and ground it into his left palm in front of Noah's face.

Noah broke out in a sweat despite the chill. He swallowed hard and nodded.

Morton returned two hours after dark, a young four-point buck slung across his shoulders.

"We shall eat well this next fortnight, my fine fellows!" he said as he dropped it on the ground in front of them, beaming. "Messers Ludden and Bancroft, ye will help me skin and dress the carcass. Messers Bursley and Jeffries, go build up the fire large enough to roast this beast."

Noah and James fetched skinning knives and set to work with Morton to prepare the deer. "I meant to return much earlier than I did, but I daresay it took me all day to track this beast. He was a wily thing, indeed! Escaped my shots three times before I finally felled him. A worthy opponent." He patted the young buck's neck as if congratulating it on nearly escaping death. "Did our Indian friends come calling today with payment for the food they took?"

Noah froze, heart in his throat. He looked across the carcass at James.

"No, sir," James said, giving Noah a warning look. "No one's called here for ages."

Morton frowned. "That is curious. I expected them today." But then he shrugged, and returned to work peeling the deer hide from the meat. "But perhaps they had an unavoidable delay."

Noah kept looking at James, who pursed his lips at Noah and looked down at his work. Noah's mouth had gone dry, and he kept silent.

Noah's conscience had begun to disrupt his sleep.

For weeks, he'd wake in the middle of the night from a bad dream. It was close to the same every time. Thomas Morton accused him and his three companions of thievery, and the magistrate's guard came to haul them off to jail. Never mind that there was no magistrate in New England to jail them, it was a frightening dream. And it always brought a stab of conscience.

He'd lay awake for hours.

Their most recent trek into the wilds of the Blue Hills to trap beaver had ended more than a week ago; and instead of returning to Weymouth Plantation with them, Morton had set off for the Indian village on the Neponset River.

His failure to return filled Noah with dread. If the Indians had killed him for calling them liars and thieves, it was their fault. They never should have cheated him out of five pelts. No matter how much they were worth. Thirty pieces of silver, or his soul?

And so when Noah emerged from his cottage on a frosty March morning, bleary-eyed from too few hours' sleep, he stopped short at the sight of Thomas Morton sitting on a stump beside a fire.

"Good morrow, Noah Bancroft!" Morton said, beaming at him. His dogs lay in a circle around the fire, and barely opened their eyes at their master's shout.

"How long have you been here?" Noah asked, turning a log on end to sit next to Morton and warm his hands.

"I arrived at dawn. I shan't tarry here long, however—I come only to settle accounts for our winter fur venture, and then I return to Mount Wollaston before the new year begins."

Noah couldn't stand it any longer. Looking all around to make sure none of the others were out, he looked at Morton and the words poured forth.

"Mr. Morton, sir—we've cheated you! The Indians came on the day you asked them to, but you were away. John Bursley, he convinced them to leave the ten pelts with us, and we'd tell you they'd been paid. But after the Indians left, the others decided to keep the pelts and tell you the Indians never came. I didn't want to do it, Mr. Morton—please believe me! But they threatened me if I didn't keep silent."

Morton listened in stony silence, his cheeks flushing pink. When Noah finished, he stood and looked down at him. "I am very disappointed in thee, Noah Bancroft."

Noah saw a glimmer of hope in Morton slipping back into the familiar form of address, and he snatched at it.

"I'm dreadfully sorry, sir. Honestly, I am! I was afraid they'd hurt me. Or take me back to Mr. Thomson. I wish I'd gone with you last week, and told you then, before you went to the Indians to demand the payment." He spoke so quickly, he nearly stumbled over the words.

Morton nodded slowly. Then he offered Noah his hand. Noah grasped it, and Morton pulled him to his feet. "I am grateful thou told me the truth, Noah. There is still time to prevent an injustice. I found the Neponset sachem away from his village, visiting the Reverend Mr. Blaxton on the Mistic River. He was surprised that I had not received the furs he had ordered his young men to send to me, but he took my word that I had not taken receipt of the payment. He promised to send them with ten more pelts in a week's time—which is tomorrow. I told him I was returning to Passonagessit—Mount Wollaston—and to bring the payment to me there. Come! We leave within the hour."

"I'm coming?" Noah asked, hardly believing it.

"Indeed. I cannot leave thee here with these blackhearts. Thou will come with me to Mount Wollaston, and stay there as a permanent member of our colony. Get thy belongings and thy dog, and be ready to leave."

They arrived at Mount Wollaston at midday.

"Welcome back, Thomas," Captain Wollaston said, regarding Thomas Morton cooly. "You are in need of a bath and a shave. Was your venture successful?"

"Indeed it was, Richard," Morton replied. "Incidentally, I am expecting some visitors from the Neponset village, who will be bringing some beaver pelts."

"They arrived an hour ago, but I told them you were at Weymouth Plantation, and sent them on their way."

Morton's face went white. "You sent them to Weymouth?"

"I did. They seemed not at all pleased, but they went."

Morton turned to Noah. "Stay here. 'Tis not safe for thee to return. I will take a boat and try to intercept them."

Noah sat on a bench next to Benjamin and several of the others, warming themselves beside the bonfire, when Thomas Morton came marching up the hill from the wharf at dusk.

"Those blackhearts did it again!" he bellowed, and plopped onto a bench nearby. "They swore the Indians had not been there—but I could see their tracks in the snow! God knows they took another ten beaver pelts from the Indians, and probably promised to give them to me, as they did the last time. But to me they said 'they did not come!' I ask ye—who is more the savage, and who the civilized?"

It was a startling question, and several of the young men gasped. But Noah knew the answer. And he was never so glad to be here.

CHAPTER 13

SPRING 1625 – MOUNT WOLLASTON

Torchlight bathed the settlement in a warm glow as twilight settled, and the heat from the circle of five dozen tar-fueled flames banished the chill of the early spring evening. On a wooden platform in the center of the village, built specially for the evening, Thomas Morton and twelve of the indentured boys lounged on tasseled cushions across a long bench. They all wore long brown robes that came to mid-shin, and were barefoot.

Morton sat in the center, six boys on either side of him, with the Book of Common Prayer open on a stool in front of him, and his Bible open on his lap. He read from the Gospel of John. *"And when Jesus had thus said, he was troubled in spirit, and testified and said, 'Verily, verily I say unto you, that one of you shall betray me.' Then the disciples looked one on another, doubting of whom he spake. Now there was leaning on Jesus's bosom one of his disciples, whom Jesus loved—"*

Leo Taylor, sitting on Morton's right, leaned onto the older man in exaggerated movement, hamming it up. He placed his cheek against Morton's chest and sighed loudly, a big goofy grin on his face. As he did so, he bent his right leg and slid the foot up past his left knee, and his now elevated right knee raised the hem of his robe toward the crowd, flashing them an unhindered view of his bare genitals.

The nineteen boys seated in front of the stage whooped and applauded. Benjamin elbowed Noah in the ribs, looking at him and waggling his eyebrows. Noah grinned.

Standing to the side, Captain Wollaston's lips tightened into a thin white line.

Suppressing his own laughter, Morton continued. *"Simon Peter therefore beckoned to him, that he should ask who it should be of whom he spake. He then lying on Jesus's breast saith unto him, 'Lord, who is it?'"*

Leo placed a palm on Morton's midsection and turned his head up, batting his eyelashes and cooed, "Lord, who is it?"

The boys in the audience laughed. Noah couldn't stop grinning. It was deliciously scandalous. Captain Wollaston rolled his eyes. Standing next to him, Mr. Rasdall and Lt. Fitcher looked unamused.

Morton nearly lost the battle against his laughter and continued reading with some difficulty. *"Jesus answered, 'He it is to whom I shall give a sop, when I have dipped it.' And when he had dipped the sop he gave it to Judas Iscariot, the son of Simon. And after the sop, Satan entered into him. Then said Jesus unto him, 'That thou doest, do quickly.'"*

Ralph Mason, seated on Morton's left, took a piece of bread and dunked it in the chalice sitting beside Morton's prayer book. From where he had been crouched behind the stage, Sam Weaver leapt out, clad in a red robe but barefoot like the others, carrying a pitchfork in one hand. A set of deer antlers perched precariously atop his curly brown hair.

Noah found it hilarious that Sam was cast as the devil, since of all of them he had the most angelic face. He was twenty years old, but one would hardly believe him older than fifteen. Cackling devilishly, Sam crept up behind Ralph Mason, stood him up and then pressed himself to Ralph's back and made lewd movements with his hips. "Entering Judas."

The audience roared with laughter, and Benjamin elbowed Noah in the side again. Then Sam pushed Ralph off the stage, slapping his buttocks before ducking back into the shadows.

Captain Wollaston shook his head and marched away.

The others onstage followed Morton offstage, reenacting the journey to Gethsemane. The eleven remaining boys lay down in the grass and pretended to sleep. Morton, as Jesus, got on his knees and cried loudly for the cup to pass, if possible; "*But thy will and not mine.*" Then Ralph, as Judas, rushed back and kissed Morton full on the mouth, eliciting another set of whoops from the audience.

Morton, struggling not to laugh, delivered his final line with added gusto. "*Judas! Betrayest thou the Son of Man with a kiss?*" Then the entire cast stood and bowed, and everyone clapped and cheered.

"That's the most entertaining Passion play I've ever watched," Benjamin said.

"It was definitely entertaining," Noah agreed with a laugh. He wasn't sure how he felt about the devil being a sodomite, but he kept that to himself. Religious folk back in his home village would have been aghast at the portrayal, so that was something.

After dinner, Noah excused himself from the table to relieve himself. He made his way to the privy by circling behind the big house, but when he neared the corner, he heard tense voices.

"You indulge them too much, Thomas," Captain Wollaston hissed. "That ill-begotten 'performance' of yours only encourages them to give in to unnatural impulses, not to resist them."

"'Twas only a bit of fun, Richard," Morton said. "There was no harm done. None of the lads descended into open licentiousness on the stage. And the whole company enjoyed it."

"Your indulgence will bring ruin upon us yet," Wollaston said in a low growl. "It has not escaped my notice—nor Mr. Rasdall's notice, nor Lieutenant Fitcher's—that many of these boys tend toward unnatural inclinations. You were naive and misjudged their natures when you recruited them. And now your light-handed indulgence only encourages them to test their inclinations rather than turn away from them. Tonight's display is evidence of that, I dare say."

"'Twas harmless fun, Richard," Morton repeated.

Wollaston's voice dropped to a hoarse whisper, and Noah crept closer to the corner to hear. "November, when I was in Virginia, a ship's captain named Richard Williams—called Cornish—was put on trial for sodomy. 'Twas all anyone in Jamestown could speak of for days. His steward, one William Couse, accused Cornish of inviting him into bed with him after he—Couse—had made it with fresh linens. When Couse would not join him, Cornish tore off the man's codpiece and put his hand to his privies. Cornish pulled him onto the bed, lay atop him and kissed him, then forced him onto his belly and buggered him."

Twin sensations of horror and excitement swirled around Noah's belly. His breath came short and fast.

"The boatswain's mate, a man called Walter Mathew, testified that he overheard Cornish and Couse arguing in the captain's cabin, Couse saying that he would not do it. But Mathews walked away, and later asked Couse what had transpired between him and the captain. Couse at first refused to say, so great was his shame; but later he admitted that Cornish had tried to bugger him, but did not say whether Cornish succeeded in fact.

"Still, the jury convicted Cornish of sodomy and hanged him the next week."

"That is a fascinating tale, Richard," Morton said, more loudly and with an edge to his tone. "But its relevance to tonight's play is not apparent to me. You speak of a man who, it is alleged, forcefully buggered another, and was hanged for that offense. There was no buggery transpiring in our Passion play, forceful or otherwise."

"I differ with your reasoning," Wollaston said, still in a hoarse whisper. "Your 'devil' pretended to do just that to your Judas Iscariot."

Morton barked out a laugh. "Do you say, then, that an action attributed to *Satan* is to be seen as an *encouragement* to these lads to investigate forbidden desires? It is a tenuous thread from which you hang your assertions."

"I am not a witness you are cross-examining in court, Thomas."

"Enough of this!" Morton snapped. "I tire of this argument. Let us return to table, where you can keep your watchful eye on the behavior of our boys."

As their footsteps through the grass receded, Noah peeked around the corner to be sure they had gone. His heart pounded. Then he hurried toward the outhouse before anyone else approached.

The second half of the passion play concluded the next afternoon, with several boys "whipping" Mr. Morton—wrapped in a sheet around his waist, bare-torsoed—with branches of soft spring leaves, driving him toward a fake crucifixion in which they tied his wrists to a door frame.

"It ... is ... finished!" Morton cried out in believable agony, and dropped his head to his chest. The boys all applauded while Sam Weaver and Ralph Mason untied Morton's wrists.

"Mr. Bancroft, a word, if I may?" Morton hurried toward Noah, who averted his eyes from the way the older man's privy parts bounced under the folds of sheet fastened around his waist. His torso was criss-crossed with slashes of red paint.

"Yes, sir?" He stared at Morton's bare feet.

"I wonder if you might accompany me on the morrow. I go to call on our Indian neighbors. And Drake is welcome to join us, of course." Thomas Morton made a show of bowing to the dog and playing at tipping an invisible hat.

Noah couldn't hide his surprise. "I would, sir. Thank you. But if I may—why me? Why not Mr. Rasdall, since he's the colony's merchant?"

Morton's smile was enigmatic. "It's an eight-mile hike, so we leave at dawn. I suggest you retire early. Good day."

Noah's breath crystalized in the pre-dawn chill of the April morning as he yawned. He briefly envied the others, asleep under their warm blankets. But they would have plenty of work to occupy them while he was trekking through the forest with Mr. Morton, so he supposed he'd gotten the better end of that.

"I hope you're well rested and prepared for our outing," Morton said, appearing at Noah's side. "Shall we?"

Noah whistled for Drake, but the pup had already joined Morton's pack and was running around with them, keeping pace with the two humans as they set out on the trail leading west through the wooded fields surrounding the hilltop village. Morton kept a brisk pace, and though Noah had no trouble keeping up, he hoped he had as much stamina as the older man. It would embarrass him to need a rest first.

When they passed into the thick forest beyond the fields, Morton pointed out various species of birds, trees, and shrubs. He could name them all.

"How did you learn all of this?"

Morton tapped his forehead. "A curious mind is as valuable a commodity as any there be. And one should never fear to inquire about things one does not know, but would like to know. I observe, and I ask."

Noah nodded. He took that as a cue to ask what was on his mind. "I presume this isn't a mercantile business outing, or Mr. Rasdall would accompany you. But I also presume it's not merely a social call. For what purpose are we visiting the Indians?"

"That is well deduced, Noah. I will make a good mercantilist of thee yet," Morton said, slipping back into the familiar address. "Business—and it matters not what business—is built upon good relations. The American tribes of this area have reasons to be suspicious of Englishmen, and it has been my calling in this country to repair what the New Plymouth militia put asunder some years ago. The effort thus far has yielded some fruit, but not the bushels we desire. Dost thou understand?"

"Yes, sir, I do indeed."

"I thought thou would. Thou art a bright lad. And I'm sure thou know our colony has backers in England, gentlemen who outfitted us with everything we would need for our first year in New England, at considerable cost. In return, they expect to earn back their investment in profit from trade—be that trade with the Indians for furs, or the fish trade, or lumber. Pannaway Plantation at Piscataqua Point sends lumber back to England, and the gentlemen on the Council sell it at great profit. The Essex colony at Cape Ann sends enormous quantities of codfish, as do the stations at Monhegan Island and Pemaquid. We at Mount Wollaston—like the Weymouth Plantation before us—are to acquire furs from the Indians. Beaver pelts in particular will fetch a grand price at the markets of Europe. Russians will pay a fortune for them."

"But Captain Wollaston took the furs to Virginia last fall," Noah said.

Morton sighed. "Indeed, he did. Our first priority is to ensure the survival of the colony. Profit cannot be made if we starve, or if we run out of supplies. So some of our furs will always need to be exchanged for what we need. These things are cheaper to acquire in Jamestown than in Bristol. And we can make the journey in an eighth of the time. Not until we acquire enough pelts to fill the hull of the ship, can we send them back to England for profit."

Noah nodded, only understanding part. "Then, we go to the Indians to build good relations, so they will trade more furs to us—but why take me, and not Mr. Rasdall? I have no experience with this."

Morton chuckled. "I believe thou hast more skill in dealing with in-tractable men than thou give thyself credit for."

It took almost three hours to hike to the Indian village on a bluff overlooking the Neponset River. The Indians' dogs announced their arrival before they'd rounded the last corner. Morton's dogs returned their barks, and Drake happily joined the chorus before looking back at Noah with a big grin on his face, tongue hanging out the side of his mouth.

Noah scratched him behind the ears and ignored the nerves tumbling around in his gut. "Good boy."

When the village came into view around the bend, a half-dozen men were running forward, hands at the tomahawks hanging from the rawhide strip at their waists. Morton's dogs positioned themselves in a tight circle around Morton and Noah, their hackles half-raised in warning. Drake remained at Noah's side, but now pressed himself more tightly against Noah's leg.

Noah raised his right hand, palm forward, the way Jimmy Hawkey had greeted the Abenaki men in the woods outside of Pannaway Plantation. It pleased him that he did it at the same moment Mr. Morton did. The Indians stopped some fifteen yards ahead of them and moved their hands from the tomahawks hanging against their bare hips to raise them in a like manner.

"*Kui kwasind*," Morton said.

"Kui kwasind," two of the Indians facing them said in return.

"That's how you say 'Good morning' to the Massachusetts or Wampanoags," Morton said to Noah.

"*Ku-i kwa-sind?*" Noah repeated, quietly, tentatively. Morton nodded forward, and Noah turned his gaze back to the men in front of them and repeated more full-throated, "*Kui Kwasind.*"

A couple of the young men looked amused, which briefly distracted Noah from their near-nakedness. He must not have said it correctly.

"We come to see Wonohaquaham," Morton said, loudly enough they might have heard him in the village.

One man motioned them forward with a wave of his arm, and they followed them. A man of about thirty stood apart from the others, and Morton made a beeline toward him. Noah hurried to keep up with Morton, and as they approached, he recognized the man's face from last summer's welcome feast.

They greeted each other with "Kui Kwasind." Then Morton added, "*Sun Kuwnay?*"

Wonohaquaham nodded. "I am well." Even in English, the words seemed to thrust from the back of his throat.

Morton put a hand on Noah's shoulder. "This is my associate, Noah Bancroft. Noah, I present the local sachem, Wonohaquaham son of Nanepashemet. His mother is the Squaw Sachem of Mistik, who leads the people since Nanepashemet's death."

To Noah's surprise, Wonohaquaham put out his right hand, English-style. Noah hesitated a second, unsure of the correct manners, before shaking it. "How do you do?"

"I am well," Wonohaquaham repeated.

"Wonohaquaham and many of his people have learned English from Mr. Blaxton, who has a mission church on the Charles River."

"I know it," Noah said, eliciting a surprised arch of Morton's eyebrows. "Mr. Maverick and I helped to build it last year."

"Ah, splendid!" Morton beamed. Then to Wonohaquaham, "May we converse with thee, friend?"

"It is not natural for the People to kill the otter and the beaver," Wonohaquaham said in response to Morton's inquiry about more furs. "Kehtannit has ordered the world that every being has purpose. We kill to eat, and use the hides for clothes and shelter; the bones we carve for tools. We do not eat brother otter or beaver. The English want only their fur, and make no use of the other parts. We can feed their meat to our dogs, but only as much as they need."

Noah's eyes had finally adjusted to the dim light of the wigwam, but the smokiness of the air still burned, and the acrid smell stung the insides of his nose. A fire burned in a shallow pit at the center of the room, and the small hole in the roof above it only swept out part of the smoke. "You brought pelts to Weymouth only last month," he said before thinking better of it.

Wonohaquaham sat next to them on a pile of deer hides; his crossed-legged pose sent a tinge of discomfort through Noah's belly. It was improper to spread one's legs in such a manner. Noah kept his knees together in front of his chest, and hung his arms around his knees. Mr. Morton had adopted the cross-legged position, though he'd grimaced when he sat. At his age, it must be difficult to try new postures.

"Our store of corn grew low, and Brother Morton has much corn, so our young men trapped beaver to trade for corn our women and children needed."

"I respect your moral compunction," Morton said. "We English have learned that the right thing or the wrong thing at any moment can be highly circumstantial." Seeing the confusion on Wonohaquaham's face, he added, "The right thing or the wrong thing to do may change in different situations, when things are different."

Wonohaquaham grunted, his expression unreadable.

Noah opened his mouth again before he could stop himself. "If you kill too much meat for the dogs, why not leave it in the woods for the wolves? Or the foxes? It's not wasted just because you don't use it your-selves." He instantly regretted saying it, and an image of his father's scowl flashed across his mind, with his stern warning against impertinence.

But when he glanced at Mr. Morton, there was a faint smile on the older man's lips.

"The furs of the beaver and otter trade for things your people need," Morton said. "That iron pot hanging over your fire. The steel knives your women use to clean the deer hides on which we sit, and that you wear. The spirits that your young men love."

Wonohaquaham nodded slowly. "We are grateful for these things, Brother Morton. But we trade what we need, and no more. What we need more than these are the guns your people use to hunt. And to fight."

Morton stiffened. "I see. It pains me to say that we cannot trade guns to you." He hastened to add, "We have only what we need for ourselves, and no more."

Wonohaquaham's dark eyes never wavered from Morton's face. "For generations, the people have warred with our ancient enemies to the north, the Penobscot and the Mic Mac. For many years now, our enemies have brought guns to the battle, and our people have not won a battle since I was a boy. Every summer we lose more young men, and our women weep. The Penobscot and Mic Mac take furs to the French at Port Royal, and come back with many guns. We are brave, Brother Morton, but we cannot fight against guns if we have none."

Morton stroked his chin beard. "I see your dilemma. *Both* of your dilemmas. Perhaps we can help you with one of them."

The daylight hurt Noah's eyes when they emerged from the wigwam. But the fresh air in his lungs smelled sweet. As ever, his eyes were drawn to the way the young Indian men moved, the graceful movement of muscle in their bare legs and half-exposed buttocks. But his cheeks heated at the thought that Mr. Morton would catch him looking at such things.

"Perhaps we should dress like the Indian men, to make the girls more comfortable when they visit us," he blurted before he could stop himself. The very thought excited him more than he'd care to admit, but the twin threads of thrill and fear wound themselves ever tighter in his belly. He looked down in embarrassment—for the thought as well as for the uncensored outburst.

"There is wisdom in thy suggestion," Morton said, though the twinkle of amusement in his eyes said that he could deduce Noah's deeper motive. "Captain Wollaston might not approve, but we can always resort to subterfuge if needs demand it."

Noah and Benjamin crept up to Mr. Morton's rear window, crouching low to keep below the sill, and pressed their ears against the frame. The wall muffled the voices inside, but Noah could still make out the words through the wood slats.

"If you're concerned about the boys being tempted by 'unnatural impulses,' as you've intimated, then this is the perfect solution, Richard. And like Daedalus we can kill two birds with a single stone. The native girls are ideal candidates for the boys' romantic distraction, and we can build a stronger relationship with our neighbors because our boys can fill an absence that they cannot fill themselves."

"It is hardly a 'perfect solution,' Thomas," Captain Wollaston grumbled. "But since we lack any English girls, and we have not the profits to purchase any, your proposal offers a temporary benefit that I will not veto. You would likely carry on with it in my absence in any event. Lt. Fitcher will see that the boys do not distract themselves too much and neglect their chores while I am away. Temper your indulgence, if you may, Thomas."

The sound of receding footsteps replaced the voices, and Noah peeked around the side of the house at Captain Wollaston marching toward the trading post.

"He and Mr. Rasdall sail next week to call at the other plantations around New England," Benjamin said. "I heard them speaking about it several days ago. For trade." He sighed. "But with Lt. Fitcher remaining behind, it shan't be the way it was when the three of them sailed for Virginia last fall. Those were good days."

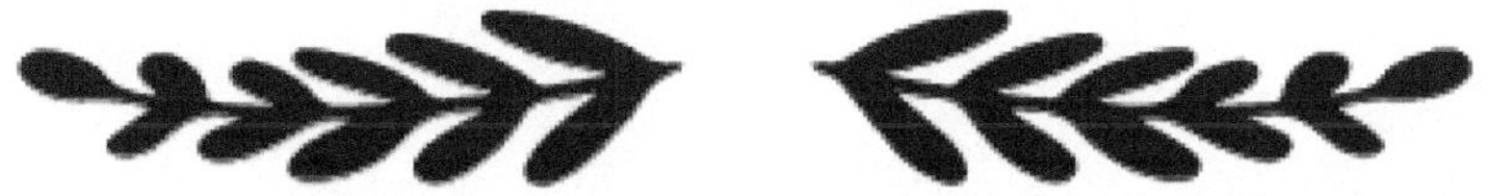

Noah returned to his quarters after working an hour in his bean patch. Sitting next to his pallet was a stack of deer skins a foot high, and a folded piece of parchment lay atop his blanket. He unfolded the paper and found written instructions, along with an illustration.

"Cut the deerskin leather into foot-wide strips, four to five-foot lengths;

Cut the remnants into two-inch strips, between thirty and forty-inch lengths;

Sew the ends of the two-inch strips to fashion a belt;

The wearer should fit one foot-wide strip through the belt in front and back and between the legs, as illustrated."

Noah counted ninety-six deer skins in the stack. This would be an awful lot of work. He'd never finish them in the next fortnight. He sighed and tossed the paper onto the hides and plopped onto his pallet. It was then, as the parchment fluttered down, that Noah noticed a bit of writing on the back side. He flipped it over and saw a brief note: "Ask Leo to help. He was once a tailor's apprentice."

CHAPTER 14

APRIL 1625 - MOUNT WOLLASTON

It was the moment of truth. Noah tingled with excitement, but at the same time his stomach tumbled with anxiety.

Taking a breath, he stripped off his clothes. He stepped into the thin belt and tugged it over his hips; then he took the long strip of deer hide and put it between his legs, keeping the soft side next to him and the suede side out. He pulled the front over his privy parts, taking an extra second to make sure it fully covered his bollocks, and tucked the front up and over the belt, letting the end drape to mid-thigh. He repeated the process in the back, and just like that, he stood in the middle of his cottage dressed in a breechclout like an Indian.

The tingle of air flow against the side of his buttocks proved how exposed he was. Goosebumps rose over his arms and torso, thrilling and frightening at the same time.

Drake watched him with his head cocked. "Well, boy, it's time. No more hiding." *This is what I get for opening my mouth.*

He walked outside, and the feel of the breeze on his bare skin made him all too aware of his near nakedness in the open. A cluster of about a dozen indentured boys stood in front of their house, clad in the breechclouts he and Leo had made. More filed out the front door every minute, snickering or giggling. Noah's eyes lingered over their muscular torsos, long legs, and half-exposed buttocks.

Thomas Morton strode into the middle of the village a few minutes later, clad in a breechclout like the others, but with leather leggings from ankle to mid-thigh, and a white shirt; the shirttails covered him in front and back more fully than the breechclout, leaving only his hips bare. Noah hadn't realized that was an option, and almost went back inside for his shirt. Mr. Morton had at least left the front unlaced, letting the top flaps hang open.

"Come, my boys, gather 'round!"

The young men collected around Morton. Noah found Benjamin, and after a couple of seconds staring at the smooth roundness of Ben's right buttock, went to stand beside him.

"In ancient times, our forebears celebrated the fortieth night after the spring equinox with dancing and revels, to honor the fertility of the season. Tonight, our neighbors from the Massachusett tribe come to celebrate with us. May the spirits of the forest bless our gathering, and lead us to create a new society, Indian and English in equal measure."

He chuckled then, looking around the circle of sheepish smiles. "And if ye are uncomfortable in your more natural state this night, remember that the Indian girls who will share the dance with ye only know men dressed thusly." This brought a cheer from many of the young men gathered around. "Do not be embarrassed, my lads! Celebrate your potency, revel in it, as the native men do."

Benjamin nudged Noah with his elbow, a sly grin on his lips. Noah's eyes roamed down Benjamin's flat belly, punctuated by a deep belly button. It was smooth, save for a trail of short brown hairs that began at the navel and disappeared beneath the breechclout. His breath caught, and he grew light-headed until he glanced away.

Wonohaquaham arrived shortly before dusk, accompanied by six young men and three times as many young women. The young men had bows slung over their shoulders and quivers of arrows on their backs. Noah was relieved to see they wore only breechclouts, like the English boys. Wonohaquaham himself wore a baggy deerskin shirt with extensive beadwork and shells in elaborate patterns. Several feathers stood at the back of his head, protruding from a headband decorated with more beadwork. A drum hung at his back from a strap across his shoulders.

While Thomas Morton welcomed Wonohaquaham with a greeting in the Massachusett language, Edward Gibbons separated himself from the other youths and strode boldly toward the collection of native women standing behind their sachem. He gave them an English bow, which made them giggle, and introduced himself.

"Edward prefers girls," Benjamin muttered to Noah. "He *says* he only took men into his chambers in Bristol for money." He leaned closer and whispered, "I suspect there was more appeal than only money, but I let him pretend."

"The six of them will take a half-dozen girls," Ralph Mason said nearby, frowning. "That leaves a dozen girls for the thirty of us."

"Who says that's bad odds?" Sam Weaver said, laughing and jabbing an elbow into Robbie Ellis's ribs.

Robbie's cheeks colored. "You go on to the front of the line, Ralph," Robbie said.

Wonohaquaham sat on a log and positioned his drum between his knees. "Keegsquaog," he said, and the Massachusett women lined up, facing the fire. "Wuskenig—young men, come." He beckoned the Mount Wollaston boys forward while the six young native men lined up facing the women, backs to the fire.

Everyone stood rooted in place for several seconds, until Edward Gibbons strutted forward and stood in front of one of the women. "What are you lads waiting for?" he called over his shoulder. Noah held his breath. Ralph joined Edward, followed by Leo and several others until the lines balanced.

Sam put one arm around Robbie, the other around Benjamin, and grinned at Noah. "We're reprieved!"

Wonohaquaham beat his drum in a steady rhythm, and strange words poured out of his mouth in a sort of hypnotic chant, sing-songy and yet not really singing. The young Massachusett men and women moved their feet, hips, and shoulders in time to the drum beat, and the indentured boys watched and attempted to emulate the steps. They looked so ridiculously awkward, Noah and his friends couldn't help laughing.

Lt. Fitcher appeared over the crest of the hill, running up from the dock, musket in hand. He stopped suddenly, mouth open and eyes widened. Then his face contorted into a deep scowl, and he marched across the clearing and stopped in front of Thomas Morton.

"What is the meaning of this?"

His voice carried over the drum and the chanting of the Indian men. Noah took a few steps closer.

"I'm not sure what it is exactly to which you refer, sir," Morton said with false innocence.

"Our boys, Mr. Morton! Dressed like savages. Cavorting like wild men. It's unseemly. I thought the village was under attack, and I hurried here to defend our plantation. Then I see our own boys, nearly naked and behaving like the American savages."

Morton's voice remained calm, but his eyes had hardened as he stared back at Fitcher. "Our *neighbors*, Lieutenant, are not savages. I find them the most noble of men. And I would ask you to kindly refrain from insulting them when they are our guests."

"And this ... display?" Fitcher waved a hand erratically at the dancing figures circling the bonfire.

Morton glanced at the dance, then back at Fitcher, nonplussed. "That is a dance of courtship, Lieutenant. Our neighbors have an excess of young women in need of male companions. Our lads suffer a lack of female companionship. It is only logical to bring the two together and let nature take her course."

Fitcher's mouth hung open, aghast. When he finally collected himself, he straightened his shoulders and said, "Captain Wollaston will hear of this when he returns." He marched off to his cottage and disappeared inside.

Morton caught Noah watching him. With a grin and a wink, he strode off to refill his mug.

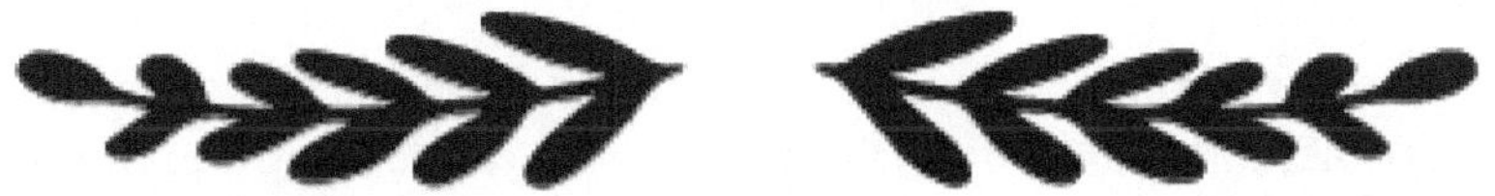

Benjamin and several of the others had gone to refill their mugs at the beer barrel, and Noah stood alone for a few minutes, watching the dancers. In particular, he watched as Leo and the Indian maid he was dancing with separated from the circle and went off alone, to the corner of the servants' house.

Leo stood close to her, and his fingers intertwined with hers. Noah's eyes stayed glued to them, to Leo's fingers stroking the girl's forearm. Those fingers that had tickled Noah's bollocks when he "measured" him for his breechclout, and teased his pillicock with a graze, now found the touch of a young woman more appealing.

Noah couldn't help the pangs of jealousy that ripped through him, even though it was hypocritical, given his own activities with Benjamin.

"They look well together, don't they?"

Mr. Morton's voice startled Noah. His cheeks heated at being discovered staring. He nodded, but kept silent.

"She is a beautiful girl, is she not? And our Leo is a beautiful boy. They would make a good match. How much more beautiful would be the offspring of such a union, should that happen?"

Noah frowned. That wouldn't be a good thing at all. Leo, he was like them—like Noah and Benjamin—not like most boys who liked girls.

"At the height of Rome's grandeur, no less a luminary than Cicero wrote, 'A true lover of beauty must be equally drawn to both sexes.' Our Leo is a true lover of beauty. As am I."

Noah's eyes widened, and he looked at Morton's face. The audacious admission hung in the air like mist.

Amusement twinkled in Morton's eyes. "Does it shock thee to hear me speak thusly?"

Noah wondered if he would seem unsophisticated to admit that it did. He shrugged, and Morton chuckled.

"At the Inns of Court, we spend a great deal of time studying the writings of the Greeks and Romans, ruminating over every minute detail of their law and philosophy. Far more than do students of the universities at Oxford and Cambridge. It is necessary for lawyers, you see. But one can't help but be struck at how *often* the ancients waxed on about the beauty of the male form, sometimes more than the beauty of women. One realizes the natural state of man is to be drawn to both."

Noah dropped his eyes. If man's natural state were to be drawn to both sexes, then he was still unnatural; he'd only ever been drawn to boys.

Morton put his arm around Noah. "Let that thought bring thee comfort, Noah. Thou art not alone in such desire. Indeed, the Inns of Court encourage a certain libertine attitude among those who are open to it. I wish thou could have known that, as I did at thy age. It might have brought thee confidence—something that I suspect was stolen from thee, by someone close. But I see it budding in thee now."

Noah nodded. "Thank you."

Benjamin and the others returned with full mugs, laughing at something.

"Come, lads! Let us make merry, as did our forebears in Merry Old England!" Morton said, beaming at them, and led them out to the circle of dancers, unconcerned that they had thrown off the male-female balance.

Noah joined a line of six young men waiting for the outhouse, a few of them crossing their legs at the ankles. A moment later, one sprinted off into the darkness of the woods, rustling through the underbrush.

A hand on Noah's shoulder startled him, and he jumped.

Benjamin laughed. "I'm sorry. Didn't mean to frighten you. I was only going to suggest we might do the same as Sam did." He nodded toward the woods.

"Let's go," Noah said. They took off to the nearby trailhead and hiked a short distance. At the trunk of a giant oak tree, Benjamin stepped off the trail, taking Noah's hand and tugging him after.

Benjamin threw up the front of his breechclout, tugged it loose from the belt, and let it hang between his legs. His genitals fell loose in the silvery moonlight, and he let a stream of piss flow.

Noah averted his eyes. Reaching inside his own breechclout, he pulled his penis out the side, away from Benjamin.

"Not that way, you lout!" Benjamin laughed. "You'll get the end of it wet." He took hold of the front of Noah's breechclout—his fingertips brushed the side of Noah's scrotum when he grabbed the deer hide, sending a shiver up Noah's spine—and tugged it loose from the belt. "That's better." His own still dragged the ground between his feet.

Noah's cheeks heated. He turned slightly away, and peed onto the trunk of the tree.

Benjamin's hand slid around Noah's back to his opposite hip. Goosebumps shot up Noah's back and down his arms. Then Benjamin turned Noah toward him and pressed his front against Noah's. His pillicock was hard against the soft skin where Noah's thigh met his groin. Noah's own stiffened.

"I'm not sorry there aren't enough girls for each of us," Benjamin whispered, his breath hot against Noah's cheek. Then their lips touched, and Benjamin ground his hips against Noah's.

His hands roamed up Noah's torso, and his thumb brushed one of Noah's nipples, causing him to gasp. Benjamin removed his mouth from Noah's and leaned down to flick his tongue over the nipple, which hardened at the wet touch. Noah gasped again and squirmed at the sensation that shot from his nipple through his belly and straight to his groin.

Benjamin's hands gripped Noah's buttocks while his tongue continued to play with his nipple. His fingertips slipped beneath the deerskin of the breechclout, traced the valley hidden there. Noah widened his legs without thinking. A fingertip teased his most forbidden spot, and a shiver ran up his spine.

Then Benjamin took him by the hand, and they lay on the ground in a crush of ferns. Noah pulled Benjamin on top of him, and the heat of their skin pressed together lit a fire in his belly that he couldn't control.

Their legs entwined, their hips ground together, erections sliding past one another in the sweat that slicked their bellies. Noah moaned at the sensations filling his body, unable to stop himself. Mercifully, Benjamin's mouth on his muffled the sound, though no one at the revel could have heard them over the chanting and drumming.

Lightning shot through him, Noah's moan rose into a cry as his body stiffened, and his seed gushed forth, warm and wet. Benjamin's hips moved faster, and a moment later his own seed joined Noah's, like a paste holding them together.

It took a moment for Noah's breathing to calm. His mind tingled. He'd never had a finish like that. Benjamin slid off him, but pressed against Noah's side, still panting. Noah looked into his eyes, and then laughed—a wave of relief washing over him, the sort of wave that starts hesitantly, but then fills the body and cleanses it.

Benjamin covered his mouth as he snickered, but then he, too, released a deep laugh of relief.

"Anyone could have come across us," Noah whispered, and giggled at the thought.

"I don't care," Benjamin said, brushing the hair from Noah's forehead. Then he kissed him.

CHAPTER 15

MAY 1625 - MOUNT WOLLASTON

Captain Wollaston and Mr. Rasdall returned from their trade voyage along the coast of New England two weeks after the revels, and he summoned the indentured boys for announcements. Noah followed, standing beside Benjamin in the bright sunshine bathing their clearing. The warmth of the May morning promised a sultry afternoon to come. "We received sad tidings from England. King James died in March. May God rest his soul. And long live His Majesty King Charles."

Noah felt strange inside at the news, almost empty. King James was the only sovereign he'd ever known. He'd been king since before Noah was born. He looked around at the indentured boys of Mount Wollaston, most of whom were twenty-two or younger; they must feel the same. How strange to have a different king!

An odd look settled on Mr. Morton's face. Of course, Morton was old enough to remember when Queen Elizabeth had died ... but it was something more than that. He looked lost in thought, but a hint of smile slowly appeared at the corners of his mouth. And that piqued Noah's curiosity about what was going on in Morton's odd brain.

"Richard, if I might have a word with you, please."

Captain Wollaston nodded and followed Morton into his house.

While everyone else went back to their chores, Noah looked at Benjamin and Leo and motioned for them to follow him around the back of

Mr. Morton's house. They crept up to the windowsill, keeping low, and pressed their ears against the wooden wall.

"As you have doubtless already been told by Lt. Fitcher, I met several times with our American neighbors, and their sachem has expressed their need for firearms in most persuasive terms," Morton was saying.

"That's against the law, Thomas."

"It is not. There was only a Royal Proclamation to prohibit it. No law was passed by Parliament—and now that the king is dead, his proclamation has died with him. We are free to sell firearms to the natives without fear of penalty."

"The new king may wish to continue the policy," Wollaston said, gruff.

"That is not the way royal proclamations work. They are unique to the sovereign in whose name they are issued. If the new king wishes to prohibit the sale of firearms to the native tribes, he must issue his own proclamation to that affect. Until he does—and until such news reaches us on these shores—-we are free to sell firearms to our American neighbors."

Morton paused, and Noah pictured him strolling around the room, preparing to deliver his most compelling argument. "It shall prove quite profitable, you'll see. The Massachusetts will pay handsomely in furs for a supply of firearms and shot. They need them to defend against northern tribes who trade for French guns at Port Royal. And our colony could use the profits. As doubtless, your recent voyage of trade has underscored for you."

Wollaston harrumphed. "We don't have enough spare muskets lying around, Thomas. At most, we could trade them but a few."

"Then we order a supply from England. I'm sure you encountered a ship on your travels that is heading back to the mother country soon. We could have guns to trade by September."

"Legal or not, I don't relish the idea of placing guns and ammunition into the hands of the Indian savages. Their motives are not to be trusted, Thomas. They may play friendly to your advances now, but then turn on the colony in a heartbeat. That's what happened in Virginia, you'll remember."

"Virginia is hardly comparable, Richard."

Morton sounded perturbed, but also off balance. Noah exchanged a look with Benjamin and Leo. The Powhatan War three years before had sent shock and horror through England when the news crossed the Atlantic. The Indian confederation had killed more than a thousand Virginia colonists in surprise attacks. Captain Wollaston had scored a hit.

"Don't let your naivete bring us to ruin, Thomas. If the same happened here, we could not resist it. It would wipe us out in a day. None would survive."

"I can't believe that." Morton's pronouncement carried a hint of petulance, and Noah's heart sank. He *was* off balance.

"Since we are on the topic of profit," Wollaston said, his voice sounding as if he were uncharacteristically smiling. "We should revisit the subject I brought up after my voyage to Virginia. The plantations there desperately need labor. We could command a high price."

"No!" Morton thundered. "This is *my* colony. I own the patent from the Council. I am responsible for populating this plantation."

"It is your colony, but they are my servants," Wollaston countered, icy cold. "*I* own their indentures. I can sell them to whomever I wish. That is my prerogative."

"We had a bargain, Richard," Morton said, sounding as if he spoke through gritted teeth. "You promised to be my partner in this venture, and to supply the young men to work it."

"And I have fulfilled that promise," Wollaston said. "But the plantation's profits have not met expectations. Must we re-litigate that point? The profit we earn from the labor of each indentured boy is far less than the profit we would earn by selling him in Virginia. You cannot argue that, Thomas, it is a fact."

Noah's head snapped toward his two companions. Benjamin and Leo looked at each other with wide, frightened eyes.

"Trading guns to the Massachusetts would bring more profit, for years to come," Morton said. "And do not forget that it was *I* who recruited most of those boys."

"And I who bore the expense of their passage," Wollaston snapped. "Therefore, their indentures belong to me, to do with as I see fit. You *know* this, Thomas! Why are you being obstinate?"

"Because your proposal is short-sighted! Yes, you will gain substantial profit by selling indentures in Virginia—but what then? The fur trade offers us *sustained* profits into the future, if we can entice our neighbors to trade more furs for what they truly desire—and that is firearms. And we must remember that if they acquire the guns from us, they will not need to seek assistance from the French."

Noah grinned. That was a point scored for Mr. Morton.

"Port Royal is too far," Wollaston said. "As long as we maintain an English presence in the Maine, we can keep the French confined to Acadia. What does it matter to us if the northern Indians are armed? They are no threat to us here. We remain safe so long as the Indians near us are not."

Heavy footfalls came through the wall, followed by the overly hard closing of a door. One of them had stormed out.

Noah and his companions crept away from the window.

"I heard Captain Wollaston talking with Mr. Rasdall about selling indentures a few months ago," Leo whispered, his voice shaky. "He said he'd argued with Mr. Morton about it. Mr. Morton was against it, and Mr. Rasdall agreed with the captain that Mr. Morton was being foolish. I thought that was the end of it."

"Hopefully it still is," Benjamin said. "Mr. Morton is still opposed."

Noah's stomach was a cold rock in the pit of his belly. "But Captain Wollaston sounded defiant. I think he's decided to do it."

Leo had gone pale. "I know why indentures fetch such a good price in Virginia," he whispered. "I heard Captain Wollaston and Mr. Rasdall discuss it after they returned from there. They say half of the colonists in Virginia die during their first two years in the colony. They call it 'the Seasoning.' It's an unhealthy place, Virginia. The swamp miasmas carry fevers and bloody flux. Men die in agony."

Benjamin took Leo by the shoulder and gave him a little shake. "That won't happen to us." His voice was firm. "We're needed here. Mr. Morton will find a way, you'll see."

Noah wondered if Benjamin were trying to convince himself as well as Leo.

And he also wished he were that certain.

Alarmed voices roused Noah from sleep a few mornings later. Drake had raised his head from their pallet and was staring out the open front door of the cottage. A couple of quiet whimpers told Noah something dreadful was happening.

Standing and stretching, Noah quickly tucked his shirttails into his trousers and around his genitals, and stepped into the morning sunlight.

About twenty of the indentured boys stood on the crest of the hill, looking toward the bay, and Noah hurried to join them. He found Benjamin at the front of the cluster. "What's going on?"

Benjamin's face was like stone, his lips set in a tight line. He pointed toward the dock without a word.

Five of the indentured boys stood on the end of the dock with Lt. Fitcher. Fifty yards out in their inlet, five more sat in the rowboat with Captain Wollaston and Mr. Rasdall, heading for the *Unity* at anchor in the deeper water. In the boat's bow, staring back at the colony, sat Leo Taylor. His face was as pale as a sheet.

Thomas Morton came storming up the hill, face red. Noah hurried to him. "Mr. Morton, what's happening?"

"Captain Wollaston sails for Virginia," Morton said, the words short and clipped. He marched toward his house and slammed the door.

CHAPTER 16

June 1625 - Essex Colony, Cape Ann

"Wake up, lad!" Floyd's voice echoed in Jimmy's brain, rousing him from a deep slumber. He raised his hand to shield his eyes from the light. "Wake up!" his father repeated. "Boats approach. Several of them."

Jimmy propped himself on his elbows. He'd said boats and not ships. On Sunday? "I'm awake, Papa." The yellow disk of the sun sat several degrees over the surface of the Atlantic, so it had to be after eight o'clock. Late indeed.

It had been a warm night, and Jimmy had slept outdoors in front of their cottage, as he often did during the warm months after a Saturday night with the community around the bonfire. He brushed the sand from his shoulders, pulled his shirt on over his head, and combed the grass from his hair with his fingers before following Floyd to the beach.

Several ketches approached from the south, sails furled, still some distance out. The Essex colonists gathered near the docks to watch, the apprehension palpable.

Jimmy counted close to thirty in the boats. They wore brown coats and hats—except for one dressed in the black clothes and white collar of a cleric—and most of them carried muskets. As the ketches got closer, Jimmy realized five of the figures were women, and ten were children. As they glided toward the wharf, the men raised their hands in greeting.

"They be from the New Plymouth Plantation," John Small muttered beside them. "I recognize the clothes. They all dress alike there. I've seen 'em many a time on the Cape Cod Bay. They be here to reclaim their wharf, ye mark my words. They came in force this time."

Jimmy grunted. John Small had a tendency to be an alarmist. This group didn't come seeking a fight, not with women and children among them. Still, a tickle of dread sank into his belly at the thought of Brownists coming to Cape Ann.

This party from New Plymouth had fifteen men, and Mr. Gardner and Mr. Tylly looked tense as they walked down the wharf to meet the visitors before they could dock.

"Grab our muskets from the hut, lad," Floyd said out of the side of his mouth.

Jimmy didn't argue. He jogged to their cottage and grabbed the muskets off the wall, hurrying back to the beach.

"Have ye come to quarrel?" Gardner called across the water at the boats drawing near.

"Not to quarrel, but to join ye," one of the men shouted. Some men aboard lowered the sails to slow the boats.

Then surprised cries of recognition rose from the gathered Essex colonists. "'Tis Christopher Conant!" one said. "And that be John Oldham!" another said. A few men hurried down the wharf to catch the ropes the passengers tossed and tied them to empty posts near the end.

The first to disembark was the one who had shouted back from the bow of the first ketch. He took a step toward Gardner and Tylly, while the other arrivals collected behind him. "We have left the Plymouth Plantation in vexation. Aye, vexation and bitterness, and we seek refuge at a friendlier plantation. I am Roger Conant, a salter, and I speak for my company here with me."

Jimmy glanced sideways at John Small, with a sense of satisfaction that his prediction had proven incorrect.

Mr. Gardner's grin radiated like the spring sun, and he clasped the hand of the man standing at Roger Conant's shoulder. "Christopher Conant, 'tis good to see you again. Welcome, my good men. Come, ye will find respite here with us."

"Well!" Floyd said with a little cackle, smiling at his son and partner. "Ain't that a fine comeuppance to those stiff-necks at New Plymouth?"

John Small looked less impressed. "The nonconformists there still be more numerous than we. There be three hundred of them. And their militia commander, Captain Standish, he be a hothead. If they seek to press their claim to the wharf, we may have no option but to submit to them. Even with these reinforcements."

Jimmy frowned. He would never submit to the rule of religious zealots. But John was probably being alarmist again.

Floyd waved it off. "The good Lord loves a fisherman more than a hypocrite. Jesus himself kept the company of fishermen, didn't he? 'Salt of the earth,' be we. That is why we prosper and they whither. And the good Lord sent us a salter!" He cackled at his own joke.

"They don't seem like fishermen, Papa," Jimmy said.

Floyd scratched his stubbled chin. The red of his beard was coming in more white these days. "Nay, they don't. But a proper town needs more than fishermen, my boy. They have all trades at New Plymouth, and perhaps now we do as well." He motioned toward where the newcomers were mingling with the Dorchester men and the fishermen. "Come, let's greet our new neighbors."

Mr. Gardner had his hand on the shoulders of two of the newcomers, laughing with them. He turned to face the gathered colonists and announced in a loud voice. "Friends! Those of you who came with us aboard the *Anne* two years ago will remember John Oldham and Christopher Conant. They were not part of our party, but travelled with us in route to New Plymouth. I am happy to welcome them, and to renew our acquaintance."

Floyd looked at Jimmy and John Small with a chuckle. "Let us meet them first." He shouldered his way into the crowd of original planters who encircled Gardner and the two arrivals.

Gardner's expression became cautious. "What news have you of your fair sister, John Oldham?"

Oldham's lips tightened almost imperceptibly. "She remains at New Plymouth Plantation. She wed one of the Brownists last year. Jonathan Brewster, son of William Brewster. The father is an elder in their separatist church." His tone grew more disapproving the longer he spoke.

But Gardner's smile returned. "Then we pray happiness for her marriage. It must please you that she did not face spinsterhood."

Oldham nodded, though his expression said he might have rather his sister be a spinster than a Brownist. Jimmy supposed he might feel the same if he still had a sister.

Noticing them standing on the edge of the circle, Mr. Gardner smiled and beckoned them forward. "John Oldham, Christopher Conant, allow me to introduce some of our fine fishermen. This big fellow is John Small. This is Floyd Hawkey, and the strapping young man with him is his son, Jimmy."

Oldham clasped Floyd's hand, looking sideways at Jimmy. After muttering "How do you do?" to Floyd, he turned to face Jimmy, staring at him through narrowed eyes. "Your *son*? How is that? He bears the appearance of an American."

"I adopted Jimmy many years ago."

Jimmy stared directly into Oldham's suspicious eyes, holding his gaze. He stuck out his hand. Oldham glanced down at it for several seconds before taking it in an overly firm grip and one hard shake. Then he turned his palm up and gazed at it for a second.

"It doesn't rub off," Jimmy said.

Oldham reacted with a silent smirk.

"I've seen you before," Christopher Conant said to John Small, shaking his hand. "You've sold fish at New Plymouth. But not in quite a while."

"Aye, the leaders there drive too firm a bargain," John said. "Our fish fetch a better price elsewhere."

Christopher Conant didn't look offended. "The colony is indeed short of funds. Governor Bradford and his cohort are fierce stewards of their resources."

The man who'd introduced himself as Roger Conant raised his arms for attention and shouted above the din of conversation. "Friends! Neighbors! On this propitious morn, I ask the good Mr. Lyford to say a blessing for us."

The clergyman stepped into the middle of the gathering with a nod at Roger Conant.

"It'll be good to have a preacher here," Floyd muttered.

Jimmy nodded, though he was ambivalent about it. He'd been baptized not long after they arrived in Cornwall in November 1616, christened James in honor of the king, and for the next five years, he and Floyd attended the obligatory Sunday services at the village church from November through April; but May through October had always found them back in these waters, where no church existed. For the three years they'd been in New England permanently, their only nod to religion was their daily prayers for protection from the sea and for a good catch.

The Dorchester men led weekly prayers on Sunday mornings, which the fishermen joined, but no formal worship. Jimmy wasn't sure he was ready for regular church services again. Or the unwanted intrusion of a clergyman into his private affairs. His private thoughts …

The clergyman, Mr. Lyford, stood in the center of the gathering, a Bible clutched against his chest, looking around with a smile. "Thank you, Mr. Conant. Brethren, it is perhaps no accident that our party should arrive on these shores on the morning of the Lord's Day. His hand hath guided us to this place and time for his purpose. Let us pray."

John Small came to their cottage stoop a few nights later, while Floyd and Jimmy prepared their supper in the evening breeze. "Let me tell ye what I've learned about the newcomers," he said under his breath, plopping onto the sand.

"What news have you?" Floyd asked, laying down his filet knife and leaning toward John. Jimmy fed sticks into the small flame at the bottom of the firepit in the sand and leaned in to blow the flame larger.

"Most of them are what the nonconformists at New Plymouth called 'Adventurers'—men who came to the colony for commerce, not to practice outlaw religion. They couldn't stand it there no longer, not allowed to dance, not allowed to drink but a little beer, not even permitted to celebrate Christmas!"

Floyd shook his head. "The poor devils. They have my sympathy. But I would not have gone there in the first place, knowin' what those Brownists are like."

Jimmy laughed. "What did they expect?"

"They expected to make lots of money, but they didn't." John leaned closer. "But that Roger Conant who makes to speak for the group, he's a Puritan, as is his brother Christopher. So is that John Oldham. That means they believe like the Brownists do, mostly, except that they still believe in the Church of England. The both of 'em—Roger Conant and John Oldham—argued with the leaders of the New Plymouth church. Oldham is banished, and they asked Conant and his family to leave with the others."

Jimmy looked down the beach, where Roger Conant played ball with his sons. It was said the Brownists at New Plymouth frowned upon sport. This Roger Conant didn't share that opinion, at least. Still, neither he nor his brother nor John Oldham had yet joined in any of the evening drinking and banter around the bonfire. And Conant didn't hesitate to share an opinion about everything.

"I can see a priggish nature in Roger Conant," Jimmy said.

"Aye," Floyd agreed, nodding slowly and stroking his chin.

John leaned even closer and dropped his voice. "'Tis said John Oldham argued with New Plymouth's militia commander, Captain Standish, and drew a knife on him. The newcomers told us Oldham and Standish are *both* hot-heads, but Standish is the commander, and so Oldham was tried for disturbing the peace."

John glanced sideways and then motioned for Floyd and Jimmy to lean in. "But the most shocking news is about the minister, Mr. Lyford. He was banished from New Plymouth, too, because they found out he was only pretending to be sympathetic to them, and wrote letters to the Council of New England, criticizing their views. So did Mr. Oldham, and that's why Standish confronted him; when Oldham drew his knife. But here's the worst part—Lyford's wife told Governor Bradford that *Lyford fathered a bastard in Ireland*; and that he fadoodles the maids, so that Mrs. Lyford could never keep one on but for him always shakin' the sheets with 'em."

Jimmy burst out laughing. The image of Mr. Lyford chasing a maid around the bed with his shriveled old prick in hand was too hilarious.

Floyd scowled at him. "'Tis not a laughing matter, James Hawkey. Mind yourself, lad."

Jimmy suppressed his laughter with effort. "I'm sorry, Papa."

Floyd fixed John with a stern stare. "How sure are you of this news, John Small?"

"I heard it from Archie, and I asked Joe about it. He told me the same tale, as did Jack."

Floyd frowned. "And they be not prone to gossip. We can trust their word is true. Ah, that is indeed a shame." He shook his head sadly. "We should report this to Mr. Gardner and Mr. Tylly. They'll want to know it before another Sunday comes."

The ruckus came several days later.

It was John Oldham's shouts that caught Jimmy's attention when he sat on their stoop mending nets in the afternoon sun.

"It's an outrage!" Oldham shouted, red-faced, in the middle of the village. He inserted himself between John and Sarah Lyford on one side, and Thomas Gardner and John Tylly. John Lyford put a hand on Oldham's shoulder, his mouth forming words that Jimmy couldn't hear. Sarah Lyford stared at the ground.

A crowd was gathering, so Jimmy dropped the net he'd been mending, stuck the needle into the ball of wax, and hurried to join the crowd.

Lyford faced the crowd, though he addressed his words to Gardner and Tylly. "It gladdens me, Mr. Gardner and Mr. Tylly, that ye came to me with the burdensome words ye heard spoke about me. 'Tis true that in my youth I committed indiscretions, for which I prayed forgiveness, and the Almighty God forgives our sins when we come to him in prayer. I confess to ye as I confessed to our Lord the sin of fathering a child out of wedlock. I assure ye, that was before my wife and I wed, when I was a young bachelor. Age and matrimony have tempered those lusts, and I deny the charges of adultery—these were *coerced* from my poor wife by the vipers and hypocrites at New Plymouth, who opposed my views on the Christian faith because I differ from their nonconformist practice."

Jimmy watched Sarah Lyford's face, still facing the ground in front of her feet. Was there extra tension when her husband spoke of coersion? Her lips tightened almost imperceptibly, as did the furrow of her brow. Her husband was lying. Jimmy glanced from her to Gardner and Tylly, who exchanged a look; they didn't believe the minister, either.

"I ask to stay and gain your trust," John Lyford said. "But if ye cannot give me your trust, then my family and I will depart on the next ship."

Roger Conant stepped from the crowd and stood beside the Lyfords, between the minister and John Oldham. "Who can ask the Lord's forgiveness if he giveth not forgiveness to his neighbor?" He looked toward Gardner and Tylly, who still appeared skeptical. "We who came with Mr. Lyford from New Plymouth would not have welcomed him to our company did we not believe in the gifts he brings to our endeavor. This colony would do well to keep a faithful minister to tend the Lord's sheep."

"Then let us have a meeting of the townsmen," Mr. Tylly said. "We shall hear from everyone who wishes to speak, and we will vote to keep or to expel Mr. Lyford from the post of minister for Essex Station."

Jimmy again crept to the open window of the meeting room at the Great House. He was twenty years old, still too young to speak or vote in a meeting of the colonists. *Next year*. But he would be damned if he was going to miss this drama. A chorus of cricket song surrounded him, along with the murmur of conversation from within the house.

Then John Oldham's voice boomed forth, loud and clear, and the crickets fell silent. "'Tis *wrong* to exclude Mr. Lyford from the discussion about his future here! He must be allowed to listen and to speak."

Mr. Tylly's voice was quieter, calmer. "Others may be free to speak their minds more openly if Mr. Lyford is not present. All should be allowed to state their opinion without fear of reprisal from the pulpit."

"An accused has the right to face his accusers and answer them," Oldham shouted. "If ye exclude him, ye deny his rights as an Englishman."

"John Oldham speaks the truth." Did this voice belong to Roger Conant? It would be like him to speak early and often.

"We will vote on that question first," Mr. Gardner said. "All in favor of including Mr. Lyford in the meeting?"

A chorus of ayes reverberated into the night.

"All opposed?"

Several nays rang forth, but without the force of the ayes.

"Mr. Conant, please bring Mr. Lyford into the room."

That resolved the first little drama. Jimmy inched closer to the wall for the main drama to begin.

"What are you doing there?"

Jimmy's heart leapt into his throat, and he spun his head. The three indentured Bristol boys watched him from a short distance. He put his finger in front of his lips, and then motioned downward with both hands.

The youths crouched down and waddled toward him. "Are they arguing?" one asked in a whisper.

"A little," Jimmy said. "They voted to let Mr. Lyford into the room to hear the argument."

"The old windbag will talk over everyone else," another muttered, and the other two snickered.

Jimmy put his finger in front of his lips again, and they fell silent. He turned his face back to the clapboard wall beneath the windowsill. His heart pounded at the proximity of the three Bristol boys. They rarely had reason to speak with him, and whenever they passed in the village, they only gave him curious glances, but never greeted him. Perhaps this was his chance to befriend them ...

Roger Conant—Jimmy was certain now it was he—gave a lengthy speech about how valuable Mr. Lyford had been as minister at New Plymouth, and the need to have a qualified clergyman deliver the word and sacrament in their new home.

"This is boring," one of the boys said, and started to stand, but Jimmy's hand shot out and grabbed his forearm.

"Wait," he whispered. The three indentured boys stared at him in expectation, but his mouth went dry. His mind raced for anything to say. "They'll hear you walk away." It probably wasn't true, but it was the best he could think of. "And they've only just started. They'll argue soon, you'll see."

This was a better argument, and he held his breath, watching the face of the boy stopped in an awkward half-crouch. The boy shrugged and crouched back down. Jimmy breathed again, but turned his face back toward the wall.

"We can write to the Dorchester Company to send us a minister," someone else said. "We are not beholden to Mr. Lyford only because he is here. We should give credence to the allegations that have been made. Fornication with a servant girl is a serious sin, even if not adultery. But as Mr. Lyford *is* married, and it is alleged these fornications happened after his marriage, it is adultery, which is a mortal sin."

"He has denied those allegations!" John Oldham's voice boomed through the window. Jimmy glanced at the three indentured boys with an 'I told you' look. They nodded appreciatively.

"A minister of God must be above reproach," Mr. Tylly said. "If there be any credence to the claims, any at all, it casts doubt on Mr. Lyford's ministry. I have heard all of ye that came from New Plymouth with Mr. Lyford speak often—and bitterly—about the hypocrisy of the nonconformists leading that colony. We cannot allow the appearance of hypocrisy here. And Mr. Palfrey is correct that we may write to the Dorchester Company to send us a minister if we vote to expel Mr. Lyford."

"We should make sure every man speaks," Mr. Gardner said. "We will go around the room, each man taking his turn. Captain Trask, you may begin."

As they circled the room, and each man spoke for a minute or five, the arguments grew repetitive. It was not quite the drama Jimmy had hoped for, though he'd gotten a taste of it at the beginning.

"Let's go," one of the Bristol boys said to his two companions, and they crept off without so much as a goodbye to Jimmy. He watched them stand at the corner of the house and disappear into the darkness, a sad aching in his heart. He could go with them; in his mind's eye he saw himself running after them, asking if he could join them, and the three of them smiling and patting him on the back and welcoming him to their group ...

He stayed where he was.

The discussion ended a few minutes later, and a vote was called. It was twenty-one to seventeen in favor of allowing Mr. Lyford to stay and minister to the colony.

Jimmy crept away from the wall, a trickle of dread running down his back.

CHAPTER 17

SEPTEMBER 1625 - MOUNT WOLLASTON

Noah held the freshly carved bed leg tight with both hands while Ralph Mason whacked the bottom with a mallet, forcing it into the notch that had been cut into the support beam on the underside of the bedframe. The vibrations ran up Noah's arms to his shoulders, which ached from the effort of holding the wood still.

Sweat ran down his forehead and soaked into his eyebrows. Back in Lancashire, the first of September was definitely autumn; here in New England, it still felt of late summer. But at least the weeks-long task of building furniture—beds, table, chairs—was nearly complete.

"Set it down, make sure it's even," Ralph instructed, and Noah eased the leg onto the ground. The bed tottered a little on three legs, but Ralph pressed down on the corner they'd been working on and shook it to test its sturdiness. He nodded in satisfaction. "On to the last one."

Several figures rounded the corner of the western trail, where it emerged from the forest into their wooded fields. Four Indians approached, two middle-aged men and two women, one considerably younger than the other.

"What do you suppose they want?" Ralph mused. The quartet didn't drag any sleds of furs or other items behind them, nor did they carry any baskets.

"That's Wonohaquaham," Noah said, nodding toward the Neponset Massachusett sachem walking a step ahead of the other three.

"The girl in the back, she's been here," Ralph said. "Ain't that the one Leo was with?"

Noah nodded, picturing the two of them standing in the firelight, fingers entwined and faces close together. As the four approached the village, he sucked in his breath at the sight of the roundness at the front of her dress.

Thomas Morton had come out to greet them with smiles and handshakes. Captain Wollaston joined them a moment later, stiff and formal.

Noah and Ralph fitted the last leg into its notch, and Ralph picked up the mallet. They were close enough to hear the other man behind Wonohaquaham—the girl's father, presumably—speak a string of guttural words to the sachem, his deep voice edged with anger. Then, to the white men, "Your boy."

Ralph struck the bottom of the leg with the mallet multiple times, forcing it into the notch. Noah strained to hear Wonohaquaham translating. "Masketpaquin finds his daughter with child from one of your young men. This young man has not called for her, so Masketpaquin demands this young man honor her with a marriage dowry."

The whacking of the mallet drowned out Thomas Morton's reply. "Ouch!" Noah said, and held his finger close to his face.

"What happened?" Ralph asked, stopping.

"I got a splinter," Noah lied. They'd sanded the wood smooth before assembling the pieces, but this was the best excuse he could come up with.

"You can use Mr. Morton's tweezers in a minute. Hey, where are you going? We're not finished yet!"

Noah glanced back at Ralph and raised one finger. He hurried to the cluster, who all turned to look at him.

"*Kui kwasind*, Wonohaquaham," Noah said.

A hint of smile stretched the sachem's mouth. "Kui kwasind. Greetings."

Wollaston scowled. "Haven't you work to finish, Mr. Bancroft?"

"I will," Noah said. "After we speak with our guests."

"This does not concern you."

"I was with Mr. Morton when we invited our guests to bring their young women to visit us, sir.

Wollaston stiffened, and cast an accusing glance at Thomas Morton. "I suggest you leave this to Mr. Morton and to me, and return to your chores at once."

"I can be helpful, sir. I can act as secretary for the meeting—as I did for Mr. Morton at the last one." That was an exaggeration, but Noah wagered Morton had told Wollaston little about it.

Wollaston's eyes narrowed. "We do not require the services of a secretary. Return to your work immediately."

"I'm not one of your servants," Noah said, crossing his arms and staring back at the captain. "You can't give me orders."

A corner of Morton's mouth twerked. "The boy is correct, Richard. He is free, you cannot command him. And since he has joined me on visits to Wonohaquaham and his people, I believe it beneficial that he join our discussion."

Wollaston's lips tightened in a thin line, almost whitening. "Very well—but do not interrupt your elders while we are speaking, young man, or I will thrash you myself. Do you understand me, boy?"

Noah frowned, but nodded without a word.

Captain Wollaston turned back to Wonohaquaham. "What proof has your man that one of *our* boys is the culprit?"

"She went off with Leo after the dance we hosted, sir," Noah said. "I saw them together, and so did Mr. Morton."

Wollaston glared at him. "I told you not to interrupt us, Mr. Bancroft."

"'Tis relevant, Richard," Morton said. "Mr. Bancroft is a witness, and I insist he tell us what he saw."

Wollaston regarded Noah through narrowed eyes, brow furrowed. "Very well. Did you witness them fornicating, Mr. Bancroft?"

Noah's cheeks heated at the imagined scene. "No, sir, not fornicating. I saw them kiss, and then they went somewhere private."

"I can confirm, Richard, that our Leo Taylor, late of this plantation, did indeed escort this young lady to private quarters on the night of the thirtieth of April, as attested by his own boasts. This occurred after displaying great affection within the public space. Within the embrace of this privacy, their subsequent behavior cannot be confirmed, save by the evidence so apparent in the young lady's belly."

Wollaston exhaled hard through the nose, eyes briefly closing. "I have not the temperament today to submit to your lawyerly rhetoric, Thomas. But since you have regaled us so, I must argue that they cannot prove the claim. An Englishman's guilt must be proven beyond reasonable doubt." A triumphant gleam shined from his eyes.

Morton held up a finger. "That standard applies only for criminal charges, my good man. As Wonohaquaham and his man bring forth a civil claim, they need not prove it beyond reasonable doubt. They need only prove that it is more likely than not that our Leo Taylor did implant the seed in this young woman that has brought forth the child within her belly."

"I believe them, sir," Noah said.

Wollaston scowled at Noah before turning back to Thomas Morton. "It matters not. Leo Taylor has been transported to Virginia, and is no longer a concern of this plantation."

A flicker of surprise passed across Wonohaquaham's dark eyes. "It is right for a young man to marry the woman who carries his child."

Morton nodded at Wonohaquaham and turned back toward Wollaston. "Richard, the incident that occasioned their claim occurred while Leo Taylor was of this plantation, and therefore the satisfaction of their claim is our concern. As this young woman's parents have the right to expect a marriage dowry due to the young woman's obvious condition, it is our obligation to pay it in Leo Taylor's absence."

"I agree, sirs," Noah said. "It's the right thing to do."

Wollaston glared at Noah again, then turned back to Morton. "Thomas, I will see you in the storehouse."

Noah followed them, but Wollaston spun on him at the storehouse door. "You have done quite enough, Mr. Bancroft. Off with you." He slammed the door shut.

Noah put his ear to the doorjamb.

"We can ill afford this, Thomas," Captain Wollaston said.

"It is the only just outcome, Richard. And we can spare the amount of one marriage dowry."

"One so far! How many others will come forward once we've paid this one?" Wollaston's shout lowered into a growl, "I was not party to this, you'll remember. I was away conducting business for this plantation when you allowed our boys to cavort about like wild Indians. Must I remind you we have come to *tame* the wilderness, not succumb to it?"

"Encouraging convivial relations with the Americans can only benefit the plantation, as indeed we have seen in contrast to the lack of trade they conduct with Weymouth Plantation."

"And yet our resulting trade has been paltry enough compared to what is required for the venture to profit."

Noah had heard this argument too many times already, and slipped away toward where a glowering Ralph Mason awaited his return to finish their work.

The others were strangely silent when Noah sat down to dinner that evening. No one returned his greeting. "What's wrong?"

Benjamin glanced nervously at the table where Captain Wollaston sat with Thomas Morton, Mr. Rasdall, and Lt. Fitcher. "We are ordered not to discourse with you," he muttered out the side of his mouth.

Noah's heart dropped like a stone. "Captain Wollaston told you not to talk to me?" He could barely get the words out. His throat constricted too much.

Benjamin nodded without another word. Across the table, Ralph and Sam stared at their plates while they ate.

Noah took his plate and sat on a tree stump at the edge of the village. He dashed away a tear from his eye with the back of his wrist. He was nineteen years old, no longer a boy, and he wouldn't let anyone see him cry.

Thomas Morton joined him a few minutes later. "'Tis always hardest on those who do the right thing in opposition to the will of the powerful," he said, placing a hand on Noah's shoulder. "But I am proud of thee. Persevere, Noah. All will be right soon."

Noah stayed several yards behind the others as they made their way down the trail to the creek a quarter-mile west of their hilltop village. When they stripped off their clothes at the edge of the sandy bank, he kept his distance and hiked thirty yards downstream to the curve where the creek widened.

The tide was out, and the brackish water was almost fresh for a while. The strip of salt marsh on the opposite shore had turned into mudflat. Low tide also meant he had to step three feet off the bank to the water without slipping in the sand. He waded out until the water reached his waist, and then splashed his chest and armpits. He looked longingly at where the twenty indentured youths splashed and played, chasing one another as they bathed in thigh-deep water.

His gaze lingered on Benjamin's lithe form, the way his muscles moved, the way his penis swung as he ran through the water, laughing. His dark brown hair looked black when wet, stuck to his face and neck.

Ben's eye caught his, and he stopped for a moment. Noah looked away instinctively and concentrated on his own bath; but curiosity made him look back, and Ben was still standing there, facing him, lazily splashing water onto his belly. They stared at each other for a moment before Ben turned back toward the others. But as he did, he motioned with his head.

Noah's stomach fluttered with hope, and he walked upstream, closing half the distance between them before he stopped.

Robbie Ellis crouched low in the shallow water by the bank, splashing and scrubbing his backside. Sam Weaver put his finger to his lips and snuck up behind Robbie. He reached between his legs with both hands and tickled the insides of his thighs next to his dangling genitals.

Robbie shot up with a squeal, and the others roared with laughter. Sam slapped Robbie's buttocks, and the smack on the wet skin echoed across the water.

The laughter rose louder when Robbie sprang a plumb branch. Robbie's cheeks turned crimson, and he pointed at Sam. "It's your fault! You shouldn't have done that!"

Sam crossed his arms, grinning. "Go on, then. Take care of it."

Robbie hesitated, sheepish, while the others hooted encouragement. Then he played with the end of it.

Noah's mouth dropped open. He was grateful the growth between his own legs was hidden beneath the surface of the water, but he turned away anyway.

"Oh, for Christ's sake, you nits!" Edward Gibbons yelled. He climbed onto the bank. "What'll happen if one of the gentlemen catches you lot like this?"

Noah hazarded a glance back. At least four of the others had grown branches and were stroking them. He looked away in a hurry.

"What would they do? Ain't nobody doing nothing unnatural," Sam replied. "Unlike the things you did for a half-crown back at the Bristol docks, Edward Gibbons!" The others guffawed, and several slapped Edward on the back after they climbed out of the creek.

Edward crossed his arms and scowled. "Don't have to do none of that no more. We've got plenty of food here."

Benjamin's hand at Noah's elbow made him jump. "Shhh." Ben tugged him around the bend and into the shallows below the sandy bank. Then he pulled Noah to him and kissed him.

Noah was breathless when they broke the kiss. And aroused. "What if the others see?" he whispered.

"Shhh." Ben put his finger to his lips.

"But Captain Wollaston won't even let you talk to me."

Ben's whisper was so quiet Noah strained to hear it. "If we must, we'll run away. The Neponset village is only five miles; the Massachusett Indians will hide us." He stood next to Noah, hip-to-hip, and slid his right hand around his waist. With his left hand, he pleasured himself. Noah slid his left hand around Ben's waist and stroked with his right.

Ben's hand slipped down to rub Noah's buttocks, sending jolts through him. Their breath came fast, and it was over in a minute.

"Supply ship coming in!" Thomas Morton's voice hollered from atop the hill behind them.

Benjamin grinned. "We'd better get back." He leaned into Noah's ear and whispered, "I'll find you whenever no one is looking." Then he kissed Noah's cheek and plunged through the water around the bend.

A pinnace anchored in their inlet, and a rowboat had tied to the wharf by the time Noah descended the hill with Drake. The dog barked at the strangers but stayed at Noah's side. Noah touched his neck, and Drake fell silent.

A middle-aged clergyman in black clothing and white collar spoke in animated fashion to Thomas Morton, while Captain Wollaston and Mr. Rasdall negotiated with the ship's captain. Noah gravitated toward Morton.

"Indeed, my wife Sarah and I had high hopes after leaving Plymouth Plantation," the clergyman said, ambling up the wharf with Morton. "The Brownists there speak of the church as an Athenian democracy, yet they enforce obedience to their collective will without regard to English liberties. They would not elect me minister, though the Council sent me for that purpose; nor would they permit me the liberty to lead worship for those that were not part of their separatist church. I had many a supporter in my conflict with those nonconformist hypocrites, and these accompanied us in our exile to the Essex station at Cape Ann. We believed God had found a home for us there among those sturdy planters. Alas, 'twas not to be." He shook his head.

"What transpired there?" Morton asked.

"I felt free for the first time since our arrival in New England to return to the liturgy of the Church of England, so reviled by the leaders of

New Plymouth. That was, until my erstwhile supporters abandoned me. Most of them were Puritans at heart, who, though less extreme in their nonconformity than the Brownists at New Plymouth, nonetheless took exception to my conformity to the Book of Common Prayer."

"It pains me to hear of your travails, Mr. Lyford," Morton said. "Return ye to England?"

"Nay, my wife and I are bound for Virginia," the clergyman said. "The two largest settlements in New England are full of nonconformists, and like Pilate, I wash my hands of it."

"The reverend Mr. Blaxton on the Charles River is a conforming minister," Morton said, stopping on the shore. "He has been good enough to minister to our boys on the holy days—though regrettably, we are without pastor most Sundays. Might we persuade you to stay with us? We would welcome your ministry here."

Noah's insides went cold. An image of Vicar Aubrey's enraged face when he caught Noah and Lance flashed across his mind. The imagined rage of this Mr. Lyford if he caught Noah with Benjamin replaced it.

Ben had said they'd run away if they had to. Noah's heart pounded. Would he ever find a home?

"'Tis a most kind offer, Mr. Morton, and I thank you." Lyford motioned up the hill toward the village. "Ye have a handsome plantation, and it is tempting to stay. But 'tis to Virginia that God calls us."

Noah's breath released in a rush.

Lyford put a hand on Morton's arm. "Be wary of crossing the Brownists. William Bradford is a vengeful devil of a man who runs the colony with a heavy hand like Sulla in the old Roman Republic. And his Captain Standish bears a most vile temper. They will not hesitate to make trouble for you."

"Thomas!" Captain Wollaston called, striding past Noah from the wharf, with Mr. Rasdall a few steps behind. "We've purchased beer, salt, and pork for the colony. We might have managed more than that had we not paid that settlement to the Indians last week."

Morton ignored the rebuke and took Lyford's arm. "Come, let us supper together before you sail for Virginia."

CHAPTER 18

May 1626 - Merrymount

Lieutenant Fitcher came to the fields before noon. One by one, he stopped a dozen of the young men in their work hoeing rows for spring planting and pointed them toward the village.

Noah and the others watched in curiosity. As more of their comrades walked back to the village, several of them exchanged looks of increasing anxiety. What was going on?

For the last hour of the morning, only nine of them remained in the fields, Noah and eight of the indentured boys.

When the lunch bell rang, Noah and the other eight hurried up the hill to find out what was happening.

Thomas Morton poked furiously at the embers in the central bonfire, stirring a bit of flame from them. He was alone in the village.

"Mr. Morton, sir?" Sam asked, looking around. "Where are the others? It's time to eat."

Morton threw down the poker, which clanged against the hearthstones encircling the bonfire. Noah jumped at the suddenness of it.

"Captain Wollaston and Mr. Rasdall departed this morn with twelve servants, again to sell their indentures to the rapacious tobacco plantations of Virginia. As they did with the ten they took last year."

Lieutenant Fitcher's head appeared over the crest of the knoll, coming up from the shore. Morton glared at him for several seconds before turning back to the young men gathered around him with open mouths.

"Ye eight remain, under the supervision of Lt. Fitcher." He marched to the table, loaded for lunch, and plopped onto the bench.

Lunch passed in tense silence. The nine young men—Noah and the eight remaining indentured boys—cast glances at each other, but none dared open his mouth.

Lieutenant Fitcher acted unaware of the tension, though he wisely kept silent while he ate. He only spoke when he got up after finishing his meal, nodded at the group, and bid them good afternoon. Then he retired to his cottage.

"Can they be stopped?" Sam asked, a note of desperation in his voice.

"They cannot," Morton said, tight-lipped. "Now get yourselves back to work, else Lt. Fitcher find ye at leisure."

The indentured youths shuffled back to the field, muttering to each other. Noah held back.

"I suppose thou fearest not Lt. Fitcher's rod," Morton said, chuckling without humor. "Thou art not under his authority."

"We have to do *something*, Mr. Morton! You can't allow him to draw down the colony so, or soon, we'll have nothing."

Morton scowled. "Do not think for a moment that I have not ruminated many hours on this possibility, Noah Bancroft." Then his expression softened. "But you are correct that it will not stop here. We must make a plan."

Noah's hands fisted at his sides. "We should go somewhere else. Somewhere Captain Wollaston will never find us."

Morton shook his head. "Running away is not the answer, Noah. This is our home. Bring the others to me, and we will discuss it together."

Fifteen minutes later, the eight remaining indentured servants stood with Noah in Thomas Morton's study. Benjamin looked at Noah with concern, and his heart broke at the apprehension in Ben's eyes. He and the others doubtless feared more bad news now that Mr. Morton wanted to talk with all of them together.

Morton took a bottle of whiskey and poured out a measure for each of them, passing cups around. "Drink up, lads. Fortitude is required."

More worried looks passed between the young men. Noah touched Benjamin's forearm and gave him a reassuring nod as Morton handed them their cups. They took a drink. The whiskey burned the back of Noah's throat, but warmed him on the way down. He took another fortifying gulp.

Morton paced in front of his desk. "You see that most of your fellows have been carried off to Virginia, and if we wait for Captain Wollaston and Mr. Rasdall's return, the same fate may await the rest of ye. You, too, will be carried away to Virginia and sold off like the others, to labor like slaves of old in the tobacco fields."

Several heads nodded, but all remained silent.

Morton spread his hands. "I am powerless to stop them. Though I have pleaded, they have hardened their hearts against persuasion, like Pharaoh to Moses. The only way to prevent this fate is to cast out Lieutenant Fitcher, send him to Virginia with a warning to the black-hearts to never return here." Morton stopped, took a deep breath, and spread his arms. "My boys, I advise you to thrust out Lieutenant Fitcher; and if ye do, I, having part in the plantation, shall receive you as my equal partners and consociates in the endeavor."

Gasps greeted this announcement. A thrill raced up Noah's spine. *Equal partners!*

"You will be free from service."

Excited murmurs ran through the group. Edward Gibbons shouted, "Huzzah!" Noah and Benjamin grinned at each other. Sam and Robbie put their arms around each other, beaming.

Morton continued. "And together we will converse, trade, plant, and live together as equals, one to another, and will support and protect one another."

Benjamin threw back the last of the rum in his cup. "Let's cast the devil out."

Edward Gibbons pounded on Lieutenant Fitcher's door. When he answered, they raised nine muskets toward his chest. Fitcher's eyes widened and his mouth opened in wordless shock.

"Lieutenant Fitcher, the free men of Mount Wollaston insist on your departure from this plantation immediately." Benjamin thrust a sealed letter at Fitcher's hand. "Take yourself to Virginia and deliver this to Captain Wollaston. The free men of this plantation forbid his return to this place or face a lashing."

Fitcher's face had gone pale. Then he stiffened and squared his shoulders in a show of false bravado. "This is mutiny. And ye will pay for your treachery."

His bluster was almost comical, and Noah might have laughed under different circumstances. He poked Fitcher in the chest with the end of his musket. "Off with you!"

"Be gone!" Sam shouted, and the others joined the chorus.

They harassed Fitcher all the way to the dock, hurling insults, and occasionally rocks if he weren't moving fast enough to suit them. By the end he was running down the dock, where he leapt onto the shallop, hauled anchor, and unfurled the sails in quick succession.

"Ye will pay for this treachery!" he shouted again, and Sam shoved the shallop off with the heel of his boot.

Noah's heart fluttered, watching the shallop disappear around the point. He turned toward his eight companions and grinned. Benjamin laughed. Then they rushed back up the hill, whooping and cheering. Thomas Morton stood at the top, beaming like a proud father.

"This plantation shall be called Mount Wollaston no longer, my boys!" Morton proclaimed when they had gathered around him. "From this day forth, it shall be known as Mount Mare."

"And a merry mount she shall be!" Benjamin said, raising his mug to the sky. The collected boys hooted and clapped at the blatant euphemism.

Benjamin's jest made Noah blush, even as he laughed with the others. The image it conjured in his mind made his cheeks burn.

"This calls for celebration!" Morton said, his face aglow as he looked around the circle of young faces. "We shall invite our neighbors to a grand revel on Saturday next. But first!" He clapped his hands together twice in quick succession. "Go find yourselves a good, tall, sturdy tree from which we can fashion the biggest maypole ever seen. Tonight, we dance around it like bacchanal satyrs."

Noah paused from hacking the branches off a felled pine tree, his shoulders aching, and set his hatchet on a nearby bench. He told the others he'd be back in a moment and went to the beer barrel to rest and have a drink. Thomas Morton was walking from the trading post to his house, and Noah hurried to catch him.

"Mr. Morton, sir?"

Morton turned back at his door. "Hallo, Noah! And do call me Thomas. Remember, we are all equal here at Mount Mare." He put his hands to his mouth and yelled toward the others, wielding their hatchets against the tree branches. "I want all of ye to call me familiar from now on. We are equals." He turned back to Noah, beaming. "Have thou come to join me for a drink?"

"Thank you, sir." Noah followed Morton inside. "I wondered what you meant earlier. When you said we would dance around the maypole 'like bacchanal satyrs.' I know what a satyr is—from Greek mythology, half man and half goat—but I don't know the meaning of the other word."

He'd asked the others this morning when they marched into the forest to find a suitable tree, but they'd shrugged and shook their heads with sardonic smiles. "He talks like that a lot. We don't know what he means much of the time," Edward Gibbons had said. Now Noah swallowed his pride and asked the man himself.

"Ah, the bacchanalia!" A gleam came to Morton's eye. He strode into his study, and Noah hurried after him. Morton ran his finger along the spines of several books before tapping one and removing it from the shelf. "Since thou art familiar with Greek mythology, I trust thou know who Dionysus is."

"The Greek god of fertility."

"Yes, and of wine." Morton beamed at him, and then opened the book and flipped through the pages. "The Romans called him Bacchus. The bacchanalia is a raucous celebration of both—wine and fertility." He stopped flipping pages and turned the open book toward Noah. "I trust thou remember that Dionysus was attended by satyrs. At ancient bacchanalia, men dressed in that role."

The drawing on the page made Noah blush. It was four bearded men—naked and quite muscular—with goat's horns on their heads and a bushy tail emerging from above their buttocks. The opposite page bore a strikingly similar image, but this time one "satyr" was on his knees and leaning back while the others poured wine into his mouth.

"These pictures adorn ancient Greek vases, unearthed along the Aegean Sea." Morton flipped the page, and that image made Noah's blush burn hotter—two naked "satyrs" surrounded two women in long Greek dresses, and this time both men had erections pointing toward the sky. Morton flipped to the next page, and this one bore a picture of a satyr—also erect—reaching inside Dionysus's robe and fondling his bullocks.

Noah looked at Morton, mouth open. "But... you mean..."

"We have no goat's horns, but I think deer antlers are a passable substitute." Morton stroked his chin beard. "We could fashion leggings from the beaver or fox pelts, and we have sufficient fox tails that we could attach to the backs of belts."

Noah's mouth still hung open, and nervous sweat ran down his back and the sides of his head. "But sir—we cannot dance *naked* in front of our neighbors."

Morton chuckled. "Not at the Saturday revels with our guests. Nay, the bacchanalia was a secret festival, open only to initiates of the cult of Bacchus. The ancient Greeks and Romans were not prudes regarding fertility rituals, young Noah. Most of Christendom has sadly forgotten their example; though the maypole is a most English invention. We shall follow the example of the ancients under the moonlight tonight when we initiate our own maypole."

Noah swallowed hard. "How will you convince the others to..." he swallowed again. "...to dance *naked*?"

Morton laughed and clasped a hand onto Noah's shoulder. "We shall warm them up, of course! With my casks of fortified wine from Portugal. They will have transformed into proper satyrs before they reach the bottom of their second cup."

Thomas Morton brought home a ten-point buck that evening, and they roasted it on a spit. They gorged themselves on venison and vegetables and downed it with copious quantities of beer. After dinner, but before they lost the evening light—or got too deep into their cups—Morton nailed the buck's antlers to the top of the denuded trunk of the giant pine tree, and together they hoisted it into a hole dug especially for it in the center of the village. It rose eighty feet into the air.

"The biggest, tallest maypole the world has seen!" Morton shouted, raising his mug. The boys cheered and drank more. Then Morton brought out his casks.

Hours later, when the moon rose over the tree line, their bellies warm with port wine and their heads abuzz, they encircled the pole, naked bodies glowing pale in the silvery moonlight, except where fox fur wrapped around their lower legs like those of satyrs. Belts of deer hide circled their waists with fox tails fastened to the back. They danced and gyrated around the maypole, laughing and play charging one another with the antlers fastened to deer hide headbands.

Even Thomas Morton, his body softer and rounder than those of his young compatriots, danced with as much energy and enthusiasm as the others. "Dance, my ganymedes! Dance!" It took little time for erections to rise parallel with the maypole, but none took any effort to hide them.

Noah's lack of shame would have astonished him had he given the matter any thought. But he only felt the exhilaration of movement, the exuberant freedom of the dance. The rigidness of his member was like a fifth limb moving to the rhythm of his own dance steps. He twirled and swayed, stomped and jumped, breathless, yet never exhausting his energy.

Hours had passed, and the moon was high above their clearing when Benjamin touched Noah's arm, drawing his attention. Ben nodded toward the darkened houses, where Thomas Morton snuck off on tip-toes with Sam; hip to hip, Morton's arm around Sam's bare shoulders. Noah collided with Ben before he could stop his dancing, and Ben laughed as their torsos bumped, rods poking each other's bellies. He threw his arms around Noah to catch him.

"That's a good idea, don't you think?" Ben said with a devilish grin. "Shall we have a merry mount, then?" His grin widened at his own pun, the whites of his teeth gleaming in the moonlight.

"We celebrate our Merrymount with a merry mount!" Noah said, his voice louder than he'd intended, the words slurring. And he was copying Ben's joke. Something in the back of his brain said that should embarrass him, and yet it didn't.

Back in Noah's room, they tumbled onto his bed. "Can I mount you first?" Ben asked. "You can mount me after I finish."

Noah nodded, perhaps a bit too enthusiastically. But then he screwed up his face. "How do we do it?"

Ben pointed toward Drake, lying on the ground, watching them with his head cocked. "You've seen dogs mount each other, haven't you? I think that's the way to do it. Here, get on your hands and knees. Then we'll switch."

Noah scrambled onto his hands and knees as fast as he could move. Benjamin flipped Noah's fox tail onto his back, causing both of them to laugh. He wrapped himself around Noah from behind and entered him.

Noah couldn't help grinning every time he passed Benjamin in the village or in the fields the next two days. His ass was still sore, something that every step reminded him of, but that only brought back to mind the unexpected tingling wave of euphoria that had swept through him the other night from an unknown place deep inside.

He hoped Ben felt the same jubilation from Noah's turn behind him. For himself, Noah was certain he stood taller somehow, and his shoulders were light. They had bitten into the most forbidden fruit there was and devoured it whole. And the energy from that fruit had radiated warmth throughout his entire being ever since.

He felt as if he were floating when guests began to arrive on Saturday evening.

"There's a change in thee, Noah Bancroft," Samuel Maverick said. "Found thy way, I'd say."

Noah's smile was so wide it made the corners of his mouth ache. "I'm happy here." This was the happiest he'd ever been in his nineteen years.

"I can see that." Maverick beamed back at him. Then he leaned in conspiratorially. "Though I must tell thee, David Thomson is outraged that a rebellion has thrown out the lawful owner of the lads' indentures.

I wish thou could have seen him sputter!" He threw back his head with laughter.

Noah could imagine it, and it made him giggle with glee. "Let it be a warning to him, should he ever learn I'm here and try to reclaim me." It struck him that he no longer feared that possibility. The absence of that long-held fear was cleansing, like the bath he'd had that afternoon.

"I shudder to think what thy friends might do to him," Maverick said with a gleam in his bright blue eyes, not shuddering at all. Then he bowed to Noah with a flourish and excused himself to find Thomas Morton.

"The natives accepted Thomas's invitation to the revels," Benjamin said when they encountered one another at the beer barrel. "There will be plenty of girls for Edward and the others to choose from. And perhaps your friend Mr. Maverick will find himself a mate."

A jolt of jealousy stabbed through Noah, erasing his smile. But he scolded himself for being silly and forced a smile. "That would be happy tidings. Doubtless Thomas will play matchmaker for him."

The natives arrived a short while later, young and old alike. Several of the men carried grouse or duck carcasses by the legs, and the young women carried baskets. As usual, Noah's eyes wandered over the muscular bodies of the young native men, clad only in breechclouts. He recalled the feeling of breezy freedom when wearing one last year. Then his mind flooded with memories of Jimmy Hawkey—which was strange, given that Noah had never seen Jimmy in a breechclout.

His belly tingled at the memory of Jimmy's lips against his at the bottom of the Hawkeys' boat, the feel of Jimmy's muscular torso against his own. And the way Jimmy's member had felt through the fabric of his trousers, thick and firm. Noah pictured himself on his hands and knees in his cottage—just like the other night—but with Jimmy Hawkey behind him instead of Benjamin, Jimmy's pillicock moving inside him...

"Noah?"

Noah's breath caught, startled, and his cheeks burned. "What?"

"You looked a thousand miles away," Ben said with an amused half-smile. "I said, your old neighbors from Weymouth Plantation are here."

"Oh!" Noah's face and neck went clammy, but he was relieved to look away from Ben's face, toward where William Jefferies, John Bursley, and young James Ludden talked with Edward Gibbons and Samuel Maverick. "Let's go greet them."

He didn't wait for agreement and strode toward their group. He told himself there was no way Ben would have known what he was thinking, or what picture had filled his imagination.

And why had his imagination conjured *that* image, anyway? He was happy, for goodness' sake! What was wrong with him?

Laughter and shouted conversations rang around the clearing. They emptied one beer barrel, and Noah joined Sam and Edward to roll another one from the storehouse, which Thomas then tapped with a great flourish to enthusiastic cheers.

"We shall make this a weekly celebration, my friends!" Thomas said, raising his refilled mug high into the air. "Every Saturday night at dusk, when our weekly work is finished, and before the day of rest, we will celebrate with a merry revel. All are welcome!"

A tremendous cheer greeted the suggestion.

Benjamin sidled up to Noah and whispered in his ear. "I was thinking—'tis noisy enough that none would hear us if we returned to your cottage and repeated the other night's activity. And as Thomas suggests, we can make it a weekly activity, you and I." He stared at Noah, eyes aglow.

Noah was glad his cheeks were already flushed with drink, so his blush didn't show. "We should not leave together, though. I'll go now. You stay and sneak away in a little while."

"Good idea."

Squeals of startled laughter caught their attention, and they looked over at Edward Gibbons emerging from his house, clad only in his "satyr" outfit from two nights before, and strutting proudly as could be toward a trio of young native women. They covered their mouths and almost doubled over in laughter.

Noah busted out laughing, while stealing more than a glance at Edward's privy parts swinging with every bold stride he took.

Ben looked at Noah and waggled his eyebrows.

"Not for all the king's gold!"

Ben grinned. "Then perhaps we don that attire when we're alone in your room."

Noah didn't argue, just turned with a wink and hurried home.

CHAPTER 19

June 1626 - Massachusetts Bay

Jimmy Hawkey stood beside the rocks some fifty yards from the cottage he and Floyd had called home for two years, staring at the ocean without really seeing it. The surf was high, and the noise of the waves crashing onto the beach nearly drowned out the calls of the seagulls, but it was all a formless buzz in his ears.

Tight in his right hand—so tight his knuckles were white—he held his father's prayer book. He pressed it so tightly against his chest that his ribs ached. He concentrated on that ache, focused on it to the detriment of all else, until the sights and sounds of the world around him faded into formless light. Only that ache mattered.

Behind him, two of the remaining fishermen still living at Cape Ann carried the body from the cottage, wrapped in a white sheet and tied at the shoulders, waist, and knees with a trio of ropes. A hand dropped onto Jimmy's shoulder, jolting him back to the here and now.

"God bless you, Jimmy Hawkey," John Small said. "And God rest your father's soul. He was a good man."

Jimmy nodded without a word. A moment later, John Small shuffled off, following the pair carrying Floyd Hawkey's body toward the village burial ground.

His reverie broken, the pain swept into Jimmy's heart like the waves crashing against the rocks. He dropped onto the sand, elbows on his knees, and cried into his hands.

Ten people attended the burial. That was all that remained here at Cape Ann. Two weeks earlier, Roger Conant had led most of the station's residents to a place called Naumkeag, some twelve miles west along the north shore of the Massachusetts' Bay. There was a protected harbor there, and Conant had declared it a better spot for a permanent plantation. Only a small group of fishermen remained behind—those who couldn't abide Conant's strict puritanical leadership.

Jimmy stood apart from the others, not looking at any of them. They'd all liked and admired Floyd, but none of them understood what Floyd had meant to Jimmy. He'd saved him when he was alone and scared, the last survivor of an entire community. He'd given him a home, a name, a place to belong. From Sennen Cove in Cornwall, to Monhegan Island, to here—wherever Floyd was, that was where Jimmy belonged.

He belonged nowhere now.

There was no clergyman, so Mr. Tylly read the funerary service from the Book of Common Prayer. Jimmy's eyes teared, blurring his vision, but he blinked them away. He wouldn't cry in front of these people.

Ten minutes later, two of the men shoveled the pile of dirt into the grave. The others dispersed to their homes, but Jimmy stayed at the side of the pit, looking down at the wrapped body until the white sheet disappeared beneath the earth. He turned away without looking at the men and walked home in silence.

He sat up most of the night, his back against the door jamb, listening to the rhythmic drone of the waves on the sand.

He couldn't stay here. Not alone. The awkward sympathy from the others would be too much to bear. Naumkeag was out of the question; Roger Conant was a hypocritical Puritan bigot. For much of the night, Jimmy considered joining the Pawtucket, or perhaps the Massachusett tribe. Their languages and traditions were much like what he had known when he was small. But he'd become too English over the last ten years to go back to native ways.

But he was also painfully aware that he couldn't walk into any other English settlement, where no one knew him; at the sight of his dark skin, they would greet him with the muzzles of their muskets.

He would be an outsider wherever he went. He would be an outsider for the rest of his life. Twenty-one years old, and his fate was sealed.

He drifted into sleep at some point, and his mind filled with visions of men of all types—English and Indian—dancing together, embracing, kissing ... and other acts he tried not to think of too often. But he felt calm as he watched; he felt the warmth of familiarity. Some men called his name, beckoned him to join them. How did they know his name? He didn't recognize anyone; and yet, he felt that he knew them. Then he saw boats on the sand between him and the men, and while he looked, the boats filled with sea bass, almost overflowing. He wondered where the fishermen sat. How amazing to catch so many fish that you had nowhere to sit! But still the men beckoned to him. Beckoned with their hands, with their eyes, with their bodies ...

Then he was among them. Their hands rubbed his back, his chest, his bollocks ...

But he had no fear. How strange to have no fear of such things. All he felt was the pleasure of their touch, the feel of their bodies beneath his hands, the warmth and excitement of the shared experience.

He belonged.

Dawn light was breaking over the ocean when he pushed off from the dock. Raising the sail to catch the stiff morning breeze, he checked the compass, and set the rudder and sail to carry him south-southeast, across the mouth of the bay. In the center of the boat sat two crates, carrying those belongings that had mattered to Floyd and to him. Everything else he'd left behind.

He was a quarter-mile off shore when he heard his name, faint over the splash of water against the hull of the ketch. He could just make out John Small at the end of the wharf at Cape Ann. Jimmy stood and waved. But then he turned away, facing the open sea.

He didn't look back.

It took most of the day to get there, but he found the place not long after spotting land. Cape Cod, this sandy curve of land was called. And if the whispered stories were correct, he'd find a cove with a rag-tag collection of temporary shelters, and a rough and tumble gathering of human flotsam that belonged nowhere.

He found the cove beyond the northwestern-most curve of the cape, and the collection of shelters on its south shore. Now he would see if the rest of the story was accurate.

He'd overheard occasional whispers about these bass fishermen at the end of Cape Cod, some of whom had been cast out of cod fishing crews, not welcome at regular fishing stations. They did things that couldn't be spoken of, things that shouldn't be found even among the loneliest of fishermen. The whispers were never specific, but the implication had always been clear.

They were like him. Or rather, like how he longed to be, deep in the privacy of his dreams.

He steered the ketch into the cove. A few men gathered near the docks, turning curious faces his way. Jimmy stood and raised his arm. "Halloo! Greetings, Englishmen! I am James Hawkey of Cornwall. May I disembark?"

Jimmy leapt from the ketch three weeks later, splashing into knee-deep water, and hauled the boat toward the sand under the blazing afternoon sun. His two companions jumped in after him, and together they brought the boat out of the water. Others already occupied the docks, bringing in the day's catch, and as often happened, it relegated them to finishing their work on the beach.

Jimmy reached inside the boat and took hold of one end of the net, waited for his two companions to grab the other ends, and together they heaved the net onto the sand with its heavy load of sea bass.

None of them wore shirts, and a coating of white salt crusted their shoulders and arms, as much from the sea breeze as from their own sweat. The two white men's shoulders and backs bore the reddish-brown hue of countless sunburns that had tanned over. Their faces bore the same sun-kissed color, and their stubbled chins gave them a rough look. Thin, wiry hair covered the pink skin of their sun-burnt and wind-burnt chests, which neve tanned as well as their backs and shoulders. Jimmy always found this curious.

"Good catch this morning," Andrew said, panting from the exertion, and wiped at his brow with a forearm. He was a lithe young man a few years older than Jimmy, perhaps twenty-five, with reddish-blond hair in thick waves that blew in the wind. He grinned a mouthful of crooked teeth. "We shall eat well and still fetch a good price."

Jimmy eyed the seagulls circling ever lower. "Let's get to work before those gulls take advantage."

The three of them hauled the net up the beach to the driftwood hut they occupied at the edge of the dune grass. It was hardly sturdy construction, though a pair of fishing nets wrapped around the walls lent it some stability. But it need only last them a season, and there wasn't any other material available.

They sat in the sand and set to work with filet knives, cleaning away the scales, pulling out the guts into a bucket, and then tossing them far into the grass to draw the gulls away. The flesh they cut into thick filets, dragged them through a salt bucket, and stacked them onto a driftwood rack.

After an hour's work, Harry stood and stretched, arching his back and placing his hands at the top of his buttocks. "After a day's catch like that, we should reward ourselves." He glanced down at Andrew. "Care for a romp in the dunes?"

"That's a great idea," Andrew said, leaping to his feet. He looked at Jimmy, who collected their tools to carry inside the hut. "You should join us one of these days."

A familiar lightness swept through Jimmy's belly. He had a pretty good idea what a 'romp in the dunes' entailed. And though he'd gladly accepted Andrew's and Harry's invitation to share their hut his first day here, he had quickly deduced they were a dedicated pair; the thought of joining something private seemed a little too forbidden.

And there was no lack of forbidden flesh on display in the tall grasses behind the huts. He need only trek a short distance to find someone—usually several someone's—lounging stark naked on the sand, pecker in hand. Or sometimes peckers in each other's hands. No one ever minded being watched. Perhaps they preferred it.

At every fishing station along the New England coast, it was not usual for a man to sneak off to some secluded spot in the woods to pleasure himself. Jimmy had often crouched in the brush and watched, secretly.

Few would have welcomed the audience, let alone a helping hand. Here, it was almost expected.

Still, he wasn't brave enough to join Andrew and Harry, though images of what he imagined them doing filled his head when he laid down to sleep at night.

Instead, he took off toward the sandy spit of land at the tip of the cape. He liked to go there to sit alone and think.

He liked this place. After initial suspicion from the men already here when he'd arrived at the beginning of June—which had made him miss his father all the more, the way Floyd introduced Jimmy as his son—he'd soon grown comfortable with this collection of cast-out fishermen. More arrived almost every day, until now, three weeks later—Midsummer's Day, he suddenly realized—there were more than a hundred of them here. And not all English, either; there were Bretons, Basques, French and Portuguese, though most were English. Even with more here, that sense of freedom in the air never waned.

The wind whipped across the point from the ocean to the bay and whistled in his ears in a not unpleasant way. He closed his eyes and listened, hoping to hear words from his guardian angels in the wind. This place was only temporary; everyone would pack up and leave at the end of September, returning to homes in England, France, Spain, Portugal, or wherever they'd come from.

And Jimmy would be alone again.

But that was three months away, and the wisdom that settled upon him from the wind was to live in this moment, and let tomorrow worry about itself. He breathed deeply, filling his lungs with the salt air, turning his face to the afternoon sun over the bay.

Satisfied, a sense of peace settling into every corner of his body, he turned toward the east and hiked along the north shore beach. The dunes hid the driftwood shelters by the cove, and he walked along the edge of the grass, drinking in the sounds of the waves and the wind.

Low moans came from somewhere in the grass carpeting the crevice between two low dunes. He stopped, craning his neck to see. Taking a few tentative steps into the grass, he spotted a man's leg on the sand some twenty yards away. He took a few more steps, closing half the distance, and now he could see the full wiry form of a man on his back, naked.

His arms crossed over his face, his body stretched out long. Another man with gentle musculature knelt beside him, also naked, his head rising and falling where the prone man's penis would be. A long wave of reddish-blond hair obscured this second man's face and the first man's penis.

Jimmy's feet rooted in place. His mouth went dry, but a thrill ran up his spine and down his arms to tingle his fingertips. He'd never seen this in waking life. It was mesmerizing and dangerous. Men caught doing this would find themselves in a hangman's noose, with their genitals cut off.

It went on for several moments, but Jimmy didn't look away. Then the man on the sand moved, his legs and arms fidgeting. His moans grew louder. The second man's head bobbed faster. The first man's body twitched, and his moans changed to cries, his mouth open, his head thrown back. His arms stretched out to grab fistfuls of sand, revealing Harry's face. Harry stiffened, hips raised off the sand, holding still and rigid for two or three seconds, gasping; and then he plopped onto the ground, panting, and wiped the sweat from his forehead with the back of his hand.

Andrew swept the wave of hair back from his face with both hands and grinned at him. Then he glanced toward the beach. His pale blue eyes caught Jimmy's and widened in surprise.

Jimmy looked away in a hurry, and took a couple of hurried steps backward, stumbling on a tuft of grass and almost falling.

"Ho there! Jimmy Hawkey!" He looked up. Andrew was grinning at him. "Did you like what you saw?"

Jimmy's mouth was dry, and he couldn't form any words.

Harry pushed himself up and strode toward Jimmy. His penis was still half-erect, waving back and forth as he walked. Jimmy stared at it a second too long, and his cheeks heated.

"He liked it alright," Harry called over his shoulder. His hand stroked the front of Jimmy's trousers, following the length of Jimmy's erection beneath the fabric. Then he took Jimmy's hand in his and pulled him forward. "Come on then, let's have a look ourselves. It's only fair."

Andrew stood with a hip cocked and an amused half-smile gracing his full lips. His erection, pale and white, rose from a mass of reddish-blond curls and aimed at the sky. Jimmy stared openly. His body was beautiful, like a Greek statue he'd seen in a book once. It was like a dream, something he'd seen in his sleep countless times, as Andrew and Harry unfastened his belt and tugged his trousers to his ankles. Then Andrew dropped to his knees.

"It's illegal," Jimmy protested. "We'll hang for it."

Harry chuckled, his lips inches from Jimmy's ear. "Ain't no one here going to hang no one else for this."

Andrew's hand took hold of Jimmy at the base, causing him a sharp intake of breath. "But it's a sin ..." Jimmy said, his voice weak and unsure.

Harry's lips nibbled at his earlobe. "We'll all be together in Purgatory, I suppose."

And then Andrew took him in his mouth, and Jimmy gasped. He'd never experienced anything like it. It was warm and wet, gentle and yet firm at the same time. The movement of Andrew's tongue tickled in a way that felt amazing, like nothing else. Harry's right hand rubbed his chest, while Harry's left hand caressed his back, and descended to his buttocks. His palms were rough from years of work and salt, and they scratched Jimmy's smooth skin in a way that sent shivers of excitement to his groin.

It was over too fast, but the sensations coursing through Jimmy's body made him light-headed. He put one hand each on Andrew and Harry's shoulders for stability, his breath coming hard and fast.

"I think he liked that," Harry said with a chuckle, lifting Andrew by the arm and then kissing him full on the mouth.

Andrew looked back at Jimmy with a wicked grin. "He wasn't the only one."

A moment of panic made Jimmy's heart race. "Are we going to hell for that?" The words came out raspy.

Andrew laughed. Harry shook his head. "I know what it says in the prayer book. 'The waters of baptism are sure protection from the fires of hell.' And we've all been baptized, haven't we? It's the law. If Heaven don't take us because of *this*, then I reckon we'll all go to Purgatory 'til St. Peter lets us in."

"And it ain't like it's buggery," Andrew said. "Harry and me, we don't do that. Some men here do, but not us. I remember what the preachers say—'don't lie with a man the way you'd lie with a woman.' This ain't fucking, so it don't count." He laughed again, and Harry laughed with him.

That made a certain amount of sense. Not all sodomy was buggery, after all.

"Andrew took care of both of us," Harry said, rubbing his rough hand along the curve of Jimmy's buttocks. "Why don't we take care of him together?"

Jimmy's stomach tumbled with butterflies, but the thought also made his mouth water. He looked down at Andrew's erection, like a maypole pointing at the sky. He put his arm around Harry's waist and the two of them dropped to their knees in the sand.

Jimmy sat alone in the dunes behind their shelter, watching the sun drop toward the surface of the bay, bathing everything in a rosy glow. He closed his eyes and asked for guidance.

He wasn't a religious man, not in the Christian sense, anyway. With his childhood people, he'd been raised to believe in the Great Spirit who had created all things and watched over all life; once he went to Cornwall with his new father and was baptized in the Church of England, he'd understood God to be one and the same. There were differences—the church's broader definition of sin, for one thing—but more consistency than difference.

As he sat in silence, eyes closed, listening to the wind and the waves, what came was a deep sense of belonging. Deeper than he'd felt in a long time. He fit in with these men.

But the summer will come to an end. Then what? Andrew would return to Weymouth in Dorset; Harry would return to Christchurch in Hampshire. The others would scatter. And Jimmy would have to find someplace else. It wasn't only that he would be alone, and isolated; there was no fresh water here, and he couldn't stay longer than his beer lasted. *What should I do? Speak to me, guide me.*

The whisper came on the wind.

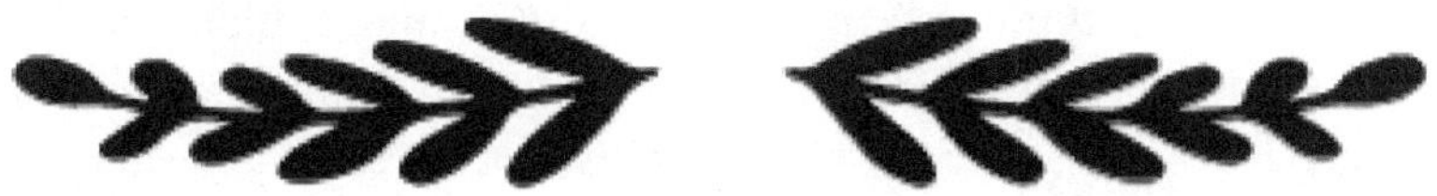

"Ho there, Jimmy," Harry said when Jimmy returned to the shelter. He was sitting in the door of their hut, sharpening his fillet knife.

"Where's Andrew?"

"I'm in here," Andrew said from inside.

"Can we talk about something?"

Harry looked at him sadly. "Are you having regret about what happened earlier?"

"No, definitely not." Jimmy didn't admit that perhaps he had, at first. But he'd dealt with that. It felt natural, what they'd done. And the feeling of belonging it brought him—that outweighed anxiety about sin.

Andrew appeared in the doorway, and the breeze fluttered the waves of reddish-blond hair around his ears. "What's on your mind?"

"How long have ye been coming to this place?" Jimmy asked.

"It's my second year," Andrew said. "Harry's been coming longer."

"Five years."

"Were ye mates last year?"

Andrew grinned and nodded. Harry shrugged. "I suppose that's true. Not at first, mind; but by the end of the first month, he was the one I kept going to. By the last month, he was sleeping every night in my hut."

"I made him promise we'd meet back here on the twenty-first of May," Andrew said with a wry half-smile. "I wasn't certain he would, but when I got here on the twenty-third he was waiting for me."

Jimmy couldn't help but smile. He wished that for himself. His mind filled with the image of Noah Bancroft, lying shirtless with him at the bottom of his boat in the Piscataqua River, and a pang stabbed his heart. "Ye never tried to see each other in England?"

Harry frowned. "Of course not. We may not be the smartest of men, but we ain't fools."

Jimmy nodded, slowly. He hesitated to say what was on his mind, for fear they would laugh. But then he plunged ahead. "Would ye consider staying in New England when the summer ends?"

Harry and Andrew exchanged a look that Jimmy couldn't read. "I don't know where we'd go," Harry said at length. "This is a safe place for men like us because there's no one else what wants to come here. It's isolated, there's no lumber or rocks for building, no fresh water. We can't stay here. It's desolate and windswept enough in the summertime, and in the winter we'd be at the mercy of every storm the sea could throw at us. This thing wouldn't shelter us." He swept his arm up toward the driftwood hut. "It won't be standing when we come back next May."

"There are other plantations," Jimmy said.

Harry and Andrew exchanged another look.

"I've been to Monhegan, and Pemaquid, and Pannaway," Andrew said. "Other stations would be the same. If we were together, they'd spot Harry and me for what we are in no time. Back home, we can slip into our old lives and no one's the wiser."

"Most men here spent time at those other stations," Harry said. "Some of 'em come here because they ain't welcome at the other places no more. Like Andrew said, it wouldn't take anyone long to figure out what we're about if we were together."

Andrew was watching Jimmy. "Where will you go when the summer ends?"

Jimmy was quiet for a moment. When he couldn't come up with an answer, he shrugged. "I can't say. But I know I can't go back to Cornwall—not after all these years, not without my father. I have to stay in New England. Somewhere."

Andrew nodded. Jimmy couldn't read the look in his eyes. "If I go back to Weymouth ..." Andrew hesitated.

He'd said *if*, not *when*. Jimmy nodded encouragement.

A sad sort of smile spread across Andrew's lips. "If I go back, my father will push for me to marry his partner's daughter. A man is expected to take a wife when he comes to my age. But in the colonies, where there are few women ..."

Harry scowled. "I'm getting married. At Christmas. It's already arranged. But that won't stop me from coming back here next May. So will you."

Andrew looked at Harry, but didn't respond.

"Consider it," Jimmy said.

A storm came through several nights later. Sheets of rain pelted the cape and blew through the cracks between the driftwood. The dried grasses that plugged the gaps couldn't withstand the wind, and scattered. The fishing nets wrapped around the hut stayed in place, keeping it standing, though its weave couldn't keep out the rain. Before long, it drenched them. The wind whistling between the driftwood chilled them, and they huddled together, wet and shivering.

The morning found their hut intact, and they set out to collect grass to stuff the cracks. At least three other huts hadn't fared as well, reduced to a pile of sticks and tangled netting.

"They all look like that in May, if you're lucky," Harry said. "Some are scattered across the beach. And every storm does that to at least a few. We rebuild. It's the price of freedom."

The price of freedom. That stabbed Jimmy's heart like a blade. Only in the most inhospitable of environments was this freedom possible. They worked in silence for a long time.

"I've been thinking," Harry said after a while. "They say there are only four men at that Nantasket station, across the bay." He scratched his chin, looking west across the endless expanse of water, gray under the cloudy sky. "I figure, if four men could make a go of it and survive these last four years, why couldn't three men give it a shot?"

Jimmy's heart fluttered. "Do you mean that?"

Harry's eyes stayed glued to the western horizon, but he nodded. "You know that country, Jimmy. You could find us a suitable place to hunker down, somewhere deep in the woods where no one will bother us. Someplace with a fresh spring, and lots of deer. Three men could make a pretty good life in a place like that."

CHAPTER 20

SEPTEMBER 1626 - MERRYMOUNT

Noah's back ached from stooping over the squash and bean plants. His arms ached from carrying bushels of the vegetables from the fields to the village. And now that the sun glowed red in the western sky, his stomach growled. But winter came early in this part of the world, and they needed to gather in what they could as soon as they could. The first frosts could be here in as little as two weeks.

His basket once again full—beans this time—he hauled it up from the ground with extreme effort and carted it toward home, his legs feeling like iron weights dragging across the ground.

It was two hundred yards to the storage house, and he was huffing with effort by the time he reached it.

Benjamin was scooping beans from a basket into tall bags of woven hemp when Noah entered. He stopped what he was doing to stand beside the scale near the door. Noah dropped his basket onto the right side of the scale and stepped back, panting.

Benjamin added stone weights of different sizes on the other plate until the beam balanced. "Twenty three pounds, eleven ounces. Almost a bushel." He walked over to the table and made an entry in the open ledger.

So close. "Is it dinnertime yet?" Noah asked, still breathing hard.

"Soon. Not enough time for you to go back and pick any more. Help me fill these bags instead?"

Noah nodded, grabbed a scoop, and shifted the beans from his latest basketful into Benjamin's open bag. The bag was three-quarters full already.

"More newcomers arrived today," Benjamin said while they scooped. "A trio of bass fishermen. One of them's an Indian, but raised in England. He talks and dresses like a white man. Isn't that queer?"

An image of Jimmy Hawkey sprang to mind. "I knew someone like that once—an Indian boy, but raised by an English father in Cornwall. They were cod fishermen at Monhegan Island." He thought for a moment, and added, "The New Plymouth planters knew a couple of others like that who helped them when they first arrived, didn't they? Squanto and ... I can't remember the other one. Started with an 'M,' didn't it?"

"Massasoit. But he was older, still talked and dressed like an Indian. He'd learned to speak English in England, though."

"Yes, that's right," Noah said with a nod. "Three more arrivals—how many does that make now?"

"Don't know ... almost a dozen, maybe? I haven't counted."

Noah looked at the bags of beans and squash around the storehouse. "Will we have enough food for the added mouths?"

Benjamin shrugged. "Probably so. You know Thomas won't turn anyone away, though. We'll all share equally in whatever we have. That's the way."

Ever since word had spread that they'd evicted Lt. Fitcher with the message for Captain Wollaston to never return, others had been arriving to join their little commonwealth. Adventurers from New Plymouth mostly, disillusioned with life in that theocracy, but also some fishermen from Pannaway. And now this trio of bass fishermen.

The dinner bell rang. Noah rushed out the door ahead of Benjamin, but then stopped in his tracks.

In front of him, surrounded by a half-dozen Merrymounters plus two other newcomers, stood Jimmy Hawkey. Noah blinked—were his eyes playing tricks on him? No, it was definitely Jimmy. It had been three years, but he'd hardly changed. Noah stared at him for several seconds before Jimmy glanced over.

And their eyes met.

It was as if someone had sucked all the air from Noah's lungs. His feet were rooted in place, his legs a tree trunk. And he couldn't look away. His gaze locked onto those dark eyes he'd so often stared into years ago.

Jimmy's face broke into a grin, and he jogged over. He threw his arms open and embraced Noah so tightly he could barely breathe. Not that he'd been breathing, anyway.

"I thought you'd gone back to England!" Jimmy said, laughing with delight. He released the embrace, stood back at arm's length, hands on Noah's shoulders, and looked him over, beaming. "We heard Captain Levett went back to Devon to fetch his family that winter, but he got caught up in the war against Spain and never came back to New England. I thought you were with him."

Noah was grinning, too, so hard his cheeks ached. "I wasn't with him." He laughed at the misunderstanding.

"What happened?"

Those memories killed Noah's smile, but he did his best to put on a cheerful face. He shrugged, as nonchalant as he could be on this topic. "Captain Levett sent me to work for Mr. Thomson at Pannaway Plantation. The next spring, I went with him to Noddle's Island, not far from here. After Captain Gorges went back to England, I went to live at Weymouth Plantation, and eventually Thomas Morton invited me to join this company. I've been here ever since."

Jimmy shook his head, a crooked grin making him look adorable. "All this time, you weren't that far away. I was across the bay, at Cape Ann."

"You were? At Cape Ann?" Noah couldn't believe it. "I would have gone there if I'd known, when I—" He stopped, having almost blurted that he'd run away from David Thomson. He smiled to cover the momentary panic. "When I struck out on my own. I went to Weymouth Plantation because it was near. Cape Ann was farther away—but I still would have gone there if I'd known you were there."

If Jimmy deduced that Noah had run away from his indenture, it didn't show. He beamed at Noah, hands still on his shoulders. The warmth of his touch radiated through Noah's chest and encircled his heart.

The dogs bounded into the village then, having come up from the marsh in response to the dinner bell. Drake split from the pack and loped toward Noah with a single bark. He stopped next to Noah's leg, standing close to him and staring at Jimmy, nose sniffing.

"This is Drake," Noah said, touching the dog's head and then scratching behind his ears. Jimmy held out his knuckles, and Drake took a couple of tentative steps toward him, sniffing audibly. Then his tail wagged, and he sat next to Noah, looking up at Jimmy with expectant eyes. Jimmy scratched him behind the ears.

"Come, I want to introduce my friends," Jimmy said. His fingers trailed down Noah's arm without shame, then wrapped around his hand and pulled him toward the other two newcomers. Noah's cheeks heated at his touch. "Andrew, Harry—this is my friend Noah Bancroft."

"The one you told us about," the dark-haired one murmured, and his eyes ran shamelessly down Noah's form and back up. A crooked grin tugged up one side of his mouth. "He's as handsome as you said."

Noah's cheeks heated even more. Jimmy had talked about him? After all this time! And he'd said he was handsome! Noah's belly went light as air.

"That's Harry," Jimmy said with a small laugh. "Harry Colburn, and this is Andrew Blanford. We met this summer at the Cape Cod station, and I convinced them to stay with me and not to go back to England. We stopped at Nantasket, and the fishermen there told us about this place."

"The way they spoke of it, it sounded like our kind of place." Andrew's tone was full of meaning, and there was a twinkle in his eyes, which held Noah's and didn't look away. "That is, I don't think they approve of the way the boys behave here."

A chill ran up Noah's spine at the implication.

"But 'twas clear they admire the plantation's success," Harry said, looking around appreciatively.

Drake wove in and out of the circle, tail wagging, tongue dangling from the side of his mouth as if he were smiling. Noah had to grin at him. He snapped his fingers, and the dog sat in front of him. "Come on, boy; let's get our dinner."

As he turned toward the big house where the dinner tables stood, he locked eyes with Benjamin. He'd almost forgotten his friend had been with him when they left the storehouse. There was a strange look on Ben's face, and an unusual coldness to his blue eyes.

"Jimmy, this is my friend Benjamin Burton," Noah rushed to say. "Ben, this is Jimmy Hawkey, an old friend from my first days in New England."

Ben took Jimmy's hand, stiff as he shook it. His eyes bore a hole through Jimmy's face. "Welcome to Merrymount." The words lacked any warmth. Ben inserted himself between Noah and Jimmy as the group walked into the communal dining space.

"He was your lover, wasn't he?"

Benjamin's words as they walked from the dinner table to the beer barrel startled Noah. They were short, Ben's tone cold.

"No." It wasn't a lie, exactly. "We never ... you know."

Ben didn't respond, but from the tight set of his mouth while he refilled his mug, that hadn't appeased him.

"It was a long time ago," Noah said with an exaggerated shrug, shoving his own mug under the tap and refilling it.

Ben scowled. "But he's here now. And I don't like the way you were looking at him."

"We only kissed, years ago." Bare torsos pressed together, hands roaming over the front of their trousers ... Noah's cheeks heated, and he looked the other direction in hopes Ben wouldn't see his blush. The growth in the front of his pants would be harder to hide.

"The other two—Andrew and Harry—they're his lovers, you know."

Noah's stomach tightened into a cold stone, and his face snapped toward Ben. "What? I mean, they're clearly friends, but why—"

Ben crossed his arms. "If you didn't have your eyes stuck on your Indian friend throughout dinner, you might have seen it too."

Noah looked toward Jimmy and his friends still sitting at the table, laughing at something. Andrew's hand rested on Jimmy's forearm. Noah's chest constricted. It was getting hard to breathe.

"I don't like the way you look at him."

Noah snapped back toward Ben. "He's my friend, that's all. I haven't seen him in three years. That's why I was talking to him so much."

Ben's icy glare struck him like a stone. He stared at Noah, arms still crossed, for several seconds. "I saw the look in your eyes. I didn't like it, Noah."

He stormed off before Noah could say anything else in his defense. But he wasn't sure what he would have said.

The frost came before the end of September, killing their bean and squash plants.

Noah and his companions spent the morning cutting back the damaged vegetation with scythes. The repetitive swing burned his shoulders and drew sweat from his brow despite the cool temperature.

"The newcomers should be working with us," Benjamin grumbled.

Noah's gut clenched, and he didn't look at Ben. It was obvious to whom Ben had directed his comment, and about whom.

Sam, pausing to wipe his forehead with the back of his arm, shook his head. "We planted the fields, and we'll clear them. The newcomers will help with everything next year."

"They're going to eat the food we planted and harvested," Ben said, petulant. "It's not fair that they benefit from our labor without contributing."

Edward Gibbons stood and pointed a finger at Ben. "Stop bellyaching. When we plant again in the spring, everyone will contribute—even the newcomers. This was our labor, and we're doing it. Now keep quiet and do your work."

Ben bent back to his work, scowling and red-faced.

They returned to the village to clean up for lunch, gathering at the rain barrel to wash the dirt from their hands and arms. From Noah's position standing between Ben and Sam, he spotted Jimmy Hawkey trudging up the hill from the river, carrying a line of four fish. Harry and Andrew hiked behind him, each with his own line of three or four fish.

Jimmy caught Noah's eye and smiled at him on his way to where Thomas Morton stoked the fire. Noah smiled back.

Ben flashed Noah a frosty glare. Noah looked down and concentrated on washing his hands.

"Trout and Pike for supper," Jimmy said to Thomas.

"Splendid!" Thomas said, clapping his hands in pleasure.

Ben flung the water from his hands onto the ground at Noah's feet and stomped off.

"You were quiet at lunch."

Noah glanced at Jimmy, but quickly looked away. "Our work has made me tired."

Jimmy was silent for a moment, so Noah started back toward the fields. Jimmy walked beside him.

"We have work to do to finish our cottage this afternoon," Jimmy said. "We wove the thatch yesterday, and now we must spread it across the roof."

The image of Samuel Mavericke shirtless spreading his thatched roof sprang to mind. It morphed into him naked in the bright sunlight, applying tar to his peer posts. Then Maverick's pale white body was replaced in Noah's imagination by Jimmy Hawkey's brown one. An involuntary stirring between Noah's legs made him look away.

He was being ridiculous. Tar wasn't needed, of course. There was no chance Jimmy would work naked.

From the corner of Noah's eye, Jimmy's face was crestfallen. His silence had hurt his friend's feelings. Guilt ripped through Noah's gut. But he could think of nothing to say.

"Tomorrow I'll be free to go into the forest and hunt," Jimmy said, his voice surprisingly tentative. "Thou could come with me."

"I'd like that," Noah said, without thinking. Then apprehension over Benjamin's reaction gave him pause. "I shall ask Thomas if it interferes with our work, though."

"Do that." Jimmy stopped then and turned back. Noah watched him for a moment before hurrying to join the others in the field.

The revels that Saturday night were particularly raucous. The long-time denizens of Merrymount sought to impress the newcomers with their merriment.

Edward Gibbons, after brazenly fondling the breasts of his favorite native girl, to hoots from all around, raised his mug in the air and shouted the names of his compatriots to join him. "A song to entertain our guests, from my cup companions and myself."

A small thrill rushed through Noah to be included in the names Edward shouted out. True, he'd been resident here nearly two years; but not being one of the original indentured boys, he still felt separate sometimes. He hurried to the end of the line, where the other eight had linked arms.

"Ye know this one," Edward said, and started the song, the others joining midway through the first line.

"Be merry my hearts, and call for your quarts,
and let no liquor be lacking,
We have gold in store, we purpose to roar,
until we set care a packing.
Then hostess make haste, and let no time waste,
let every man have his due,
To save shoes and trouble, bring in the pots double,
for he that made one, made two!"

They downed the contents of their mugs, rivulets of beer trickling down their chins and dripping to the ground. Then Thomas made a great show of refilling the mugs from a pitcher, laughing and dancing, spilling surprisingly little. And then came the second verse.

Each verse ended with a call for another round, draining their mugs, and Thomas again gamely refilling. By the end of the twelfth and final verse, they were all slurring the words to near incomprehensibility:

"Then Hostess lets know, the sum that we owe,
twelve-pence there is for certeen,
Then fill t'other pot, and here's money for thot,
for he that made twelve, made thirteen!"

The belch that escaped Noah's throat after he downed his twelfth mug brought the burn of acid to his throat, but he wiped his mouth with the back of his hand. He stumbled toward the table where Jimmy sat with Harry and Andrew, applauding the song. He tripped on a root and dove forward, the uneven ground zooming toward his eyes in startling focus.

Strong hands gripped him under the arms before he landed. Strong arms tugged him upward, the world spinning before his eyes. He lost his balance and his face crashed into Jimmy's chest. He giggled, taking the woolsey fabric of Jimmy's shirt between his teeth, growling like a dog and shaking his head.

Jimmy's fingers on his face nudging him back sent a tingle through him. He looked up at Jimmy's face, and his amused grin spread warmth through Noah.

"You drank too much beer," Jimmy said.

"And too fast," Harry said with a chuckle.

"We've done that one many times," Noah said with an exaggerated shrug, referring to the song. He became aware of Jimmy's hands on his shoulders, holding him up, and he giggled again.

And then he planted a kiss on Jimmy's cheek. "Thank you for helping me," he slurred, and plopped onto the bench next to Andrew, who regarded him with undisguised amusement. Jimmy took a seat next to Noah—very close indeed, their thighs touching—and put an arm around his shoulders to steady him. Noah hadn't realized he was almost leaning into Andrew.

And before he could think twice, he leaned the opposite way and laid his head on Jimmy's shoulders. He closed his eyes and sighed in contentment.

But then he opened them, and stared into Benjamin's glaring face, standing right in front of him.

"There is nothing between me and Jimmy Hawkey except the affection of friendship," Noah said the next morn, quietly due to the dull ache in his head.

Ben pursed his lips and arched an eyebrow. "'Tis obvious there was more than that before. And the way you look at him, 'tis clear there still is."

Noah frowned. The possibility that Ben saw more clearly than he stung. He squared his shoulders. "I was but seventeen then. I'm a man of twenty years now." Old enough to control his yearnings.

Ben crossed his arms. "You acted the lovelorn seventeen-year-old last night."

Noah's stomach dropped, the image of Jimmy's chest inches from his face while he gripped his shirt in his teeth flooded his mind. He looked away so Ben wouldn't see the shame in his eyes. "'Twill not happen again."

"See that it doesn't."

CHAPTER 21

October 1626 - Merrymount

Jimmy stared out the glass window at the cold rain driving hard against the ground, splashing into gray puddles and shooting back inches into the air. Behind him, the firewood crackled in the hearth as Harry blew the flames to life.

Andrew called his name. "Come sit by the fire with us."

Jimmy didn't look away from the window. This was the kind of hard autumn rain that would last all day, robbing them of one of the few remaining opportunities to gather food for the coming winter. "'Tis a wasted day, this is." Strange how much he sounded like Floyd when he said that. An ache settled into his chest and wouldn't leave.

"So we'll work twice as long tomorrow," Harry said. "The fish always swarm the surface after a hard rain. Easy catch tomorrow."

Jimmy grunted, nodding, but didn't take his eyes off the rain. Looking across the clearing at the house Noah shared with the eight others.

Andrew's voice beside him startled him. "A rainy day always makes the heartache worse for the lovelorn soul." He put a hand on Jimmy's shoulder.

Jimmy didn't have the strength to deny it, and kept silent. Staring out the window. The heavy rain was a curtain between him and Noah's house, making it fuzzy at the edges.

"Either tell him how you feel, or find yourself another," Harry's gruff voice said behind his other shoulder. But there was kindness behind the blunt words.

"*He* has another," Jimmy said before he could stop himself. He almost cringed at how petulant he sounded. Like a child.

"Aye, I think perhaps he does." Harry's voice was softer now, gentler. He put a hand on top of Andrew's on Jimmy's shoulder and squeezed Jimmy's neck muscle between thumb and forefinger.

"We have each other, the three of us," Andrew said, kissing Jimmy's cheek. Then he stroked his chin. "Forget those bygone days. Let us distract you." He slid his hand down Jimmy's torso and beneath the waist of his trousers.

Jimmy peeled his eyes from the window and looked at Andrew. His physical reaction to Andrew's ministrations was undeniable. Some distractions were more effective than others.

Harry's hand rubbed his back, slowly circling down to rub his backside through his trousers. Jimmy pulled his shirt over his head and tossed it aside. Putting a hand on the back of each housemate's head, he pulled their mouths to his.

They lay in a three-sided pile on the deer hide spread in front of the hearth, their sweat-covered bodies glistening in the flickering firelight, bellies rising and falling with heavy breathing.

Andrew ran a fingernail languidly across Jimmy's chest, with Jimmy's head lying against his belly. "That's better, ain't it, Jimmy?"

"Mmm," Jimmy said, eyes closed.

Harry turned his head from where it lay on Jimmy's thigh and rolled onto his side to look at Andrew. "Who could ask for more than this? We found paradise here, my boys. This is where we belong."

"Here's to Merrymount!" Andrew said, grinning and raising a hand in salute. "May it shine as a beacon to every lost soul in New England."

"Here, here!" Harry said, propping himself up on an elbow.

Jimmy's smile was more muted. If this place had existed three years ago, perhaps he and Noah could have come here then ... and they'd be together today.

If they'd known to fight for what they had.

"Sounds like the rain's let up some," Harry said, looking toward the window. Then, overly loudly, "Hallo there! We have ourselves an audience!" Harry sat up and pointed at the window.

Half a face peered past the side of the glass, watching them. It disappeared in an instant, but not before Jimmy recognized the eyes and the wavy brown hair beneath the hooded cloak.

"I told you they were lovers," Benjamin said with a triumphant gleam in his eye. "Now we have proof. I saw it with my own eyes. There they were, the three of them all together, taking each other in their mouths."

"What's so shocking about that?" Sam asked from the other side of the house. "I remember the Bristol docks. It ain't as if you've never had someone in your mouth, Ben."

Robbie covered his mouth to mute his giggle.

"*That's* not the point," Ben said, scowling. "It was all *three* of them, all together."

Noah sat on the edge of the hearth, hugging his knees to his shoulders. Staring at Benjamin's feet.

Sam shrugged. "What do we care about that? Let 'em do what they want. We're all free here, remember? This ain't New Plymouth."

Ben crouched in front of Noah, the swoop of brown hair falling into his eyes. He pushed it back from his forehead and put a hand on Noah's arm. "I know you think about him still. But he's moved on to others, and we know it for certain now. He doesn't care for you like I do. And I do care for thee."

Ben had slipped into the familiar, but Noah just nodded without a word. The sharp stab to the heart from the news had dulled into a numbness. Even Ben's tender words now didn't bring any warmth. He felt nothing at all.

"Wampanoag men take two wives," Ralph said, stirring the coals in the hearth with an iron rod. A salacious grin spread across his mouth as he turned toward the room. "Ye think the gals always take turns?"

Robbie giggled again, louder this time, and covered his mouth with both hands.

Ben glared at Ralph. "And do you want two wives, Ralph Mason?"

A crack of laughter escaped Ralph's lips. "Wives? No—but some nights I wouldn't mind the attentions of two gals at the same time."

"I'm going out," Noah said, standing.

"In the rain?" Robbie asked.

"I'll go with you," Ben said, also rising.

Noah shook his head and grabbed a cloak off the hooks beside the door. Ben's damp cloak hung next to it, smelling of wet wool. "I need to think."

Only a light rain fell when he crossed the clearing and hiked toward the wooded fields, and he didn't immediately pull up his hood. The cold raindrops on his face and scalp gave him the jolt he needed to rise out of the numbness. His boots splashed into big puddles and sucked up mud, but he ignored all that.

He hadn't believed it any of the times Benjamin had suggested the possibility that Andrew and Harry were Jimmy's lovers. It seemed so preposterous. He remembered the innocent way Jimmy had kissed him three years ago, so tentative at first, and it was unimaginable that he could have strayed so far off a normal path. No, he'd thought—Jimmy, Andrew, and Harry were good friends, and there was nothing more between them than that.

But hadn't he told Ben that he and Jimmy were no more than good friends?

His cheeks heated. He'd been a fool. A naive fool.

The rain had knocked most of the leaves from the trees, and their branches waved bare in the wind. Piles of brown leaves covered the cabbage patch where they'd been working this week. That would complicate the rest of their harvest. Time was of the essence—they needed to bring all the cabbage heads in before the first freeze.

"Noah!"

Jimmy hurried toward him from the village, his cloak billowing behind him and the front of his shirt getting wet. And clinging to him. Noah forced his eyes upward to Jimmy's face. "Hello."

"I have to speak with thee."

"Why didn't you tell me?" he asked, refusing to return the familiarity.

Jimmy stopped in his tracks. He looked down, but didn't answer.

"Why didn't you tell me?" Louder this time, harsher.

Jimmy took a long breath, his chest rising against the wet woolsey and then falling again. He kept his eyes down. "Because I still wanted thee. Because I thought perhaps thou wouldst tire of thy other beau, and if thou knew the truth about me and Harry and Andrew ..." His voice trailed off. He made a weak little shrug and then looked up at Noah.

"I wouldn't want you anymore," Noah finished for him. "You were right." He pulled his hood over his head and turned away.

But as he trudged across the carpet of wet brown leaves, the heaviness of the lie tugged his heart into the pit of his stomach, and the tears flowed harder than the rain.

CHAPTER 22

NOVEMBER 1626 – MERRYMOUNT

"Your eyes are closed again." Benjamin rolled off the top of Noah, plopping onto the mattress beside him. "You're thinking of *him*."

Noah's thoughts tumbled. "I always close my eyes when we kiss. So do you."

Ben frowned. "You close your eyes all the time now. When I'm on top of you, when you're on top of me—you never look at me anymore. You're imagining being with him."

"No, of course not!"

"You're lying." It was a lie, of course. Noah often imagined Jimmy's hands on him instead of Ben's, the feel of Jimmy's lips, Jimmy's hips grinding into his ...

Ben rose from the bed, tugged on his trousers and shirt with his back to Noah. Noah lay still, watching, unable to think of anything to say. Ben turned around with his stockings in his hand. "I think you should stay in one of the other houses from now on."

Noah bolted upright. "What? Why?" He swung his legs over the side of Ben's bed, took Ben's free hand in both of his. His throat was tight, but he managed to croak out, "Don't send me away. I want to be here with you."

"No, you don't." Ben looked away, stared at the floor. His eyes glistened, and he blinked rapidly.

"I do!" Noah yanked on Ben's hand, then again until Ben looked at him, scowling. "My home is with thee." It was only then, slipping into the familiar, that Noah realized they'd stopped using it. When had they done that?

"There are others. You can't stay in this one. I don't want to see you every time I turn around."

Noah screwed up his face. Ben was being silly. Theirs was a small settlement. Even if he moved to a house across the clearing, they would still see each other multiple times a day. "Where will I go? It's too late in the season to build a new house."

Ben's lips tightened into a thin white line. "Ask your friend. I'm sure he'll take you in." He pulled his hand from Noah's grasp and left the room, grabbing his boots by the door.

It only took a few minutes to stuff his few belongings into a canvas sack, but Noah couldn't concentrate. His mind buzzed, but not in a pleasant way. Every inch of his skin itched, and the strange aching sensation penetrated to his bones.

Ralph, Edward, and Benjamin sat around the table in the common room, glasses of dark apple cider in front of them. Edward yawned without covering his mouth. Ben wouldn't look at him. Ralph and Edward eyed the sack he'd slung over his shoulder.

"Where are you off to?" Ralph asked.

Noah shrugged.

"You're leaving?" Ralph stood, the scrape of his chair on the wooden floor echoing.

Noah shook his head. "Just finding other quarters."

Ralph and Edward glanced at Ben. Edward shook his head. "Worse than women," he muttered, and took a drink of his cider.

That stung. Noah looked away and took a step toward the door. "I'll see you at work."

Outside, snowflakes swirled in the breeze, but melted on the grass. They'd need to dig up the carrots and parsnips now, before the ground froze. Noah turned up the collar of his coat and tucked his chin down, heading for Thomas Morton's house. His foot slipped on the wet grass, and he slowed, planting his feet flat.

At the edge of the forest, on the trail leading down to the creek, Jimmy moved through the bare trees with Harry and Andrew. Noah paused to call out to him, but the shame closed off his throat and he looked back at the ground in front of him, trudging forward. Drake raised his head from the pile of dogs near the smoldering remains of the night's bonfire, took a few steps into the open, stretched, and trotted to Noah's side.

"Good morrow, Noah!" Morton beamed when he opened the door, and stepped aside and making a sweeping motion with his arm to beckon Noah inside. "I made oatmeal porridge for my breakfast—would thou like to share it?"

Noah muttered thanks and set his sack on the floor. Morton glanced from the sack to Noah's face. "I hope thy plan is not to leave us, Noah. We value thee. Thou art one of us, a true member of our commonwealth. A part of our little family in the wilderness."

Noah couldn't force himself to look Thomas in the face. He focused on the ruffled collar at his throat instead. "I've come to ask for new quarters."

Thomas stroked his chin beard. "I don't understand. Has there been damage to your quarters in the boys' house? Does the wall need repair?"

"No, sir."

"Ah, then there is some quarrel with one or more of the other boys, I presume."

Noah's cheeks heated. "With Ben, sir."

"I see." The words hung heavy with meaning. Morton moved around the table, removed a bowl from the cabinet, and scooped oatmeal porridge from the pot. "Ye cannot avoid one another, Noah. We are but a small company, still, even with the new arrivals. If ye have a quarrel, 'tis best for all that ye resolve it quickly."

Noah pursed his lips. "Moving quarters wasn't my choice." He hadn't intended the hard edge in his voice, but he wasn't sorry, either.

"Mmmm." Morton nodded slowly, looking up in thought. "The guest cottage sits empty most days. Thou may bunk there until we find more permanent lodging for thee. Now come and eat."

The tiny cottage was sparsely decorated—only a bed and a single chair adorned the one-room space—but it was more luxurious than his cottage at Weymouth Plantation had been. Noah uttered no complaint.

Wampanoag visitors often stayed for two or three days, and so they had built a cottage where they could shelter from the rain while here. As long as none came calling while Noah encamped here, it was an ideal situation.

The snow stopped mid-morning, and the sun occasionally peaked through holes in the gray sky while the boys pulled the root vegetables. The ground was cold, but still soft, and after a while Noah's fingers ached. He glanced often at Ben, who never looked back, always keeping himself on the opposite end of the patch.

Noah's irritation mounted. How childish Ben was acting.

He hurried to catch up with Ben after the lunch bell rang. "I'm staying at the guest house for now," he said.

Ben barely glanced sideways at him. "I'm surprised you're not staying with your friend Jimmy Hawkey. That's where you want to be, isn't it?"

The bitterness in his tone stung, but then Noah's pain morphed into rage. He stopped in his tracks and watched Ben walk toward the village, glaring at the back of his head.

Robbie was serving lunch in the storehouse when Noah got a plate. He was in no mood for the sympathetic look Robbie gave him. Of course they'd all heard. Rather than sitting with everyone else, he took his ham and coarse hunk of bread outside and sat by the fire. Drake trotted after him and laid across his feet, chin between his paws.

Jimmy, Harry, and Andrew entered the clearing carrying lines strung with fish. They waved and smiled at Noah on their way to the storehouse. Noah returned the wave, but not the smiles. Jimmy's gaze lingered on him until he went inside.

A few minutes later, Jimmy came out with a plate and took a seat beside Noah. "Why are you out here all alone?"

"I suppose you haven't been here to learn the latest gossip," Noah said, staring at the fire. He hated how bitter he sounded. He took a deep breath, closed his eyes for a moment, and then turned toward his friend. "Benjamin told me to find other quarters. He doesn't want me staying in the same house as him and the others."

Jimmy frowned. "But won't he see you in the fields, and at meals?"

"That's why I'm out here."

Jimmy's frown deepened. "Don't let him drive you out. This is your home, too. You are not some outcast to be pushed aside, Noah."

"I know that!"

"Then don't let him bully you."

That gave Noah pause. He was about to protest, but thought better of it, and instead asked, "You think Ben's a bully?"

"Isn't he always the one who decides what you two do?"

"No ... well, I guess usually. But I don't mind that; he has great ideas." He scrutinized Jimmy's face, but his friend's expression gave away nothing. "How do you know that?"

"I watch you two. I watch everyone," he hastened to add, and looked down at his plate to cut his ham. "And I know what I see," he added after he took a bite.

Noah finished his lunch and held the plate down for Drake to lick the remnants. He stood, but turned toward Jimmy before returning his plate. "I want to be alone for a little while."

He dipped the plate in the rain barrel, left it on the bench outside the storeroom, and hiked off into the woods with Drake.

He walked faster than usual, hands shoved into his coat pockets, nervous energy propelling him forward. It was a while before he calmed enough to look away from the trail ahead of him and gaze up at the clouds, the birds in the bare branches, the last brown leaves dangling from the ends of branches.

The tumble of emotions calmed. The cacophony of thoughts stilled into a coherent thread.

Ben was angry that he thought about Jimmy while he and Ben enjoyed each other's bodies? That sort of jealousy made Noah's skin crawl. What right did Ben have to his private thoughts? His thoughts were his own, his desires his own, and they were *no* one's business but his own.

Damn him for thinking he had the right to control how Noah felt! No more—he was twenty years old, and he would control his own feelings from now on.

The first big snowfall came two weeks later. Big fluffy snowflakes fell, blurring the view of the distant woods.

The men spent the afternoon throwing snowballs at each other, slipping and sliding in the wet accumulation, their coats and hats turning white as the flakes kept falling.

Noah and Jimmy crouched behind a rock, ducking with each barrage of snowballs Sam and Robbie heaved their way. They obliterated on impact with the stone, sending cold sprays onto Noah's face.

"Are you ready?" Jimmy asked, grinning.

Noah nodded, and together they sprang to their feet and lobbed their own collection of snowballs back at Sam and Robbie. Robbie squealed with laughter, turning his head and letting the snowballs hit his back and shoulders. Sam, kneeling to compress one to throw back, took a shot right in the privies. He doubled over, both hands on the front of his pants, groaning.

"Sorry!" Noah shouted, and then covered his hands laughing.

"I'm going to get you back for that, Noah Bancroft!" Sam yelled. But then he laughed and plopped onto his back in the snow, hands on his chest.

Across the field, Benjamin snuck up behind Ralph with an armload of snow. Ralph was too busy throwing one snowball after another at Edward, the two of them pelting each other nonstop. Then Ben grabbed the back of Ralph's trousers and dumped the snow down his backside.

Ralph howled, grabbing the seat of his pants with both hands. Ben roared with laughter, and dashed off when Ralph and Edward turned their fire on him.

"Don't even think about it!" Noah shouted to Robbie, nervous at the mischievous look on his face. Robbie knelt to scoop up an armful of snow, and Noah and Jimmy raced back toward the village, slipping and sliding and laughing the whole way.

Jimmy grabbed Noah by the arm and tugged him toward his house. "Come on, let's warm up. Looks like Harry and Andrew have the fire going already." Smoke rose from the chimney, black against the falling white.

"No, not there," Noah said, shaking his head. Then he motioned toward his cottage. Drake, bounding over from where he'd been frolicking with Thomas's dogs, went through the door with them.

Inside, they loaded some wood into the hearth, and Jimmy struck a flint until it lit. They hung their soaked stockings from the mantle and sat on the floor beside the hearth. Drake plopped down next to Noah.

"That was a great time," Noah said, nudging Jimmy with his shoulder.

"We make a great team," Jimmy said.

Indeed we do. Noah scooted closer to Jimmy, so their legs touched. Jimmy didn't pull away, so he put his hand on Jimmy's back, stroking the valley of his spine with his thumb.

Jimmy sat very still for a moment. Even his breath had stopped moving his back. A chill ran up Noah's arms. Had he overplayed? Then Jimmy pulled his shirt off and spun on his rear to face Noah. For a second, everything stopped. He touched Noah's cheek, and Noah leaned into his hand. He kissed the palm, then stared into Jimmy's eyes.

When Jimmy's lips touched his, it was as if a cannon exploded inside him. He put his hands around Jimmy's smooth, muscular back and clung tightly to him. All the pent-up longing of three years came out in that kiss, and he opened his mouth fully and let his tongue explore.

The fire had warmed the entire cottage by the time they broke the kiss. Or was that the fire burning inside him that made Noah so warm? It mattered not, and he took Jimmy by the hand and stood. They undressed and sat on the bed, side-by-side. Their hands explored, and then they kissed again, slowly lowering themselves to the blankets.

Noah kissed a trail from Jimmy's neck, down his chest and his belly, to the crook of his legs. Jimmy grabbed fistfuls of the blankets when Noah's tongue ran across his scrotum, and he gasped when it ran up the length of him. Their eyes locked and held.

They took their time exploring each other with hands and mouths. Eventually, the tension inside Noah had wound tighter than a pocket watch. He got onto his hands and knees and turned his backside toward Jimmy. He reached back to guide him, but Jimmy took him by the hand and pulled him up.

"No, like this," he whispered, and lay Noah on his back. He eased Noah's knees back toward his ears and hooked his ankles over his shoulders. Then he lowered his face to Noah's and parted his lips.

Jimmy's mouth on his muffled his cry when Jimmy entered him. But he was slow and gentle, concentrating all their focus on their kiss; and before long, Jimmy was all the way inside him, and there was no air between their bodies. They stopped to take a breath, both holding still, and Noah stared deep into Jimmy's dark eyes. Jimmy's fingers stroked the side of his face, and multitudes of meaning passed between them without a sound.

And then Jimmy started to move again, slowly at first, gradually building. Noah had never done this face-to-face, and he couldn't take his eyes off Jimmy's, touching his chin, his cheek, his hair. Jimmy kissed his fingers, sending tingles down his arm and right to his belly, and the tension inside him became too much. He arched his back, pushing his hips tighter against Jimmy's, and stars filled his vision.

Drake sat beside the bed, head cocked and tongue hanging out the side of his mouth, looking for all the world as if he were grinning. His tail swept the floor. Jimmy dropped his forehead to Noah's and they laughed.

After, Noah lay in Jimmy's arms, his cheek resting on Jimmy's chest. It rose and fell with Jimmy's deep breathing, but the thump of Jimmy's heart by his ear slowed into a comforting cadence. It could lull him to sleep.

"I love thee," Jimmy said, quietly, stroking Noah's hair. "I always have."

Noah pulled himself away from the comforting heartbeat long enough to look into Jimmy's eyes and place a kiss on his chin. "And I love thee."

CHAPTER 23

MARCH 1626/1627 - NEW ENGLAND

Thomas Morton's voice calling his name roused Noah from a deep slumber, and he had to wipe drool from his mouth as he sat up. He looked around the cottage, bleary-eyed, but Jimmy had already left.

"Noah Bancroft!" Morton's shout repeated across the village green.

Noah sprang from the bed, the chill of the late winter morning seeping through his nightshirt, and he pulled on his trousers under it. "I'll be there presently!" He donned his stockings and shoes, and didn't remove the nightshirt until he was ready to pull on his shirt in quick replacement. He was tucking it into his trousers and wrapping the front tails around his privy parts when Jimmy opened his door.

"Mr. Maverick is here. He's asked for you, but he doesn't look cheery this morning."

That *was* odd. Samuel Maverick was the cheeriest person Noah knew. And why on Earth would he be calling at this early hour? He had to have set out before dawn. "I'm just coming."

The open space encircling the crest of the hill was still mostly white with snow cover, but a few bare places had appeared here and there over the last several days. Boot-prints frozen solid in the silver-hued dirt made walking treacherous. It was a breezy morning, and the shadow lines of clouds moved across the ground faster than a man could run.

Maverick stood next to the smoldering remains of last night's bonfire, a brown woolen cloak draped across his shoulders. A serious expression lined his face as he talked with Thomas Morton. He didn't smile when he saw Noah walking toward them with Jimmy.

"I am sorry to wake thee, Noah," Maverick said, his tone somehow gentle and yet ominous at the same time. "I have come to ask thy help. Since thy father was a physician, our hope is that thou would know certain remedies we might give to David Thomson to break his fever. The sickness is severe—dire, even—else I would not ask thee to do it."

Icy dread radiated from the center of Noah's gut, and he stood rooted in place, staring at Maverick but unable to answer.

"I know what thou fearest there." Maverick held up both hands in reassurance. "Please come. I have assurance from Mrs. Thomson that they will not attempt to reclaim thee."

A tingle of apprehension swept through Noah's belly. "Thou said my name?"

"She already knew of whom I spoke when I said I know the son of a physician." Maverick took a step toward him and put a hand on his shoulder. "Amias Thomson is an honest woman—if she gave her word not to reclaim thee, she will not go back on it. And her husband is feeble of body, and often not of conscious mind, given the state of his fever."

Noah hesitated, and looked to Thomas Morton for advice.

"I would not have called for thee if I thought it unsafe," Morton said.

"I told them not of your whereabouts, only that I can fetch thee to them," Maverick added.

Noah imagined his mother telling him he must do his best in this world, and the next would take care of itself. David Thomson might be a stern and oppressive master, but he was a man, a fellow child of God.

He took a deep breath, and then nodded. "I'll go."

Jimmy's hand touched the small of his back. "I'll go with thee."

"As will I," Morton said.

Noah took a moment to think back over all the fever patients he'd seen his father treat. "We need to collect willow bark, a lot of it." He turned to Jimmy. "Find a stand of willow trees and collect as much bark as thou can." Then to Maverick, "Go to the creek near the shore and pull up two marshmallows by the root. Bring them to me, root and all."

While Jimmy rushed into the woods and Maverick hurried down the hill, Noah took a moment to think. His hands trembled. He'd forgotten something, he was certain of it.

"Leeches cleanse the blood," Morton said.

That was it! There was a stagnant pond out past their fields, less than a mile. If it wasn't frozen over, they'd find leeches there, hiding in the mud. "Dost thou have a jar we can use?"

"I do indeed."

It was about a half-mile trek, down the more gently sloped backside of their hill to where the pond sat in a little divot surrounded by tall stands of bare trees. Part of the shoreline was rocky, and other areas had strips of wetlands with cat-o'-nine-tails. Noah made for the boundary between the two.

"Not long after we arrived in this country, some of our boys took a dip in this pond on a hot afternoon. They came out of the water covered in leeches. We could hear their cries from the village." Morton cackled. "City boys don't know that stagnant water carries leeches. The rest of us had a good laugh at their expense. It covered them in red welts for days."

Noah tugged at a midsize rock, discouragingly stuck to the ground. Still partly frozen. Morton helped, groaning with effort, and it gave way with a reassuring sucking sound as it separated from soft mud. Noah took Morton's long iron tweezers from inside his cloak and plucked out two leeches. Their slow squirm as he dropped them in the jar told him they were barely awake from winter slumber. But they would do the job. He and Morton moved on to other rocks.

By the time they returned to Merrymount with a jar full of leeches, Maverick was already waiting for them with two tall marshmallows. Their roots dripped muck onto the still frozen ground. "We'll prepare them when we get there," Noah said, looking toward the woods. No sign of Jimmy yet.

Jimmy appeared several minutes later, arms clutching a gigantic pile of willow bark to his chest. "This was all I could carry," he said. "I dropped a few pieces on the way back."

Noah almost laughed in spite of the nerves tumbling around in his stomach. "That's plenty. Let's put it in a sack."

Roger Hodges waited on the wharf to meet Maverick's shallop, and his eyes widened when he saw Noah. "We thought you were surely dead," he said after tying off the ropes. He looked past Noah at Jimmy. "Or gone over to the Indians." That carried an unmistakable note of disapproval.

"Neither is true," Noah said after jumping onto the pier. He bore no hostility to Roger. But no warmth, either. "Take us to Mrs. Thomson."

Amias Thomson's smile was obviously strained, but she welcomed Noah back to Thomson's Island. Noah resisted the urge to tell her the sailors' charts still labeled it Noddle's Island, and instead said he was happy to help. A lie, but it seemed to please her.

"We've applied leeches," she said, looking at the jar in Morton's hand. "But the fever worsens."

"What do we need to do first, Noah?" Maverick asked.

"Ye have boiled water?" Noah asked Amias Thomson.

"We have a pot heating for the laundry," she said. She turned to Roger. "Add wood to the fire, bring it to a boil."

Noah looked at Maverick. "Strip the leaves from the marshmallows and chop them up as finely as you can. Then do the same to the roots. Toss away the stems. When the water boils, put them into a bowl and ladle water over them."

Then he looked at Jimmy. "While Mr. Morton and I go to the sickroom with the leeches, cut two handfuls of bark into strips. Soak them in the boiling water for ten minutes, and then bring the pan to me."

Jimmy nodded, but glanced sideways at Amias Thomson waiting midway up the stairs. His eyes brimmed with worry.

"I won't leave him alone with them." Morton put one hand on Jimmy's shoulder and used the other to pull aside his jacket to reveal the pistol tucked at his side.

Jimmy's eyes hardened, and he nodded. He touched Noah's hand on his way past.

Noah mounted the steps behind Amias Thomson, his heart rising into his throat. He followed her to the back bedroom, where David Thomson lay beneath a stack of woolen blankets, pale and thin. His eyes were closed, his mouth open. Amias touched his forehead, which glistened with a sheen of sweat.

"He's burning up, hot as ever."

Noah stood rooted in place several feet from the bed, staring at the hated man lying there. For several seconds, he couldn't make his mouth or his feet move. Then Morton touched his back, and it was as if he'd awakened from a bad dream.

"Let's put leeches on his chest, and one on each side of his nose," Noah said, picturing patients in his father's study, where he'd often stood at the door as a child.

Amias lowered the blankets and raised the nightshirt, revealing two red welts on her husband's chest. Morton opened the jar, and Noah carefully removed four leeches with the tweezers, applying them to the four corners of Thomson's chest. Then he took two more and put them on the sides of Thomson's long and narrow nose.

That woke him up, and Thomson's pale eyes searched until they rested on his wife. She placed a hand on his shoulder, and his gaze shifted to Noah. It took several seconds before they registered recognition, and then they widened and he sucked in a breath through his mouth. "The runaway returns," he said, voice raspy.

The words sent a shiver up Noah's spine and raised goosebumps on his arms. But he squared his jaw and stared back at the sick man, defiant. "I've come to treat your fever."

A cough raked the man, and he turned his head away from Noah. He looked frail, pathetic, and Noah's fear vanished.

Maverick entered with a steaming bowl. He extended it to Noah, who nodded toward Amias Thomson. "Have him drink this. It's marshmallow," he said when she took it.

"All at once?" she asked, brows knit in doubt.

Noah shook his head. He wasn't certain, but he must appear so. "A little at a time." At least, that's what he remembered seeing his father's patients do. He couldn't remember his father's instructions to them, though.

He didn't know how long the leeches were supposed to stay in place, so he hesitated to remove them. Better to let them suck too much blood than too little, wasn't it? That made sense, so he waited until Thomson had finished drinking the marshmallow broth before he told Morton to remove the leeches.

Jimmy arrived then with the pan of soaking willow bark. Noah had him set it on the table, and then he took the tweezers to remove a strip of bark from the hot water. It steamed in the chill air, and he waved it a few times to cool it before extending it toward Amias.

"Have him chew this until it's mush. Give him another one in an hour." That's what his father had instructed patients, wasn't it? It sounded right.

Maverick stood next to Amias Thomson and put a hand on her shoulder. Morton and Jimmy went downstairs with Noah.

"We should wait here until his fever breaks," Morton said.

The idea of remaining in this house made Noah's skin crawl, but he nodded and took a seat at the table between them.

Maverick came down a half-hour later. "His fever's not broken, but it's lower." He took an empty chair and pulled it next to Noah. He sat and took Noah's hand in both of his. "Thanks, my friend. It was very brave of thee to come here, and it was an honorable thing. I'm proud to know thee."

"I'm glad it helped." In truth, he wasn't confident it would.

"Mrs. Thomson will keep giving him the willow bark, and I'll fetch more marshmallow from my land. She has leeches at hand, so there's nothing more thou can do here, Noah. I'll take ye home."

Noah, Thomas Morton, and Jimmy climbed onto Maverick's shallop. Noah's heart pounded, fearing that any second someone would come rushing out of the house to seize him and drag him back. A pair of the

Thomsons' servants pushed them off, casting sideways glances at Noah. While Morton and Jimmy conversed in the ship's bow, Maverick called Noah to join him at the wheel.

"Thy Indian friend, Jimmy Hawkey," Maverick said quietly, nodding at the pair standing in the bow. "He kept his eye on everyone in the house. He was on his guard every minute ye were on the island. I suspect if anyone had laid a finger on thee, your Jimmy would have knocked him out cold. He cares for thee, that one."

Noah nodded, a lump in his throat making it difficult to swallow.

"I'm glad thou found someone special."

Noah froze. He dared not look at Maverick, and stared instead at the sail flapping in the icy wind. But the curiosity became too much, and after what seemed an eternity, he ventured a glance sideways. Maverick's bright blue eyes held no malice, no condemnation—only warmth. The relief that washed over Noah like a wave from the bay choked up his throat, and he looked across the gray water so his friend wouldn't see the tears flow.

Maverick put an arm around Noah.

When he'd regained his composure and wiped away the wetness from his cheeks, Noah looked back at Maverick and forced a grin. "What about thou, my friend? Was there a special someone in England? Or someone who returned with Captain Gorges? Thou could send for them."

A sad sort of smile graced Maverick's lips, and he looked back toward Noddle's Island. "Alas, my heart is set on someone I cannot have. She belongs to another. And for her sake—and by the grace of God—I'll do my best to help her husband recover from his illness." He looked back at Noah. "To send for someone else to join me here would be a prison sentence for both of us."

Samuel Maverick didn't join the Merrymount colonists for the New Year's feast on the twenty-fifth. But he came up their hill at dusk on three days later, while the company came in from clearing the winter fluff from the fields. He removed his hat.

"Mr. David Thomson passed from this life to the next this morning, the twenty-eighth of March in the year of our Lord sixteen-hundred and twenty-seven. We pray for his widow, Amias Thomson, his two sons, and three daughters. May God rest his soul."

The colonists bowed their heads, and Thomas Morton removed his hat. "God rest his soul," everyone echoed.

Noah ate supper in silence, rarely looking up from his plate. He had no words for the emotions swirling and battling within him. He was officially free at last, but also ashamed that he had failed to save Mr. Thomson's life. He had failed. They would all judge him for that, and he couldn't bear to look at anyone.

David Thomson had mistreated him, and he hated him for it; but if God forgave the man for that—and he certainly did—then it was Noah's duty to forgive him, too. The peace of forgiveness eluded him, however.

Birdsong greeted him when he opened his eyes, the warm yellow light of a spring dawn shining through his window. He yawned and stretched, the promise of a new day filling his chest like the fresh spring air he inhaled. March the twenty-ninth would be a new start.

Jimmy was approaching his door when Noah stepped outside a few minutes later. The look on his face chilled Noah's contentment, and Jimmy's dark eyes flashed a warning. He nodded backward over his shoulder.

At the table next to Thomas Morton sat a young man with flowing waves of blond hair, a long face bearing a serious expression, and the black clothing and white collar of a clergyman. Next to him sat a young woman with a plain round face framed by brown hair pulled back under a white bonnet, her pale hands resting on the enormous bulge beneath her russet brown dress.

"Ah, here is our last man, Mr. Cheswick," Thomas Morton said, motioning Noah to join them. "Noah Bancroft, I present the reverend Mr. Jonathan Cheswick, newly arrived from London with his good wife, Miriam. Mr. Cheswick has been appointed minister for Weymouth Plantation."

"Good morrow," Cheswick said, rising to give Noah a firm handshake. His deep blue eyes seemed to bore into him, as if reading the secrets in the deepest part of his soul, and Noah had to look away. "You are a late riser, Mr. Bancroft."

"Not usually, sir," Noah said.

"Mr. Bancroft received some troubling news yesterday, and I fear he had a fitful night," Morton said.

"Ah, then we pray God's peace will find you this day." Cheswick's eyes still bored into him. His words carried the harsh nasal accent of the eastern shires, and it grated Noah's ears.

Noah muttered thanks and took a couple of steps away. Jimmy appeared at his side, but kept a larger distance than usual.

"Now that we've made introduction to all at this plantation, my wife and I will take our leave," Cheswick said to Morton, nodding. "We thank you for the breakfast, kind sir. But now we must sail up the bay to call upon our other neighbors." He took his wife's hand and helped her carefully rise from the bench, her back arched until she found balance.

Only after the minister and his wife had their backs to them did Jimmy touch Noah's hand, briefly, for barely a second. They exchanged a look. A minister at Weymouth Plantation—a mere five miles away—was a troubling development.

Morton escorted the Cheswicks across the clearing, where John Bursley, Will Jeffries, and James Ludden stood with unreadable expressions on their faces. The three of them accompanied the Cheswicks down the hill toward the wharf, but the minister paused to look back at Merrymount and the men who watched him leave.

"A very fine plantation you have, Mr. Morton. We shall visit ye often. Good day."

PART THREE

"THY LIBERTINE WAYS WILL DAMN THEE."

"Thy libertine ways will damn thee."

CHAPTER 24

Spring 1627 - New England

Noah and Jimmy wove long strands of flowers into a garland before dinner. Others were stringing floral garlands from house to house, encircling the center of the village and its giant maypole. "If this is like last year, Mr. Morton will have us all dancing naked tonight under the moon," Noah said.

Jimmy stopped working momentarily to run his eyes down to Noah's lap, and then slowly back up with a grin. Noah whacked him on the arm, laughing. But his mind flooded with the images from last year—of him and Benjamin running back to his bed. Of how it was the first time they'd ever... he gulped and hoped Jimmy didn't notice.

"This will be our biggest revel ever," Sam said when he and Robbie came for their latest garland. "Thomas expects more than two hundred Indians tomorrow, from all directions, plus the white folks from up-bay, and the men from Weymouth Plantation and Nantasket."

"Not their pastor, I hope!" Noah said with more levity than he felt.

Robbie laughed, but Sam shrugged. "I doubt he'll want to attend. Thomas says Mr. Cheswick's a Puritan, and they don't approve of maypoles and dancing."

"Besides, his wife just had a baby not a week ago," Robbie said. "He'll want to stay at Weymouth Plantation and look after 'em."

"Noah says we dance naked tonight," Jimmy said, very matter-of-fact, and Noah's cheeks heated.

Robbie giggled and covered his mouth. Sam's grin was crooked, but he shrugged. "Not *completely* naked. Our legs were covered." Robbie burst out laughing, almost doubling over.

"We dressed as satyrs," Noah said to Jimmy.

"I don't know what that means."

"Neither did we, until last year," Robbie said.

"Satyrs are from Greek mythology. Half man, half goat." Noah swallowed hard. "And always naked." And according to the pictures in Mr. Morton's book, always with enormous erections. He left that unsaid, but his face burned hot.

Jimmy looked at him with an amused twinkle in his dark eyes. "Then I look forward to tonight's adventure."

Noah had never seen Merrymount so crowded. Massachusett Indians from the Neponset and Charles River villages; Samuel Maverick and the Walfords from up-bay; the four fishermen from Nantasket; John, Will, and James from Weymouth Plantation; plus others from Naumkeag across the bay that he'd never seen before but that the other boys knew from Bristol. Indentured boys that Thomas Morton had recruited in Bristol, but Captain Wollaston had sold at the Essex station before they landed here, Noah was told.

Some danced around the maypole, others engaged in raucous and bawdy conversations that echoed across the clearing, and everyone drank more beer or fortified wine than necessary.

Around mid-afternoon, Thomas brought out casks of whiskey to whoops from dozens of the Indian men who rushed to him, cups in hand.

Noah curled his nose. "I don't like that nasty brew."

"Why not?" Jimmy asked.

"It burns. And it goes right to your head, makes you crazy."

Jimmy laughed. "I think we have enough of that here already!"

Next to them, Edward Gibbons buried his face in the cleavage of an Indian girl, making loud gobbling noises like some sort of rambunctious child. She squealed with laughter and thrust her chest forward, tugging the top of her deer-hide dress lower.

Jimmy took Noah by the elbow. "Let's get something to eat."

While they ate wild turkey and washed it down with beer, Sam Weaver came galloping through the clearing shirtless, carrying Robbie Ellis on his back. Robbie was shirtless and barefoot, and swung his shirt over his head while smacking Sam's chest with the other hand. "Gidd'up!" Sam neighed like a horse.

Noah laughed, but Jimmy glanced nervously at a cluster of their white visitors. "This isn't Cape Cod," he muttered.

"What do you mean?"

But Jimmy just shook his head. "They're getting a little bold in front of strangers, that's all."

Not far away, James Ludden lay in the grass, chin in his hands, rubbing noses with an Indian girl who lay facing him. On the other side of the clearing, Edward's hands were all over the girl he was with, even sliding up her legs under her dress. Ralph was kissing two Indian girls at the same time, arms entwined, barely pausing for a breath.

"I think everyone gets bold on May Day," Noah said with a grin, nudging his elbow into Jimmy's ribs. Jimmy grunted, and Noah cocked his head at him. "What are you thinking?"

Jimmy was silent a moment, and then drained his mug. "It doesn't matter. Let's get some more beer."

The celebrants grew ever louder as the evening shadows stretched across the clearing. The Walfords bid everyone farewell and descended toward the wharf; Samuel Maverick shook Noah's and Jimmy's hands a while later before returning home himself.

Noah's head buzzed from too much beer, and his whole body was warm and tingly as he leaned against Jimmy. The latter had lost his shirt somewhere, at some point. Noah had barely noticed until he laid his cheek on Jimmy's shoulder.

Benjamin took the hand of one of the young men from Naumkeag across the bay, looking back to make sure Noah noticed. With his other hand Ben stroked the young man's arm, holding Noah's gaze for several seconds before leaning close to the young man's ear, lips moving but no sound reaching Noah. The pair hurried off toward the woods, and Ben looked over his shoulder at Noah with a smirk.

Noah rolled his eyes and sighed. That might have hurt a few months ago. He laid his head back on Jimmy's shoulder and rested his hand against Jimmy's firm belly, the warmth of Jimmy's smooth skin radiating through his hand and up his arm.

He'd gotten the better end of the deal.

Thomas Morton's dancing around the maypole grew ever more exuberant, arms gesticulating every which way. A distance away from the village—but hardly out of vision—Edward Gibbons lay buck naked atop his girl in the grass, her hide dress hiked above her hips, his pale buttocks a stark contrast to her brown legs wrapped around them. Ralph had retired to his cottage with four Indians—three women and a man—all of them in various stages of undress and physical affection, and none of them having remembered to close the door.

Noah could only giggle at the spectacle, followed by a hiccup. He clamped a hand over his mouth but then hiccuped again. This time Jimmy laughed, and Noah had to laugh with him, interrupted at regular intervals by additional hiccups, which only served to fuel their laughter.

"Mr. Cheswick, welcome! I'm so pleased you joined our little revel!"

Thomas Morton's booming voice grabbed their attention, and Noah's face snapped toward the young clergyman standing at the crest of the hill on the path from the wharf, mouth hanging wide open and the whites of his eyes clear even from this distance.

James Ludden released the hand of the Indian girl he'd been holding, and surreptitiously slipped his shirt back on. John Bursley and Will

Jeffries both dropped their mugs, spilling beer onto the ground, the foam spraying onto bystanders. John and Will disappeared between the houses. Noah craned his neck and spotted them sprinting down the eastern trail toward Weymouth Plantation. A moment later, young James hurried after them, calling for them to wait for him.

"Mr. Morton! I... I..." Words seemed to escape Jonathan Cheswick, and he stood there gaping at the activity, which hardly paused to acknowledge his presence.

Thomas took Cheswick's hand in both of his, pumping it too hard and making his arm swing. "May Day is still upon us, Mr. Cheswick! Let us make merry to mark the occasion, as has been done in merry old England since time immemorial. Come! I will fetch you some food and drink."

Cheswick wrested his hand from Morton's grip. He swept his arm across the gathering. "What a display, sir! Must I remind ye that drunkenness is against the law in England, and in all of her realms?"

Jimmy put his arm around Noah and tugged him backward. "Let's get away from here," he whispered. The warmth of his breath on the side of Noah's neck made him smile before he recognized the danger facing them.

His brain was working slower than usual, but when it finally hit him, the fear chilled him to the core. It was a forgotten, yet all-too-familiar fear, something he hadn't felt in over a year now—not since they'd cast out Lt. Fitcher and told Captain Wollaston never to return. They'd been free for all of that year, free even to act on those most forbidden impulses. And he'd grown too accustomed to that, too lax.

Jimmy pulled his hand, and together they ran behind the storehouse.

"'Tis indeed unfortunate that such copious amounts of drink are required before men and women feel free to return to their natural state," Morton was saying, his voice fading into the background as they fled.

They stopped short before colliding with Philip Davies hidden behind the stone well with a pair of their Native guests. Phil had his left hand up the dress of a young woman, and his right hand inside the breechclout of a young man. He grinned at Noah and Jimmy. "Don't mind us." Jimmy pulled Noah along to the far side of the storehouse, out of sight.

It was as if everyone else on the other side of the building disappeared into nothingness. All Noah could see was Jimmy standing in front of him, panting from the run, sweat glistening on his chest and belly. Everything else blurred. His heartbeat roared in his ears. He grabbed Jimmy round the waist and pulled him to him, smashing his mouth against his.

He broke the kiss long enough to pull his shirt over his head and toss it aside. The hunger in Jimmy's dark eyes matched that within him, and his fingers flew to Jimmy's belt buckle, then to the buttons on the front of his trousers. Jimmy's hands did the same to Noah's.

Jimmy tugged Noah's pants down, then dropped to his knees and took Noah in his mouth. Noah leaned his head back against the storehouse wall, closed his eyes, and let his mouth hang open. He dug his fingers into Jimmy's thick hair and allowed all of the sensations to course through him—the physical, the emotional, all of it swirled inside his belly and his mind as a warm and colorful mélange.

Just when Noah thought he was about to explode, Jimmy rose slowly, kissing a trail up his belly before flicking a tongue over his nipple and then kissing the crook of his neck, sending shivers down Noah's spine. "We have an audience," he whispered, his voice husky, almost hoarse.

Noah glanced sideways. Jonathan Cheswick stood in the shadows at the corner of the storehouse, his eyes locked on them. But instead of hanging open in shock, his lips were barely parted; and his hands at his sides weren't clenched in fists, but hung relaxed. He seemed almost fascinated by what they were doing.

Jimmy took his open trousers and wiggled them over his hips, letting them drop. Then he pressed his body fully against Noah, slowly grinding his hips into Noah's. His face was turned toward their observer. One hand on the small of Noah's back pushed him harder against Jimmy, while the other dropped to his buttocks and squeezed, the fingers tracing the space between. More shivers ran through Noah, raising goosebumps everywhere, from his arms to his ankles.

"Just like Cape Cod," Jimmy whispered.

"What?" Noah's voice came out breathless.

"This is just like at Cape Cod, last summer," Jimmy said, brushing his lips along Noah's jawline. "Always an audience. Always someone wanting to watch. Wanting you to give them a show."

Alarm bells went off in the back of Noah's brain. Images flashed. Vicar Aubrey watching him and Lance; not looking for a show. David Thomson catching him in the closet with his pillicock in his hand; not looking for a show. But the warm buzz enveloping his mind muted the alarm, and the touch of Jimmy's body and hands silenced the rest.

Forget the past. Jimmy would protect him. He closed his eyes and surrendered.

Jimmy's hand turned him around, and then he was pressing himself against Noah's back and backside. His manhood slid between Noah's buttocks, rubbing up and down. Noah opened his eyes and looked at Jonathan Cheswick, still standing in the same corner, unmoving except for the way his breath visibly rose and fell. Noah's eye flicked down to the obvious protrusion at the front of Cheswick's trousers, and he looked back at the minister's face and smiled at him.

Jimmy found his forbidden entrance and pushed inside him. A cry escaped Noah's lips, and then he grinned even bigger at Jonathan Cheswick. The minister's eyes widened—but not in shock. No, there was something else in those eyes, but it wasn't horror. The rising and falling of Cheswick's chest quickened.

Then all of a sudden his shoulders squared, his hands fisted, eyes narrowed into slits, and his mouth tightened and contorted. An unintelligible, almost animalistic cry rose from his lungs, ringing in Noah's ears and drowning out the rush of his own pulse.

Then Cheswick stalked off toward the woods and disappeared into the deepening dusk.

Noah's heart turned to ice and sank into the pit of his stomach. They had been careless.

CHAPTER 25

SUMMER 1627 - MERRYMOUNT AND PLYMOUTH

It was almost a week before Noah could bring himself to talk to Thomas Morton about it. He was ashamed of how careless they'd been. He was ashamed of how foolish he had been. The one lesson he'd learned above all others in his nearly twenty-one years was that he must always hide his desires.

Always.

He approached Morton after breakfast, when everyone went out to their assigned work. "May I have a word with thee, Thomas? In private?"

Morton's smile faded when he studied Noah's face. "Come with me. We go into the forest. We shall hunt for the night's supper." He grabbed two muskets and whistled for the dogs.

They'd gone at least a half-mile into the forest before Noah summoned the courage to put words to what he needed to discuss. "Last week ... at the revels ... Mr. Cheswick saw Jimmy and me ... we were naked, and, well, paying amorous attention to each other. The way a man would to a woman."

Though they'd talked around it many a time, Noah had never stated it directly before. Once the words left him, his nerves evaporated. It was as if someone had loosened an invisible belt around his chest. His breath released. Drake, trotting beside him, cocked his head at him, ears perked.

"I see," Morton said, remarkably calm, stroking his chin and looking off through the trees. "And how did our Mr. Cheswick react to such a spectacle?"

Noah snorted. "He watched us. He watched us for a long time. And then he got mad angry."

"Mmmm," Morton said. "I might have guessed."

Noah wouldn't have. Not in a hundred years. "We've put the plantation in danger. Mr. Cheswick will tell others, and Jimmy and I will hang for it." Despondency came rushing back like a gust of wind when he vocalized the dreaded punishment, and his shoulders slumped.

Morton put a hand on his shoulder. "No one under the protection of *my* colony will hang, I assure thee."

"But Mr. Cheswick will insist."

"Mmmm. He might. But there be no one here with the authority to hang ye, Noah. At worst, Mr. Cheswick will write to the Council about our misdeeds, and the Council will write to me that I must hang the 'deviants' and rid the colony of the vile cancer that threatens to eat us alive. I will consign the letter to the fire, and that will be the end of it."

"How could that be the end of it?" Noah asked, eyebrows bunched.

Morton chuckled. "Unless the Council see fit to come hither themselves—which, after these many years, they show no inclination to do—then they cannot truly oversee us so far afield from them. For all of their grand schemes, New England will remain a wilderness sparsely populated, and we will be left to our own devices, young man."

Jonathan Cheswick marched into Merrymount two weeks later, leather Bible clutched to his chest, looking uncomfortably hot in his black clothing. That wasn't likely the reason for his fierce scowl, however.

"This don't look like a social call," Harry muttered as they sat at the table in the center of the clearing, gathering for lunch. Noah's heart pounded despite Morton's assurances during their talk in the woods. He exchanged an anxious look with Jimmy.

Thomas Morton ignored the minister's demeanor entirely, and beamed greetings.

Cheswick nodded as his sole acknowledgement. He strode to the head of the table and opened his Bible. His voice as he read was loud enough to echo off the walls of the surrounding houses.

"And when the people saw that Moses delayed to come down out of the mount, the people gathered themselves together unto Aaron, and said unto him, 'Up, make us gods, which shall go before us; for as for this Moses, the man that brought us up out of the land of Egypt, we wot not what is become of him.' And Aaron said unto them, 'Break off the golden earrings which are in the ears of your wives, of your sons, and of your daughters, and bring them unto me.' And all the people brake off the golden earrings which were in their ears, and brought them unto Aaron. And he received them at their hand, and fashioned it with a graving tool, after he had made it a molten calf: and they said, 'These be thy gods, O Israel, which brought thee up out of the land of Egypt.' And when Aaron saw it, he built an altar before it."

He looked up with eyes full of fire, and swept his arm toward the eighty-foot pine trunk at the center of the village.

"This *symbol* ye have made for yourselves, this *maypole*, is but an idol like the golden calf of Horeb! When the children of Israel made for themselves an idol instead of trusting in the Lord their God, and danced and feasted before it, the Lord suffered them to wander in the wilderness until all of that generation were gone. When the children of England—the new Israel—make for themselves an idol, and dance and feast before it, they do show forth the *depravity* of their natures, in violence against the love of God. Repent of your wickedness, lest ye fall before the Lord's hand!"

The chirping of distant birds, and of crickets in the tall grass, was the only sound. Everyone at the table stared at Cheswick, some with mouths open, others scowling. Noah broke out in cold sweat, his pulse rushing in his ears. But then he crossed his arms and glared at the minister. How dare he come into their home and insult them so?

Thomas Morton alone appeared unmoved. "I see that you are a man of great eloquence, Mr. Cheswick. Your gift of oratory does without doubt lend itself to many a fine sermon. But 'tis a false analogy you make between our maypole and the golden calf of Horeb. We ascribe no divine power or insight to this maypole, my good man! 'Tis a symbol of nothing more than timeless tradition in the shires of old England. We feast and dance around said maypole in celebration of the bounty of spring, which we rightly ascribe as a gift of our most gracious God after the fearsome winter months. And we share that feast with our neighbors, as indeed our Lord and Savior commanded that we love our neighbors as ourselves. What could be more Christian than such sharing, I ask?"

"Dancing is a sign of wickedness, Mr. Morton." Cheswick's eyes narrowed to slits. "The dancer's movements, of hip and of belly, mimic the movements one makes in the marital bed, and is therefore unfit for public view, and a danger to the moral rectitude of an upright citizenry."

A thin smile stretched Morton's lips. "Your fears are unfounded. No less a luminary than the great King David, most righteous before the Lord, did write in the Psalm: *'Let them praise his name with dancing.'*"

Cheswick's lips pursed. "Marital relations between unmarried persons—as I witnessed at your debauched 'revels'—is fornication, and Paul lists fornication among the sins that will keep the unsaved from the kingdom of heaven. And far worse even than that ..." he flipped his Bible several pages and read. *"Thou shall not lie with mankind as with womankind; it is abomination."* He flipped another page. *"If a man also lie with mankind as he lieth with a woman, both of them have committed an abomination: they shall surely be put to death; their blood shall be upon them."*

Morton raised a finger. "Aye, but the Lord Jesus himself taught, *'Blessed are the merciful, for they shall obtain mercy.'* We are merciful Christians at this plantation." Then he pointed his finger at Cheswick himself. "And Jesus also said, *'Let him who is without sin cast the first stone.'*"

Noah leaned forward, a smile slowly spreading. Had Mr. Cheswick gone pale? He was certainly angered—Cheswick's exhale through his long nose was audible at the opposite end of the table where Noah sat.

"Even the devil can quote scripture to suit his own purposes." He stretched taller. "As indeed he did when he tempted our lord. But our savior in his righteousness prevailed against the perversion of God's word."

"Aye—but which of us is the devil in this analogy, Mr. Cheswick? You, or I? I know which *I* believe it to be."

Cheswick's brows shot skyward, and his mouth opened without words. The boys hooted laughter, and some slapped their hands on the tabletop in appreciation.

A thrill rushed through Noah, and he couldn't help grinning.

"We should pray," Cheswick said, and without waiting for agreement he bowed his head.

If he'd expected a simple blessing on the food, Noah was mistaken. After the blessing, Mr. Cheswick launched into a request for God's grace to repent and see the light. The prayer went on and on, and eventually Noah opened his eyes and peeked around. Others around the table were doing the same. Only Thomas Morton and Edward Gibbons still had their eyes closed, though Edward shifted in his seat and fidgeted his folded hands.

When at last Mr. Cheswick said "Amen," the boys dug into their food. The ham had gone cold, though Noah didn't mind that; he made a face after shoving a bite of beans in his mouth, though.

Jonathan Cheswick remained standing.

"Please take a seat and eat with us, Mr. Chewick," Morton said. Cheswick looked around the table, hesitant. His eyes landed on Noah and stared.

"Jesus ate often with sinners, Mr. Cheswick," Noah said, smiling as sweetly as he could manage.

Cheswick nodded, one firm motion, and sat. "If I am to minister to the lost souls I find, it is best if we nourish ourselves for the endeavor." He took a knife and stabbed a slice of ham from the platter, dropping it onto the plate Morton put in front of him.

"I noticed you did not make the sign of the cross when blessing the food, Mr. Cheswick," Morton said.

A gleam came to Cheswick's blue eyes. "The cross is but a symbol; it bears no power of its own. Its use in prayer is a distraction from true piety."

"Mmmm. A Puritan you are, then?"

Cheswick stiffened briefly, but then forced a smile. "I preach the Reformed faith. Some in England call that devotion 'Puritan.'"

"*Reformed* by definition of John Calvin, I presume, sir?"

"Among other reformers, yes. John Calvin's writings illuminate the Christian faith and practice in a most remarkable way. We in England who carry forth the Reformed tradition work to purify the Church of England of its latent papist rituals. Our efforts are opposed by bishops who cling to papist ways, for their own power, and who seek to keep England in darkness."

"Then why venture forth to New England, if you have work yet to do in England?" The gleam in Morton's eye said that he was enjoying this taunting.

Cheswick sucked in a breath. His brow knit. "I was called here after several months spent as a prisoner of His Majesty in the Tower of London. I was consigned there after a disagreeable appearance before the Star Chamber."

"Star Chamber?" Noah asked. The name sounded familiar, but he couldn't place where he'd heard it.

"A court in the Palace of Westminster, used to bring the king's justice when judges and magistrates refuse to do so," Morton said. "Powerful men who remain out-of-reach of the shire courts can be brought before the Star Chamber, where the king's Privy Counsellors adjudicate." He looked at Cheswick. "Given that you are not a powerful lord, Mr. Cheswick, one assumes that your magistrate sympathizes with your Puritan views—I mean, Reformed religion."

Cheswick stared back, tight-lipped.

The rest of the meal passed in uncomfortable silence.

The company returned to their chores after lunch. Noah and Jimmy walked, hoes in hand, toward the fields, where they were assigned weeding the bean patch. Sam and Robbie, on their way to weed the wheat field, walked beside them, and Sam made a joke about fornication, hands clasping at the air in front of his hips and moving back and forth. They all laughed, and the tension of the meal evaporated.

"Don't let that parson see you," Robbie said, grinning.

"I suspect he could use the lesson," Sam quipped, and they laughed again.

Feeling someone watching, Noah glanced over his shoulder. Jonathan Cheswick followed a dozen paces behind. He raised his hand in greeting. "I'd appreciate the opportunity to observe your labors."

Sam shrugged, stone-faced. "If it suits you."

They reached the edge of the field, parting around the statue of Priapus. They rubbed the end of his enormous erection as they passed, Sam and Robbie going right toward the wheat field, while Noah and Jimmy went left to the bean patch. Jonathan Cheswick followed a few paces behind Noah after skirting wide around Priapus.

"Ye have excellent fields," the minister said, nodding at the expanse of green rows between the trees. "God will bless your efforts even more if you turn your faces toward his countenance."

"I pray every night," Jimmy said.

This startled Mr. Cheswick even more than Noah, whose eyes only widened half as much as the minister's.

"I am most pleased to hear that, Mr. Hawkey," Cheswick said through a tight smile. "Might I suggest when you pray that you add the entreaty, 'Remove the desire for abomination from my heart, oh Lord, and strip away the loathsome curse that staineth my soul.' Pray it diligently, and the Lord will reward you."

"Are those the word you pray, Mr. Cheswick?" Noah had to grin at the image of Jonathan Cheswick stripping away his clothes while praying for the Lord to strip away his curse.

Cheswick scowled. "You are an impertinent young man, Mr. Bancroft."

"You watched us for a long time," Jimmy said, staring down the minister until he took a step back and looked away. "I saw the look in your eye, and it wasn't loathing you felt."

"Impertinent!" But Cheswick's voice was little more than a hoarse whisper. Then he straightened, and stared back at them. "'Twas a hangable offense, what ye did. I would overlook it, if ye repent of it."

"And if we don't?" Noah put his arm around Jimmy's waist and looked back at Cheswick with defiance.

Cheswick's lips pursed. "Then I will have no recourse but to report the offense to the authorities at Plymouth Plantation, and let their sheriff deal with ye according to the law."

Jimmy slipped from Noah's grasp and stomped toward Cheswick, not stopping until a mere foot in front of him. He jabbed his finger at the minister's long nose. "If anyone comes to hang my Noah, I will kill you myself." He raised his hands in a circle around Cheswick's neck. "I will kill you with my hands while you watch me do it."

Cheswick went as white as a sheet and stumbled backward several steps. Then his face and neck turned crimson. "Devils!" he shouted, pointing at them. "The Lord God will not let your evil rest unanswered. By one means or another, the land will be cleansed of ye!" He spun on his heel and marched back up the hill.

The meeting house at Plymouth Plantation was spacious, big enough to hold all of the colony's three hundred residents, but only two men sat across from one another a week later.

"I did not expect to see you again so soon, Mr. Cheswick," Governor William Bradford said in his nasal Yorkshire twang. "What trouble brings you here?"

"Forces of evil are at work in the land, Mr. Bradford," Jonathan said. "I am steadfast in the Lord's work, but I confess that alone I am not able to counter this evil and protect the people of God from it."

Bradford leaned back, lips pursed, and exhaled slowly. "You speak of Mr. Morton's plantation—his Mare Mount, or Merrymount, or whatever name he calls it this year." He shook his head. "I believe I know of which you came to speak to me. We have heard reports from many quarters concerning the drunkenness and dancing at Mr. Morton's weekly 'revels.' I have written to the Council concerning these things—but Mr. Morton has many friends on the Council, and my pleas fall on deaf ears. They do naught to restrain his excess."

"Drunkenness be the root of it, but there be far worse to convey to your excellency," Jonathan said.

Bradford's eyebrows rose. "Oh? What more did you witness, Mr. Cheswick?"

"They invite the savage Indians among them, the near nakedness of their menfolk an affront to Christian souls, though they at Merrymount worry themselves not for it. Then they invite these Indians for their consorts—both *men and women*. 'Tis a shocking display, the lot of them dancing and frisking together ... and worse practices, as well." Jonathan looked away.

Bradford leaned forward, hands gripped so tightly his knuckles turned white. "What worse practices? Speak, man! Declare the sin so that the Lord may absolve thee of complicity in it."

Jonathan swallowed hard. "I have seen men and women fornicating in plain sight. And I have seen ..." his voice faltered, but Bradford's stern unwavering gaze pushed him on. "I have seen men fondling and ... and buggering one another like the demons of Hell."

Bradford held up a hand. "Speak no more of it, lest it burn thy tongue and my ears."

Jonathan nodded, sweat beading on his forehead and upper lip. "And they have carved for themselves a pagan god to look over their crops and bring fertility."

Bradford exhaled hard. "'Tis a serious charge—though I daresay traces of paganism abound, what with all of Mr. Morton's references to Greek gods every time he opens his mouth."

He snatched a piece of parchment and a quill, and furiously scrawled several lines of script before folding it and hiding it inside his coat. "Mr. Morton is himself a barrister of some note, so we must gather evidence of his crimes as thoroughly as we may. Continue your ministry to the Weymouth and Nantasket colonists. As you are moved, call upon Mr.

Morton and his lot and do what you can to turn them from their evil ways—or report what they refuse to repent. We will build God's city only by cutting the cancer from the body."

CHAPTER 26

APRIL 1628 – MASSACHUSETTS BAY

Noah strained against the horizontal oak trunk they used as an axle for the millstone. His legs and buttocks burned with the effort, and his shoulders ached. Ralph Mason pushed on the opposite side, and together they spun the millstone in a slow circle. Robbie Ellis stayed a few steps ahead of it, tossing the newly-harvested winter barley onto the grindstone. Their breath crystalized in the chill air, but Noah felt as hot as a summer day from the labor.

They'd been going at this all morning. Thomas wanted to brew a half-dozen barrels of beer before the May Day revels, and that required grinding a hundred and twenty bushels of barley—six acres' worth.

"You men are slowing down!" Sam said with a grin, on his way to the storehouse from the field with another basketful of newly-picked barley. He paused to slap each of them on the buttocks as they passed. "Push harder! Grind faster!" He laughed and resumed his march to the storehouse.

"He won't be laughing anymore when we lay his pillicock under that millstone, that's certain," Ralph said, huffing with the effort.

"I'd miss it, but it would serve him right," Robbie said.

Noah didn't have the energy to laugh.

"Visitor!" Sam called from the front of the storehouse. Noah and Ralph stopped pushing the axel, and Noah hung his arms over it, panting.

Samuel Maverick hiked up the hill from the wharf, raising his arm and calling "Halloo!"

Noah pulled himself upright and stepped around the end of the axle, waving at his friend. Thomas came out from the storehouse. "Welcome, Mr. Maverick! What brings you calling today?"

Maverick swept his hat off and bowed with a flourish of his hand. When he stood he had a cheeky grin, and plopped his hat back on his head, tilted jauntily to the side. "I have come to invite ye to my wedding on Sunday next, to the widow Amias Thomson, née Cole. I would be honored if ye joined us, Midday at the Thomson home on Noddle's Island. The Reverend Mr. Blaxton will solemnize the rites when Mistress Thomson becomes my wife, and we will celebrate with a feast."

Noah beamed at his old friend. "Congratulations!"

"Congratulations, indeed!" Thomas shouted. "Come, join us for a midday repast, and we will toast your upcoming nuptials."

Maverick bowed. "I thank you for the kind invitation, but alas, I have many more plantations to visit this day before my toil is complete. Good day." He touched the rim of his crooked hat, and sauntered back down the hill toward his waiting shallop.

A dozen Merrymounters sailed on Thomas Morton's shallop to Noddle's Island on the appointed morning. Samuel Maverick was at the wharf greeting arrivals, while the Thomsons' servants tied up the vessels. They ignored Noah when he stepped off the ship, not even looking at him. Envious of his freedom when they still had two years left of their indentures?

Mr. Blaxton looked a little thinner than Noah remembered him, but the minister recognized him. "My, but you have grown up, Mr. Bancroft. How old are you, now?"

"Twenty-one years, sir," Noah said. "May I introduce my best friend, James Hawkey?"

"*Kui Kwasind.*" Mr. Blaxton said a few more sentences in the Massachusett tongue.

Jimmy said something back in that strange, guttural language, before switching to English. "You're a well-known person in this country, Mr. Blaxton, and I'm pleased to meet you at last."

Blaxton's eyes widened at the unexpected Cornish lilt. "Ah! You've spent time in England. That is excellent. I endeavor to translate the scriptures into the Massachusett tongue, though my knowledge of it be limited. I must rely often on assistance from Indians who speak English. And if my ears do not deceive me, Mr. Hawkey, you speak both tongues with equal eloquence. Am I correct?"

Jimmy nodded. "You are correct, Mr. Blaxton."

"Would you make yourself available to me one morning each week? I would gladly pay you for the work."

Jimmy glanced at Noah, but Noah only gave him a little shrug. It sounded like boring work, and they didn't need money, but perhaps Jimmy would enjoy it.

"I would be glad to help you, Mr. Blaxton. Perhaps Noah could come with me, if that would not trouble you? He's eager to learn the ways of this country."

"Yes, of course. Tuesday?"

They agreed, and Mr. Blaxton moved on to another conversation. Jimmy turned to Noah. "Perhaps you could wear the breechclout you made, and fit the role."

Noah almost missed the tiny curves at the corner of Jimmy's mouth. He whacked him on the arm.

Another shallop arrived shortly after, carrying about twenty men and women from Naumkeag, on the north shore. Jimmy went to the wharf to greet them, catching Noah by surprise. He shook hands with a man in a modest brown suit and tall hat, about mid-thirties. He walked with the man and his wife onto shore, and motioned Noah over.

"This is Thomas Gardner, and his wife Margaret. Mr. Gardner was one of the overseers of the Essex Station on Cape Ann, who welcomed my father and me. Mr. and Mrs. Gardner, this is my best friend, Noah Bancroft."

"How do you do, young man?" Thomas Gardner said, shaking Noah's hand. Mrs. Gardner bobbed her head.

"It seems only the original Essex colonists have come to Mr. Maverick's wedding," Jimmy said, looking over the group. "Not either Mr. Conant, or Mr. Oldham, or any of the others?"

A strange look came to Gardner's eye. "Roger Conant does not approve of Mr. Blaxton's conformity to church ritual."

Jimmy looked over the score of others who'd come from Naumkeag. "There is a difference of opinion among the planters, then?"

Did Gardner wince? It was subtle, so Noah couldn't be certain.

"We are of accord on Reformed practice and belief," Gardner said, seeming to weigh his words. "But most of the original planters sent by the Dorchester Company tolerate the Book of Common Prayer, though we do not embrace it. Roger and Christopher Conant, Mr. Oldham, and others who came with them, are less inclined to accept its practice by others."

Jimmy grunted, and Noah wondered what he was thinking. His dark eyes gave away nothing. "How do ye fare in your new settlement?"

Gardner's expression relaxed. "Quite well, thank you. The soil at Naumkeag is more fertile and less rocky than that which we tried to cultivate at Cape Ann, and our harvests have been bountiful. Our fishermen bring in as many cod as they did at Cape Ann, which brings the colony profit."

"Mr. Tylly and the others, they still reside at Cape Ann?"

"Aye, a small company still resides there, and Mr. Tylly oversees them."

Noah couldn't help wondering what more they left unsaid. After Mr. and Mrs. Gardner had moved on to talk with Samuel Maverick, Noah asked, "What was that all about?"

"Roger Conant, who leads the colonists at Naumkeag, is a prig."

"Is he as priggish as Mr. Cheswick?" Noah asked, nodding toward the ketch arriving with the six residents of Weymouth Plantation, including Mr. and Mrs. Cheswick and their infant.

Jimmy's eyes narrowed. "'Tis himself that offends himself."

Jonathan Cheswick's eyes scanned the crowd after helping his wife onto the dock. His eyes stopped when he spotted Noah and Jimmy, and rested on them for several long seconds. There was something intensely disquieting about the intensity of his stare; but Noah resisted the urge to look away, staring back in as much defiance as he could muster. Then Cheswick scowled and looked away.

Amias Thomson came out of the house then with her five children in tow. She wore a bright green frock to match the season and carried a bouquet of fresh daffodils in her hand. Samuel Maverick hurried to her, offered her his arm, and together they walked toward Mr. Blaxton. The crowd collected in a crescent around them.

At the feast following the wedding, the new Mrs. Maverick smiled at her guests, but snapped often at her three daughters, and thrashed her two rambunctious sons. She even tongue lashed her new husband for failing to rein in the boys in front of their guests.

At their table, Thomas Morton shook his head and made a "tsk-tsk" sound. "Our Mr. Maverick is as strong as Samson, and as patient as Job. But I fear Amias Maverick be a difficult Delilah who will take his masculine virtue."

Noah glared at the new Mrs. Maverick before he remembered himself. "He loves her so."

"Aye, he does at that. If only she loved him as well."

Noah looked at Morton, cocking an eyebrow. "If she loves him not, why would she marry him?"

Morton chuckled, a twinkle coming to his eye. "She had many a suitor over the last year since her husband's demise. Suitors came by water from all about the bay to court her, English women being in short supply. And she with a rich inheritance from her Mr. Thomson. But she demurred until came a letter from her father, ordering her back to England and threatening to deprive her of her property. So she gave her hand to our Mr. Maverick, removing herself from her father's command, and giving the property to him and thus keeping it from her father's clutches."

Noah stared at her. He could hardly blame her for doing what she must to keep her freedom. Such that it was as a married woman, that is. She had chosen a gentle husband, one who would not take a strong hand against her will. And yet, he was furious that she'd pulled the wool over his friend's eyes.

"'Twas a willing blindness," Morton said, as if reading Noah's thoughts.

Noah's cheeks heated, but he couldn't argue.

Jonathan Cheswick approached Thomas and Noah a moment later. Thomas greeted him with a big phony smile. "What did you think of Mr. Blaxton's performance, Mr. Cheswick?"

Noah nearly laughed at the pointed question, and how Cheswick stiffened.

"He strayed not from the Rites of Marriage in the Book of Common Prayer, as I expected," Cheswick stated. "Many of us of the Reformed persuasion have little quarrel with the marriage rites, though there are a few small things that we omit."

"Indeed," Thomas said, smile never fading.

Cheswick cleared his throat. "I learned from the men in my flock—the three at Weymouth Plantation, and also the four at Nantasket—that you plan to host a pagan festival on May the first."

Morton's smile remained steadfast. "I would not fashion a traditional May Day revel as a pagan festival, Mr. Cheswick."

Cheswick frowned. "Young master James Ludden told me you announced that you seek to ring in the 'Reign of Comus.' He knew not the reference, being but an innocent."

Noah had had to explain the reference to several of the Merrymount men, as well. Comus, the son of Dionysus, was the Greek god of excess and of nightly dalliances. The Reign of Comus was an Italian painting from a hundred years ago, featuring a naked drunken revel.

"You can't possibly believe he meant that *literally*, can you?" Noah said with as much derision as he could summon. Next to him, Morton grinned.

Cheswick scowled. "I suppose not—but even metaphorically, it is troubling. Drunken debauchery, fornication—you lead these young men into the arms of Satan, Mr. Morton. Thy libertine ways will damn thee."

His use of the familiar struck like a glove to the face, and Noah's hands fisted.

Morton was unperturbed. "My dear Mr. Cheswick, let me assure you that we observe the Sabbath at Merrymount, with Sunday morning scripture and prayer as ordered by the Book of Common Prayer. You need not fear that any of our lads be bound for Hell—though in probability a spell in Purgatory awaits a great many of us before we see the gates of Heaven."

Cheswick's lips pursed as tight as a cat's ass. "Purgatory! Bah! The Church of England would do well to purge itself of that unchristian belief. There is no basis for it in scripture—only Heaven and Hell are attested by the Lord Jesus Christ, and Hell awaits those who forsake his righteous teaching."

Morton closed his eyes and nodded graciously. "Time will prove it."

"Indeed it will. You have been forewarned Mr. Morton. I pray ye heed the warning. Good day, sir."

As the Puritan minister marched away, Morton chuckled and turned back to Noah. "I suspect a night of Dionysian excess would do him well, were he ever to relax enough to partake of it. But he will not, because the public expects that he would never. Fear not—our aim shall steer us clear of religious busybodies, who are only motivated by appearances."

Thomas Morton clapped his hands for attention after their shallop sailed away from Noddle's Island.

"My boys, I have an excellent idea! 'Tis time to make official what I have proposed for the last few years—that Englishmen should take

Indian maids to their bosom as wives. As Mine Host of Merrymount, I have authority to wed any who belong to the plantation. This May Day we will solemnize marriages between ye and the fair Indian maids."

A cheer arose from many of the young men surrounding him. But icy fingers of apprehension rose from Noah's belly to encircle his heart. Surely Thomas didn't mean *all* of them. He exchanged nervous glances with Jimmy, Robbie, Sam, and Benjamin.

Thomas put a hand on Noah's shoulder. "If it be in a man's nature to want a wife, then a wife he shall have. If it be not in his nature to desire this, then it will not be forced upon him here."

Jimmy was quiet all evening, barely speaking at dinner, or after dark when he and Noah sat by the fire. After they got into bed, he laid his cheek against Noah's belly, and placed his hand on the inside of Noah's thigh.

Noah stroked his hair. "What is it?"

Jimmy sighed, and didn't answer right away. Noah waited.

"I have never wanted to marry," Jimmy said at last. "At twenty-two years, it's expected that a man seeks a wife, to share his home and his life. I've never looked forward to that. Harry and Andrew were resigned to it, and I talked them out of submitting to it."

He paused, and turned to look up at Noah, resting his chin on Noah's navel. "But seeing Mr. Maverick's wedding, I wished something. I don't know how to describe it. I don't want a wife, but I want thee. I don't want thee to be my wife, though—I just want thee, as thou are, as we are ... but forever. I wish ... I don't know. We can't marry, but I still want to be with thee forever. I want thee to be with me forever, until I die. Just like married people, except like us instead." He closed his eyes and sighed again.

Noah touched his cheek, and Jimmy opened his eyes. "I think I know what thou mean. I promise thee, I will stay with thee forever."

Jimmy kissed his belly, and slid up his body slowly, planting kisses until he reached his mouth. "And I promise I will stay with thee forever."

CHAPTER 27

MAY 1628 - MERRYMOUNT

Sunlight glinted through the leaves above them. Three couples stood in front of Thomas Morton in the center of the village, wreaths of flowers on their head. Ribbons connected the wreaths of bride and bridegroom. Thomas read from the Book of Common Prayer. The couples said the church-approved vows, everyone prayed the official prayers, and with an impish grin Thomas blessed them with the sign of the cross like a vicar and pronounced them wed.

The crowd raised their beer mugs and toasted the happy couples. It was early, and no one was too far into their cups yet.

Noah took Jimmy by the hand. "Come with me."

He led Jimmy past the houses to the wooded fields, where Harry and Andrew stood with Thomas in front of the Priapus statue. Floral wreaths decked Harry and Andrew's heads. Jimmy looked at Noah, open-mouthed, and Noah grinned. Jimmy looked behind them at Sam, Robbie, Benjamin, and a few others following.

"After our promises the other night, I asked Thomas if he would do this for us," Noah said. "I thought thou would like that."

Jimmy's mouth still hung open, but he closed it and swallowed before nodding.

Thomas handed them a pair of wreaths, and Noah placed one on Jimmy's head before donning his own. Then Sam, Robbie, and the others gathered behind them. Jimmy looked at Sam and arched an eyebrow. Sam laughed and shook his head. "Not me!"

Thomas cleared his throat. "While ye cannot wed your beloveds, in ancient times the bonds between pairs of beloved men were solemnized before the gods. The Sacred Band of Thebes were elite soldiers, one hundred fifty pledged pairs of lover and beloved, who swore their allegiance and fealty to one another unto death. All of Greece lauded them as the bravest and most loyal of men, and sang their praises across the land." Thomas opened a dusty book. "Let us begin. Give your beloved your right hand, if you will."

Noah's belly tingled when he took Jimmy's hand. Jimmy looked calm and composed, contrasting with Noah's pounding heart. Jimmy had to feel his pulse through his hand.

"Look at your beloved. Do ye swear an eternal oath to protect your beloved with your life, and to never surrender your position together? If ye swear it, say 'I do.'"

"I do." Noah's grin was so wide it hurt his cheeks, but he didn't mind.

"Then let us raise a cheer for the lovers and their beloveds. Cheers!" Thomas raised a glass, and everyone behind them shouted "Cheers!"

After drinking their toast, the group headed back to the village. Edward Gibbons stood above them on the path, arms crossed and scowling.

"Hallo, Edward!" Thomas said, still beaming. "What brings you here?"

"Curiosity at what you lot were doing," Edward said, biting. "Fake weddings? For pairs of men?"

"Not weddings, my good man—shared oaths, in the ancient fashion of the Sacred Band of Thebes."

Edward rolled his eyes. "What in the world is that?"

"Only the most feared and beloved company of soldiers in ancient Greece."

"Looked just like the weddings earlier to me."

Thomas clapped a hand on Edward's shoulder. "Come! Let me get you another glass of beer."

A sudden clap of thunder rattled the house. The mugs and flatware in Thomas Morton's cabinet clinked against one another as it shook. The simultaneous flash of light illuminated the rain pelting the windows.

Noah looked up from the book he'd been reading next to a candelabra in Thomas's library. "That was a close one."

"A tree's fallen near here, that's certain," Jimmy said.

"I don't envy Thomas, staying at Weymouth this night. There's bound to be leaks in those houses, after sitting uncared for these four years."

Another flash of light illuminated the space, followed by a boom of thunder. At least this one didn't rattle the house.

When Thomas went to Weymouth Plantation to trade for supplies, he asked Noah and Jimmy to look after his house in his absence. It had been two weeks since the May Day revels during which they'd sworn their loyalty oath to one another. Noah had spent those weeks on top of the world. He couldn't get over his amazement that this kind of happiness was possible for someone like him.

Jimmy stood and stretched, yawning. Noah unashamedly lifted his eyes from the book to the way Jimmy's shirt rose to reveal his belly as it stretched. "Storms like this are only good for going to bed. Are thou coming?"

Noah flipped the book closed. Jimmy didn't have to ask him twice.

A pounding at the door caught their attention. They looked at each other in disbelief, and the pounding repeated.

"Who could be out in this?" Noah hurried to the door and unbolting the lock.

Thomas Morton stood on the other side, soaked clothing stuck to his skin. Rivulets of water ran down his face and dripped from his hair. He marched through the door and slammed it behind him.

"The swine! The filthy swine!"

Noah watched him rush by, then hurried to catch up with him. "What happened?"

"Captain *Shrimp* and his militia surprised me at Weymouth," Morton said, using his nickname for Captain Miles Standish. "They held me in a house and questioned me about supposed 'crimes' I have committed. Mr. Cheswick was their witness, though he confessed under my cross examination that he had not witnessed any of the supposed misdeeds of which he accused me. I demanded from whence he'd obtained his information, and he would say only that it was someone who attended our revels on May Day."

Morton stopped at the cabinet and poured himself a glass of fortified wine. He took a solid gulp before setting down the glass too hard, making Noah and Jimmy wince at the crack of the glass on wood. How the glass didn't break, Noah would never know.

"I pressed him for the identity of his informant, but he would not yield the name. No matter how much I insisted that English liberties guarantee the accused the right to face his accuser, *still* he would not relent. And nary would Captain Shrimp compel him."

"They let you go, then?" Jimmy asked.

Thomas scoffed. "Not at all. They insisted I go with them to New Plymouth to face trial. A trial without the key witness, I reminded, but nonetheless they locked me in the house, planning to take me thither on the morrow. Their worthy guards fell asleep, and masked by the noise of the storm I broke the lock and ran free. I did not stop running until I reached our fair Merrymount, and indeed the good Lord sent lightning aplenty to illuminate the path hither. Finding this door locked for the night, I was compelled to pound my fist until ye answered. I apologize if I woke ye from slumber." A wry smile graced his lips. "Or disturbed other activities."

Noah blushed, but Jimmy said, "Not yet."

Morton threw his head back and laughed. A flash of lightning at that second cast his face in a garish light, and the booming thunder masked his laugh.

"Come! We must prepare!" Morton said, throwing an arm forward and leading them to a storeroom. "I have four good guns and three pounds of dry powder. Should Captain Shrimp and his six worthies brave the storm to come hither, we will be ready for them. Do I have your pledge to aid me in this quarrel?"

"Of course," Noah said. He owed everything to Thomas Morton. "You have it without need to ask it."

Evening shadows spread long across the village when Jimmy came sprinting in from the Weymouth trail.

"They're coming!" he shouted, breathless, and skidded to a stop in front of Thomas and Noah. "Nine of them—Captain Standish and eight others."

A crowd of Merrymounters gathered around them, and several nervous faces turned toward Thomas.

"If they be nine in number, then we are the more numerous, my boys. We shall face them down in defense of our fair plantation. Get your guns!"

Morton hurried into his house, and the others went to their own houses to fetch their guns.

"It's *him* they want, not us," Edward said. "Why risk our own necks? If we don't fight them, they'll leave us in peace."

"Shut your mouth, Edward Gibbons, you craven bastard," Ralph snapped, reaching for the musket his new Indian wife handed him.

Edward stiffened. "I'm only being practical. Thinking of the whole plantation, I am. We're all of us coequal partners, remember? Why risk that? If he's innocent of what they say, then let him face the trial and go free."

Something clicked in Noah's brain. "It was you, wasn't it?" he said, pointing his finger at Edward. "You were the one that told Mr. Cheswick whatever it was that they accused Thomas of. Confess it!"

Edward smirked. "Let a judge and a jury decide if he did what they accuse."

Noah stomped right up to Edward's face. "A jury of Brownist hypocrites! He can't get a fair trial, and you know that. You knew it all along. What are you after?"

Edward turned away. He went into his room and slammed the door.

"Forget about him," Sam said, taking Noah by the arm and turning him away.

Noah, Jimmy, and the rest of the men collected in Thomas's house, and he barred the door.

"Here they come," Jimmy said from the window.

A fist pounded on the door. "Thomas Morton! Surrender yourself, and we will grant you quarter." That was Miles Standish; Noah would recognize his Lancashire accent anywhere.

Thomas looked calmly at the young men gathered around him. "Let us show them what they are facing by coming against our plantation, my boys. Put your guns through the port holes."

Noah and the others flipped open the port holes and thrust the gun barrels through.

"Lay down your arms, and we will grant ye quarter!" Miles Standish shouted, switching to the plural.

"And face prison for these supposed 'crimes?' We say 'nay!'" Thomas shouted back.

"We mean not to detain ye," Standish said, "but to send ye back to England."

"I am the son of a soldier, my good man. I will not lay down my arms, having taken them up in just defense of our plantation. And if ye plan to send me over to England, they be needful while at sea."

"Unless you plan to shoot a leviathan with your musket, Thomas Morton, you need it not. Lay down your arms, and we grant ye quarter."

In the silence, Jimmy cocked his musket, so Noah did the same. He aimed through the port hole at the only militiaman he could see through the tiny space. This man also had his musket raised and aimed at the house; but he could not see within, and Noah could fire right into his belly.

After several interminable seconds of silence, Thomas shouted to them, "I wish not to see the shedding of your worthy blood, as would issue if we played upon ye out these port holes. If offer myself to yield upon your quarter, so long as no violence be made upon my person, my possessions, or the members of my household. Ye take me, and let my men remain at liberty. And that ye leave me my arms to take with me to England. With those terms, would I capitulate."

Seconds ticked off before Standish shouted, "Come out of the house, and we will accept your terms, Mr. Morton."

"Don't do it," Noah said, taking Thomas by the arm. "Do not trust them."

"I am a man of my word, Noah Bancroft. And I will hold them to theirs. Lower your weapons." When all of the muskets had been pulled out of the port holes and lowered, Thomas unbolted and opened the door.

They fell upon him immediately, yanking the gun from his hands, and then forcing him face-down to the ground. Standish stood over him, arms akimbo. "Thomas Morton, you are under arrest for the crime of selling firearms to the savage Indians, and for the crimes of drunkenness and lewdness. The rest of ye, disperse at once."

One militiaman put his knee between Thomas's shoulder blades and pushed down hard, eliciting a yelp, while another bound his wrists.

"You swore no violence against him!" Jimmy yelled.

Miles Standish regarded Jimmy through narrowed eyes. "One does not make a bargain with a monster, but takes the monster down by any means necessary." Three militiamen surrounded Jimmy. Two of them seized his arms, and the other snatched his musket. Jimmy struggled, and it took all three of them to hold him, but they gripped him tighter, forcing him to his knees.

Noah rushed to them. "You promised no harm to his household!"

"If ye leave quietly, no harm shall come to ye," Standish said. Noah towered over the man, but he glared up at Noah uncowed.

"Then what about him?" Noah nodded at Jimmy. "He did nothing to resist ye, yet ye seize him like a criminal."

"He is an armed Indian, a hostile, and proof of Thomas Morton's crime of selling firearms to the savages." Standish motioned to his men, and the three of them drug Jimmy out of the house. Two more raised Thomas by his bound wrists and marched him out. The remaining three took their muskets from the rest of them, and then rummaged through the cupboards, tossing Thomas's silver into empty sacks.

"Thieves," Ralph muttered. "No better than common thieves." Noah barely heard him as he rushed past on his way out the door.

Outside, Standish and his men marched Jimmy and Thomas down to the wharf. A shallop tied up there, and Jonathan Cheswick climbed the hill toward them. "Is this the savage what threatened your life, Mr. Cheswick?" Standish called, pointing at Jimmy.

"That be him," Cheswick said, and stopped to wait for them. "He's called James Hawkey. He said he would kill me with his own hands, a year ago at this very plantation But I remember it as though it were this morning."

"Then you are under arrest for threat of murder, James Hawkey."

Noah stood at the crest of the hill, fists clenched in impotent rage, watching them march Jimmy and Thomas to their ship. Jimmy looked back, and their eyes held until they forced him onto the boat facing toward the bay.

CHAPTER 28

MAY 1628 - PLYMOUTH AND MERRYMOUNT

It took two days to journey overland to Plymouth Plantation, thirty-five miles southeast over the Blue Hills, pulling three sleds loaded with beaver pelts. When Noah asked for help, Harry, Andrew, Sam, and Robbie had agreed at once. Benjamin agreed after Harry and Andrew strongly suggested he join them.

Drake trotted along beside Noah when they left, and it broke Noah's heart to order him to stay. But it was too dangerous to have him along, not when silence and subterfuge were required. The dog sat obediently, but watched him go with his head cocked and ears perked, his eyes sad and confused. Noah turned around often to tell him to go home, but the dog sat in the same spot until Noah could no longer see him.

He tried not to think of that during the journey.

Noah had never been here. More than any other colony or station in New England, New Plymouth looked like a proper English village, with a church, a mill, several smithies, and dozens of houses lining straight dirt lanes.

"I've been here, once," Harry muttered as they hiked through the plantation's fields. "Sold some fish here a few years ago. We'd heard from others that they were in dire need, and so we brought a boatload to them. They treated us like lepers, but they took our catch. Never came back. Never had to."

A man in the field who identified himself as John Billington assumed they came to trade and directed them to the storehouse in the center of the village.

"It's a safe bet they're keeping Thomas and Jimmy somewhere near there," Sam said after they left Billington behind.

"I'd wager it's that house," Noah said, nodding at a cottage on the central square with stocks in front of it. Thankfully, the stocks sat empty. At least they'd spared Jimmy and Thomas that humiliation.

"We'll investigate the back of it." Harry nodded for Andrew and Benjamin to come with him.

Noah, Sam, and Robbie continued to the storehouse, passing between the empty stocks and the cottage door. The only window was small and high set, so nothing within was visible.

"You two go in and barter the furs," Noah said. "I'll wait out here and watch for signs."

"Shout for us if anyone makes trouble," Sam said, and disappeared inside with Robbie and the three sleds.

Plenty of comings and goings kept Noah's attention. New Plymouth was home to three hundred people, and the daily business of an English village continued steadily. Several people cast curious glances in his direction, which turned more suspicious the longer he stood there. This might end up a waste of time.

But at last his patience was rewarded when Jonathan Cheswick emerged from the suspected jail house. His face was bright red, and he stomped the other direction. Noah eased back into the shadow of the storehouse door. That building was far too small to be the Meeting House, or the home of Governor Bradford; it *had* to be the jail house. There could be no other reason for Mr. Cheswick to be calling there, since he was not the plantation's minister. And something Jimmy had said had infuriated Cheswick. Or shamed him.

Noah slipped inside. Sam was deep in negotiations with the man in charge of the storehouse that day, but Robbie caught Noah's eye. Noah nodded once to indicate that their assumption was correct.

The three of them left the storehouse a short time later, sleds loaded with supplies of cloth, pewter dishes, and copper kettles. They found Harry, Andrew, and Benjamin near the edge of the fields.

"That's the place, I'm certain of it," Noah said. "I saw Mr. Cheswick leave."

"Harry got on the tips of his toes and peaked inside the back window," Andrew said. "Our Jimmy sat upon a bed, with two armed militiamen keeping watch."

"I didn't see Thomas," Harry said. "So after we returned to the lane we asked a woman we passed if it was true they'd arrested the scoundrel Thomas Morton. That got us an earful!" He chuckled.

"They're taking him to the Isles of Shoals," Andrew said. "The ship left this morning."

Damn! They'd missed him. "Not to England, then?"

Harry grunted. "That was a lie. They never intended to pay his passage back to England. They wanted all along to strand him on the Isles of Shoals with no provisions, and 'let God decide his fate.' The hypocrites."

"We'll see to that later," Noah said, mind racing. "First, we free Jimmy and get back to Merrymount. Then, we'll rescue Thomas."

They crept back into the village after dark.

It was easy enough avoiding the night watchman, though they had to wait several minutes behind the storehouse while he strolled through the village square. Once he'd moved off, they took positions on both sides of the jailhouse.

While Robbie and Sam hid in the shadows on either corner where they could watch the square, Noah went with Harry, Andrew, and Benjamin around the back. Harry stood on the tips of his toes and stretched his neck to look inside the high window. He watched for a full minute before dropping down and whispering, "The guard's eyes are heavy, and his chin keeps dropping before he jolts awake. Wait five minutes and he'll be sound asleep."

Those five minutes felt like an hour. For all Noah knew, it might have been. When Harry stretched up for another peek inside, he looked down and whispered, "He's asleep."

Andrew handed him a wedge and hammer, and Harry worked it as quietly as he could, barely tapping the hammer against the wedge. The progress was slow, but eventually he pried the bottom of the glass away and raised it to the eave.

"Ho there, Jimmy Hawkey!" he said, in a hoarse whisper. "Wake up, man! We're here to rescue you."

The silence was deafening, and Noah held his breath, straining to hear any movement from within. Finally, there was a scratch of shoes on wood, and fingers on the window ledge. Harry grabbed his hands, and Jimmy's torso thrust through the window with a quiet huff. Noah hurried forward to help Harry and Andrew catch him, and Jimmy's feet landed softly on the ground.

"I missed thee," he said to Noah, who threw his arms around him and held him tight.

"Sorry, gents, but we'd best be on our way," Harry whispered, and they followed him around the building.

At the front corner, Robbie frantically waved them down, and they crouched in the shadows behind him. The night watchman was strolling along the opposite side of the village square, some twenty yards from where they hid. The flame-light from his torch danced along the fronts of the houses, and Noah prayed that he'd move on and not circle around to their side of the square.

He circled around and strolled toward where they hid.

Robbie almost fell over Noah in his haste to get behind the house. Everyone fled as silently as they could, pushing the one in front of them. Harry was the last to round the corner, seconds before the watchman's torchlight flickered in the space between the houses.

"That you, Sam?" Robbie whispered at the dark shape on the opposite side of the back wall.

"You're lucky it is, you loud-mouth," Sam whispered back.

"Let's get away from here before anyone else catches us," Harry said, and led the way.

Noah's breath was fast and shallow until they passed the last house on the lane and crossed into the dark fields. They dropped to their hands and knees and crawled between rows of Indian corn. The stalks were only two feet tall, and the moon had risen over the trees.

They were almost to the end of the row, with the forest beckoning twenty yards ahead of them, when a shout arose from far behind them. Someone had raised the alarm.

"No sense hiding now. Run!" Harry said, rising and making a dash for the trees.

Noah's heart pounded. The tension in his head ached as he sprinted behind Jimmy. From the distance of a quarter-mile, a gun cracked at the edge of the village, just a few steps before he dove into the brush. His heart skipped a beat. He tumbled into Jimmy, and they fell to the ground, Noah landing on top of him with a thud.

"It's not the best time for that," Jimmy said, a twinkle in his eyes.

"Hold thy tongue!" Noah said, but accepted Jimmy's hand as they heaved themselves up.

The braying of hounds sent a chill through him.

Harry grabbed them by the shoulders and pushed them forward. "We've got to get to the brook."

With spots of silvery moonlight filtering through the canopy, they kept on the trail until it crossed the brook a hundred yards above the grist mill. The mill pond to their right reflected the moon, and they plunged into the shallow water and hurried to the left, upstream and away from the village. The splash of their boots in the water made a terrible racket, but Noah prayed that the braying of the hounds overpowered all other sounds in their pursuers' ears.

Five minutes later, panting with exhaustion from the extra effort of running through water, they finally paused for a few seconds.

"We should split into two groups," Jimmy said. "They'll know we followed the brook once the hounds lose our scent."

"Then we'll leave the water first," Andrew said. "They'll chase us when the hounds find the scent. Ben, you come with us." He took Ben by the shoulder and pulled him along with him and Harry, slipping northward through the trees. "We'll meet you back at Merrymount!" he called over his shoulder.

"We should keep going in the water a while longer," Jimmy said. "When they find Harry and Andrew—and Benjamin—they'll leave them alone when they don't find me."

"Hopefully," Noah said, not too sure about that.

"Why wouldn't they?" Jimmy said. "They won't know who they are. They're looking for me."

"We'll talk about that later, men," Sam said, nudging them upstream. The hounds had only just fallen silent, doubtless sniffing frantically along the banks of the brook for the lost scent. That would only last a few minutes, until their handlers caught up with them and directed them upstream.

Noah's thighs ached from the effort of moving through the water, but he forced himself forward with all the strength he had left.

It was quite some time later when the hounds suddenly raised the alarm. They'd found Harry, Andrew, and Benjamin's trail. Noah, Jimmy, Sam, and Robbie kept moving, and slowly the sound of the dogs faded into the forest.

Noah and Jimmy held back in the forest when they reached the edge of Merrymount's wooded fields two days later. Sam and Robbie crept forward slowly, looking all around. They'd nearly reached the statue of Priapus when Benjamin ran out to meet them. The three of them huddled for a moment.

Drake came bounding down the hill, yelping with joy, tongue lolling as he ran. Noah beamed, and leaned down to meet him. The dog jumped up, paws on Noah's shoulders, and licked his face. Noah laughed and told him to stop, but Drake continued licking for several minutes.

Jimmy touched Noah's shoulder and pointed. Ben ran back to the village, and Sam and Robbie hurried back to Noah and Jimmy.

"Ben says it was still dark when they arrived this morning," Sam said, breathless. "But Captain Standish and the Plymouth militia arrived by boat not an hour ago, rousing everyone. Only Edward was awake. They're questioning everyone about you, Jimmy."

Noah looked into Jimmy's eyes. "They won't leave soon."

"I know."

The solution struck Noah like lightning from the blue. "We'll go to Samuel Maverick. He'll shelter us."

"We're coming with you," Robbie said with a decisive nod.

"Aye," Sam agreed. "They'll suspect us the moment we set foot in the village. And Robbie ain't a good liar."

Noah looked at Jimmy to decide. Jimmy nodded. "Then we go to Samuel Maverick."

CHAPTER 29

June 1629 – Shawmut Peninsula

Noah and Jimmy stayed at Maverick's old house on Shawmut peninsula for three weeks. Sam and Robbie returned to Merrymount on the third day, returning hours later to say that the Plymouth men had left; but Noah thought it best that Jimmy continue to hide for a while.

The first time Jimmy fished off Maverick's pier, Noah got so aroused at the memory of Maverick naked while tarring the posts, they made love right there on the planks. He kept to himself what had put him in the mood.

Maverick came over from Noddle's Island every other afternoon to check on them. The Walfords' farm and smithy lay about a mile to the north, on the Mystic River, and Jane Walford brought them fresh bread several times. "Mr. Morton was a kind soul, and he didn't deserve what those Brownists did to him," she said every time she visited.

Maverick came early that morning, and in his shallop. "Halloo!" he called, tying up at the dock.

Noah and Jimmy left their half-eaten porridge and came out from the cottage. "Why the bigger vessel?" Noah asked. "Traveling somewhere today?"

"'Tis time to fetch our Mr. Morton, my boys!" Maverick said with a grin, swooping his hat off his head and bowing. "Come aboard, lads, we sail for the Isles of Shoals. Captain Standish and his minions haven't returned, so the time is right for Mine Host to return to Merrymount. Mistress Maverick has packed us provisions for two days. Come! We must depart at once, to arrive by dusk."

Drake leapt aboard with Noah, and dashed up and down the ship, tail wagging. He jumped at the bow and put his paws on the rail, looking across the water, and Noah laughed. This was a great adventure.

The brisk salt breeze off the water cooled them against the intense sunshine. Noah and Jimmy worked the sails while Maverick manned the rudder, and before long they were cruising at eight knots.

"I propose we stop at Pannaway Plantation to inquire on Mr. Morton's whereabouts," Maverick shouted over the wind. "We might waste an entire day searching the Isles for signs of him, but I'd reckon the fishermen of Pannaway know where he lodges."

Noah agreed. He looked over the endless blue swells to the east, and the unease of past sea voyages rushed back upon him.

A brown dot appeared on the horizon after they rounded Cape Ann and headed north. Noah squinted to see it better. "Supply ship coming in."

"Mistress Maverick knows what to buy if it calls before we return," Maverick said, waving it off.

"He left not three days ago," one of the Pannaway fishermen said when they docked late in the afternoon. "Supply ship come by, and he hopped a ride back to England. Told us he aims to file a complaint with the Council against them Plymouth troublemakers. Said he'd speak to Sir Ferdinando Gorges himself about it."

"He will, too, I reckon," another fisherman said, chuckling. "Determined, that one. Said he'd be back before the new year to settle scores and reclaim his plantation."

Noah's heart sank. He'd been looking forward to seeing Thomas more than he'd realized. "I hope the Council listen," he said.

"They know what sort the Brownists are," the first fisherman said.

Maverick clapped his hands once. "Then there's no call to continue on. We stay here tonight. Is the manor house open?"

A pinnace sat at anchor in the harbor at Naumkeag when they passed early the next afternoon on their way back to Noddle's Island. But the size of the crowd on shore, plus the number of horses, cattle, and goats unloading in rowboats, told them the *Abigail* wasn't a supply ship.

"Perhaps we'll call on Mr. Gardner in a few days," Maverick said. "First, I take ye back to Merrymount."

Shouts of welcome greeted them when they put into the harbor below the hill of Merrymount, and Drake barked in answer. Their friends ran down to meet them. Harry and Andrew embraced Jimmy, and Noah was surprised with Benjamin embraced him.

"We were all worried for ye," Ben said.

Noah looked around and sighed. "It's good to be home."

"Two hundred Puritans from Dorchester," Samuel Maverick reported a few days later. "Men, women, and children, all in family groups. They came under a new charter from the Council, and their leader, a gentleman by the name of Captain John Endicott, is appointed Governor over all of the Massachusetts' Bay."

Harry crossed his arms. "I don't like it. We don't need no more damned pious nonconformists in this country. And sure as the sun rises each morn, we don't need a Puritan as governor over us."

"We'll be fine once Mr. Morton returns from England," Robbie said.

Noah was troubled. "That won't be for months, perhaps almost a year."

Maverick chuckled. "They've renamed the place Salem. That's a biblical word for 'peace.' They believe we have a peaceful future to look forward to!" He threw his head back and laughed.

Snare drums announced their arrival before they appeared a week later. Fifty armed men marched into the clearing in rows of five.

The men of Merrymount rushed out of their houses, gathering in the center of the village, in front of the eighty-foot maypole. "Hey, that's Edward!" Sam said, pointing. Edward Gibbons marched in their ranks, but kept his eyes forward and didn't look at any of his fellow Merrymounters.

The drumbeat changed from every other step to every step, four times to announce the end of the march, and the column halted. A man at the front stepped forward.

"By order of Governor John Endicott, this plantation is closed. Words of the misdeeds of this place have reached the Governor's ear, and he has declared the place forfeit in the name of our most dread sovereign, King Charles of England. You will disperse at once."

The fifty militiamen fanned out, entering every house. Ralph's wife screamed at them in her native tongue, but he held her back. Noah looked down the hill to the wharf. A boat sat tied up, and Mr. Cheswick stood on the pier and stared up at them.

"In the name of the King and his appointed representative, Governor Endicott, gather your belongings and leave!" the militia leader shouted.

There was no time to argue. Noah and Jimmy rushed to their cottage, stuffing their few possessions into a canvas sack. Noah rolled their barrel of oats out the door, but Edward stopped him, aiming his musket at Jimmy's chest. "Foodstuffs beyond what ye can carry yourselves are forfeit."

At the center of the village, four militiamen with axes chopped at the trunk of the maypole. With a fierce crack, it leaned toward Harry and Andrew's house, and the four axe men backed off. After two agonizing seconds suspended at an angle, the maypole crashed onto the thatched roof and fell through.

"You bastards!" Harry yelled, and a militiaman struck him on the head with the butt of his rifle. Blood ran down Harry's face, and Andrew ran to him, holding a handkerchief to his forehead.

The militiamen rolled all of the barrels out of the storehouse—food, utensils, supplies of every kind. They hauled out the racks of beaver fur. They took all of the furniture they wanted from Thomas's house, and then set fire to the structure. Men with torches moved from house to house, setting all of the alight. Great clouds of black smoke billowed into the blue sky.

"Disperse! All of you, disperse!"

The men of Merrymount scattered into the forest, in every direction.

Noah and Jimmy ran through the fields, their sacks over their shoulders beating against their backs. Drake bounded beside them, occasionally looking back toward the burning village and barking. The acrid smell of smoke and ash filled their nostrils. They didn't stop for a mile, until they reached the pond. Noah leaned forward, hands on his knees, and vomited into the water.

Once he'd stopped heaving, Drake leaned against his leg and licked his fingers.

"We have to get far away from this place," Jimmy said, rubbing a hand on Noah's back.

Noah wiped his mouth with the back of his hand, and slowly straightened. Over the forest canopy, clouds of black smoke met the westerly wind, swirling into dark wisps over the sun.

"Where will we go?"

"We can stay at the Neponset village tonight. Wonohaquaham will shelter us."

"But then where?" Noah asked. "Mr. Cheswick wants to see us hang. He won't leave us in peace."

"Then we go far away. They can't stop us. And they can't change us, Noah." Jimmy's dark eyes held a determination Noah hadn't seen in a long time. "We won't let them keep us apart. We'll go somewhere far."

He took Noah in his arms, and they held each other tight. Noah couldn't help the tears that poured forth, and he buried his face in Jimmy's shoulder for a long time. When the sobs stopped, he looked up into Jimmy's face.

"Together until death, remember?" Jimmy said. "We swore an oath."

Noah leaned his forehead against Jimmy's. Drake scratched his paw on Noah's leg, and he scratched behind the dog's ears. Come what may, they had each other.

EPILOGUE

1631 – Manhattan Island, Nieuw Nederland

It was three and a half miles to the palisade surrounding Nieuw Amsterdam. Noah made the hike with Jimmy and Drake every Saturday to go to market. The trail from their cottage followed a bluff overlooking Hudson's River. It descended toward the low-lying tip of the island where the Dutch colonial capital sat.

The palisade gate stood open during the day, but a pair of armed guards in shiny steel breastplates watched the comers and goers. They nodded at Noah and Jimmy. It had taken a while before they stopped watching Jimmy with suspicion, but after three years, theirs were familiar faces.

The merchant houses rose three stories over the wharfs, with the imposing steep-roofed Fort Amsterdam looming behind them. This was the busiest part of the bustling little village, and Drake barked and wagged greetings at several dogs.

Jimmy opened the door of Jan Pier, a merchant who had always treated them fairly, but stopped midway, staring at the quay.

"What is it?" Noah asked, and looked where Jimmy was looking.

Jonathan Cheswick came down a nearby dock carrying a large wooden crate, dressed in the faded blue trousers and dingy woolsey shirt of a common laborer. His eyes grew wide when he saw them, and he looked away in a hurry.

"Where in the world did he come from?" Noah said, more to himself than to Jimmy. The tight set of Jimmy's jaw turned his insides cold, and he put a hand on his arm. "Don't."

But Jimmy marched off anyway, storming toward the waterfront. Noah hurried after him. Jonathan Cheswick wouldn't look up from the ground in front of his feet, hauling his crate toward a half-loaded wagon. Jimmy grabbed him by the arm when he reached the wagon, and his crate tumbled sideways against the others already loaded.

Cheswick winced. Jimmy's knuckles were white. "You destroyed our home," he said through gritted teeth. He shook his arm. "You didn't light the torches, but you destroyed it. Your words lit those torches. Your words about us."

"Please!" Cheswick said, voice cracking. The whites of his eyes stood out in sharp contrast to the bright blue. "I'm a broken and despised man, hated by those I love. I have paid an awful price for my iniquities, and God will yet judge me for them. Leave me alone, I beg ye."

"What price have *you* paid?" Jimmy hissed, spittle flying onto Cheswick's cheek. "We lost our home and our friends. Everyone scattered, and we never found them."

"God has repaid me in kind. I lost my ministry. I lost my wife and son, never to see them again. The temptation was too much to bear. I stopped myself, I swear I did, but we were seen. I had to flee, lest they keep me in jail for the rest of my miserable life." He bent forward, putting his face in his hands, and sobbed.

In spite of everything, Noah's heart broke for the man. He reached out tentatively, fingertips touching Cheswick's shoulder.

Cheswick looked up at him. "You were right about me," he whispered through sniffles. "I am a vile sinner, like ye. And for my abomination, God has turned away from me." He looked away. "Please, leave me be."

That word, *abomination*, cut Noah to the core. He stiffened, scowling at the former minister. "Be on your way then, and we'll be in ours." He looked at Jimmy and nodded toward Jan Pier's door. They would sacrifice no more happiness on this self-loathing hypocrite.

Drake followed them, but looked back at the bent form of Jonathan Cheswick, a single small whine escaping his mouth. But then he trotted through the door with them, the sad man forgotten.

THANK YOU FOR READING OF WILD AND MERRY MEN!

If you enjoyed this book, please tell a friend, recommend it on your social media, and/or write a review at your favorite book retailer, Goodreads, or other forum.

If you want to know more about Jonathan Cheswick and how he came to be at the dismantling of the Merrymount colony, you can read his story in **The Reformer's Tale**. Click here to read it for free.

Every "villain" is the hero of their own story. While Jonathan Cheswick may have been a villain to Noah and Jimmy, he has his own story, his reasons for acting as he does. He is not a villain to those he loves.

Want to find out when my next book comes out? Sign up for my monthly newsletter to receive updates about what I'm working on, reviews of what I'm reading, and upcoming appearances.

Questions or comments? Feel free to contact me at www.garretthutson.com.

Also by Garrett Hutson

Exciting LGBT Historical Fiction

Death in Shanghai (mystery series):

The Jade Dragon

Assassin's Hood

No Accidental Death

The Pink Lotus

Martin Schuller, Spy Catcher (thriller series):

Hidden Among Us

Spy Tango

The Swiss Conspiracy

Tales of the Bohemian Resistance (LGBT thriller series):

Gray Paree

Each Hidden Passage

Standalone novels:

In a Safe Town

About the Author

Garrett Hutson writes upmarket historical fiction featuring realistic LGBT characters. He lives in Indianapolis with his husband, three adorable dogs, one odd-ball cat, and more fish than you can count. He has one grown daughter. You can usually find him reading about history, and day-dreaming about being there. This is where his stories are born, and he hopes they transport you the way his imagination transports him.

Want to know more? You may contact him at his website, www.garretthutson.com with any questions. Sign up for his monthly newsletter to find out what he's working on, what he's reading, and get access to exclusive bonus content.

f   facebook.com/Garrett-Hutson-Author-536759483052341

BB   bookbub.com/profile/garrett-hutson

y   twitter.com/GarrettBHutson

HISTORICAL NOTE

T his is a work of fiction. While the Merrymount colony was real—as were the other English outposts mentioned—I have filled in the blanks of the known history and fictionalized the story. I've stayed as true to the actual history as possible, though there are many gaps that leant themselves well to fictional depiction.

Almost nothing is factually known about the indentured youths who lived at Merrymount (aside from Edward Gibbons, who would join the Puritan colony at Salem), so I have relied on general statements made by Thomas Morton in his 1637 memoir *New English Canaan*, and by William Bradford of Plymouth Plantation. I find these general comments both intriguing and illuminating, and so I believe my depiction of life at Merrymount to be as realistic as can be from the limited sources available.

The fates of these unnamed young men is unknowable, beyond the general statement that they scattered (or were scattered). Anything more is conjecture. I have imagined what might have happened, and readers can judge for themselves.

According to Thomas Morton's memoir, New English Canaan, the Merrymount colony had one documented woman (the unnamed "doe of Virginia") who came for a while, delivered a baby, and returned to Virginia after the baby died. Dates aren't stated, but it's implied that she was pregnant prior to arrival, likely making her stay brief. I have not included that episode in the novel, since it's a side story to the overall narrative and felt like a distraction.

This story includes several people who really lived, as well as fictional characters. I rarely fictionalize real people, since there is no way to know for certain if we're being true to the way they acted and spoke; but New England in the 1620s was a tiny society—fewer than five hundred English colonists alongside a much-diminished Native American population—and it's impossible to tell this story without including the real people who did the things being described. Fortunately, many of them are well-documented in the literature of the time, including statements of their character, and I have relied on that as my basis for fleshing them out:

- Christopher Levett is described in the travel narrative of his 1623 voyage as warm and jocular.

- Samuel Maverick is described by many contemporaries as good-hearted and generous, but oddly eccentric; he is, after all, the origin of the term "maverick" to refer to someone who does their own thing and doesn't follow the crowd.

- Thomas Morton has been well-documented as a lawyer seeking social justice for the poor and forgotten; as well as a generous, outgoing, and savvy leader and businessman. The merriment of his revels is documented both by his detractors and by Morton himself, giving us a 360-degree view of the man and his Merry-mount colony. In his younger years in London, he moved in the same circles as William Shakespeare and Christopher Marlowe, so I felt comfortable showing him quoting their work, though those scenes are my specific inventions.

Morton's bisexuality is easy to surmise—it was darkly hinted at by his detractors at Plymouth Plantation (Governor Bradford, Miles Standish, and others), but Morton himself also gave a coded clue in his own memoir (*New English Canaan*) by referring to his indentured boys frequently as his "ganemedes" or "gamedes" which (given the nature of that specific

Greek myth) could **only** be a coded reference to same-sex relations with the much younger men.

Morton returned to England in 1628 to lodge a complaint against the Separatists of Plymouth Plantation. The members of the Council of New England were too preoccupied with politics in England to take definitive action against Plymouth, but they confirmed Morton's charter and sent him back. Morton arrived at Boston in 1630, presented himself to the governor of the new Massachusetts Bay Colony (the famous John Winthrop), and was promptly sent off to the isolated fishing stations of Maine. He lived out his days there, dying around 1647. It was here that he would have written his memoir of the Merrymount colony, *New English Canaan*, which he sent back to England for publication.

Within the legal records of the Massachusetts Bay Colony concerning Morton, there are references to "sodomical boys" at his Merrymount colony; and yet I'm not aware of any records of these young men actually being tried for either sodomy or buggery. While one interpretation is that these were unfounded accusations of homosexual activity, I don't believe that; given Morton's own references to Ganymede in his memoir I find it much more likely that the Puritans simply lacked sufficient proof to seek conviction of sodomy, and so they let the small fish go and concentrated on the big fish, Morton himself, throwing everything they had at him. Presumption of innocence was a cherished principle for *all* English, even the strict and judgmental Massachusetts Puritans. In fact, after their experiences at the Star Chamber in the years immediately preceding their mass migration, the Puritans may have clung to that presumption of innocence even more tightly than most of their contemporaries.

History is written by the victors, and the Merrymount colony faded from collective memory, not fitting into the prevailing narrative of America's founding. It was fictionalized a few times—most famously by Nathaniel Hawthorne in his 1836 short story, "The May-Pole of Merry Mount" published in *The Token and Atlantic Souvenir*. Unsurprisingly, there was zero mention of same-sex relations in Hawthorne's story, which focused on the Puritans' suppression of drunkenness and interracial relations. Hawthorne satirized both the repressive Puritans and the free-wheeling excess of Merrymount.

Nineteenth-Century artists sometimes depicted Merrymount and its revels as white men dancing and amorously frolicking with Native women, or drinking with Native men. One 1900 illustration by Bertha May features the wedding of a white man and a Native woman.

In the early 20th Century, H. P. Lovecraft fashioned Thomas Morton as the originator of a secret esoteric pagan cult—a wildly ahistorical portrayal.

The first scholarship I read about Morton and Merrymount was a brief entry in Richard Slotkin's 1973 treatise *Regeneration Through Violence: The Mythology of the American Frontier, 1600-1860* (pp. 58, 61-62, 64, 452), which mostly concerned the sale of firearms to the Native American tribes. Shortly afterward, I came across Jack Dempsey's 2000 book, *Thomas Morton of Merrymount, The Life and Renaissance of an Early American Poet*. Dempsey's was the most in-depth study of the man and his forgotten colony to date, and he came at the subject from a queer sensibility.

Since then, many posts have been written by LGBTQ bloggers reclaiming a forgotten piece of queer history. The level of source documentation naturally varies, but I found many blog posts that lead me to primary sources that I found useful. I encourage readers to judge for themselves.

In 17th Century England, membership in the Church of England was mandatory, as was weekly attendance at Church of England services. However, actual belief was much more open and varied than we might suppose by that legal mandate.

When Queen Elizabeth I created the modern Anglican church in January 1559 (new style), she deliberately made it a "middle road" between Protestantism and Roman Catholicism. This was a practical compromise, but probably also reflected Queen Elizabeth's own preferences—a modified Catholic liturgy paired with a more-or-less Protestant theology.

The Act of Uniformity that re-created the Church of England only mandated uniformity of practice, not of belief—Queen Elizabeth famously said that she had no desire to "make windows into men's souls." So it came to be said that the Church of England was a "broad church," one that could encompass people who considered themselves Protestant, as well as those traditionalists who might feel closer to Catholic.

That was not without some friction, however. By the reign of Elizabeth's successor, her cousin James I, people in England had sorted themselves into three broad parties:

1. High-Church Anglicans—those who favored the ritual and tradition of the Catholic mass, stressing those elements within the Anglican liturgy, and often also clinging to a more Catholic theology.

2. Low-Church Anglicans—those who favored the more preaching-based liturgies of the Protestant churches, and a generally more Protestant theology. You might think of these as being close to what we now call Methodists (and indeed, the Methodist church arose out of this movement a century-and-a-half later).

3. Puritans—those within the Church of England on the far Low-Church end of the spectrum, who favored getting rid of the episcopal hierarchy (bishops and archbishops) in favor of governance by elected Elders (*presbyters*).

   - The more moderate faction of Puritans favored replacing the episcopal hierarchy with a Presbyterian hierarchy;

   - the more extreme faction of Puritans wanted to jettison the hierarchy altogether and have each congregation governed independently (Congregationalism).

The fervor of their belief led many clergy of the Puritan party to ignore certain ritualistic portions of the Anglican liturgy, in violation of the Act of Uniformity. Some were jailed for these offenses. At the same time, the power of their preaching led to some being invited to preach to the royal family at the chapel in St. James's Palace.

And of course, a very small contingent of Congregationalists (not much more than a thousand people) felt so strongly that they left the Church of England entirely, and established independent (i.e., illegal) congregations. Since this violated the Act of Uniformity in its entirety, they were persecuted from the start. These "Brownists" (named after their founder, Robert Brown) fled to Holland, and later (1620) founded Plymouth Plantation in New England. Today we know them as the Pilgrims, or "Separatists" rather than "Brownists." This latter is what they were called at the time, so it's the term I have used in this book.

As we know, it was the Puritans who founded the colonies that became the bases for the New England states. After 1625, King Charles I used increasingly draconian measures against Puritan clergy who wouldn't conform, which led to the Puritan Great Migration of 1629 to 1640, in which 75,000 Puritans left England—and 21,000 of them settled in New England, in a single decade becoming the largest English population in the western hemisphere.

It's important to note that the distinctions between High Church and Low Church Anglicans were a spectrum, and there was a whole continuum of people who would have considered themselves somewhere in between. I have portrayed Reverend Blaxton and Samuel Maverick as middle-of-the-road Anglicans, which is what the contemporaneous writings about them imply. But over the course of the early seventeenth century, these distinctions between high and low church became increasingly polarized, eventually leading to the English Civil Wars of the 1640s.

Merrymount is today the name of a mid-century suburban neighborhood in Quincy, MA. The site of Thomas Morton's settlement is today a park in the middle of that neighborhood, aptly named Maypole Park. There is a historical marker there to commemorate it. You can find many photographs of the park online, and these made it easy for me to imagine the setting as it might have been in 1624-'28.

As always, I have endeavored to be as historically accurate as possible in this novel. Any errors are mine and mine alone.

Acknowledgments

No novel is written in a vacuum, and many people played roles large and small in helping me craft this story.

When I first read about Thomas Morton and Merrymount in 2008, of course I imagined a story set among the free-thinking young men of Morton's settlement. Who were they? What were their lives like? They were nameless in the historical record. I decided I had to write a novel set in this early queer enclave, and I dove right in. I talked about it at parties, and Brenda Havens asked to read it. She was kind enough not to tell me until years later how bad that first draft was. "Excruciating" I believe was the word she used—and rightly so. I must have intrinsically known this, because I didn't even finish the book before I set it aside for years. Thank you, Brenda, for both your kindness and your honesty. When you finally confessed how bad it was (in contrast to how much better my later novels were), you unknowingly gave me the impetus to pull this story out of the proverbial drawer and get to work.

I owe tremendous thanks to the incomparable Hannah Vanvel Ausbury, editor extraordinaire, who made fantastic suggestions. Of course she was right in almost every instance. Without her, this story might never have been finished. She's also the reason Jonathan Cheswick has his own story.

A special thank you to my fantastic beta readers, who read the whole manuscript and provided invaluable feedback: Pattie Horwood, Roxx Tarantini, Christopher Riese, and Christine Weald. Their suggestions and encouragement helped make the book better.

And last but never least, a million thank yous plus all my love and devotion to my husband, David Lee. You make my life so much better in so many ways, and I couldn't do any of this half as well without you.

-Garrett B. Hutson, August 2023